Claudia Gray

The Fatal Unpleasantness at Netherfield

Claudia Gray is the pseudonym of Amy Vincent. She is the author of the Mr. Darcy & Miss Tilney mysteries, which began with *The Murder of Mr. Wickham*. She is also the writer of multiple young adult novels, including the Evernight series, the Firebird trilogy, and the Constellation trilogy. In addition, she's written several *Star Wars* novels, such as *Lost Stars* and *Bloodline*. She and her husband, Paul, live in Turin, Italy, under the benevolent rule of a small dog named Peaches.

claudiagray.com

Also by Claudia Gray

The Murder of Mr. Wickham
The Late Mrs. Willoughby
The Perils of Lady Catherine de Bourgh
The Rushworth Family Plot

GRAPHIC NOVELS

House of El: The Shadow Threat
House of El: The Enemy Delusion
House of El: The Treacherous Hope

CONSTELLATION SERIES

Defy the Stars
Defy the Worlds
Defy the Fates

STAR WARS

Journey to Star Wars: The Force Awakens: Lost Stars
Bloodline
Leia: Princess of Alderaan
Master & Apprentice
Star Wars: The High Republic: Into the Dark
Star Wars: The High Republic: The Fallen Star
Star Wars: The High Republic: Into the Light

FIREBIRD SERIES

A Thousand Pieces of You
Ten Thousand Skies Above You
A Million Worlds with You

SPELLCASTER SERIES

Spellcaster
The First Midnight Spell
Steadfast
Sorceress

EVERNIGHT SERIES

Evernight
Stargazer
Hourglass
Afterlife
Balthazar

STAND-ALONE

Fateful
The Haunted Mansion: Storm & Shade
The X-Files: Perihelion

The Fatal Unpleasantness at Netherfield

A Mr. Darcy & Miss Tilney Mystery

Claudia Gray

VINTAGE BOOKS
A DIVISION OF PENGUIN RANDOM HOUSE LLC
NEW YORK

A VINTAGE BOOKS ORIGINAL 2026

Copyright © 2026 by Amy Vincent

Published by Vintage Books, a division of Penguin Random House LLC, 1745 Broadway, New York, NY 10019.

Vintage Books and colophon are registered trademarks of Penguin Random House LLC.

Library of Congress Cataloging-in-Publication Data
LCCN 2025942784

Vintage Books Trade Paperback ISBN: 979-8-217-00807-0
eBook ISBN: 979-8-217-00808-7

Book design by Nicholas Alguire

penguinrandomhouse.com | vintagebooks.com

Printed in the United States of America
1st Printing

The authorized representative in the EU for product safety and compliance is Penguin Random House Ireland, Morrison Chambers, 32 Nassau Street, Dublin D02 YH68, Ireland, https://eu-contact.penguin.ie.

To every one of the many friends we've come to know since our move to Torino in 2024: Thank you for so quickly making our new place a true home.

THE FATAL UNPLEASANTNESS
AT NETHERFIELD

Chapter One

September 1823

Netherfield Park, a fine estate near the town of Meryton, had nearly twenty-five years prior been let to a most desirable tenant: one Mr. Charles Bingley, a gentleman of means, and possessed of an open and amiable character. Although some among his family and friends found Meryton and its environs appallingly backward, Mr. Bingley made himself so very much at home that he eventually wedded the loveliest of the local young women, Miss Jane Bennet. As her temperament was as obliging as his own, they were well-liked by all their neighbors, and it seemed as though the Bingleys would long reign over Meryton as its foremost citizens. This prospect displeased no one—not even the former holders of that position, the Lucas family, as Sir William's good nature eclipsed even his considerable pride in his knighthood. Indeed, the ascendance of the Bingleys seemed to give delight to nearly everyone.

However, rather too much delight in this matter was taken by Jane's mother. Mrs. Bennet possessed little sense and less tact. She could not be made to see that, while her daughter's new place in society enhanced Mrs. Bennet's own, the two were not the same. Nor could Mrs. Bennet perceive that her position could only be harmed by such pride and ostentation as she began to regularly display. Most husbands would have spoken with their wives in an effort to curb the worst excesses, but Mr. Bennet was not one to much trouble himself with the concerns of his town or his family, nor to deny himself such amusement as his wife's behavior afforded. He thus limited his remarks to a few dry jokes over the evening meal. As she lacked the wit to comprehend his humor, Mrs. Bennet continued unchecked.

Therefore it was not long into the Bingleys' marriage that Jane began to wonder whether she might not be happier dwelling farther from her parents. The very notion filled her with guilt, for Jane's first desire in life was to promote the happiness of those around her. Embarrassing though Mrs. Bennet's behavior might be, there could be no denying how happy her mother had been made by Jane's marriage.

Yet soon, other reasons for a change presented themselves. The Bingleys became aware of a fine house for sale in Staffordshire, an easy distance from Derbyshire and the great estate of Pemberley, where Jane's sister Elizabeth lived with her husband and Charles Bingley's good friend, Fitzwilliam Darcy. This information was swiftly followed by a gentle suggestion in a letter from Elizabeth to Jane, which hinted that within a few months, she would have need of a sister living near. No more was required. Charles and Jane Bingley had quitted Netherfield for their new home swiftly enough that Jane was able to attend her sister Elizabeth in her confinement and to be present at the birth of her first nephew, Jonathan.

Mrs. Bennet was gratified enough by her new status as the grandmother to the heir of Pemberley to recover from the loss of Jane's society. In truth, the Bingleys served her purpose nearly as well from afar. Rarely did Mrs. Bennet fail to brag upon the great marriages her two eldest daughters had made—nor the rather good one her middle child, Mary, unexpectedly entered into some years later—or even the misbegotten match of her youngest daughter, Lydia, whose shameful elopement and subsequent penury were blithely ignored. (The fifth daughter, Kitty, had simply married the local clergyman,

Mr. Brooks, who, though wholly respectable, was too ordinary for even Mrs. Bennet to expound upon.) Whenever Netherfield Park gained a new tenant, Mrs. Bennet could compare them to the Bingleys and find them not nearly so elegant nor so worthy. She had the opportunity to do so often, for the house found no long-enduring residents for nearly another two decades.

Yet Jane was to learn that, no matter how far we may travel, we are never beyond the reach of that which has the power to call us home.

First, Mr. Bennet took a fall from his horse, and though his leg healed well enough, he was henceforth obliged to walk with a stick. Then Mrs. Bennet's health, long complained of, began at last to deserve her descriptions. Although their daughter Kitty strove to help them, she had young children that required much of her time, and more was needed.

So it was that Netherfield Park was let once more, and the Bingleys had returned five years prior to the night our narrative begins.

"As long as you were obliged to live here once again, I wonder that you have not done more with the place," opined Mrs. Hurst, the eldest sister of Mr. Bingley, between hands of whist.

"You might add some modern furnishings or some fringe to the drapes," added Mrs. Lofton, the youngest sister of the Bingley family. "The new style is not so plain, you know." She brushed one finger along the extra row of ruffles upon her sleeve.

Jane, unable to see any blemish in a home she shared with her husband, defended it with her usual gentleness. "We have added a few little tables in the rooms and halls, you see, and a bit of ornament here and there. The longcase clock, too."

"Well, it is better than nothing, but that is all it is better than," Mrs. Hurst said. It might have been wondered why she cared about the decoration of a place in which she heeded little beyond the card table. Not once did she look up from it as she continued: "One could never call a house so isolated *truly* fashionable, of course, but it could be made so much more fit to be seen!"

"It is fit for our purposes," said Charles Bingley, not for the first time. He was an exceedingly patient man, both for good and for ill. "I have always found Netherfield a most charming and comfortable place and do not plan to change it one jot. You must like it well enough, sister, to have come to stay again!" He did not intend this remark to be pointed, though Mrs. Hurst might have taken it as such had she not been distracted by the dealing of the next hand.

"Really I suppose there is little point to spending too much on matters of style when one lives in the country," said Mrs. Lofton. "City life is for fashion, flirtation, all that is bright and lively. Country life should be more sober and respectable. Do you not agree, Mr. Lofton?"

"I would not presume to dispute any lady on a matter of fashion. *That* is a fool's errand." Her husband never glanced away from his cards; Mr. Lofton was not nearly so avid a player as Mrs. Hurst, but a cleverer one, so he did not allow himself to be so easily distracted.

"An errand? What? At this hour?" This came from Mr. Hurst, who sat on the nearby divan with a cup of wine. His hearing had worsened over the years, and his comprehension had never been strong. "Late for any errand. Cannot a servant be sent?"

"Do not trouble yourself," Charles said kindly. "All is well. Is that not correct, Mrs. Bingley?"

"Of course. Do not be bothered, Mr. Hurst." Before Jane had done speaking the words, Mr. Hurst had already slumped back down upon the divan, paying her no more heed than he ever had. The players remained with their cards, and Jane sat at the writing desk quite alone.

She did not mind this, for she was a faithful correspondent with her two grown daughters, as well as her two sisters who lived afar. (Kitty and Mr. Brooks visited nearly every evening of late, and often in the day as well, though on this night they remained at home.) Jane also honored her husband's desire to visit often with his sisters and their husbands, even those whose company she found less congenial. Yet the prospect of housing both the Hursts and the Loftons for another two months—and being soon joined by the Allerdyces as well—could daunt even the sunniest of spirits. In previous years, Jane had borne such lengthy visits by devoting herself even more fully to her adored children. However, her two eldest daughters were both married women now and a county away in either direction, Thomas had just left to rejoin his tutor's household in Berkshire for the autumn, and young Martha Elizabeth was learning dancing and comportment at a girls' boarding school in Surrey. To Jane, Netherfield felt at once far too full and very empty.

So it was that Jane continued her letter to Elizabeth by doing that which she nearly never did: requesting something for herself.

You must not think, dearest Lizzy, that I am mournful.
Abigail and Sarah have made matches that satisfy all
the needs of both head and heart (and I hope for greater
joy with Abigail in the new year). My younger children
enjoy a wider society than Meryton can afford them,
and thus are well situated for their happiness. Though
I miss our dear Whitebeam Dower, Netherfield has
claims upon my affections, too. Also, I have long since
forgiven Mrs. Hurst and Mrs. Allerdyce for their

undue protectiveness of Charles during our courtship, while ever heeding your wise caution that forgiveness may thrive, and even thrive best, without being mistaken for trust. My situation, you see, is not so very bad.

Yet I should so relish your company at this time! If you are entirely free, will you perhaps consider a visit? With the Allerdyces' impending arrival, only one bedroom at Netherfield remains unspoken for, but it is yours if you wish it.

"Oh, Jane!" Elizabeth Darcy put one hand to her cheek; the other cradled her sister's letter. "To be deprived of her most beloved companionship at the same time she is subjected to the most burdensome—disagreeable fate indeed."

Mr. Darcy let his newspaper fall, revealing an expression of concern. "Will you then go to her? Georgiana would understand."

Husband and wife shared a long glance, one that suggested the exchange of thoughts without words. Jonathan Darcy had learned to recognize, though never to interpret, his parents' silent communication.

He sat in the chair nearest the fire, which was lit despite the warmth of a September afternoon that felt more like July. Nearby sat a tray with the remnants of tea and toast that he had been given between meals, even though he had been able to join the entire family for breakfast, lunch, and dinner for months. Although Jonathan had thus far been able to dodge having a shawl draped around his shoulders, one sat at the ready, folded very near his mother.

Jonathan had noticed how many people desired to be at the center of others' attention. It seemed that the best means of accomplishing this was to get oneself shot.

The shooting was his own doing: He was the one who had challenged Laurence Follett to a duel. The wound he'd received had not been a serious one, and he had been fortunate enough to suffer only minor infection afterward. Jonathan would concede that he had indeed taken a great risk with his life, that his parents must have endured wretched terror both when learning of the duel and when discovering he had indeed been shot, and that it was therefore natural that the event should cast a long shadow over their lives. What he refused to concede was that his parents should now treat him as though he were a porcelain ornament upon a mantelpiece.

All the more maddening was the fact that, while his mother and father could not forget the event of the duel, they simultaneously appeared unable to remember the reason for it, namely, Miss Juliet Tilney. The one time Jonathan had managed to raise the subject with his father, more than a month prior, had proved woefully unhelpful.

"Do you blame Miss Tilney for this?" Jonathan had said, gesturing in the general direction of his abdomen, where his blue waistcoat concealed the scar of his wound. "The duel was of my creation, not hers. Yes, it was done for her sake, but only because she had been cruelly treated by Follett in so outrageous a manner that no man of honor could have done less than defend her."

(This crime had been exceedingly wicked: A former schoolmate of Jonathan's, and a rising artist, Follett had painted an entirely proper portrait of Miss Tilney, but then later modified it so that her face was instead shown as that of a woman from Greek mythology who had behaved in a most scandalous way. The painting had portrayed this behavior in shocking detail, as indeed it showed a young woman's unclothed person and the natural—if incorrect—inference was that Miss Tilney had willingly posed so. Not content with this mischief,

Follett had further seen to it that the painting was displayed in one of the largest art exhibitions in London. Once Miss Tilney was recognized publicly as the girl from the portrait, her reputation had been ruined. Ruination was the death of all social and marital hopes for a young lady, or so it was said.)

"I do not blame Miss Tilney," Mr. Darcy had replied. "You must recognize that your actions were rash and irresponsible, and that they worked against your own aims, and against Miss Tilney, too. Her infamy is the greater for having been the cause of a duel. Many who would never have seen the offending portrait heard of its existence only through the inevitable gossip excited by such an event."

This had occurred to Jonathan already—had done so even before the duel itself—but it seemed beside the point. "If you do not blame her, why will you not speak of her? Of my desire to—"

"Jonathan." Mr. Darcy could sound very stern when he wished. "Miss Tilney is not a good influence on you. It is your behavior that has demonstrated this, not hers."

"That is unfair, Father. I have made mistakes enough in life, but they are not of her creation, nor shall her absence render me infallible." Jonathan realized that pointing out his own weaknesses might not constitute his best argument, so he altered his approach. An injustice had been done, and he could not allow this to stand. "Although my actions may have spread word of the portrait's existence, so did it the information of Follett's wrongdoing. He has acknowledged his misbehavior publicly, and, but for the duel, I do not know that he would ever have done so."

"So I have seen. For her sake, I am glad of it. There is now some small chance that Miss Tilney's prospects are not forever destroyed. However, any future connection between the two of you would mean that her shame could never be forgotten." Mr. Darcy hesitated, and his countenance gentled.

"I realize it is an unhappy circumstance for you both. Yet it is done, and what is done cannot be changed, and must therefore be faced."

No other substantive conversation on the topic of Miss Tilney had been possible. So for months, Jonathan had found himself unable to speak of what he most thought about, forced to endure the constant heat of the unnecessary fires and the distracting pressure of the shawls and blankets his mother and the servants kept ever at the ready, prevented even from riding his beloved Ebony. On this warm September afternoon, as sweat beaded upon his brow, he felt as though he could bear little more such treatment. Yet, one way or another, deliverance seemed to be at hand.

His mother, who had been considering quietly, finally shook her head. "No," she said. "I cannot go to Netherfield. We must hold to our plan. Yes, Jane wants companionship—but Georgiana *needs* it, desperately so."

Jonathan understood this to be some reference to his aunt Georgiana's stormy marriage to the Earl of Oxford. "Stormy" was perhaps an unjust term, as for long periods, his uncle and aunt would seem very happy, and at such times, all the Darcys might be welcomed at their stately house, Maidencourt. Yet clouds always came, and every few months or years, the earl's mood would darken, his temper foul. From Jonathan's earliest childhood, he had been wary of the earl for this reason. Inevitably some manner of crisis arose that demanded the presence of one or both of Jonathan's parents, or that brought Aunt Georgiana to stay at Pemberley for a long while. In the past weeks, it had seemed clear that this cycle was renewing itself.

How long would his parents be gone? More than a month, possibly, in which case Jonathan would have time to take exercise, to escape from the servants' caution, to resume normal life—and, perhaps, to conceive of a way to take himself off to Gloucestershire, where Miss Tilney lived. Yet not all such visits to Georgiana endured so long. His parents never knew how long these visits would be, and once they had returned so quickly that Jonathan realized they had spent more time in carriages going to and fro than they had at Maidencourt itself.

He consoled himself by thinking, *They may be with Aunt Georgiana quite a while, but if they leave sooner, surely Mother at least will go to Netherfield Park after. They will be far from Pemberley for some time, and I should be at liberty.*

This inspired a second thought, one far better, and so he quickly spoke: "Why do I not go to Netherfield instead?"

His parents exchanged another silent glance, though this time he did not have to guess at their thoughts. Rarely did Jonathan wish to leave home; almost never did he suggest such a journey himself. It was his mother who said, "You have never been eager to visit that part of the country."

She was referring to his grandparents, who were not understanding of Jonathan's particularities. Still, if their presence were the price of escaping Pemberley, it must be borne. "I could be of service to my family. Is not that reason enough?"

"Indeed." Mr. Darcy had begun to smile. "You understand your duty very well, Jonathan."

Mother remained cautious. "Your health—traveling is such an exertion. Can it be right?"

Jonathan wished to retort that he was fully healed, that he was a twenty-four-year-old man in excellent health, and above all that he was tired of being coddled like the runt puppy of a litter. Yet none of these would persuade his mother, so he instead replied, "I believe myself capable of the journey, and then I shall be with Aunt Jane."

"Of course." His mother's eyes brightened. She must have been wary of leaving him, even still, and was comforted by the thought of her eldest son instead being in the keeping of her most beloved sister.

Jonathan felt a pang of guilt, for he was not being wholly honest—and his was a forthright nature, sometimes to the point of impoliteness. Yet where persons refuse to acknowledge a truth, they make the way ready for lies.

Not everyone in his family was so easily deceived, however. That night, on the way down to dinner, his younger brothers, Matthew and James, fell into step beside him. "Off to Netherfield?" Matthew said. "With Grandmama so near? Not like you at all."

"'Tis all the murders," opined James, with a grin that belied his words. "Everywhere Jonathan goes, someone gets murdered. Maybe he hopes someone will give Grandmama a push off a high cliff."

Jonathan tightened. "You cannot really think that I would ever—"

"Oh, of course he thinks no such thing," Matthew said, flicking James's hair to mock scold him. "Besides, they haven't any high cliffs in Hertfordshire."

James protested, "They have hills! One could be pushed down a hill."

"Then Grandmama would simply bounce like a ball." Matthew laughed at the image, then nudged his elder brother. "You only want to get away from all the shawls, do you not? Well, never fear, we won't tell."

Probably that was true. Jonathan more or less trusted his younger brothers, who despite their constant noise and japery were generally considerate of his feelings. Yet they seemed to him the most impenetrable of minds—as though the entire confusing world would make sense to him before Matthew and James did. They even anticipated their imminent return to school with delight, though to Jonathan the place had seemed more like a prison. How he envied their ease with the world!

But that envy was not so strong as once it had been. Jonathan understood that his minute observations of the peculiarities of behavior had helped him in the investigation of murder—the activity that had first and ever united him with Juliet Tilney.

I will find a way to write her from Netherfield, he resolved. *Or to visit Gloucestershire. In some manner, once I am free from my parents' oversight,*

I will *be with Miss Tilney again.*

"There's a letter for you, Juliet!"

Within her room, Juliet Tilney slowly lifted her head from her book. She had been rereading *Rob Roy*—or pretending to—for the third time since January. There was little to do besides read when one received no invitations to dinners or parties, when one was spoken to in public only rarely and then with only the barest civility, or when one felt conspicuous even in church.

Such was the nature of ruination.

Social ruination, of course. Juliet knew her honor and her character to be as true as ever they had been, but in the eyes of society, her reputation was severely damaged. Even though she had come to realize that almost no one truly believed that she had posed nude for Laurence Follett, that all understood she had been the victim of a vicious prank and that the picture reproduced no more of her than her face, the shame lingered regardless. The difference, her mother had told her, was that for Juliet, this would most likely fade somewhat in time. Thanks to Mr. Follett's belated confession and destruction of the offending painting, her isolation might not be permanent. This level of exile might last no more than two or three years.

Two or three years! To a young woman nearing twenty-one, this might as well have been eternity. She would scarcely be an old maid upon reaching the age of twenty-four, but her prospects would be diminished even in the best of circumstances. Given the scandal, finding any match would be a struggle. Finding a good match would be an impossibility.

To think she had been so close—so very near indeed—to a marriage that would have satisfied every expectation of society and every hope of her heart!

Yet Juliet did not let herself think of Jonathan Darcy too long. He was alive and well. With that, she must somehow content herself.

"Yoooooo-hoooo?" sang her younger sister, Theodosia, whose footsteps thudded upon the stairs. "Did not you hear me? A letter is come for you!"

Juliet left her room as little as possible these days, but a letter was reason enough to budge. It would not of course be from Mr. Darcy—the only person from whom she truly wanted to hear—for unmarried men and women could not correspond absent an engagement. Still, any amusement would make a change. So she opened her door at the very moment Theodosia had raised her hand to rap upon it.

"I heard you," Juliet said, holding out her hand. "And thank you."

With a tiny smile, Theodosia very primly dropped the letter into Juliet's hand. Her younger sister had just turned fifteen, and only in the past few weeks had begun wearing her hair up. How odd to think that Theodosia might well be wed, with a household of her own, before Juliet could even dream of it!

Insofar as any expectations about this letter had been formed, Juliet had had a vague notion that it might be from her aunt Eleanor, inviting her to come for a visit. Yet she saw the handwriting of the address was entirely unfamiliar and the letter had been sealed with purple wax, not the deep blue her aunt normally used. The initial embossed upon the wax was an *F*. Whom did she know with that last initial? Juliet remembered the kindly Edward and Elinor Ferrars, whom she had come to know during her visit in Devonshire. Why should they write now?

Upon breaking the seal and opening the letter, however, Juliet discovered that the Ferrars were not her correspondents. The letter was from Laurence Follett.

It contained a proposal of marriage.

Chapter Two

Dear Miss Tilney,

Forgive the impudence of my writing to you in this manner—though, given such impudence as you have already endured from me, a mere note must not seem so great a sin. Still, men and women do not correspond unless they are engaged to be married. There exists however one exception to this rule, of which I now avail myself: A man may propose marriage through a letter, and so I do.

Through your famed investigations, you have proved yourself a clever creature, Miss Tilney. Therefore I will not insult your intelligence by pretending that I am overcome with love for you, or that you are likely to feel such sentiments toward me. The fact is that, through my bad manners and ill-considered humor, I have wrecked both our reputations in a manner that only marriage is likely to cure. Were we to wed, it would be presumed that any liberties taken during the painting of the portrait were those readily excused between two affianced persons. This would restore your honor, and though the public might consider us intemperate, even shocking, they would no longer punish us for such a minor impropriety as that.

My own situation is not what a bride would most desire, yet I am not so reduced as to be ineligible. I am not to inherit any grand estate, but my fortune should *be sufficient to take a very respectable house, perhaps even to purchase one. You would not be among the first figures of fashion, but nor would you be shabbily or inelegantly supported.*

It is possible, indeed, that my situation would be much improved by our marriage. My wretched "joke" at your expense has harmed my situation at least as much as it has yours, for I had only just begun to establish myself as a portraitist. To have abused your trust—to have portrayed you in a scandalous manner, entirely contrary to your actual pose—has ruined any confidence future clients might have had in my discretion. I have had no commissions since that unfortunate incident in London, and though I have managed to sell a few allegorical works, my portrait-painting days are at an end—at least, for now.

Were you to marry me, however, it would cast my behavior in an entirely different light. All would understand that a painter takes liberties with his own wife that he would never presume with any other. In time, I could resume my career and paint many persons in fine society, and in so doing, I should be able to add to our income and comfort.

As for fondness, we should have to trust that marriage would in time make us companions of the heart. Many generations have wed so, and many have been made happy. We have each, I think, known other feelings—deeper sentiments toward persons now lost to our hopes. Yet should this not awaken a certain sympathy between us? If we did not enter marriage joyfully, we could do so honestly, and that alone is more than many accomplish.

Let me also apologize to you personally, as I ought to have done before (and did attempt in London,

only to find that you had already quitted the city).
Although it is no excuse, I had not the slightest thought
of causing such harm. With no suspicion that either
you or Mr. Darcy should be in London for the season,
I imagined your face would go entirely unrecognized.
I thought it a private joke—a rude one to be sure, but
one that assuaged my pitiful sense of humiliation after
Mr. Darcy, the old schoolfellow I had once teased for
his foolishness, solved the murder of the woman I had
once loved. That he should avenge her, while I had
been blind!—though for the sake of her memory, I ought
to have been grateful for this rather than resentful.
Regardless of your reply to my letter, know that I deeply
regret my actions in this matter and always shall.

I am well aware of the damage I have done to your
reputation, Miss Tilney, and I am ashamed of it. Let it
not also be said that I have robbed you of your chance
to marry. Let us make an alliance that can heal many
wounds and offer us every chance of prosperity.

You will of course wish to speak of the matter with
your good parents. Please let them know that I have
written to your father for permission; my letter to him
should arrive within a day or two of your own. I felt
it most proper to speak first to you, as it is your answer
I am more uncertain of receiving. Take whatever time
you require to decide whether my suit shall find favor.

Yours in sincerity—
Laurence Follett

From this missive, Juliet could not swiftly recover. To think
that Laurence Follett, the man who had destroyed all her
hopes, should compound his impudence by wishing to make
her his wife!—no, no, it was not to be borne.

Yet the worst of the letter was that the arguments Mr. Follett made were not unreasonable. He had offered the one cure for her situation, the only path back into society and respectability.

Surely Papa and Mama would not expect me to wed against my inclinations, she thought. *They would not wish me to become the bride of such a man.*

But they would wish her to become a bride, and it was entirely possible that Mr. Follett's offer constituted Juliet's last and only chance to do so.

As the Darcy carriage turned at last upon the drive of Netherfield Park, Jonathan looked out the open window to take in the scene. His usual trepidation regarding new places did not apply here, for he knew this corner of Hertfordshire nearly as well as he did his home in Derbyshire; and Netherfield had housed him on more than one occasion. Of all people outside his immediate family, almost no one was so gentle and welcoming as his aunt Jane.

"You are come to us at last," she said, hurrying out past the butler; Aunt Jane did not stand upon ceremony when it came to greeting those she most loved. "Though we were afraid you might not be well enough to travel—but then, we knew that if you needed nursing and your dear mama was away, that of course you should be with us."

Jonathan submitted to her embrace; even from Aunt Jane, he sometimes found such touches unwelcome, but he could prepare for them, and from experience knew she would not linger unduly. "I do not need any more nursing, as you shall soon see for yourself. Mother refuses to believe that I am returned to health, but you may be able to convince her better than I can—even better than the evidence of her own eyes."

Aunt Jane replied, "You will remain at Netherfield until such time as *all* of us are assured of your complete recovery."

That might mean weeks, even months. Much could happen in a few months' time. Jonathan had been sure to bring his writing box, and this very night, he could begin work on the most important letter he was ever to write.

His pleasant mood was, however, swiftly tempered upon his entering the Netherfield drawing room and encountering so many persons there.

"Jonathan! Good lad!" His uncle Mr. Bingley rose to his feet and shook Jonathan's hand with both warmth and brevity. "How happy I am to see you, and in excellent health, it seems! Come, come, you remember my sister and her husband, the Hursts?"

Mr. Hurst slumped on a nearby chaise, well into his cups despite the midafternoon hour. This was, indeed, exactly how Jonathan always remembered him. Mrs. Hurst sat alone at the card table, playing a round of patience. Though Mr. Hurst did no more than lift his half-empty glass of port as a sort of salute, Mrs. Hurst did look up long enough to smile. "Well, Mr. Darcy, you have come. Perhaps at last we can gather a table for whist."

"Good L—d, woman," groaned Mr. Hurst as he motioned to a servant to pour him more port. "How much more money can you lose before dinnertime?"

"It is early in the day for cards, is it not?" Jonathan said. He was wary of playing cards, mostly because he was very good at it. In his experience, people never liked him any better after they owed him money.

"I do not see why we may not play whatever games we wish at home!" Mrs. Hurst cried. "Why, we are all family here, are we not? Except, of course, Mr. Lucas. I suppose the Brookses must be said to count."

Mrs. Brooks—Jonathan's aunt Kitty—did not take well to

this. "If you are family by being sister to one of the Bingleys, then surely I am family by being sister to the other." Only then did she add, "It is good to see you, Jonathan. You have long been absent from Hertfordshire."

"Indeed," said her husband, Mr. Brooks, the local curate. His smile was slight, but not insincere. "How glad we are that you have returned."

In his considerations of the Netherfield visit, Jonathan had not thought much about the presence of the Brookses. His aunt Kitty had always been pleasant enough to him, he supposed—neither teasing him in the manner of his grandparents nor achieving the warmth and welcome of Aunt Jane. The Brookses had visited Pemberley on a handful of occasions in his childhood, but not since. To his embarrassment, he hardly recognized his aunt Kitty; his memory had not done justice to her bright eyes and open manner.

His uncle Mr. Brooks, however, proved difficult to recall even when standing directly in Jonathan's sight. He had been handsome in his youth but now appeared entirely ordinary, neither tall nor short, thin nor fat. His attire was that befitting a country parson, modest and plain. Jonathan remembered only one companionable incident between himself and Mr. Brooks from childhood, when Mr. Brooks had showed him some interesting mathematical puzzles. (Interesting to him, at least: Matthew and James had immediately effected an escape to play in the Pemberley attics instead.)

Mr. Bingley gestured toward the couple sitting nearest Aunt Kitty. "You are not so familiar, I believe, with my youngest sister and her husband, Mr. and Mrs. Lofton."

"We have met," Jonathan said, "but only many years prior. It is a pleasure to see you again." This had to be said, whether Jonathan was pleased or not. However, he had no particular prejudice against the Loftons, who greeted him with every show of civility. Like the Hursts, the Loftons were dressed as people of wealth and fashion; unlike the Hursts, they did so with good taste and restraint.

"Mr. Darcy!" Mrs. Lofton cried. She was a small woman, rather younger than her siblings present. "We are in need of a new source of interest, so you are come to save us from the evils of idle minds. I shall be wanting to hear all about some of your famed *investigations*. They say you have caught murderers hither and yon!"

"The credit cannot belong wholly to me, for I had invaluable help." Juliet Tilney's face filled Jonathan's mind again, and it was with difficulty that he prevented himself from sighing.

"Yes, yes, you must tell us everything." Unfortunately, Mrs. Lofton was proving to be one of those persons who very much want to look someone in the eyes at all times while speaking, a habit Jonathan particularly abhorred. She kept angling her head to try to stay within his gaze, no matter how hard Jonathan tried to avert it. "Nothing *improper*, of course. I suppose much of the truth of such things must be improper."

Mr. Lofton laughed as he drew his wife back. "Mrs. Lofton, if you wish to observe propriety, follow the example of Mrs. Brooks, who as you see has held at least one of her questions for her nephew until later!" Polite chuckles answered this, though Jonathan thought he detected Aunt Kitty taking especial pleasure in the comment, no doubt due to Mrs. Hurst's earlier incivility.

"Then last comes Mr. Lucas," Uncle Bingley finished, "though the two of you, I know, are friends of old."

"Indeed," said Isaac Lucas, standing and offering his hand to Jonathan. "Admittedly, I, too have heard of your adventures, Mr. Darcy!"

"That is not the word my mother uses to describe my experiences," Jonathan said in all seriousness, though everyone laughed. He realized that this was not mockery; instead, he had been taken for a wit. This did not at all comport with what he next wished to say: "My condolences upon the passing of your father last winter."

Mr. Lucas's smile dimmed somewhat. "Thank you. It was a great shock to us—not yet sixty and in fine health, and only two years after Grandpapa's death."

"It must make a great change for you," Jonathan said, "to become master of Lucas Lodge at so young an age."

"Indeed. Fortunately my father taught me how to manage an estate, beginning even before I was ready for school. Do you not remember how he walked the fields with us, talking about signs of a good harvest?"

"Yes, I do." The late Mr. Lucas had been patient with Jonathan's many questions and hunger for detail. "He was an excellent man."

Isaac Lucas was but a year older than Jonathan. Both his mother and Isaac's aunt Charlotte Collins had determined that the two boys should be playmates in their youth, and every journey into Hertfordshire for Jonathan had involved a great deal of time spent in Isaac's company. Though they never became the bosom companions their female relations would have wished, they had nonetheless got on well. Jonathan's oddities of temperament had never much bothered Isaac; and for his part, Isaac was too good-natured a fellow to indulge in any of the mockery that had so bedeviled Jonathan's time at school. Sometimes Jonathan thought he would find it much easier to spend time with strangers if more of them would comport themselves as Isaac Lucas did.

"Now I will make my confession," said Mr. Lucas. "The Bingleys had spread word of your coming, and you see, I have paid a call upon them precisely so that I might be here for your arrival and, if you wish, accompany you to Longbourn."

Jonathan had been dreading the visit to his grandparents—

specifically, to his grandmama—from the beginning. Yet he knew that she would behave herself better in the presence of anyone outside the family; Mr. Lucas had understood this, too, and had most tactfully offered his assistance. "Thank you, Mr. Lucas. Let me change from my dusty traveling clothes, and we shall go at once."

Mr. Lucas smiled, an open, artless expression. *Perhaps*, Jonathan thought, *we are better friends than I realized.*

For Juliet, the ideal disposition of Mr. Follett's letter would have gone as follows: She would have discussed it with her mother, and only with her mother. Her mother would have said that of course the proposal must be refused and that she herself would assist Juliet in the writing of this missive. (Her imagination went so far as to specify that this letter should be tenderly solicitous of Mr. Follett's feelings, even though he quite obviously had none. This was simply a matter of good taste.) The task swiftly accomplished, her mother would immediately send a servant to put the reply in the post while Juliet tossed the offending proposal into the nearest fireplace, rendering it into ash.

However, even the best-laid plans can fall afoul of a talkative younger sister and a grandparent's ill-timed visit.

Theodosia meant no mischief, but where news was to be given, she found silence unendurable. Scarcely had Juliet done reading Mr. Follett's letter than both their parents were at her door, and even they had got no more than half through it when notice came that her grandfather—the stern, phlegmatic General Tilney, then visiting the family at Woodston— had heard that Juliet had received a letter. In her current state of social exclusion, such a missive could only be extraordinary, and he demanded to know its contents at once. Having been so informed, he then wished to discuss the matter with all of them at once.

Juliet had always feared her grandfather's displeasure and had always been correct to do so. On this day she learned that his pleasure could be worse by far.

"Well, then," General Tilney announced to the family members gathered in the study. "We have an end to all the difficulty, all the trouble. It is as good a match as *she* is fit for now, and that marriage will clear the path for Theodosia to make a far better one in another few years."

The Reverend Henry Tilney had, to his great credit, never failed to speak his mind to his father on matters of principle. "This Mr. Follett has shown himself to be of low character, and he has caused Juliet tremendous suffering. Can this be the sort of man you would wish to welcome into your family?"

The general's usual scowl deepened. "Certainly I would not say that this Follett will prove any ornament to us. A *painter*! One can scarcely imagine a profession more ridiculous—for a working man, it might be the best trade available, but for a gentleman? No, no. Under normal circumstances, his proposal would not be countenanced for an instant."

Juliet's mother, Catherine, seeking an opportunity, pounced upon this one. "Consider that it has not yet been even one year since the incident at the art exhibition. When more time has passed—as knowledge of Juliet's innocence spreads—"

"No time will wash away such a stain as that," General Tilney said with such disgust that it might have been assumed he had actually seen the offending painting. Yet in this matter, Juliet could not blame him. Mr. Follett had put her face in a picture portraying the myth of Pasiphaë, who had disguised herself as a cow all for the amour of a bull. This work of art would have been shocking in any exhibition anywhere in England; she even thought it might have been considered immoral in *France*.

Finally Juliet dared to speak. "Mr. Follett said that we should take our time considering his proposal. He does not expect a swift reply."

She had understood her grandfather's pride well, for he instantly replied, "Indeed he shall not have one. Let this man Follett not think that our family is so eager to admit him. After all, Juliet could simply remain a companion to her sister, or a housekeeper to her brother. We must not be thought too impoverished to support one spinster."

Such were the fates she could contemplate! Juliet might have wept.

Though the worst fate was unavoidable—it lay all about her, in every direction—for it was simply that she would not marry Jonathan Darcy, the only man she believed herself able to love. And that, now, could never be changed.

Longbourn was one of the more respectable houses in the vicinity of Meryton. Certainly it lacked the grandeur of Netherfield, or even that of Lucas Lodge, but it was nonetheless a proper country home. Though Jonathan's mother said that Longbourn had often seemed small and crowded with five daughters in residence, it offered more than enough comfort for an elderly couple who entertained but seldom. This fact was evident to all except the elderly lady in question.

"I have told Mr. Bennet time and again that the chimney needs repairing, but he never listens," said Mrs. Bennet, who sat in her chair, waving a small handkerchief as though to punctuate her thoughts. "Come wintertime, we shall scarce be able to see each other for all the smoke! Like as not it shall spoil all the furnishings, and my clothing, too."

"You believe, then, that my clothes will prove equal to the challenge," said Mr. Bennet, who had not looked up from his book since only a few minutes after Jonathan had arrived with Isaac Lucas. "But yours, you despair of? Take heart, madam. I never yet knew a woman who complained of a reason to order new dresses."

Mrs. Bennet was not diverted. "Well, Mr. Lucas, you are grown quite the gentleman now. How I do remember you gamboling about the meadow with a kite or playing on your hobbyhorse. But now! Head of the family, magistrate of the county, all very proper. You do not run around like *some* of the young bucks do that are grown up so very wild."

Jonathan had the distinct impression that he was being classed as one of the young bucks, an implication so patently false as to be unworthy of argument. As a child and adolescent, he had often attempted to correct his grandmother's erroneous assumptions, which had convinced her of nothing save that her eldest grandson was willfully impudent and terribly proud.

Luckily, Isaac Lucas possessed better manners than anyone else in the room. "When a man inherits a house, he also inherits a responsibility to his family, and his conduct must change accordingly."

True and rational as this statement might be, it displeased both the Bennets in different ways. Mr. Bennet was reminded that he could have attended more to his own responsibilities as head of household, but such thoughts never occupied him for very long, and within moments he was once again absorbed in his book. As for Mrs. Bennet, she was freshly irate that Longbourn would someday be inherited by their cousin Mr. Collins and his wife, Charlotte—Isaac Lucas's aunt. This prospect did not daunt her so much as it had before three of her daughters had married exceedingly well, guaranteeing her comfort in old age, but she continued to resent the entailment of Longbourn on general principles.

Mrs. Bennet changed the subject to another of her dissatisfactions. "My good Jane remembers her family, to be sure, though we have not seen her in ages—"

"Jane visited three days ago," Mr. Bennet said, with no expectation that this fact would be acknowledged, as indeed it was not.

"She has many responsibilities, and so many guests! Those ladies expect her to cater to them and entertain them whenever they please, for as long as they like. How such a good man as Bingley came to have such disagreeable sisters I am sure I do not know." Mrs. Bennet sighed. "At least we do see our Jane. Kitty has not set foot in this house in a month." She continued on in this vein for some time, happy to be heard and uninterested in hearing; Jonathan was grateful not to be forced to make more conversation.

With Mr. Lucas's deft assistance, escape was accomplished by the late afternoon. The two young men rode together for the first half a mile, until the time came for them each to turn toward their respective houses. "Thank you for your companionship today," Jonathan said. "My grandparents were pleased to see you, I think."

"It was but a small thing; yet I will claim it as a kindness, for I wish to beg one of you in return," said Mr. Lucas. "Mr. Darcy, would you be so good as to inform me immediately upon the arrival of the Allerdyce family at Netherfield?"

Jonathan's heart sank. "The Allerdyces are coming?" There had been something about that in Aunt Jane's letter, he now recalled, but he had not heeded it as well as he should have done. Mrs. Allerdyce—the former Caroline Bingley—had plans for Jonathan, plans he intended to disappoint.

"Indeed, they are to be here within three weeks. I know

not the date, and I do not wish to excite undue curiosity by asking . . . but it is my hope you will remedy that."

The shy smile on Mr. Lucas's face suggested a motive he would not speak aloud. Jonathan had in recent years made more practice of studying the unspoken wishes of others, which allowed him to now deduce that Mr. Lucas was interested in one of the Allerdyce daughters. He very much hoped it was Priscilla, whose mother seemed intent upon making Jonathan's bride, whether he liked it or not. "Certainly. As soon as the information is mine, it shall also be yours."

With that Mr. Lucas rode off toward Lucas Lodge, and Jonathan enjoyed the best moments of his entire day, the few during which he was able to be alone. At last—liberty, privacy, room in which to breathe! He kept his horse at a slow walk, the better to savor these simple pleasures, which had been denied him ever since the duel in London.

Thoughts of the duel brought forth thoughts of Juliet Tilney, and this, too, gave Jonathan reason to linger in his leisurely ride back through fields painted in rosy sunset light.

But he did return to Netherfield, and to dinner, and to the company assembled there. Aunt Jane and Uncle Charles had always provided the kindest, most genteel, most feeling companionship, but the same could not be said of all those who sat at table.

"It is so fine a thing to see," said Mrs. Lofton, "when sisters are so close that they never wish to be parted, even in adulthood. Why, Mrs. Brooks, you have dined at Netherfield four times this week, all to be near Mrs. Bingley."

Aunt Kitty's cheeks seemed very pink. "My sister has been so good as to invite us."

This struck Jonathan as odd, for it had never struck him that his aunt Jane and aunt Kitty were particularly close. It was his mother who had attended Aunt Jane's confinements, who traveled distances to see her, who wrote letter after letter. Furthermore, on past visits to Netherfield, Jonathan had of course seen the Brookses, but he did not recall them being so often in the company of the Bingleys. Then again—he had become fonder of his brothers once they had aged out of preadolescent barbarity and could at last hold civil conversations. Sibling relationships might, perhaps, wax and wane.

It struck Jonathan then that Mrs. Lofton's comment might have been a veiled jab at her sister Mrs. Hurst. If so, it had gone unheeded. "The larger the party gathered in the evening, the livelier the diversions that follow," Mrs. Hurst declared. "Whist tonight? Or brag?"

"Could have some music," said Mr. Hurst, gesturing impatiently at the servant to refill his wineglass. "We need not always have cards."

"They weary me," said Mrs. Lofton. "I cannot see the point of sitting up all hours in search of knaves or deuces or whatever is not in one's own hand."

"Card games provide much exercise for our powers of reason," said Mr. Brooks, a comment that no one seemed to have any interest in following up on.

"Tonight we may be able to set up two tables!" Mrs. Hurst said brightly. "You will play, will you not, Mr. Darcy?"

"Not this evening, I think. The journey was long, and I am much tired."

Jonathan suspected he would not be able to escape Netherfield without winning at least some of Mrs. Hurst's money, but he did not intend to begin tonight.

A whist table was nonetheless convened, with the Hursts, Mr. Brooks, and Aunt Jane set to play (though Aunt Jane seemed to participate only out of politeness). Uncle Bingley busied himself at the writing desk, saying only that he needed to write a letter. Jonathan fancied he once or twice saw Aunt Jane peer toward her husband curiously, or perhaps she only longed to escape from whist. The Loftons conversed with

Aunt Kitty, and Jonathan was free to take up a book; most of Mr. Bingley's library was kept in Staffordshire, but volumes enough were present for his old friend Tacitus to be found.

As much as Jonathan enjoyed Roman history, this work was familiar enough to him that he attended somewhat to the conversation around him.

Aunt Kitty: "Your father must have had many stories to tell of his adventures in the West Indies, Mr. Lofton. Why have not you shared more of them with us?"

Mrs. Lofton: "When gentlemen have ought to do with the navy, they should leave all such behind upon returning to their lives and estates. So I have always held."

Mr. Lofton: "My good wife means, of course, that I am meant to conceal the less genteel sources of our wealth. But I am not ashamed of my father's naval history nor its role in our prosperity."

Mr. Hurst: "What are trumps again?"

Aunt Kitty: "One should never be ashamed of serving the crown. Indeed, I have always held so. Whether in army or navy! When the militia was stationed here in my youth, how I swooned over a red coat."

Mrs. Lofton: "The army is the proper pursuit of a gentleman."

Aunt Jane: "Oh, no, no, we must not wager. That is not the way of a friendly game."

Mrs. Hurst: "It is the way of society."

Mr. Lofton: "Some boys have tree houses, but I had a tree ship. My father let me use old ruined tablecloths as sails, taught me to tie rigging, quizzed me on direction of the wind."

Aunt Kitty: "How delightful that sounds!"

Mr. Brooks: "I believe the hand is mine."

None of this fitted together for Jonathan, and he was grateful not to be obliged to make sense of any of it. More grateful yet was he to be able to retire for the evening. Once in his bedchamber, eagerly he took up his writing desk, ready to begin the fateful letter to Miss Tilney . . . but what, precisely, did he intend to say?

So preoccupied had he been with finding the opportunity to write this all-important missive that he had not properly reckoned on what he would include. Jonathan wished to propose marriage, but on what terms? Certainly he did not have his parents' approval. Jonathan was accustomed to think of himself as an eligible bachelor—everyone he met did so—but without Pemberley, how would he support a bride? He had considerably more savings than most young men in his situation, as he neither gambled nor drank his allowance away, but these means could hardly provide the living of a wife and family.

My parents would not disinherit me, Jonathan thought, *unless I wed without their consent*. His father could be stern but never cruel, and his mother had shown more sympathy toward Miss Tilney. Where Mrs. Darcy approved, Mr. Darcy's opinion often followed. This could take some time, however. Months. In so grave a matter as this? Years might pass. Could he truly ask Miss Tilney to endure so long an engagement?

Ultimately, Jonathan's inkwell remained stoppered that night. He went to sleep determined to think again upon the practicalities of the matter tomorrow. He *would* write—would propose, would find a way—but the doing of it must require as much pragmatism as passion, as much delicacy as hope.

He awoke early the next day and submitted to the assistance of an unfamiliar valet. Jonathan often found the constriction of clothing a great distraction, at times even troubling; his tailor had relaxed the seams and collars of Jonathan's shirts, jackets, waistcoats, and trousers as much as possible while maintaining fashion and decorum. The valet at Pemberley went through the dressing process slowly, giving Jonathan time to accustom himself to every layer. This new man's speed made Jonathan feel uneasy—the pressure at his waist, at his neck. As the cravat was being tied, he remembered the sight of a strangled man—one of the murders he had helped to solve in London—and Jonathan thought he might be overcome. He raised one hand, then stopped, resisting the urge to swat the valet away—when a scream from below startled them both into stillness.

"Who was that?" Jonathan said. His nerves, already strained, made him feel taut enough to snap.

"I know not, sir," said the valet. A second scream sounded, as shrill as the last and even longer, and Jonathan could wait no longer. He dashed from his room toward the sound of the screams, which seemed to be coming from downstairs. Most of the others remained abed; only his aunt Jane stood at the broad doorway of the breakfast room, one hand at her chest, her eyes wide. Next to her stood a servant girl who had been carrying a plate of pastries—and had dropped it with a thud upon the discovery of Mr. Hurst lying dead upon the floor.

Chapter Three

"Oh, no," Aunt Jane whispered. "Oh, Mr. Hurst! He is unwell— A doctor, we must call—"

"I believe he is dead," Jonathan said, putting one hand on his aunt's arm before stepping further into the room to stoop over Mr. Hurst's body. The sight was rather grotesque: Mr. Hurst stared vacantly at the fine plaster medallion on the ceiling, his tongue lolling slightly from his mouth. Two fingers against the man's wrist confirmed Jonathan's fears. "Yes, he has died."

The serving girl swooned so that she might have fallen, but Aunt Jane went to her side immediately, catching her by the elbow. "Sit down, Becky," Jane said, even though her own voice shook so much that she seemed equally likely to fall. "You must take care. You are so apt to fall, but who could blame you? Oh, how shocking, how wretched!"

Jonathan Darcy was no stranger to death; four times, he had been called upon to investigate murders, and in so doing he had seen and heard much that was generally shielded from members of the gentry. Yet he was more shaken by the sight of Mr. Hurst's body than he had been since the very first occasion. That had been the murder of Mr. Wickham, Jonathan's uncle who had been married to Aunt Lydia, his mother's youngest sister. He had attributed his composure at the incidents of homicide since to experience and greater maturity, but now Jonathan realized that he had neglected to consider another significant point: That first time, as now, he had long known the victim.

It was not as though Jonathan had been intimately acquainted with Mr. Hurst; insofar as observation could inform, Mr. Hurst's interests had been limited to eating rich foods, playing cards, and drinking massive quantities of wine and port. As Jonathan relished none of these diversions, their conversations over the years had been necessarily brief and invariably dull. Yet the mere fact of having known Mr. Hurst as long as he could remember—having encountered him at his uncle Bingley and aunt Jane's homes throughout the years—rendered this death more disruptive to Jonathan's peace of mind than most of the others he had beheld.

By this time, his uncle had come to the door, with Mr. Lofton standing just behind. They both wore their dressing gowns: Bingley's plain, Lofton's silk with a tasseled belt. "Dear G-d!" Bingley exclaimed. "He is dead? Are you certain?"

"Very much so," said Jonathan.

Mr. Lofton, though pale and evidently shaken, retained enough composure to say, "I shall go to my wife, and together we will inform Mrs. Hurst."

Jonathan had occasionally wondered why the Hursts were married, so little attention did they pay to each other—but no doubt Mrs. Hurst would be very sorry to be made a widow. He nodded to Mr. Lofton before turning back to Mr. Hurst's body.

Brief though the diversion had been, it allowed Jonathan to look at Mr. Hurst with fresh eyes. It had become evident that the man had lost control of his bodily functions either just prior to his death or upon the moment of it; furthermore, beneath his arm lay a puddle of what could only have been digestive effluvia. Jonathan was familiar enough with death, by this time, to be certain that this last was not common at the moment of decease. In fact, he had seen it only once before.

His attention turned next to the china cup that lay several inches from Mr. Hurst's hand. A splash of coffee on the carpet suggested that Mr. Hurst had not quite finished drinking it when the fatal spasm came upon him. Jonathan took the cup in his hand, and though he had dined in the Bingleys' home at least a few times every year of his life, the pattern of the china seemed new to him. The pale sky blue of the exterior was spangled with small gilt flowers; the interior was a light ivory.

In this cup, that ivory was clouded—too pale. Jonathan reached in with one finger and dabbed the coffee-stained sludge sticking to the bottom, which revealed a bit of fine white powder at the base, which had not fully dissolved into Mr. Hurst's coffee. Yet enough had been drunk to prove fatal.

"Poison," he said.

He had spoken to himself, more than to the others, which was why he was startled by the gasps and cries of alarm that met his statement. Jonathan looked up to see Aunt Jane with her hands to her face, Uncle Bingley clutching the doorjamb as if to keep himself from collapsing, and the serving girl Becky slumped in her chair as though she already had.

"Poison," Bingley repeated. "Are you certain? Quite certain?"

"I would stake much upon it," Jonathan said, looking down again into the china cup.

"It must be sugar," Aunt Jane protested.

Jonathan shook his head. "The powder is too fine and soft for that. I believe you will find it to be very similar to the arsenic kept for poisoning rats."

Aunt Jane cried out, "But we keep so little! We have so many cats in the yard and stable—we scarcely see a mouse."

"If you had as much as is in this cup, then that has proved sufficient," Jonathan said. "Last night, I believe, Grandmama said that Mr. Isaac Lucas is the new magistrate. Is that correct?"

Bingley nodded. "Though I believe he has yet to be called

upon to oversee any serious matter. Certainly nothing so dire as this."

"He must be notified as soon as possible," Jonathan said.

Aunt Jane had taken a napkin and now carefully draped it over Mr. Hurst's contorted face. Her pleading gaze sought Jonathan as she said, "You have knowledge of such things, do you not, Jonathan? You will get to the heart of it, of that I am sure. Surely it was an accident—some mischance—"

"Few accidents would lace a coffee cup with arsenic," Jonathan said. Jane covered her face with her hands. Perhaps she felt she could bear to hear this only if she did not also have to see Mr. Hurst lying dead upon the floor.

"If some villain has crept into this house," Bingley said, "if such has been done to my guest and brother—then I am glad indeed you are here, Jonathan. The truth must be known, and as soon as possible. We have heard much of your investigations from your parents' letters, and surely you are the most proper person to help us in this matter. How can we assist you? What else should we do?"

Do not blame Jonathan Darcy for what then came into his mind. Think, instead, of the fineness of spirit necessary for a young man so desperately in love to look upon such a situation and only after several minutes realize it has made a reunion possible.

"The first thing you must do," he said, "is to summon she who has been my partner in every such investigation of murder. You must send for Miss Juliet Tilney at once."

Had Juliet known that she was soon to be called from Gloucestershire to another murder inquiry, her feelings would have been rather more mixed than Jonathan Darcy might have supposed—but she would, nonetheless, have eagerly wished the express to ride even faster, the swifter to learn all that there was to know. Yet as soon as the rider did arrive, and she had read the missive sent from Netherfield Park, Hertford-shire, Juliet felt that longing all the more sharply. For, had the rider come but three hours earlier, her parents and siblings would have been present. The information would have first been shared with her mother and father, and together, they could have discussed what was to be done.

However, two hours earlier, Mr. and Mrs. Tilney had left in her grandfather's second-best coach to take Albion to his boarding school, where he would learn Latin and Greek, and Theodosia to the far less demanding school for girls, where she would learn dancing and deportment. During an absence of but a week or two, they would previously have left Juliet in the parsonage, attended by their few servants, to amuse her-self as she saw fit (generally, with novels and long walks).

However, young women whose reputations are in tatters are not to be left alone to their own devices. In Juliet's case, her parents fully trusted her; what they did not trust was the direction town gossip might take. Thus the express rider found her in the keeping of her grandfather and uncle, whose visit was indeed wholly intended for this purpose. Worse yet, the letter's arrival coincided with that of her uncle, the eldest son of the general, and the only relation Juliet liked even less than her grandfather.

This uncle, Major Tilney, studied the letter coolly. "You have never met this Mrs. Bingley?"

"No," said Juliet, "though I have met her sister Mrs. Darcy, and of course I know Mr. Jonathan Darcy, who is already at Netherfield."

General Tilney's cold, sharp gaze remained fixed on Juliet. "You wish to go, then, for you could have refused the invita-tion without my consent."

So astonishing had the arrival of Mrs. Bingley's letter been that Juliet had scarcely even asked herself whether or not she wanted to accept the invitation. Yet her grandfather—while a difficult, dictatorial man—was not a fool. "Yes, Grandfather," she said. He had informed her that she was too old to call him "Grandpapa" when she reached eight years of age. "I would wish to leave at once, sir, and to travel as swiftly as possible. The sooner one begins such an investigation, the better."

"I could not be less interested in the Bingleys' family troubles," General Tilney said. "What you have here is another opportunity to catch the Darcy heir. I take it you will endeavor to seize your chance?"

Juliet had been thinking of Jonathan Darcy since she had read the first paragraph of Mrs. Bingley's letter, which had explained who she was and who had asked that Juliet be summoned. But she had not considered this an "opportunity," as she had no intentions of "catching" him or anyone. This, surely, was not the way to think of matrimony! Nor was the matter as simple as her grandfather suggested. "Mr. Darcy could scarcely wed without his parents' approval, sir, and *that* shall never be given, no matter how many murders I may solve."

Her uncle, Major Tilney, laughed as he refilled his pipe. "Come, girl, you have more tricks than that, do you not? There are situations in which a gentleman's honor may be compromised nearly as much as a lady's. Bring one such about, and I believe the Darcys could be made to see sense."

He was, in effect, suggesting that Juliet seduce Jonathan Darcy—that she should disgrace them both to such a degree that his parents would hurriedly consent to the match rather than have such disgrace be known. This was so vile, so dishonorable, that Juliet would not have expected it even from her uncle, a most venal and base man. Her cheeks flushed hot, as though she had been slapped. "I would not stoop so low!"

General Tilney's scowl deepened. "You will not 'stoop' to

marrying Mr. Follett, nor to ensuring that Mr. Darcy will marry you? Then you will stoop further yet, child. Do you long, then, to become a governess? A lady's companion? Neither gentlewoman nor servant, there only to nod and smile and be forgotten? For those fates are not far from you."

Better a governess than a whore, Juliet thought but did not say. "Am I to be allowed to go to Hertfordshire, sir?"

After a moment, her grandfather smiled, a thin, tight expression devoid of any mirth. "Indeed, you must go. Prepare as quickly as you can, and I shall arrange for the carriage to take you at the best possible speed. We shall have you at Netherfield Park on the morrow." This was a long and difficult journey, one during which Juliet was unlikely to have one moment's rest, but she felt a distant pang of joy.

Yet this faded as her uncle added, "Perhaps you need not employ my stratagem, but you no doubt have a few of your own. Catch Mr. Darcy if you can. If this proves impossible, then you will have a letter to write to Mr. Follett, will you not?"

To this Juliet could scarcely reply. She simply gave them a swift curtsy before hurrying to summon the maid who could help her pack.

Eager though Jonathan was for Miss Tilney's arrival, he did not neglect his duties as an investigator. Not one hour could be wasted, especially as he had come to understand that the period immediately following a murder could prove crucial to understanding it.

First, he confirmed that Netherfield, like most great houses, kept a small supply of arsenic on hand in order to kill any rats that might enter the kitchen, barn, or stores. (Thanks to Aunt Jane's beloved cats, this was more a theoretical concern than a practical one, but the housekeeper, Mrs. Mulgrew, believed in the value of preparation.) This box was to be found in one of the pantries, and as the pantries were not locked, any person could conceivably have accessed the arsenic at any time. For that matter, it would not have been difficult for anyone to purchase more arsenic in town, and the shopkeeper would have thought nothing of it—most likely, such a commonplace transaction would not even be remembered. Jonathan had investigated an arsenic poisoning before, and as such he knew the futility of tracking the killer by its trail alone.

Second, he sat down with Mrs. Mulgrew and the cook, Mrs. Gooding, to discuss who might have been seen in the kitchen that morning other than the servants normally working there.

"Becky came in—she's an upstairs maid, but was helping in the kitchen today because Louise, that's one of my usual girls, had need to go see her mother in Meryton, as she's poorly," said Mrs. Gooding, who was eager to give any relevant information and much that was irrelevant as well. "So that's no wonder."

Jonathan said, "Any of the staff not accounted for?"

"No, sir," Mrs. Gooding said.

"What about the Bingleys or their guests?"

Mrs. Gooding seemed puzzled. "We saw Mr. Bingley, of course, but it's his kitchen, ain't it? He likes a well-kept kitchen, he does; and a few times a year, he walks through on his way outside, says good day to all, has a look about."

Though it was unusual for a gentleman to enter his own kitchen, it was not unheard-of, and at Netherfield, it appeared to be a common practice. Nonetheless, Jonathan felt obliged to note it.

Mrs. Gooding went on: "Mr. Lofton, too, but we see him once or twice a week. That wife of his, she wants a bite here and a bite there all throughout the day! He has to fetch her toast or a biscuit early morning, late at night, one never knows."

Mrs. Mulgrew, more genteel as befit her position, added, "Mr. Lofton passed me in the hallway this morning and mentioned he was fetching toast for Mrs. Lofton."

"Why did they not simply ring the bell?" Jonathan asked.

"When Mrs. Lofton is alone, she does," Mrs. Mulgrew replied. "Mr. Lofton will make the trip himself, however, no matter how often I assure him we are ready to assist." She seemed to take Mr. Lofton's lack of pretension as an intrusion upon her proper sphere.

All of these behaviors, if neither daily nor common in society, were nonetheless habitual within Netherfield. Jonathan tried once more: "You saw no one else in the kitchens this morning?"

Mrs. Mulgrew and Mrs. Gooding exchanged a look. It was Mrs. Mulgrew who said, "Not in the kitchens, sir—but early this morning, I saw Mrs. Hurst upon the grounds. Her maid had not yet attended her, so I could scarcely believe she had ventured from her room. Certainly she hurried within quickly enough afterward. Where she went immediately following, I do not know, but she entered through the door nearest the kitchen."

Mrs. Gooding added, "Didn't see her myself, but as early as she was up, I would have been in the dairy, and my maids would have been in the scullery."

That meant Mrs. Hurst—or potentially some other person—would have had opportunity to enter the kitchen and procure the poison. Jonathan felt he had got somewhere at last.

Third, he discussed these facts, his general plan, and the imminent arrival of Juliet Tilney with Mr. Isaac Lucas, who appeared quite astonished to suddenly be responsible for catching a murderer. "We have two constables, but they serve only when called upon, and I believe it has been years since this was the case," Mr. Lucas admitted. "Meryton and its environs have not required such since the militia days—we govern each other adequately enough, or so we did until now. A murder by poison! I can scarce believe it."

"As you are the proper authority, you need not allow Miss Tilney and me to lead the investigation," Jonathan said, "but I hope that you will do so. I promise, we are thorough, and we act without prejudice. All possible culprits will be questioned and studied, regardless of my relation to any given person."

Mr. Lucas appeared quite pale. "You think, then, that the killer must be one of the residents or guests of the house? Not a servant nor an intruder?"

"Few strangers travel to this area," Jonathan said. "None of the busier roads pass through, and there are no inns where a stranger might stay. Had any unusual person ridden or walked through, it would have aroused much comment, would it not?"

"Indeed, for we must make the most of whatever novelty comes our way," Mr. Lucas said with a sigh. "And I have heard none such about a wanderer these past few days."

Jonathan had suspected as much—had expected Mr. Lucas to mention any unknown travelers—and as there were none, he felt confident in eliminating the possibility of any homicidal intruder. "As for the servants, I do not yet know. I will speak to them and ask my uncle and aunt about their staff, but I know that the Bingleys pay handsome wages, and as such the servants here tend to be devoted. If any member of the staff had harsh feelings toward Mr. Hurst in particular, if he was unkind to any of their number, hopefully this shall soon be determined."

Mr. Lucas nodded. "Very well. As you have instructed, I sent a rider to the local physician, with instructions that he is to retrieve Mr. Hurst's remains and either conduct this—you called it an 'autopsy'?"

"Yes," Jonathan said. He had had occasion to learn of this in Devonshire. "Do not ask more, for I assure you, the particulars are indelicate in the extreme."

"To conduct this procedure," Mr. Lucas said determinedly, "I shall send for a doctor who can come as quickly as possible. Now, as magistrate, it is my responsibility to ensure that your intention of questioning the servants does not mean that you will fail to question the houseguests or the master and mistress of Netherfield." More quietly he added, "Though of course it is impossible that Mrs. Bingley could be guilty."

"Of course," Jonathan said. "Nor do I think my uncle likely. The others must be considered in turn. You have been a guest at Netherfield, have not you? Have you noted any particular strife regarding Mr. Hurst and any of the others?"

"No, I think not." But Mr. Lucas considered the matter closely, rather than simply changing the subject. "Well. Mr. Hurst seemed apart from the others at nearly all times. He had few interests, so far as could be seen, and even these he pursued rarely, preferring to . . ." Mr. Lucas's words trailed off in evident embarrassment.

There could be no point in tact when the truth must be had. Jonathan said, "You mean, I believe, that Mr. Hurst did little other than drink more than was good for him. I have known him—I should say, I knew him—most of my life, and this habit of his I beheld myself."

"One does not wish to speak ill of the dead," Mr. Lucas said, "and certainly I enjoy a glass of wine or whisky as much as the next man. But it appeared to me that Mr. Hurst enjoyed nothing else. Knowing the Bingleys as I do, it did not surprise me that they did not speak to him of it. The Loftons are not so circumspect, and I might have thought one or the other would comment—but they never did. Mr. Brooks never quoted Scripture on the evils of drink, for which I was generally grateful. And Mrs. Hurst, whom one would expect to be much aggrieved in this circumstance, took no notice of it whatsoever."

"She never has, that I can recall," Jonathan said.

Already Mr. Lucas appeared to regret having spoken. "Then it is unimportant. I ought to have remained silent."

"Do not apologize, Mr. Lucas. Acquaintance leads to some insights, but obscures others. I do not know that I would have considered this particular facet of Mr. Hurst's character as carefully as I should, had you not encouraged me to do so. A fresh perspective is ever useful."

Jonathan was still dwelling upon this a few minutes later, when he heard his uncle speaking with Mrs. Hurst in his study. "I realize how terrible it must be for you," Bingley said, his voice kind. "Whenever this procedure is complete—I can arrange for swift transit, even ample ice from our icehouse, to ensure that—"

"There can be no question of transporting Mr. Hurst's body back to Essex," Mrs. Hurst said briskly. "In this heat? It would prove abominable to all, and the church here is as sacred as any other."

Bingley's hesitation suggested that he was taken aback by Mrs. Hurst's lack of sorrow following her husband's demise. "Surely it would be a greater comfort to you to read his inscription in your own church, to know that you might be near him every Sabbath."

"In the Meryton church, however, Mr. Hurst will have pride of place," Mrs. Hurst said with apparent satisfaction. "No, it is entirely proper for him to be buried here, and the better for us all."

These were not the considerations of a grieving widow. Mrs. Hurst was more interested in the importance of her husband's grave than in the fact that he was dead. Jonathan wondered whether her lack of sorrow hinted at her guilt—or did it suggest the opposite? Would not a murderess be sure to at least feign sorrow for her late husband, to disguise her culpability in his death?

Jonathan would ask Miss Tilney this at his next opportunity, which he hoped would be very soon. He had taken notes on all he observed, and would continue to do so, in order that the investigation would not be delayed.

And they had so much more to speak of—so very much. He wished her carriage all speed and smooth roads, so that it might bring Miss Tilney more swiftly to his side.

Meanwhile, within her grandfather's carriage as it jolted and bumped along the road, Miss Tilney sat alone with her thoughts. (It was not surprising that neither her grandfather nor her uncle had accompanied her—whatever concern for her delicacy either had ever possessed had dissolved along with her reputation—but she still felt conspicuous in her solitude. What must the coachman think?)

She was not going to Hertfordshire to "catch" Jonathan Darcy. A loving son, he would never marry without his parents' consent; he did not have such and was unlikely ever to receive it; thus all hopes must be at an end. Yet how could she not be glad of seeing him once more? To be with Mr. Darcy again would be both happiness and sorrow, both balm and wound.

However, it was not only for him that she went. Juliet wanted to solve one more murder.

Investigations were so much more interesting to her than any "proper, ladylike" activity had ever been. To study human nature, both at its best and its worst—to examine every facet of a crime, whether of evidence or motivation—it was the most fascinating activity she knew. So often women were expected to concern themselves with being pleasing, being decorative, and no more. To investigate a murder was to step beyond the narrow boundary society had laid all about her.

Let me be ruined, then, Juliet thought. *Let me have no prospects, or only very few and very dim. Let my grandfather judge me, my parents despair of me, my siblings undertake the care of me later in life.*

But let me once more do this work, solve this crime, and do so with Mr. Darcy by my side. That will be enough.

It has to be.

Chapter Four

To Jonathan it seemed that Netherfield remained frozen during the short time it took for the physician to examine Mr. Hurst's body, and for Miss Tilney to arrive—as though every person present had joined the late Mr. Hurst in the icehouse, impervious to the last summer warmth. Most kept to their rooms, even taking their food on trays. Jonathan did the same regarding his meals, but remained on watch in the house . . . though for what, he knew not.

Finally, the word came: The autopsy had found the telltale signs of poison. Mr. Hurst had indeed been the victim of murder.

Jonathan and Mr. Lucas broke this news to the Bingleys that evening. Although Aunt Jane had scarcely ceased weeping, her tears came afresh, and Uncle Bingley seemed as sad as Jonathan had ever seen him. "A pity, a great pity indeed," he said. "You truly believe someone in this house has done it?"

"I cannot see any possibility of an intruder," said Jonathan. "Additionally I must state that I have spoken to various members of your staff since the fatal event, and none of them know of any problems between Mr. Hurst and any of the servants. Therefore, the culprit is almost certainly a person not only known to us but also an intimate of the family."

"Unthinkable," his uncle Bingley said, but as an exclamation rather than denial. "How very terrible. At least you are here to assist us, Jonathan. I do not know what we would do without you."

"And Miss Tilney, too," added Aunt Jane, between sniffles. "Oh—Mr. Lucas—please do not think we fail to value your—"

"I know nothing of investigating murder," said Mr. Lucas, "so I have no pretensions to expertise and am as grateful for Mr. Darcy and his friend as you can be."

After this there was nothing to do but to retire. However, Jonathan lingered a moment longer to speak privately with Aunt Jane. "I wished to ask—when you wrote my mother about all this, did you mention—had you yet mentioned that Miss Tilney—"

"I have not yet written Elizabeth," Aunt Jane said. "How terribly I have neglected my duty to her as your mother!—but every time I tried to begin, my tears would spoil the ink. And I know they are much concerned with the earl and countess at present. I did not wish to add to their concerns, though I know I must."

He could scarce believe his good fortune. "Do not do so yet, please," he said. "You know how worried my parents have been regarding my health, though you see for yourself I am entirely recovered. There can be no cause yet to disturb them."

Aunt Jane agreed entirely, and Jonathan felt guilty—for while he did wish to avoid alarming his parents, his chief desire was to conceal Miss Tilney's presence in Hertfordshire as long as possible. Its importance made the deception imperative, no matter how regrettable.

After a long journey, much jostled and ill-rested, Juliet Tilney arrived at Netherfield Park shortly following dawn. Sore and weary, aware that she must look bedraggled at best, she descended from the carriage in front of a fine country house—not so grand as some she had visited, but elegant all the same, situated upon a small hill that overlooked the verdant countryside. Dew still glittered upon the grass.

Naturally, Juliet had anticipated that a servant would show her in. To her surprise, however, a genteel woman bustled out, showing no sign of discomfiture at welcoming a guest hours before breakfast time. "Miss Tilney, is it not? I am Mrs. Bingley. How good it is of you to have come! What a journey you must have had, to arrive so swiftly. We cannot thank you enough."

Juliet had not been received so graciously by anyone outside her family since she had been "ruined." In her current state, this unexpected kindness moved her greatly. "Thank you, Mrs. Bingley. I am gratified that you wished for my assistance at this difficult time, and I shall do my best to help in any way I can."

Mrs. Bingley looked her over, head to toe, not with judgment upon her disheveled state but with an almost maternal solicitude. "You must be tired, and thirsty and hungry, too. Cook is still preparing breakfast, but we can offer you tea and toast, and the cakes shall be done very soon. We will have your room ready later today—"

"It is being prepared as we speak, Aunt Jane." Jonathan Darcy appeared at the front door, and Juliet saw him for the first time since the aftermath of his duel with Laurence Follett.

Her first thought was only that Mr. Darcy looked very well—as hale and handsome as he had ever been, and perhaps even more so. This was a great contrast to their last encounter, when he had been wounded and weak. Her second thought was that she scarcely knew what to say to him, the person to whom she had once felt freest to speak in all the world.

Mr. Darcy, at least, was more at ease. "I have vacated what was my room here at Netherfield that it might be made ready for you," he said. "I shall stay nearby with my grandparents at Longbourn, and— Oh, I ought first to have said welcome, Miss Tilney."

"Thank you, Mr. Darcy." Juliet heard her calm voice almost with wonder. "That is most kind of you."

"It is the least that I could do. You have come a very great distance to help solve the murder of Mr. Hurst, and I am most thankful that you have." Mr. Darcy smiled at her then, and Juliet ought to have smiled back, but all her weariness seemed to have settled upon her at once, and she felt as though she might swoon.

Mrs. Bingley must have glimpsed this, for she took Juliet by the arm. "Come. While the maids make up the room fresh for you, you shall have some tea and food. After that you must rest."

"Not for long," Juliet said. "I wish to begin as soon as possible."

"I have made preliminary inquiries and taken notes," Mr. Darcy said. "These we can discuss after you are refreshed. I look forward to it."

"Come, now," Mrs. Bingley said gently. "Let us get you that cup of tea."

Mr. Darcy seemed to realize that Juliet was in no state to converse with him, at least not to any purpose, and he made a small bow as Mrs. Bingley shepherded her inside. The rest was a haze of politeness and orange pekoe, until at last Juliet was free to bathe herself with a cloth and basin of water, then to sink onto the comfortable bed that awaited her. For an instant, as she lay there, she recollected that Jonathan Darcy had slept in this bed only an hour or two before. How strange, yet how easy, to imagine that he lay beside her—

But exhaustion was more overwhelming than even this novel image, and within seconds, Juliet was fast asleep.

Jonathan Darcy intended that Miss Tilney should never know the level of sacrifice he had made so that she might stay in comfort at Netherfield. This sacrifice was great indeed, for there were few houses in which he felt more uncomfortable than he generally did at Longbourn.

"Well!" Mrs. Bennet said upon his arrival. "Not that Longbourn should not be good enough for you to stay, but I see you will only come to us at a time of extremity. Only to make way for that Tilney girl, of which so much has been said in the papers! Make no mistake, I know well what 'Miss T—' stands for, and so does everyone else."

"You must forgive your grandmother," said Mr. Bennet, who was already settling back into his armchair with a book. "Anyone else would be more struck by the fact that a murder had been committed than by a young lady's crimes against propriety. One would think that the latter, no matter how egregious, could scarcely eclipse the former."

Jonathan had worked hard at becoming an easier conversationalist, at being able to speak readily upon topics beyond his principal interests (namely, the Roman Empire and the works of Sir Walter Scott). However, his grandmother's remarks often left him at quite a loss, disrupting his best efforts. "I cannot tell whether you are unhappy that I did not ask to stay with you at first, or that I am to stay with you now."

"Of course we are most happy to see you at any time," said Mr. Bennet, never looking up from his reading, "for you are our eldest grandson. Even if you are abundant in the caprices with which wealthy young men amuse themselves, to be sure, you are far from the most bothersome person I have known. Indeed, you are not even the most bothersome person in the room."

Mrs. Bennet took little notice of this. "I wager you now 'twas no murder at Netherfield Park. Mr. Hurst simply took sick and died. Little wonder, as he drank more than was good for him. This is but a mistake, mark my words, and thus all this upset and change is for nothing."

"Then it is most striking that arsenic should have been put in Mr. Hurst's coffee cup on the very morning illness struck," Jonathan said. He did not bother quoting the results of the autopsy, as this would only extend the conversation. "I shall spend most days at Netherfield, the better to investigate what has happened there. But I thank you for your generous hospitality." Jonathan said this last because he had noted that expressing gratitude for behavior not yet exhibited by a person often inspired that individual to behave in precisely that manner. People generally wished to live up to good expectations of themselves.

Mrs. Bennet was not particularly susceptible to this attempt, as it would have required her to reflect upon her own behavior, a task she seldom undertook. However, she did at least sense that the time to protest his stay had passed. "All well and good, then. Not that I do not wish to see my grandchildren as often as possible—how I do miss little Susannah!—but to be sure, you will be less in the way if you spend your days elsewhere."

From this it could easily be seen that all of Mrs. Bennet's grandchildren were not equal in her sight. Jonathan had long ago ceased to hope for, much less expect, affection from her—so this was not the reason her words stung him so terribly. That was the mention of his late cousin, Susannah.

All at once he felt too exposed, too vulnerable, too intimidated by his grandparents' uneasy welcome. "I shall go to my room and undertake the unpacking."

"What? You, unpack your own trunk?" Mrs. Bennet's ire felt sharper to him, almost unbearably so. "I assure you, we have servants enough in this house to see to such tasks, even if Pine shall have to leave off making the marmalade to—"

"I wish to do it myself," Jonathan said. "Pine need not be troubled."

With this he hurried upstairs, increasingly desperate to be alone.

In point of fact, Jonathan had never unpacked his own trunk, not once in his life. This was simply the first excuse he thought of to ensure quick solitude. As soon as he shut the bedroom door behind him, he sat down heavily upon the bed, closed his eyes, and breathed deeply. But calm would not come.

Susannah had been Jonathan's cousin, the daughter of his uncle Wickham and aunt Lydia, born late in their marriage. As Lydia and Wickham had little money for servants and less patience for the more tedious aspects of caring for their child themselves, they were all too happy for Susannah to visit relations as often as possible, for as long as possible. The Darcys had welcomed her more often than any others, for by this point, they had realized they would be blessed only with sons, and they delighted in the presence of a little girl. When Lydia died of smallpox, Wickham surrendered Susannah all but completely. Therefore the little girl spent far more time at Pemberley than she did at her home.

By that point, Jonathan had been enduring the miseries of boarding school so he had seen his young cousin only out of term time. Most other children had intimidated him, annoyed him, or both, but he had adored Susannah from the start. She had been quieter than his wild brothers, even solemn. He was used to mockery for his particular ways, the order in which he liked to place things, his dislike of any casual unexpected touch, but Susannah had taken Jonathan as he was. If she ever realized that his behaviors were peculiar, she showed no sign of it. They had played games together, croquet or hide-and-seek, and he had even been willing to swing her around on the lawn. It seemed to him sometimes that he could still hear her laugh.

So much time did Susannah spend at Pemberley that it seemed possible, even likely, that eventually she would live there permanently. Jonathan had overheard his parents discussing their intention to provide her with an ample dowry, something Wickham could not supply. This had made Jonathan happy, for it clarified Susannah's place in the family; she was to be considered a sister, as much as though she had been born to his parents.

Yet Mr. Wickham had not agreed with this—had allowed pride to dictate his actions far more than paternal love. This pride, combined with one simple, terrible mistake, had led Susannah to an early grave.

It might have struck an observer as strange that Jonathan sat in his room, mourning a death that had occurred years ago, while the demise of Mr. Hurst barely entered his thoughts. Such is the difference between those we love and those we only know. Mr. Hurst would receive his due shortly; Susannah could never receive hers, and so Jonathan would not deny her this place in his heart.

When Juliet awoke, she quickly took better stock of her situation than she had been in any condition to upon her arrival. Her room was exceedingly pleasant; the angle of the sunlight suggested she had only dozed until just before midday, and a fresh basin of water and cloths had been placed nearby. Her first impression of Mrs. Bingley, though clouded by exhaustion, had proved true: Juliet was being most generously received.

Yet that could be no more than a guise, could it not? After Juliet's past experiences in investigating murders, she had learned never to assume that anyone—however civil and obliging—was innocent.

Still, the Bingleys' hospitality proved even more gracious than she had realized. When she descended, Mrs. Bingley and her husband welcomed Juliet, asked about her journey with such interest that their questions seemed sincere rather than commonplace, and repeatedly thanked her for her goodness in coming such a long way to help them.

Did they not know of the scandal of the portrait? This seemed impossible, and yet the only alternative was that the Bingleys truly refused to judge her on so unjust a basis—so rare a stance that Juliet could scarcely credit it.

The Bingleys assured her that, as soon as the house knew she had awoken, a messenger had been sent to Mr. Darcy at his grandparents' home, and indeed, after but a few minutes, Juliet heard the thump of approaching hooves, the jingling of stirrups and bridle. She did not allow herself to look out the window. Instead she stood with the Bingleys as Mr. Darcy was again shown in.

"Miss Tilney," he said, inclining his head toward her. "You are refreshed?"

"Sufficiently so for our purposes." Juliet next addressed the Bingleys: "I thank you for your kindness, but much of what Mr. Darcy and I need now to discuss is best spoken of in private. This room will do, or another similar—so long as the door is left open, and a servant is not too distant, propriety can be maintained."

"Of course," Mr. Bingley said. "You must have the use of my study for the duration of your efforts."

So it was that, within but a few minutes, they were shown into the room, and Juliet found herself with Mr. Darcy again for the first time in months, all but alone.

"Miss Tilney," he said, his voice rather low. "Have you been well? I have been much concerned—"

"My situation is unimportant, compared to the murder of this Mr. Hurst." Juliet would not have it said that she had used the death of a gentleman as no more than an excuse to "catch" Jonathan Darcy! Though he seemed surprised by her refusal to confide in him, he did not object, so she continued. "First, I think, you should explain to me who all these persons are, and how they relate to one another. To you, I believe, they have all been well-known for many years, but to me they are strangers."

He swiftly summarized the persons currently staying in the house: his uncle and aunt, the latter of whom had been born and raised very near; Mrs. Hurst, the sister of Mr. Bingley now suddenly widowed; and the Loftons, another of Mr. Bingley's sisters and her husband. Mr. Darcy described Mrs. Hurst as proud, Mr. Lofton as unpretentious, and Mrs. Lofton as being—"I have no right, as an investigator, to point any fingers, and my father would deplore the slang, but . . . I would call her 'nosy.'"

Miss Tilney almost smiled before catching herself. "Then that is to the good. Mrs. Lofton may have 'nosed' out some information that will be of use to us."

"As well as much that has not," Mr. Darcy said. He hesitated, then added, "I realize, of course, that all potential suspects must be investigated in turn, and fondness cannot be allowed to play a role—but I would be remiss if I did not say that I consider it highly unlikely that either of the Bingleys would ever take the other life of another. For my uncle, the mere suggestion is strange; for my aunt, nearly farcical. She is as kind and mild a creature as has ever been born, I should say."

Juliet knew she must remain objective about the Bingleys, in order to counterbalance Mr. Darcy's affection . . . and yet, based on her acquaintance with them so far, she could see the likely justice of his opinion. "If your aunt and uncle are as blameless as you suggest—"

"It cannot be Aunt Jane," Mr. Darcy said. "Almost certainly not my uncle either, but it is *not* my aunt Jane."

As Juliet had no information with which to challenge this assumption, she did not argue. "Are there other frequent guests at Netherfield? People who were there the night before, perhaps?"

"Mr. and Mrs. Brooks. She, too, is my aunt, a younger sister of my mother, and he is the local clergyman. They have two sons who attend a boarding school in the next county." Mr. Darcy had become very thoughtful. "On my first night here, the last night before Mr. Hurst died, there was some comment to the effect that the Brookses came to Netherfield almost every evening. This caught my attention slightly, Miss Tilney, because my aunt Kitty was never particularly close to Aunt Jane when they were girls. Nor had I believed their relationship to be much altered in adulthood. I may simply have been wrong, of course, but I should be interested to know why the Brookses are so often here."

This seemed promising. "And Mr. Brooks?" Juliet asked. "What of him?"

Mr. Darcy shrugged. "I must admit that I know Mr. Brooks shockingly little. He is quiet but not dour, methodical in his habits, deft with cards and with dancing, and insofar as I have ever seen, otherwise utterly unremarkable."

"Is there anyone else we should consider, Mr. Darcy? Anyone at all?"

"The only other guest present earlier that day was Mr. Isaac Lucas, a gentleman close to my own age, who recently came into his inheritance. That said, I cannot think why Mr. Lucas should have any interest in Mr. Hurst whatsoever. Moreover, he is the local magistrate."

Juliet felt grateful that there should be little need to investigate the very person charged with administering justice! They would ask questions, of course, but the difficulties presented by a murderous magistrate would be considerable indeed. "Very well. Take me to the place of the murder, if you will, and we may begin to determine more of what happened on that day."

She began to rise, only to hear Mr. Darcy say—with a new note in his voice, one that arrested her completely—"Miss Tilney, will you not tell me how you are? How you have been these past months? I have so often thought of you, longed to hear your voice."

"Do not." Juliet held up a hand, forestalling him. "Please, Mr. Darcy, do not speak of any such thing. What is gone— what is lost—we must continue on. Do not compromise what we are called upon to accomplish here, for it would but tarnish whatever scrap of reputation I still possess."

"I would not do that for the world," cried Mr. Darcy, "but we cannot be strangers to each other, can we? I do not wish that, any more than I believe you do."

Shaking her head, Juliet rose and straightened herself. "The past months have taught me how little our wishes are worth. The only desire left to me is that I should prove to the world that I can once again help to capture the guilty, to avenge the dead. You have always helped me in that before, Mr. Darcy. Do not abandon me now."

Mr. Darcy's gaze met hers, so intently that Juliet felt heat coming to her cheeks. He said only, "I have no intention of abandoning you, Miss Tilney—now or ever."

Oh!—but Juliet caught herself. She would find the murderer, and all else . . . at the very least, all else must wait.

Chapter Five

Miss Tilney's refusal to speak of their connection discouraged Jonathan Darcy, but only briefly. The look in her eyes, the tone of her voice suggested that her sentiments were much the same as his. A few years prior, he would not have trusted his judgment in this matter, but that had changed—partly because of Miss Tilney, and the greater experience and confidence he had gained from their investigations. The difference between word and feeling both tantalized and tormented him. Most young persons in similar straits would have been rendered nigh unintelligible with suspense.

However, Jonathan had learned that he had a superior ability to set aside such upset for a moment—as though placing it in a box, to save for later—and to attend to more important matters, such as the precise circumstances of Mr. Hurst's death.

"It happened here, in the breakfast room," he said to Miss Tilney as he showed her in. "The room has not been set for breakfast since, as you can well imagine."

"Indeed. I should suppose all would insist on taking their morning meal elsewhere for months to come."

"To the contrary—now that you are come, Aunt Jane has ordered that normal dining is to resume. With two investigators at hand, I believe she feels safer." Jonathan hoped his aunt's faith was justified. He stepped farther into the room, gesturing to the oaken sideboards. "On this longer wall, the breakfast is set out to be taken whenever guests choose. Over here, opposite the window, are set out china cups and an urn of coffee. Those who prefer tea instead obtain this, freshly brewed, from the servants."

He was unsurprised when Miss Tilney immediately understood the importance of this. "Was Mr. Hurst known to drink coffee at breakfast instead of tea?"

How proud Jonathan was of the notes he had taken! "Yes, invariably, but he was not unique in doing so. My uncle and the Loftons both take coffee in the mornings as well. My aunt Jane drinks only tea. Apparently Mrs. Hurst's choice varies from morning to morning."

Miss Tilney had walked to the coffee stain on the rug, which had gone uncleaned at Jonathan's request. "Was Mr. Hurst the first to enter the breakfast room that day, besides the servants?"

"Yes, so far as is known. Yet it would not have been difficult for anyone to slip in after the room had been made ready, for the door would have been open, and the servants are required to enter and remain only after the first guest arrives." This was generous of his aunt and uncle, for many fine houses required servants to stand at the ready for hours before guests appeared for breakfast, if indeed they appeared at all. "The servants are of course alert for the guests' arrival, but anyone familiar with the patterns and schedules of the household would have known when an opportune moment was likely to arise."

"Which indicates that the poisoner was indeed a long-time guest of the household or a servant." Miss Tilney frowned. "Often magistrates and constables are too eager to believe that a servant must be the villain, rather than a member of the gentry, a prejudice most unjust. And yet we have learned that the staff cannot be excluded from our considerations . . ."

"Indeed not," Jonathan said. "Though the generous wages of this household strongly suggest that none of the servants would strike out at random in any attempt to discredit the Bingleys."

"So if our killer is a servant, it would be one with a grievance against Mr. Hurst alone." Miss Tilney's mental energies appeared to be fully awakened, as she proved by asking, "He was overtaken by the poison swiftly?"

"Very much so—after perhaps half an hour's time, perhaps more, according to the servant girl. He died as rapidly as did the late Mrs. Willoughby."

Miss Tilney grimaced at the reminder of that unfortunate woman's gruesome demise. "Were the coffee cups aligned in such a way as to make it clear which cup was to be first chosen?"

"Indeed they were. In a sort of triangle, one cup in front, two behind, so on and so forth. The arsenic was placed in the foremost cup. That would not make it absolutely certain to be the first used, but highly likely."

"Nonetheless, it suggests a disturbing nonchalance on the part of the poisoner. One would think that *any* chance of killing the wrong person would discourage most. But then, anyone willing to commit murder is already careless of human life." Miss Tilney tapped her fingers on the sideboard, an unexpected gesture, informal, the sort of thing genteel people reserved for their family and intimates. Jonathan was therefore encouraged. She turned to him, eyes alight with realization. "Was Mr. Hurst always the first to rise in the morning?"

Jonathan had known she would ask. "Indeed, no. In fact, he was almost always the *last* to rise, probably due to his overindulgence in drink. In other words, we cannot be certain Mr. Hurst was the intended victim."

How this information struck her! For the first time since her arrival at Netherfield Park, Miss Tilney smiled—not the expression of happiness but of astonishment and wonder, of eagerness to learn more. Though the great injustice she had suffered had left its mark, her character and courage remained the same. "Then who *was* generally first to appear?"

"My aunt Jane, but as she invariably drinks tea in the mornings, the poisoner would have known her to be safe from it."

"You must realize this would also give her opportunity."

"Miss Tilney, I must say again: Let us investigate thoroughly, but I am *entirely* certain the culprit is not Aunt Jane." Grateful for evidence to support this assertion, Jonathan added, "Besides, it was her cry of alarm upon discovering Mr. Hurst's body that drew me and others to the breakfast room. Were she guilty of the deed, would she not have delayed until she could hide or clean the offending cup? Why alert others before removing all evidence?"

"You make an excellent point, Mr. Darcy. It is not conclusive of her innocence but highly suggestive of it." With every minute that passed, with every question she asked, Miss Tilney's spirits and color seemed to improve. "Next we must learn whether anyone would've had reason to expect Mr. Hurst to be up early that morning, or whether that person believed someone else would rise even earlier."

Jane Bingley had been told by her nephew that questioning must occur, that this was a critical part of every investigation, a key to finding the truth. Though still she found it difficult to believe that any of her guests could be a murderer, she was determined to cooperate in every possible way, so that the truth might be known beyond any doubt. Alone among her family, Jane had never considered Jonathan's temperament anything so out of the ordinary as to be worthy of comment, and since his majority she had always put much faith in his judgment. If he determined that questioning was necessary, then she would comply, and as hostess encourage all others to do so. Such encouragement took the form of offering to answer questions first.

"How very strange it all is," Jane said, looking at Jonathan and Miss Tilney, each of whom sat in a chair opposite her in Charles's study. She thought only how kind it was of them to allow her the pretty view from the window, never realizing that they wished to watch her expressions in the best light possible. "To think that anyone would be so unkind to Mr. Hurst!"

"Did you ever find him to be a difficult guest?" Miss Tilney asked.

Ever tactful, Jane chose her words carefully. "Mr. Hurst was clear about which pursuits did and did not interest him. As his hostess, I made certain that his every visit would contain a shooting party if weather allowed, card playing in the evening, and handsome meals and drink. With this he was ever content."

Jonathan asked, more boldly than was his wont, "Mr. Hurst often drank to excess, did he not?"

"I do not care to sit in judgment," Jane said, "but I did sometimes think that it would have been much better for his health had he been more moderate."

Her nephew would of course have known this for himself, as he proved by then asking, "In my recollection, when Mr. Hurst had drunk too much, he became quiet and inattentive. Was this invariably so? Or did he ever become agitated, perhaps argumentative?"

How awful to think on it, and how much worse to have to tell it! Yet Jane would not fail to do her duty. "On occasion, yes. But his pronouncements were always—oh, which horse was likely to win at the races, or his opinion of which were the best shoemakers in London, that sort of thing. He could be forceful in such matters, and sometimes it seemed to me he wished conflict for its own sake. Yet the subjects involved were not the sort that cause any lasting ill feeling. Certainly I cannot imagine them inspiring anyone to so grievous an act as murder."

Miss Tilney's bloom had returned. Jane saw this with relief; how wan the girl had looked this morning! Tea and a nap had done the trick. With confidence, Miss Tilney asked, "Forgive me, Mrs. Bingley, but was there truly no one with whom you felt Mr. Hurst did not get on with well?"

Jane considered this. "On the rare occasions he became difficult, he could be very challenging toward the men in the party, regardless of who they were. Women, he did not take so much account of."

Jonathan was taking notes, which seemed to Jane admirably purposeful if not entirely genteel. "Did he ever challenge Uncle Charles?"

"Oh, at times." Jane's face felt hot. "Shortly after they arrived for this visit, there was some manner of discord between them—I know not what. To Charles, I know, the difficulty was of no great account, but Mr. Hurst could be single-minded on occasion."

Miss Tilney said, "You have no sense of the subject of this discord? None whatsoever?"

"None," Jane promised, "and whatever it was, it was smoothed over within a week's time."

"What of the other gentlemen?" Jonathan asked.

"Mr. Brooks could become very annoyed with Mr. Hurst, for when Mr. Hurst was in his cups, he did sometimes take the name of the Lord in vain. As for Mr. Lofton, he did not take much note of Mr. Hurst's behavior at such times. Between them, I recollect no disharmony greater than a conversation in which Mr. Lofton strongly defended the merits of Rhenish wine, versus Mr. Hurst's preference for French."

None of these appeared to Jane as likely reasons for murder, but she supposed Jonathan and Miss Tilney's greater experience allowed them to see more within this than she could do.

"What of the servants?" Miss Tilney said. "Was Mr. Hurst difficult with them?"

"Indeed no. I do believe he sometimes—that on occasion, there were messes that required more cleaning." How terrible to think of that! One did not even wish to admit to oneself that a guest had drunk to the point of sickness. Yet she carried on. "No doubt that was troublesome for them, but Mr. Hurst was not unkind. Of that I feel certain. Our servants know that they can come to us with their worries, and that we will help them if we can. Not one of them had anything to say regarding Mr. Hurst."

The two young people exchanged glances, and Jane recognized the deep understanding between them as a kind of intimacy she normally observed only in husbands and wives—usually, not even then. From letters, she knew that the elder Mr. Darcy opposed this match, and that even Elizabeth was uncertain. Yet Jane was too tender of heart to stand in the way of such affection.

"Thank you, Aunt Jane. That will be all," Jonathan said, unaware he had just gained a great ally.

The next to enter was Mr. Lofton, a gentleman utterly unknown to Juliet and none too familiar to Jonathan. Together they had determined that, when questioning those not well-known to either party, this should be led by the person of the same sex. Therefore it was Mr. Darcy who asked Mr. Lofton a question to which they already knew the answer: "On the morning of Mr. Hurst's death, had you left your room at any time?"

"I did, sir," said Mr. Lofton. He was a tall man, very slender and very genteel. His fair hair was shot through with silver, but otherwise he would have appeared younger than his years. "My wife sometimes wishes for a bit of bread or a biscuit or some such thing at an odd hour of the day. As she was hungry that morning, I came down and fetched her some toast. The servants were no doubt busy with breakfast—quicker to have done it myself."

This sensible attitude, so unusual and refreshing for a member of the gentry, made Juliet feel more warmly toward Mr. Lofton. However, she swiftly rebuked herself; some of the murderers she had encountered in the past had been entirely capable of conducting themselves in a civil manner when not actively engaged in homicide. She could, however, credit him with honesty: Mr. Lofton had not attempted to conceal his visit to the kitchen, even though he was unaware they had already learned of it.

Mr. Darcy asked, "What was the nature of your relationship with Mr. Hurst?"

"We married sisters," Mr. Lofton said, "which meant we were obliged to be friendly whether or not we felt any particular warmth toward each other. I will confess now that I did not, and I feel quite certain Hurst did not, either. Let me be frank: His favorite companion was drink; and where that is so, no friendship can exist entirely beyond it. As I am not overly fond of spirits, we had little to say to each other. That said, there was no real harm in the fellow; and it is hard, very hard, to think of him dying in such a manner." Indeed, he did seem to be much moved.

Yet Juliet felt she had detected a discrepancy that needed clarification. "We had heard that Mr. Hurst could be argumentative with the gentlemen of the party," she said. "Even belligerent, at times. Was he not so with you?"

"Oh, from time to time. But only over trivialities. I never

took much note of that, for I knew that come the next morning, Hurst would have forgotten the matter entirely." This corresponded to what Mrs. Bingley had told them.

Mr. Darcy continued. "On the morning of Mr. Hurst's death, or the evening before, did you see any person in a place you would not have expected them to be? Behaving in a manner that struck you as unusual?"

Mr. Lofton considered this. "I must think—Hurst's death overshadows all else in my mind regarding those days. But you were there, too, Mr. Darcy, so perhaps you can aid my recollection. Was that the night that Mrs. Hurst and Mr. Brooks were so much in conversation in the front hall?"

"I did not note that, and I believe I would have done so," Mr. Darcy said.

"Ah, well. That must have been another recent evening." Mr. Lofton shrugged.

Juliet, however, was not inclined to ignore this. She said, "Will you tell us more of this conversation between Mrs. Hurst and Mr. Brooks?"

"I know nothing of its substance," Mr. Lofton said, "and in all honesty, I regret having mentioned the matter, as I cannot see what bearing it would have upon this tragedy."

"We will not place undue importance upon it," Mr. Darcy promised, "but any detail you have noticed could prove useful to us. If nothing else, it may tell us what else Mr. Brooks and Mrs. Hurst were in a position to see or hear."

Mr. Lofton did not seem convinced, but he spoke: "One evening very recently—perhaps the night before your arrival, Mr. Darcy, certainly no more than a day or two prior to that—as all made ready to go upstairs, Mrs. Brooks and I were speaking of a book we had both read. Then Mrs. Brooks became much confused upon realizing that her husband had slipped from the room without saying anything to her.

She walked from the drawing room, and I followed, and so I saw that she found Mr. Brooks and Mrs. Hurst whispering together."

Juliet glanced at Mr. Darcy, who seemed as avidly interested in this matter as she was herself. He asked, "What were they whispering about?"

"I do not know," Mr. Lofton said. "Indeed, Mrs. Brooks did not even ask. Many wives would turn shrewish upon seeing their husband talking with another woman so clandestinely! However, Mrs. Brooks is of a finer character. She simply said that they should return to their home, and though Mr. Brooks seemed displeased at the interruption, he agreed."

"How did Mrs. Hurst react to this?" Mr. Darcy asked.

"She appeared startled, perhaps even flustered, at having been seen in private conversation," Mr. Lofton replied, "but beyond that, I could not speculate. It might be that she simply felt the need to speak to a clergyman on a matter dear to her."

All that Juliet knew thus far of Mrs. Hurst made this possibility seem remote. Still, she had to admit that Mr. Lofton's idea was, if not persuasive, at least plausible.

"Thank you, Mr. Lofton," Mr. Darcy said. "That will be all for now."

Mrs. Lofton immediately followed her husband into the study. Wisps of curly hair, barely touched with gray, peeked from her ornate lace cap. Her dress was in the latest style, with layers of ruffles at cuff and hem, and longer sleeves. So eager did Mrs. Lofton appear to be for the conversation that one might have thought her the investigator.

It was Juliet's turn to lead the questioning. "Mrs. Lofton, can you describe your relationship with Mr. Hurst?"

This was met with a scoff. "What 'relationship' can there

be, with a man who never once remained sober after four in the afternoon? We were often in the same room together, and he was rarely in enough sobriety to know I was there. That is as much as can be said on the matter. It is a shameful thing, to be so taken with drink. One almost thinks the Baptists have the correct idea."

Though a clergyman's daughter, Juliet was not to be distracted by doctrine. "It sounds as though you were not very fond of him."

"Indeed I was not." Mrs. Lofton spoke freely, so much so that it seemed she had no thought of being considered as guilty of the murder. "Though it would be most correct to say, I did not care for him at all—for beyond irritation with his habits, what was there in him to like or dislike? My sister could have done much better, and indeed I tried to tell her so when the match was being made, but would she listen? Mr. Hurst had money and a fine house, and she cared for nothing else. I do not believe she ever did care." Mrs. Lofton showed some feeling in this, at least, as she went on, "Yet, one would wish to *talk* with one's husband occasionally, would one not? To have some manner of conversation, warmth, fellow feeling? What is a marriage, without this?"

Juliet was in agreement, but she knew better than to say so. They needed to remain on the topic at hand. "You said, Mrs. Lofton, that Mrs. Hurst placed a high value on her husband's property and fortune," said Juliet. "Do you think she disregarded his drinking entirely? Or did it pain her?"

"I never saw her take the slightest notice of it, beyond some momentary irritation," Mrs. Lofton said. "Whatever pain she might ever have felt upon the subject surely died many years ago, as they were married for nigh three decades."

This was a good point, yet Juliet felt as though surely there must be more to the matter. If Mr. Hurst were only a drunkard, one every other person had learned to ignore, then why should anyone have decided to murder him? She asked, "Did you ever get the sense— Mrs. Lofton, did you ever think that Mr. Hurst's drinking was affected by some other factor in his life? Some pain or difficulty that he wished to forget?"

"So far as I could ever see, he drank when times were good, when times were bad, when it rained, when the sun shone." Mrs. Lofton had become nearly gleeful in her disapproval.

Mr. Darcy interjected: "Mrs. Lofton, had you noticed any particular conversation between Mrs. Hurst and Mr. Brooks?"

How puzzled Mrs. Lofton then appeared! "Whatever would those two have to say to each other? My sister is not an especially pious woman. For that matter, I do not believe Mr. Brooks is an especially pious clergyman, though he is strict on proper language." A lack of piety in a clergyman was not very unusual, Juliet knew; many younger sons in the gentry took clerical orders merely because it was one of the few professions suitable for a gentleman. "To answer your question, Miss Tilney, no, I had not noticed any such thing. Though—well, it had seemed to me that Mrs. Brooks had some anxiety on this point. She was often asking where her husband was when he was but briefly absent from the room. So very nervous about where he might be! Do not you wonder why?"

Her tone was most pointed. Juliet again exchanged glances with Mr. Darcy, and she saw he too had noticed Mrs. Lofton's insistence. But did she mean to incriminate Mrs. Brooks, who seemed an unlikely culprit?

Or was there some other matter to which she wished their attention to be drawn?

Juliet decided that the next question should be broader— and, if she understood Mrs. Lofton's character correctly, nigh irresistible to her: "To speak more generally, Mrs. Lofton, in the days prior to Mr. Hurst's murder, had you overheard or observed any behavior you found especially . . . curious?"

She had hit her target, as surely as though she were back at Rosings Park with bow and arrow in hand. Mrs. Lofton brightened. "Indeed, there is much that I have thought of greatly, very greatly, since the terrible event! For briefly, at the beginning of our stay, there was some strife between Charles and the Hursts."

"Both of the Hursts?" Mr. Darcy asked. Yes, he had caught it, too!—for Juliet had noted the difference between this and what they had recently been told. "Not only Mr. Hurst?"

"Indeed, both of them made some pointed remarks about, oh, what was 'due'—something of that nature. It cannot be money, of course, for none of our family has any need of that nature, so whatever could it be?" Mrs. Lofton's glee continued to increase. There are few greater pleasures for a busybody than the arrival of a fresh audience to hear all. "Then Mrs. Bingley—only the day before you came, Mr. Darcy— I heard her speaking to my brother in a very sad tone, truly mournful, as though someone had died." Mrs. Lofton caught herself at the awkward turn of phrase, but this would not be enough to dismay her. "Well. I could not overhear what it was all about, save for one phrase she spoke. Mrs. Bingley said that nothing had been the same '*since Nancy.*'"

At this Mrs. Lofton looked triumphant, probably due to the surprise on Mr. Darcy's face, which was no doubt reflected on Juliet's own. Already she had come so to believe in the fabled goodness of the Bingleys that she felt nearly wounded by the implication that Mr. Bingley might have been unfaithful.

But this Nancy—whoever she was—was not necessarily a mistress. Juliet rallied. "How was that connected to Mr. Hurst?"

Mrs. Lofton looked confused. "I would not assume it connected to him at all. But it is curious, is it not?"

Of all the ludicrous charades! Mrs. Hurst could scarcely believe that she was expected to submit to impertinent questions from two young persons. She would have thought it obvious that no widow should be troubled with poking and prying so soon after a husband's death. What had become of manners? Of common decency?

If she was obliged to endure this, she determined to do so on her own terms. So Mrs. Hurst swept into her brother's study—a room she had been familiar with since before either of these two had been born—wearing her best day dress and a necklace she would normally have reserved for a more elegant occasion. Let them see whom they had dared to summon like a servant!

"Mrs. Hurst," said Jonathan Darcy. "Thank you for coming."

"I suppose it must be done," Mrs. Hurst replied, as civilly as she could. It would not do to offend the heir to Pemberley, regardless of his impolite behavior. "What would you wish to know?"

Then the Tilney girl, the one who had no place even showing herself in decent society, had the effrontery to ask the questions herself. "Our sympathies upon the death of your husband, ma'am. I take it you were very happy together?"

"We were as happy as any husband and wife," said Mrs. Hurst, who had given little thought to the foundations of marital intimacy. For many years, she had existed in the same house as Mr. Hurst without being unduly troubled by him; this she considered the limit of reasonable matrimonial expectation.

Miss Tilney pressed. "Had he any habits or tendencies you regretted?"

"Why should I regret anything that was his action alone? I do not see that his behavior should reflect upon me. That would be very unjust."

"Forgive me, Mrs. Hurst, but the way that you phrase this—" Miss Tilney hesitated, as she should have done, yet continued with her rudeness: "It sounds as though there was indeed some aspect of your husband's behavior that you were unhappy with."

Mrs. Hurst could scarcely believe this was happening. "No person is ever entirely happy at all times with the actions of another, no matter how near their relation. Though I expect *you* know little of matrimony and are unlikely to learn."

That did the trick: Miss Tilney's cheeks flushed scarlet as she understood the allusion to her own infamy. Mrs. Hurst would have taken greater pleasure in this had Mr. Darcy not then become unaccountably sharp with her. "I shall speak plainly, Mrs. Hurst; we have been told, and I have myself observed in the past, that Mr. Hurst regularly drank to excess. Would you agree that this was so?"

"He drank nothing that his hosts did not offer him." Mrs. Hurst pursed her lips. "A fine thing, to judge a man for accepting that which is offered."

Mr. Darcy continued to press. "You have not yet assumed mourning attire, nor withdrawn from company."

"I have not ventured beyond my brother's home," cried Mrs. Hurst, "where all know my widowed state, so there is no need yet of donning black. And I have sought no company beyond this house, nor shall I for some time to come. Do you demand that I suffer more for your satisfaction? For we do not bury wives with their dead husbands in the manner of some ancient potentate of Babylon."

"Of course not, Mrs. Hurst," said Miss Tilney, who had forgotten her rebuke so swiftly that she felt free to resume her impertinence. "Will you tell us the nature of your acquaintance with Mr. Brooks?"

"He is the clergyman of the parish," Mrs. Hurst replied.

"His wife is Mrs. Bingley's sister. Therefore it is entirely natural to see much of them when visiting Netherfield."

Miss Tilney said, "Have you had private conversations with Mr. Brooks at any time, away from the rest of the party?"

"No conversations of any moment. I am sure that once or twice we have spoken apart from the others, either because they had gone on ahead or because we had, but no occasion was significant enough for me to recall it."

Still Miss Tilney went on unchecked. "We had heard there was some dispute between you, your husband, and Mr. Bingley shortly after your arrival here. A matter of something 'due.' Can you explain to us what that meant?"

"*That?*" Sputtering with laughter, Mrs. Hurst replied, "We teased each other about the money we won and lost at our nightly card games. Charles will never play for more than sixpence, you know! I do believe the teasing went on a bit too long, though. Mr. Hurst became irritated. It is possible to tell a joke once too often."

Mr. Darcy seemed to find his tongue once more. "Did you leave your room at any point after retiring the night before your husband's death or earlier that morning?"

"Why would I have any cause to do so? No, no, of course I did not." Mrs. Hurst very much hoped that would be all—and it proved to be so. Within but moments she was free to leave the study.

As soon as she was sufficiently far along the hallway to be certain of remaining unseen, Mrs. Hurst paused and put one hand against the way, as if to steady herself.

They do not know, she thought. *They do not know, and they never shall.*

Chapter Six

Together, Jonathan and Miss Tilney had unearthed many lies and the truths behind them—but rarely had they caught so blatant a falsehood so soon. As soon as Mrs. Hurst had departed, Miss Tilney whispered, "She lied about leaving her room!"

"Indeed, and it is surely significant." Jonathan felt the same excitement that illuminated Miss Tilney's face, rendering her so lovely he would have remarked upon it—would it not have distracted her from the accomplishment that had made her so happy. "That said, alone I do not think it would convince a jury of her guilt."

"Then nor should it convince us," said Miss Tilney. "There may be an innocent explanation for her movements that morning—not innocent, or she would have told us of it, but unrelated to the murder."

Her tone suggested she doubted this, as did Jonathan himself, but he agreed: "We shall not cease asking questions until we have every answer."

At the open doorway appeared Aunt Jane, with a basket over one arm, covered with a checkered cloth; from the cloth peeked the neck of a bottle of wine or spirits. "I go now to have luncheon with Mamma and Papa at Longbourn," Aunt Jane said. "Are you both well? Mrs. Gooding soon will send up a tray of cold meats and cheeses, a few other nice things. Is there anything else you could desire?"

Jonathan, freshly attentive to the power of discrepancies, said, "When you have a moment, please consider carefully the morning of Mr. Hurst's death. Do you recollect anything else unusual, anything at all?"

"Even if it seems unimportant, Mrs. Bingley," added Miss Tilney. "No matter how trivial or how silly. It might prove of use to us, if you would please tell us of it."

"Not at this second," Jonathan hastened to add. "Grand-mama can become quarrelsome when a meal is delayed."

"How true. I must not keep her waiting. But I promise to think very hard!" Aunt Jane smiled openly at them, and Jonathan was jarred by the memory of what Mrs. Lofton claimed to have overheard regarding "Nancy," and what this might mean.

Surely that could not be so—could it?

His thoughts must have been very clear, for even as Aunt Jane left to take her place in the carriage, Miss Tilney asked, "Shall we next speak to your uncle?"

"I think we must."

Charles Bingley had ever been of the most obliging temperament. Gracious, kind, and unassuming, he was exactly the sort of gentleman who might have been ruined by the wrong marriage, or at least made extremely unhappy by it, as his great desire to please could have rendered him ineffectual in counteracting the pettiness or greed of a lesser woman.

Indeed, he had been as fortunate in his choice as Jane Bennet had been in hers. She, too, would have struggled in a marriage less fortuitous, as her gentle and selfless nature might have been taken advantage of by a sterner spouse, or even one benign but unaccustomed to thinking first of others. As it was, however, the Bingleys shared a deeply joyful union, one in which neither party could possess any greater delight than in seeing the happiness of the other.

Yet, strange though it may seem, this in itself led to certain difficulties. The Bingleys, absent any need to oppose each other, had never fully gained the ability to oppose anyone else. In their earnest desire to see all their family and friends as contented as they, both husband and wife would attempt any assistance, offer any enjoyment as was within their power, even at the sacrifice of their own peace of mind. Nor could either readily refuse requests, even when both the thing asked and the person asking were unwelcome.

The Bingleys were at least spared the injustice done to so many obliging persons, who rarely receive the full appreciation that is their due. Both Charles and Jane were cherished by most of their family and acquaintance, and even the few exceptions still regarded them with some measure of respect.

So it was that Mr. Bingley had never in his life undergone questioning on so difficult a subject as the death of Mr. Hurst, and yet he would have never dreamed of attempting to avoid the experience.

"Shocking thing, this," Bingley said to Jonathan, before recollecting that Miss Tilney did not know him so well as his nephew, and thus more polished speech must be appropriate. "We are of course most distressed for my sister's sake, but Mr. Hurst had been a guest in our home at least once a year for more than two decades. His absence shall be greatly felt."

Most young ladies would have murmured some general sort of agreement, but Miss Tilney did not. "What in particular will you miss about Mr. Hurst, sir?"

How Bingley wished he had more to say! "Why, he—as husband to my sister—well, he was a very familiar figure in our lives."

Ever forthright, Jonathan said, "You would not have been his friend, I believe, had he not married your sister."

"No. I suppose we would not have been, as we shared few interests, but it is quite beside the point, for he *did* marry my sister, and they seemed to suit each other very well. So it signifies little that his company was—that it was not—"

"That his company did not suit you?" Miss Tilney asked.

Bingley, though pained, felt honor bound to admit, "Not particularly, no. But I knew no harm of the man."

Jonathan asked, "Would this be equally true for those who were not Mr. Hurst's social equals? For instance, did you ever observe any occasion on which Mr. Hurst was particularly unfair or unkind to one of your servants?"

"I do not recall one. This is not to say that such an event would be impossible, for Mr. Hurst could be somewhat intemperate in speech when in his cups." How Bingley disliked speaking ill of the dead! Yet it was not so very ill, as he then pointed out, "This is hardly uncommon, you know. I should scarcely think Mr. Hurst the worst exemplar of such behavior. Regardless, I know of no conflict between him and any of my servants, and I do believe they would have told me of any egregious action on Mr. Hurst's part."

"We have heard," said Jonathan, "that there was some minor discord between you and the Hursts—in particular, Mr. Hurst—soon after they came. Will you tell us of its nature?"

"Louisa—Mrs. Hurst, I should say, always wants to wager at cards. Normally I do not allow substantial sums to be wagered in my household, as it can only lead to ill feeling." Charles had seen more than one fistfight between former friends while at university, merely over a hand of cards. What could be the point of it? "On this occasion, however, she teased and teased me until I finally agreed, and she won thirty pounds. Of course I would have swiftly made good the debt under any circumstances, but for whatever purpose, she was very insistent upon being immediately paid. I rarely keep such a large sum of cash on hand, and thus it took two days for me to give her what she sought. The Hursts were rather pointed about it, which I found"—this was some of the harshest criticism Charles would ever utter about one of his kin—"not entirely congenial."

Miss Tilney said, "What of the Loftons, sir? Were they on very intimate terms with the Hursts?"

"Well, of course, Mrs. Lofton is my sister, just as Mrs. Hurst is. They are more than ten years apart in age—Mrs. Hurst is the eldest in our family, and Mrs. Lofton the youngest—so they were perhaps not as intimate as most siblings. But there is hardly any wonder in that, and I believe their relations to have been congenial." Bingley had never before particularly considered these two sisters' husbands as independent personages—these men seemed to exist more in the role of eccentrically chosen ornaments—but he wished to help, and so he thought hard. "I cannot say that Mr. Hurst and Mr. Lofton had any special affinity. But nor did I ever detect any sign of discord between them."

Jonathan seemed to be taken by a sudden notion. "Did they only ever meet at your home, sir? Or did the Hursts travel to visit the Loftons, and vice versa?"

"Why, I believe they generally only met here—once or twice, I believe, holiday festivities took place at Stevenage Court, which is the home of the Allerdyce family. Mrs. Allerdyce is another of my five sisters, you see, Miss Tilney."

"I am familiar with Mrs. Allerdyce," Miss Tilney replied in a very low voice. "We met in London earlier this year."

Bingley wondered why the young lady should be so downcast at the memory. Only then did he recollect the scandal of the painting. He had heard of it, of course, as had any reader of the London newspapers, but how heartened Miss Tilney would have been to realize that Charles Bingley had not given the matter one thought until this moment! "Ah, yes, of course," he replied, eager to hurry past a topic that might cause his young guest pain. "I meant only to point out that, although the Hursts and Loftons would have met elsewhere on a few other occasions, they generally came together here, or in our home in Staffordshire. That is only natural, as I have been head of the family since the death of our dear father almost thirty years ago."

Jonathan and Miss Tilney seemed not to find this fact as natural as Bingley did. Come to think of it, he supposed the siblings might well have met in one another's homes more often, rather than always looking to him as their host for several weeks—sometimes months—of the year. Once or twice, Jane had even tentatively suggested it to him, and they had gone so far as to think of how they might hint to this effect to the Loftons, the Hursts, and even the Allerdyces. And yet, as was so often the case, they had borne all, lest his sisters think themselves not welcome.

"I believe we have no other questions at present," said Jonathan. "Thank you, dear uncle, for obliging us."

Happy to be thought obliging, Mr. Bingley took himself off, much relieved.

Though Juliet thought it likely that the murderer would prove to be someone staying at Netherfield, and knew Mr. Darcy to agree with her, they could not neglect those persons often present who would therefore be familiar with the house, its routines, and the late Mr. Hurst. The Bingleys had undertaken the difficult task of inviting these individuals to Netherfield that day for questioning, and the first two to appear were Mr. and Mrs. Brooks.

Mrs. Brooks entered the room first. As she was not a direct relation of Mr. Hurst, mourning attire was not expected, but she had shown delicacy in wearing a simple gray dress with minimal trimming. Yet as Juliet took in the cheapness of Mrs. Brooks's dress, its few trimmings some years out of date, it had to be wondered whether this modesty was truly thoughtful or merely necessary. Several small signs—the lack of any jewelry, the wear on her shoes—suggested that the financial situation of the Brooks family, although not impoverished, did not come near that of any of those currently staying at Netherfield, nor of Juliet herself. This was to be expected from a clergyman who had but a small parish and who presumably possessed no family wealth to augment his coffers.

No ready resemblance could at first be found between Mrs. Brooks and the two of her sisters whom Juliet had come to know, namely Mrs. Bingley and of course Mrs. Darcy. Yet a moment's study allowed the recognition that Mrs. Brooks's heart-shaped face was very like that of Mrs. Darcy; furthermore, Mrs. Brooks's pale blue eyes and delicate chin were very like that of Mrs. Bingley. So why had the recognition of these similarities been so difficult to achieve?

Juliet realized, *Both Mrs. Darcy and Mrs. Bingley are happy women. Even when engaging with them at times of turmoil, I can detect in each woman a faith in herself, in her husband, and in her situation that is somehow whispered within every gesture, every expression.*

This faith, Mrs. Brooks does not possess.

"Thank you for agreeing to assist us in our endeavors, Aunt Kitty," said Mr. Darcy. His tone suggested warmth toward his relation but no true intimacy with her.

"Of course," Mrs. Brooks said. "I am always ready to do what I can for my family."

Juliet began, "Let me see if I understand rightly. You are the younger sister of Mrs. Bingley, yes?"

"Yes," Mrs. Brooks said, looking down at the hands she kept folded in her lap. "I am the fourth daughter of five."

"Mrs. Darcy is known to me, and of course we are both the

guests of Mrs. Bingley," Juliet said. She knew a bit of the rest, but found herself interested to hear how Mrs. Brooks would put things. "Your other sisters?"

"Mrs. Wheelwright is the wife of the Dean of Tunbridge Wells." Mrs. Brooks sounded unaccountably sharp as she said this, but then a flicker of true grief became apparent upon her face. "My younger sister, Mrs. Wickham, passed away some years ago. Did not you learn as much when looking into the murder of her late husband?"

Mr. Darcy said, "Forgive my speaking of such personal matters, but I had always felt that Aunt Lydia was more your particular companion than my mother or your other sisters."

"Very much so." Mrs. Brooks tucked one of her curls beneath her cap, an unnecessary gesture that hinted at disquiet. "The elder two—Jane and Elizabeth—they had little enough time for those of us who were younger."

"That is not so uncommon, I think," said Juliet, "for the siblings closest in age to be nearer in temperament and confidence. Yet I note that you seem to have become much more intimate with Mrs. Bingley in adult life, for it is said that you and your husband dine here at Netherfield a few times a week."

Mrs. Brooks did not smile, nor betray any other sign of fond remembrance. "The Bingleys returned to Netherfield in order that they might be more in attendance upon my parents, when required by their age and ill health. It was more than Mr. Brooks and I could manage alone, as he has the needs of his parish to attend to and our children were yet young."

Yet Mrs. Brooks does not dine with her parents nearly so often as she does here at Netherfield, Juliet noted.

Mr. Darcy had cocked his head, studying his aunt with a newly sharpened gaze. Had he, too, noted that Mrs. Brooks had not actually answered her question? He said only, "Aunt Kitty, your time spent here at Netherfield would have made you better acquainted with the Hursts, no doubt. Had they become particular friends of yours?"

A small twitch at the corner of Mrs. Brooks's mouth might have been amusement—or was she, perhaps, flinching? "I would not say that. Certainly we had become much better known to one another, but not intimately so. Mostly we play cards together. Mrs. Hurst is an enthusiastic cardplayer, you know. As I remember you once were, Jonathan. Is that still the case?"

"My aptitude is unchanged," said Mr. Darcy, forthright as ever. "But I play seldom. People do not like to lose, nor do they care for the company of those they lose to very often."

She endeavors to distract him, Juliet thought. *Or am I grown overly suspicious?* "Mrs. Brooks," she said, "I understand the Meryton vicarage is not far from this house. Did you return to Netherfield either later on the night before Mr. Hurst's death or earlier on the morning of the day he died?"

"Indeed not." Mrs. Brooks's tone was sharp. "Why should I ever do such a thing? What purpose could there be for it?"

The purpose was of course entirely clear—to poison Mr. Hurst—but although Juliet found Mrs. Brooks to be overly cautious in her responses, nothing she had said tended to suggest any motive for that murder. "Thank you, Mrs. Brooks," Juliet said. "I believe we need not trouble you further today."

Mr. Brooks followed, giving both Jonathan and Miss Tilney the same polite nod of greeting, despite the fact that he had been Jonathan's uncle for nearly fifteen years. They knew each other scarcely at all, a fact that had never before struck Jonathan so forcibly. Even the late, unmourned Mr. Wickham had from time to time taken Jonathan riding during his boyhood. Mr. Brooks, on the other hand, he could scarcely remember at any occasion beyond weddings, funerals, and some hazily recalled dinners. Card games were the only amusement they had ever shared, and seldom at that. Indeed, at no prior point had Jonathan realized that he always addressed Mr. Bingley as uncle . . . but almost never Mr. Brooks.

"You wish to know of my doings around the time of Mr. Hurst's death, I surmise," said Mr. Brooks, not waiting to be asked. "We dined here at Netherfield that night, as often we do, and played cards and listened to music afterward, which is also our custom. You had gone to bed at this point, I believe, Mr. Darcy. All of Mr. Bingley's sisters are accomplished at the pianoforte, and Mrs. Lofton is in addition a fine singer. She gave us a few Irish airs between rounds of whist. All ended at the usual hour, at which time my wife and I returned home. Neither of us had left the vicarage again before word came of Mr. Hurst's death."

This was all summarized very neatly, which pleased Jonathan's instinct for order—yet also allowed Mr. Brooks to be more cautious with his words. Miss Tilney never took her gaze from Mr. Brooks; but merely from the set of her shoulders, and the quality of her silence, Jonathan knew she shared his instinct about his uncle's pointed clarity. "Thank you, Mr. Brooks," he said simply. "Did you speak in particular with Mrs. Hurst that evening?"

"Briefly, as we were departing, but only about her strategies at the card table. As you know, whist is not at all a game of chance." Mr. Brooks did not alter either his tone or expression as he continued, "I fear that Mr. Hurst was apt to miss church many Sundays, yet I feel sure that his immortal soul is now in the keeping of our Savior."

How difficult it was to follow such a pronouncement with any comment remotely to the purpose! Jonathan struggled for a moment before Miss Tilney managed, "Thank you, Mr. Brooks." They watched him go, and as soon as he had departed, she whispered to Jonathan, "He is remarkably unmoved, is he not? To be in constant companionship with a person for weeks on end, year after year, and yet to be so blithe upon his passing!"

"Indeed," Jonathan said. "Yet I cannot but think that this tends to exculpate Mr. Brooks, rather than the reverse. We have seen murderers successfully feign surprise, grief, and even fear. To feign nonchalance is, I should believe, far more difficult, at least to do so as thoroughly as Mr. Brooks has done."

"True. Nor can I conceive of a motive for Mr. Brooks to harm Mr. Hurst. Yet he did forestall our questions so readily, so firmly!" Miss Tilney had become livelier, more engaging—more *herself* at last. Jonathan knew that to mention this would damage the very thing that had so benefited her, namely her interest in the mystery before them. So he simply nodded as she continued: "The Brookses have no fortune to equal that of the Bingleys, I take it? Or the Hursts, or the Loftons?"

Jonathan said, "Not at all. That said, while their situation is not exceedingly prosperous, I believe the Brookses' income to be steady, and a reasonable support for a small family. Meryton vicarage is not grand—nor is its parish—but nor would it be found deficient. In size and aspect it is not much smaller than Longbourn, my mother's family home."

"The difference in prosperity is felt, I think," Miss Tilney mused. "Yet, I cannot see how it would signify in this matter. Mr. Hurst's demise cannot add to the prosperity of Mr. and Mrs. Brooks."

"He claimed he and Mrs. Hurst spoke only of cards. Do you believe him?"

Miss Tilney tapped her lips with one finger, as she sometimes did when deep in thought. Jonathan had not forgotten this detail about her, but had not called it to mind in months. Yet he could not let his joy in her presence prove distracting!

She, seemingly more disciplined, kept to the topic. "It seems unlikely, does it not? Even so, whatever else might they have to say to each other?"

In point of fact, Juliet Tilney was not without her own moments of distraction regarding Jonathan Darcy. However, her fascination with the case animated her in its own right. Her mind had been freed from the confines of remorse and shame, as sure a liberation as any prisoner has ever felt walking away from gaol. It was in such fine spirits that she awaited the entry of the final person they were to question upon that day.

Mr. Isaac Lucas, a gentleman of roughly the same age as Mr. Darcy, proved pleasing in both his person and his address; if he knew of the scandal attached to Juliet (and how could he not?), he showed not the slightest sign. So open and artless was his manner that she found herself speaking to him far more frankly than she had intended. "You must know, Mr. Lucas, that you are not very high on our list of suspects, having no particular tie to the family or the house beyond having attended the final dinner of Mr. Hurst's life. Yet you are also the local magistrate, and therefore, a meeting between us is important, as it is by you we must be directed."

"I have been the magistrate for but a few months," Mr. Lucas replied, "and in that time, there has been but one investigation, regarding the theft of old Mrs. Philips's lace shawl, and that was resolved upon its being found in the hedge of her own home, where the wind had blown it. So you see, Miss Tilney, I am thus entirely without the sort of experience of which you and Mr. Darcy have so much. Given that, and my uncomfortable proximity to the time and place of Mr. Hurst's murder, I would be grateful were the two of you to conduct all necessary inquiries. We should take care to gather every few days, however often is necessary to see that I remain informed of your progress. Thus it can be said that all is proceeding under the aegis of the law."

Mr. Darcy's relief was evident, and the match of that within Juliet herself. She even saw him smile as he said to Mr. Lucas, "That would be ideal, sir, and I thank you on Miss Tilney's behalf as well as my own."

It appeared that Mr. Lucas was the most relieved of all persons present. How odd, Juliet thought, that one should not be interested in investigating a murder!—before recollecting that she herself would have responded in much the same fashion before having experienced it for herself. She said, "I do beg your pardon, Mr. Lucas, but still, we must ask you what you noted on the night before the murder. Did any conversations or actions strike you as out of the ordinary? Think carefully, for the oddest details are sometimes clues to more than you might imagine."

"I have thought of little else since word first came that Mr. Hurst's death might prove to be murder," Mr. Lucas said. "Yet try though I might, I can recall nothing that could not have been seen on any other evening. Mrs. Lofton was at times a shade . . . waspish, shall we say? But not with Mr. Hurst in particular. She occasionally had a sharp tongue with almost all in attendance, from her husband to both the Hursts, both the Brookses, and once or twice even with Mr. Bingley."

Juliet, intrigued, forgot entirely the agreement between herself and Mr. Darcy regarding the questioning of persons of the same sex. "So Mrs. Lofton was difficult with everyone?"

"Everyone save Mrs. Bingley, and I cannot imagine the creature wicked enough to speak harshly to so sweet a lady as she." Mr. Lucas smiled at a portrait upon the wall, one that Juliet now recognized as the young Mrs. Bingley. How worshipful everyone seemed of Mrs. Bingley! Juliet could not but wonder at it, even having observed her hostess's kindness for herself. "Yet these were but stray comments—I cannot remember the particulars of any of them—and most of her behavior was ordinary. Certainly none of her momentary irritations would have seemed likely to presage a turn toward the murderous."

"So we are left not much better off than when we began, Mr. Darcy," Juliet said once Mr. Lucas had left. The afternoon sun, low in the sky, slanted through the window at the perfect angle to form a sort of halo around the head of Mrs. Bingley's portrait. "We know that Mrs. Hurst enjoys cards. That Mrs. Lofton was in an ill temper, but not remarkably so. And that almost none of these persons who spend so much time together truly know one another intimately—that, or many of them are unwilling to speak the full truth."

"My supposition is the latter," Jonathan replied, "but it seems clear that while many may be concealing much, only one is concealing the guilt we wish to discover. The difficulty will lie in determining which one that may be."

"I agree that there is no conspiracy afoot." Juliet sighed. "It is hard enough to discern even *one* motive for the murder of Mr. Hurst, so it beggars belief to posit that multiple people should possess such."

"Tomorrow, we must go through all anew, and look further into the operations of the household," said Mr. Darcy. "As for tonight—my grandmother will certainly expect me to dine with them, and they dine at an early hour. But I could return to Netherfield, perhaps, without causing undue offense."

She felt her cheeks flush with warmth. "We could scarcely excuse ourselves from the activities of the house, even on such business as this."

"Then we need not." Mr. Darcy stepped somewhat closer to her, enough for Juliet's breath to catch. "Let us play the pianoforte for each other, or join Mrs. Hurst in her card games—let us even read books side by side—that alone would be such a—"

"Mr. Darcy." Juliet rose to her feet, even as she lowered her gaze to the floor. "I am allowed in this house for one purpose only. You must go. You must."

She hurried toward the study doorway, wondering how she could be both relieved and disappointed that Mr. Darcy made no move to follow. Yet as she went through it, he said, "You underestimate my family, Miss Tilney, and you underestimate me."

"You underestimate my grandfather," Juliet said, hating the words she spoke for their truth, "for he will see me wed before you can hope to do so."

Mr. Darcy's consternation was great, as well it might be. "What can you mean?"

"I mean, Mr. Darcy, that Mr. Follett has sought to repair our reputations—and, more significantly to him, his painting career—by proposing marriage."

"You would not." How horrified Mr. Darcy appeared! "You could not bear it!"

Juliet struggled for composure. "It is not my wish, but it is that of my grandfather. I do not think my parents would ever consent, but both Mr. Follett and General Tilney speak truth when they say it may be the only means of escaping my current predicament."

"It shall not stand," said Mr. Darcy. "It must not be."

As much as his feelings in the matter resembled Juliet's own, she could scarcely bear to hear him speak them aloud. The trap of hope was too near being sprung. "We should talk of it no further. The investigation is our main concern, and that we will speak of tomorrow."

Mr. Darcy seemed as though he would like to talk more on

the matter, much more, but he accepted her dismissal with grace. "Until tomorrow."

Why must the tone of his voice pierce her so? But Juliet kept her resolve, neither pausing nor looking back until she was up the stairs and in her own bedchamber. Only then did she allow herself the relief of tears.

Chapter Seven

Jonathan Darcy was in no tranquil state of mind that evening as he rode back toward Longbourn. The confusing early stages of their investigation had their own claims on his attention and spirit, but above all he was preoccupied by personal concerns.

Laurence Follett, proposing marriage to Miss Tilney? Absurd. It could not possibly come to pass. Despite her refusal to discuss the matter, Jonathan sensed that Miss Tilney had rejected this idea as vehemently as he, if not more. Still, when she spoke to Jonathan, Miss Tilney seemed to wish to put him at a distance, to consider the potential for a match between them as irrevocably ended, as if she had lost all regard for Jonathan already.

Yet, if he judged correctly, her protests were too fervent to be sincere. If she truly had put aside any hopes for a shared future life, if she had any real notion of wedding Mr. Follett, then there would be little need for protestations.

Or would there? Jonathan hesitated, doubting himself. His fundamental tendency was to assume that people meant what they said—to take them rather literally. (This tendency was one of his "peculiarities," though Jonathan personally felt that, if it were truly odd to assume honesty, this was more an indictment upon society than upon his comprehension.) Yet the more he considered the matter, the more assured he felt in his judgment. He believed that he had, during the previous three years, improved greatly in his understanding of the nuances of behavior—and into that of Miss Tilney most of all.

So he returned to Longbourn in better spirits than he was accustomed to having upon his entering that house. Better yet was the sight of one of the Bingleys' carriages, suggesting his aunt Jane remained present; she generally tempered his grandparents somewhat. Yet Jonathan's pleasant temper was not to be of great duration.

"Well, and here you are, after spending all the day bothering those at Netherfield, and without learning anything of consequence," said Grandmama, who sat by the fire, a half-forgotten bit of knitting in her lap.

"You are impatient, my dear." Grandpapa smiled at her, but not fondly. "I understand it may take two or three days to solve a murder, occasionally even more. We must not hold Jonathan to a standard even higher than that set by the London constabulary."

Jonathan stopped himself from protesting that generally even more time was required. All his hard-won knowledge of behaviors such as "sarcasm" and "exaggeration" seemed to dissolve when he was in the presence of his grandparents. "We have only just begun our efforts. It is important to be careful in such matters."

"I should think it important to be quick, too, if murderers are to wander about slaughtering whomever they will," Grandmama insisted. "Like as not we will all be killed in our beds before you have made heads or tails of it! Though I still think it must all come to nothing. Mr. Hurst drank himself into his grave, mark my words."

Grandpapa turned toward Jonathan as though they were conversing warmly. "You see that Mr. Hurst's complicity in his own demise does not save us from the danger of being slaughtered in the night."

"Oh, you will laugh and make your little jokes," Grandmama retorted, "but when we are all dead, you will be sorry!"

From the back entry came his aunt Jane, doffing the simple

smock she wore over her gown. "There, now, Mamma, the herbs are hung to dry in just the way you like. I am sure Pine sees the correct method now."

"That is as may be," said Grandmama, "but Pine ever wishes to do things in her own way, as though she were the mistress."

Jonathan said, "Aunt Jane, I had thought you came only for luncheon."

"As did I, but Mamma and Papa needed me to look after a few things, and of course I read them our latest letter from your cousin Sarah. She settles into married life very well, which is a great comfort to her father as well as to me." Aunt Jane had begun readying herself to return to Netherfield. "Good evening to you both, and I will be back. Come, Jonathan, will not you walk me to the carriage?"

This seemed unnecessary, as her driver stood at the ready not twenty feet from the door, but he was happy to have another moment's liberty. "Are you well, Aunt Jane?"

"Indeed I am," she said, glancing back at the door behind them, where a diffident servant paid them no notice. "I have given much thought to the matter of any peculiarities on the morning of Mr. Hurst's death. Three have come to mind, though they are all so small—irrelevancies, I am sure, but you did say anything might be of use."

"Anything at all," Jonathan affirmed.

Aunt Jane stood next to the carriage, and began counting off points upon her gloved fingers. "First, I remembered the peacock."

"Peacock?"

"It is a little china ornament, on one of the tables in the first-floor hallway. When I went down that morning, I saw it had been knocked on its side. Most likely that was only Becky's doing. She tries very hard, but I fear she is a clumsy girl."

If this was the best their inquiries were to solicit, Jonathan's hopes were not high—but he had asked. "Very well. The peacock had been knocked over."

"Then, second, I remembered that something had disturbed the hens." Aunt Jane seemed very pleased to be helping, so Jonathan would not discourage her, though going from peacocks to chickens did not seem a promising direction. "Of course, our roosters always greet the morning, and one expects the poultry yard to be lively early in the day, but as my maid did my hair, we heard the chickens squawk and flutter mightily. I feared a fox might have got at them, and I meant to check, but then Mr. Hurst— Well, I did not even remember until the next day, and then Mrs. Mulgrew assured me all the poultry and livestock were well."

Jonathan realized he had judged too quickly: This might prove useful. The Netherfield stable, dairy, coop, and other outbuildings were somewhat closer to the house than was commonplace for such an estate, close enough to sometimes hear a whinny or cluck from the rear of the house. Therefore, someone slipping out of the house—Mrs. Hurst, to be specific—could well have disturbed them.

And yet, he wondered, *how could that action have related to the murder of Mr. Hurst?*

"Third, and last," said Aunt Jane, "as we were waiting for Mr. Lucas to arrive that terrible morning, I saw that someone had taken out my latest copy of *La Belle Assemblée*. It sat in Mr. Bingley's study, and you know he has no interest in such things. Someone had gone through my own private sitting room upstairs and brought it down. It lay open to a page describing the new Limerick gloves. Perhaps one of the maids wished to daydream, but why not do so in my sitting room itself?"

"That I cannot say," Jonathan admitted. Could gloves possibly be important in this matter?

"I am sure nothing will come of any of it, but at least I have told you." Aunt Jane's smile widened. "Now, I will return to Netherfield. Do not fear, for I shall look after Miss Tilney." Her carriage had rolled away, onto the country lane, before Jonathan realized his aunt understood the nature of his interest in Miss Tilney and did not disapprove.

He might have thought upon this discovery at more length had he not walked back into Longbourn to find dinner about to be served, and the Bennets once again in dispute.

"Jane should insist upon proper deference," Mrs. Bennet said, "from Mrs. Hurst and Mrs. Lofton and Mrs. Whomever-you-like. They have her running about after that as though she were one of their servants!"

"It was you who had tasks for her all afternoon, madam," Mr. Bennet pointed out mildly.

Mrs. Bennet did not receive the comment in the same way. "Why should she not help her mother? Is it not in the Bible, to honor one's parents?"

Confusing as his grandparents' bickering ever was to Jonathan, his dismay had fixed upon another source entirely. Their first course was pea soup, a dish he had ever found repellent; its vivid green color and usual texture damaged his appetite. His parents humored him by seldom serving this, and on the rare occasions when they wished to please a guest for whom it was a favorite, they made certain that the cook strained the soup over and over again until it was entirely smooth. The version served at Longbourn was altogether more grainy, and it was this that changed the soup from one Jonathan disliked to one he abhorred.

He had mentioned his displeasure with pea soup to his grandparents before—rudely, during childhood, to his parents' dismay, then more politely as he grew older. At no time had his grandparents taken any heed.

I must eat it, Jonathan told himself. *When I turn down food at their table, they see it as an insult.* So did many people. The extremities of disgust he endured when faced with certain food textures were not those he could easily express, not with any degree of decorum. So he forced a spoonful into his mouth. Then another. And another. His throat tightened convulsively, but Jonathan managed to get it down. At least his parents would have been proud, had they seen him.

However, he had not taken care to disguise his expression as he did so, and to judge by his grandmother's pointed sniff, his loathing must have been all too clear.

I must eat this and be unhappy, Jonathan thought, *and she must watch and be unhappy, and somehow this is all preferable to my simply asking to skip the soup course.* It comforted him somewhat to think that Miss Tilney might be given a more palatable dinner at Netherfield—though what could be truly palatable in a house where poison recently had been served?

Indeed, Juliet Tilney's evening meal proved to be a trial. The food itself (pork braised in red wine, spiced mushrooms) tasted so delicious that it much revived her appetite, which had weakened greatly during the past months of shame. However, even this could not distract her from the general temper at the table, which was—put as kindly as possible—wary.

All of Juliet's prior investigations had obliged her to spend considerable time at the premises of the crimes, and with the persons suspected of having done the wickedness. However, she now realized how thoroughly, in every such prior situation, those present had convinced themselves that the miscreant could only have been an unknown intruder, or that the death had been but an accident. In other words, they had most often believed that no murderer was in fact in their midst.

Such assurance was lacking at Netherfield. Despite the Bingleys' best efforts to remember any anecdote in which the late Mr. Hurst seemed somewhat congenial, and otherwise to make brighter conversation about such mundanities as the weather, talk remained subdued. Mrs. Lofton glanced from person to person—in suspicion, or afraid of it—but spoke rarely. (The only other individual concerned, Mr. Isaac Lucas, had wisely taken himself back to Lucas Lodge to dine in safety.)

Propriety dictates that young unmarried ladies should be the quietest at table, speaking only to answer questions or compliment the hostess. Juliet sometimes thought whoever had determined "propriety" had not actually met many young ladies. Certainly, in practice, the best conversation included all those present, and she had never felt shy of volunteering a comment when she felt she had an observation worth the saying—until this evening. Made uneasy by the unspoken disharmony at the table, and burdened by the occasional sharp glance from Mrs. Hurst, Juliet finished her meal as silently and swiftly as courtesy allowed. Afterward she pled a traveler's weariness to escape what promised to be a long, mirthless evening.

Once in her chamber, she breathed out a sigh of relief to be alone, but this was followed by a rap at the door. Her visitor proved to be Mrs. Bingley.

"I wished to ask— I meant to before, but the tumult regarding poor Mr. Hurst—" Mrs. Bingley put her hand over her mouth. "I should not even mention him when you are seeking rest. But, Miss Tilney, I have realized that you traveled without a maid to attend you. However did you manage this morning?"

Like many young ladies of gentility, Juliet could manage a simple bun well enough; if the style was somewhat outdated, it was nonetheless proper. She had lost so much weight the past few months that her stays were unnecessary. Juliet said only, "I am come here to help if I can, and no finery is needed for that."

"We do not speak of finery, Miss Tilney, but of your comfort," Mrs. Bingley insisted. "I shall send my own maid to you as soon as she is free, and as of tomorrow morning, you shall have someone of your own to attend upon you."

Her promise, though civil, was not beyond the normal duty of a hostess. However, the gentleness with which Mrs. Bingley spoke, her evident desire for Juliet to be taken care of— this was more than uncommon, and unquestionably sincere.

Paradoxical though it may seem, during times of travail, we are often able to endure even the greatest cruelties with fortitude, only to be completely undone when shown kindness. So it was with Juliet, who to her mortification felt her eyes welling with tears. Within but moments, she found herself sitting on the edge of her bed, her hand clasped in both of Mrs. Bingley's, and her head upon that lady's shoulder.

"I am so very sorry," Juliet said, between sniffles. "You will think me a hysteric."

"I think no such thing." Mrs. Bingley petted her hand. "You have been through a great deal. In your place I should be all but insensible—and yet, you are here, taking on such difficult work only to help us! It is very good of you, and I think you a most courageous young lady."

"You know, then . . . about the portrait, the scandal . . ."

"Yes, all of it, from the papers but also from my dear sister Lizzy. How very shocking for you! How very wrong of the painter, too, so unkind."

"Unkind indeed," said Juliet, "and yet, my grandfather would have me marry him."

This information had the most extraordinary effect upon

Mrs. Bingley, who rarely demanded anything of anyone, but who insisted upon hearing more of this at once. After Juliet had explained all regarding Mr. Follett and his misdeeds, she then took the letter from her writing box and allowed Mrs. Bingley to read it.

"Note how he thinks our marriage would help him resume his career as a portraitist." Juliet pointed at the offending line on the page held in Mrs. Bingley's hands. "Were he still obtaining commissions for his paintings, I suspect Mr. Follett would have no thought of my shame as any motivation for matrimony."

Mrs. Bingley's generous temperament would not allow her to ascribe such mean motives to anyone. "He may be both concerned for his own welfare and for yours. I am sure he would not ask to marry you for so purely venal a purpose. Indeed, his words suggest that he is truly sorry, as well he should be."

Juliet dabbed her damp cheeks with her handkerchief. "You advise me to marry him, then?"

"No, indeed I do not. You do not love him!"

"Love is said to come after marriage for most, not before. Many a woman has married to oblige her family, or to maintain her place in society, with no great feeling toward her intended." Juliet sighed. "I confess that I never wished to be among their number, and yet—"

"You love another, do you not?" Mrs. Bingley blushed. "Forgive my forwardness. Yet it is alluded to here in the letter, and today I myself observed the great affinity that exists between you and my nephew."

"The Darcys will not hear of our marrying, and there is an end to it," Juliet said, straightening and again wiping her cheeks. Here, she must be strong. "Those hopes are all in the past now."

Mrs. Bingley would never be so swift to dismiss the possibility of love. "You must not think so! My sister is not so unkind, nor Mr. Darcy either. He can be proud, but he will always do what is right in the end."

"The Darcys are defending their son's honor and reputation, precisely as they should." Juliet gently took back Follett's letter from Mrs. Bingley and folded it shut.

"She bade me speak of it no more, so I fell silent, for what else could I do?" Jane said later, lying in bed next to Charles. "Still, she must not marry that dreadful painter! To have a spouse one could neither trust nor respect, to say nothing of love— that is a cruel sentence indeed, particularly for a girl who has committed no crime."

"Good heavens," said Charles. His heart was very nearly as tender as his wife's, and his distress scarcely less than her own. "A dreadful thing, to oblige a girl to marry the man who has disgraced her! One hears of it from time to time, but I shall never think it any less than barbaric. Surely Darcy and your sister would not wish such a fate upon her."

"Surely not." Yet Jane was uncertain. Few situations could be more vexatious to her than those involving the conflicting desires of two people she cared for deeply. "Elizabeth wrote so little to me of Miss Tilney herself—so upset was she by the duel and its aftermath that she scarcely mentioned its cause. I cannot think why they should wish to discourage Jonathan's marriage to anyone so brave and so clever, particularly when they are so very taken with each other."

Bingley considered this. "Perhaps they do not wish to discourage the match at all. Sentiments run hot after such an event as a duel. The Darcys may look at the matter very differently now."

How this brightened Jane's spirits! She would not be obliged to keep Miss Tilney's presence a secret forever. Everyone she cared for would be reconciled, and happiness might yet reign over all.

The mere act of having confessed her feelings and concerns to a sympathetic person did much to restore Juliet's spirits. Nothing could entirely dispel the gloom—Mr. Darcy was no doubt still lost to her, the question of Mr. Follett's proposal was by no means resolved, and the fact that she almost certainly slept in the same house as a murderer was no less disquieting for being a circumstance she had encountered before. Yet kindness is a balm for almost all wounds, and so Juliet rose in better temper than she had known in some time.

True to Mrs. Bingley's promise, a soft rap at the door heralded the arrival of her maid. "Though I can't say I'm truly a lady's maid as yet, miss," said Becky, "I'd like to become one, and Mrs. Bingley has let me practice on her a few times when no company's expected."

This was not the most reassuring testimonial to Becky's skills with brush and comb, but Juliet was not overly governed by vanity. Besides, what Becky lacked in technique, she promised to compensate for in enthusiasm.

The young girl did indeed assist Juliet in dressing, exclaiming at the ill fit of her stays ("You'll be needing new, miss! The gowns this year are even lower at the waist, you'd hardly believe it. Scandalous, my mam says."), and doing her best with Juliet's hair. Becky dropped the comb once, and was clumsy removing the curl papers, but the end result was not too bad. If the ringlets on either side of Juliet's face were not precisely symmetrical, as fashion recommended, they were nonetheless flattering. Juliet caught herself wondering what Mr. Darcy would think when he saw her—

He will think of the murder of Mr. Hurst, as you should do. There is no other topic that unites you, not now nor ever again. It had become more important to remind herself of that fact since she had realized that it was a fact Mr. Darcy did not know.

Juliet asked, "Becky, were you not attending upon breakfast on the day of Mr. Hurst's death? Did I not hear Mrs. Bingley say something to this effect?"

Becky's smile faltered. "Indeed, miss. It was something terrible to see."

It struck Juliet that many servants in such a situation, probably most, would have been frightened by such an inquiry and quick to deny any potential blame. Becky's confidence that she was trusted—that her employers did not and would not assign any measure of the guilt to her—spoke more to the Bingleys' kindness than anything Juliet had yet seen. Many who seem generous toward their equals become far meaner creatures when dealing with those of inferior wealth and social station.

"Will you tell me exactly what you remember of that morning?" Juliet went to her little writing box, readying paper, ink, and pen. "Please share every possible detail. Even those you believe irrelevant may ultimately be of some use."

Becky had no chance to reply, for that moment, a voice came from the hallway. "Miss Tilney?"

"Oh—yes?" Juliet nodded for Becky to open the door wide, which revealed the Loftons, arm in arm, clearly heading down for breakfast themselves. Mrs. Lofton behaved as though nothing were at all peculiar about her willingness to intrude upon Juliet's time in her private room; it was Mr. Lofton who seemed to recognize the awkwardness of the situation, glancing from Juliet to Becky to the floor and back again.

"Are you coming down for breakfast?" Mrs. Lofton said. "We are of course pleased to walk with you, should you desire."

There was no way in politeness to refuse such an offer, even though it bordered on impudence. Did Mrs. Lofton mean to suggest that, through allowing her door to be opened, Juliet had abandoned all expectation of privacy? "Of course," she said. "Thank you for asking. I must exchange a few further words with Becky first—"

"What more could I tell you, miss?" Becky said. "It was any other day up until then, wasn't it? Anyone who'd been in the breakfast room earlier that morning, early enough to see who came in and out, why, then that person would have something worth saying. But as it is . . ." She sighed, then smiled. "You do like your hair, miss?"

"Very much, thank you, Becky," Juliet said. Bereft of any further means of delay, she joined the Loftons to walk downstairs, have breakfast, and drink coffee out of very quietly, but carefully, inspected cups.

After the dismal Longbourn dinner the night before, which had not improved following the loathsome pea soup, Jonathan Darcy awoke hungry. Breakfasts were more reliably enjoyable, Mr. Bennet being fond of good bacon, and thus great was Jonathan's temptation to linger long over the morning meal. However, his desire to return to Netherfield overruled all other impulses. Both the investigation and Miss Tilney awaited there, and thither he would go as soon as possible. (Lest Jonathan sound too fervent in his longing, it should be noted that he was also aware that Netherfield would have breakfast enough for him as well.) His grandparents were, as ever, glad enough to spare him, and so the grass still sparkled with dew as he set out on his horse for his aunt and uncle's home.

The ride was a pleasant one, and autumn rains had smoothed the roads to the perfect state between the extremes of dust and mud. Jonathan wondered what his parents would say if they knew he was riding every day instead of remaining swaddled by the fire as they would have insisted upon at home. Best, of course, that they should know nothing until he had already proved himself fully recovered, hale, and furthermore the suitor of Miss Tilney . . .

Unless they came to stop him.

Aunt Jane said she would not write immediately, he remembered, *but she must do so eventually. She will conceal Miss Tilney's presence, but the investigation alone will summon one of my parents, and then all will be known.*

His great alarm upon this realization distracted him sufficiently that he only very belatedly realized he was not the only person on the way to Netherfield this morning. A carriage on the main road—lower than his gently hilly path, and thus clearly visible—bumped along at good speed, hinting at more haste than was seemly at breakfast. Jonathan's first guess was that this would be Mr. Isaac Lucas, perhaps with some word regarding the case. However, as the carriage passed him, he caught a glimpse of the liveried coachman and the silhouette of his passenger. Yet it was that passenger's hand upon the window, a gaudy ring shining upon it, that identified her beyond all doubt.

Where should Mrs. Hurst have gone so early in the morning? Jonathan asked himself. *It appears she is come from Meryton, but why should she go to the village?*

It was, of course, possible that this early errand was not of a nefarious nature, that it had nothing whatsoever to do with the recent demise of Mr. Hurst. Perhaps Mrs. Hurst had suddenly, unaccountably, decided she wished to be out and about of a morning. Well did he recall Miss Tilney's wise maxim: If a fact would not convince a jury of guilt, it should not convince them.

But what one fact alone could not do, many together could achieve—and this was one more unexplained action by Mrs. Hurst that must be considered in an increasingly suspicious light.

Chapter Eight

Mrs. Lofton, having come with her husband to collect Juliet for breakfast, apparently intended to remain her companion throughout the meal. "How did you rest, Miss Tilney?"

"Very well," Juliet said, which was as true as it could be under the circumstances. "It is very peaceful countryside."

"My sisters made this part of Hertfordshire sound positively wild, when Charles first settled here. As though one would find mud huts and Druids strewn about." Mrs. Lofton laughed as she took her cup for coffee. "But, as usual, Louisa and Caroline had made much out of nothing."

Juliet possessed sophistication enough to know when she was being baited to speak unkindly of another. Wisely, she instead asked, "Is Mr. Lofton well?"

"Oh, very well indeed. He has become rather fond of Hertfordshire, it seems. I believe he would gladly never leave." Yet now that there was no chance of tricking Juliet into maligning Mr. Bingley's other sisters, Mrs. Lofton's enthusiasm for the conversation seemed to have waned. She turned her attention back to her food, and Juliet most happily released her.

Even more pleased was she when Jonathan Darcy arrived midway through the breakfast hours. He told her of his conversation with his aunt Jane, and she agreed that, while the peacock and the lady's periodical seemed to be of little value, the information about the disturbance in the poultry yard might prove useful. She, in turn, told him of her brief conversation with Becky.

"So the servant girl could tell us nothing beyond what we

already knew?" Mr. Darcy said, looking remarkably disappointed for a young man who had just had a second helping of bacon.

"Perhaps," said Juliet. "Though I have reflected upon it much since then, and I do not know whether Becky had no more to tell me—or whether she did not wish to tell me anything while Mr. and Mrs. Lofton stood nearby."

Mr. Darcy dropped his voice to a whisper. "Do you mean that she feared them?"

Juliet shook her head. "It was not fear I sensed in her—at least, not the mortal fear of one who believes a killer to be near. She may have been concerned that the Loftons would believe her to be speaking out of turn, or above her station. That said, the likeliest circumstance is that Becky has no more information than that which she has already shared."

"Which does not differ substantially from what Aunt Jane told me, or what I myself observed in the immediate aftermath," Mr. Darcy said, between bites of toast. "In short, the poison could have been put in the foremost cup, with the rational expectation that the first person to come to breakfast and drink coffee would take it. The arsenic powder in the cup would have been all but invisible against the pale china, meaning that anyone—particularly a person very newly awake—might not have seen it while pouring in the coffee."

"Yet you told me before that Mr. Hurst was rarely the first to rise in the morning," Juliet said. This had bothered her late at night, as she determinedly thought of the case and not Mr. Darcy. "Either someone had to have been keeping watch on him at that time—seeing that he rose early, and acting accordingly—or else Mr. Hurst was not the intended victim, as we conjectured before."

Mr. Darcy replied, "I recall as well as you that the first case of poisoning we witnessed struck down the wrong individual. Yet I feel it important that we do not allow our past experiences to color our perceptions in our present circumstance. The earliest to rise in the mornings were generally Aunt Jane, who does not drink coffee, and the Loftons, for whose potential murder we have as yet determined no possible motives. For that matter, we have as yet discerned no compelling motive for any person in this house or regularly visiting to harm any other."

Conundrum though it was, Juliet found the puzzle oddly bracing. After months on end of having little to occupy her mind beyond her disgrace, her dashed marital hopes, and her grandfather's excoriation, she felt almost unfathomably grateful for the sheer liberty of thought—the freedom only found in questions without answers.

Mr. Bingley entered the breakfast room then, as cheerful as a man could be in mourning black. "What a party we shall be tomorrow morning!" Bingley said as he went for coffee (swiftly, but definitely, checking his cup). "I shall have to tell our cook to prepare food enough for an army. She will think Buonaparte resurrected."

Juliet frowned in confusion, and Mr. Darcy gently said, "You will recall, the Allerdyces are coming."

Well did she recall it, but this did not make the announcement of that family's imminent arrival easier to hear. It was Mrs. Allerdyce who had led them all into the art exhibition in London, who had made certain to shame Juliet before all the world, and most particularly before Mr. Darcy, with the wicked portrait Mr. Follett had painted. It seemed to Juliet as though she stood in the gallery again, her humiliation fresh.

Rather than betray any sign of her turmoil, Juliet rose and left the breakfast room. If she lost her chance at determining a new clue—lost her chance to stay longer with Mr. Darcy—so be it.

Only belatedly did Jonathan realize that the day of the exhibition would be Miss Tilney's strongest recollection of the Allerdyces. So much had he thought upon his own desire to avoid that family that he had not fully reckoned with how very much stronger her response would be. How painful to be brought back into the presence of those who had witnessed such a spectacle!

(Of course Jonathan had witnessed the event, too, but Miss Tilney evidently trusted him to know the truth of the matter and behave well. The faith she had shown in him struck him greatly, though not so much as the sight of her pain.)

Swiftly he took the final sip of his coffee, then set out to follow her. His haste was not undue, but enough that Mr. Bingley raised one eyebrow at the proof that his wife had been correct about the bond between these two young persons. (As to the cause of Miss Tilney's disquiet, however, Bingley remained oblivious for the moment.)

Jonathan headed for the garden, in particular toward a folly his uncle had given his aunt, a miniature Grecian temple that could comfortably house a small picnic. He believed Miss Tilney would be drawn to the beauty of its surroundings and the sense of privacy and calm. Of course he could not be certain she would choose this precise spot to retreat, but as the only other possibility was her bedchamber, a place he could not follow, he must at least hope—but it was not hope that had led him to the folly, where indeed Miss Tilney sat, looking out at the green rolling hills. It was his understanding of her heart.

"Miss Tilney?" Jonathan called, not too loudly, just before he reached the steps. "Are you well?"

"As well as could be expected with that—that horrid—" Miss Tilney caught herself. "I must admit that I do not see how any person so grasping and cruel as Mrs. Allerdyce could be sister to a man as good of heart as Mr. Bingley appears to be."

That Mrs. Allerdyce was "grasping" could not be denied, but as for cruel . . . ? Then Jonathan realized that Miss Tilney believed the discovery at the art exhibit to have been deliberately staged by Mrs. Allerdyce, a belief that, upon consideration, he was inclined to accept. He came up, closer to Miss Tilney's side; still, she did not turn to face him. "If it is of any consolation, in my experience, Mrs. Allerdyce behaves more civilly in her brother's presence than otherwise."

"Then consoled I must be."

"Miss Tilney, please!" They could not continue on in this useless way. Jonathan wished to be sensible of her feelings, but he would not accept her conclusion. "Mrs. Allerdyce has done great harm, but she has taken nothing away from you. Do you not comprehend? All my wishes, all my plans, they remain steadfast."

She wiped her cheeks with the back of her ungloved hand. "My wishes might be unchanged, but plans—we have nothing more of plans, Mr. Darcy. Your parents will not allow the match, and that is the end."

"So you say, but I do not believe it, and you should not either."

To his surprise, Miss Tilney's response to this gentle entreaty was near ferocity. "You do not believe it, Mr. Darcy, because you are *a man*. Your position, your wealth, your freedom to choose your own future: These remain unaltered. To some extent they are unalterable. It is not so for a lady! *You* could seduce a maid and abandon her, as Mr. Willoughby did, without receiving one visiting card the fewer. You could drink to excess every night, as did Mr. Hurst, and still they would call you a fine fellow and invite you back to drink once more. You do not feel the shame of what has happened because society gives you no part in that shame. No, that is mine to bear, mine alone, and for eight months now I have borne it. The contempt, the callousness, all the severity society can possess, it gladly bestows upon a woman who has done no wrong greater than be the victim of a wicked joke. Why should I think that this destroys all my hopes? Because I have seen it! I have felt it! Do not lecture me from the seat of Pemberley on the limitations of disgrace."

These were, by far, the sharpest words Miss Tilney had ever spoken to Jonathan. Worse, he immediately understood they were, in large part, justified. "Forgive me, Miss Tilney. I did not wish to underestimate the cruelty that has been visited upon you."

"Then spare me the cruelty of reminding me of what I have lost." Miss Tilney's words, now spent, trailed into silence. After a moment she ducked a short curtsy, then walked away across the grounds.

Jonathan hardly knew where to look or how to think for many minutes afterward. When he could collect himself, he finally made himself consider the possibility that Miss Tilney was correct—that, indeed, his parents never would consent to their marriage.

If that proved to be true, then what was he willing to sacrifice? And how much could he ask Miss Tilney to sacrifice by his side?

Head abuzz, he wandered back into Netherfield. By habit his steps took him toward his uncle Bingley's study, which had become the de facto office for the investigation. One small part of his brain, calm amid the chaos, reminded him that he owed a note to Mr. Isaac Lucas, which he should write promptly. However, while still in the hallway, Jonathan heard his uncle speaking with Netherfield's steward. Jonathan went on to write the note for Mr. Lucas and handed it to a servant for delivery, almost absent any attention to what he was doing, so preoccupied was he with what he had overheard.

"There, Burton—beware the blots, and take the check to Mr. Peck immediately, and remind him that there is to be not a word of this to anyone," said Mr. Bingley. "We don't want Mrs. Bingley to find out, do we?" At that, Burton the steward chuckled.

Jonathan did not bother hiding as Burton walked out; and for his part, Burton simply ducked his head and carried on with his errand.

What was it that Aunt Jane could not know?

Meanwhile, Jane Bingley sat at the desk in her study upstairs, looking out over the rear grounds. She had inadvertently witnessed some manner of impassioned conversation between Miss Tilney and Jonathan, one that led Miss Tilney to flee before being wholly overcome. How very much in love they were!

Elizabeth had written very approvingly of Miss Tilney after their first acquaintance at Donwell Abbey. (*I should not say that I wished Mr. Wickham to be* avenged, *for surely he earned the fate he met, but what a gift it was to us to have the truth, so that there should be no undue suspicion, no unjust conviction! Proud though I am of the part Jonathan played in this, I must admit that Miss Tilney shared in this endeavor from beginning to end. She is a clever and resourceful girl, pretty in a dark sort of way, and best of all, she may have awakened Jonathan to the possibilities inherent in womankind. This awakening, I had begun to doubt would ever take place—but, as ever, Jonathan finds his own path in his own time.*) Another letter had come after Jonathan and Miss Tilney discovered who had been attempting to murder Lady Catherine de Bourgh at Rosings, and some kind words for Miss Tilney had appeared there, too, though Elizabeth's sense of fun had driven her to write far more about the unlikely circumstances of Lady Catherine's escape from a house fire.

The longest passage regarding Miss Tilney had come in

the epic letter—nigh a novel—Elizabeth had written after Jonathan's return to Pemberley after his duel. Only after much description of his wound and his convalescence had she finally written: *It is much to be regretted that Miss Tilney became mixed up in this business, as it exposes her to ridicule and censure she does not deserve. Yet mixed up in it she is, and Mr. Darcy is convinced that her ignominy will not be of short duration. The match between her and Jonathan was all but made, but that is over now, and for the best, for she appears to inspire him to a certain level of recklessness that cannot add greatly to his happiness and has already subtracted substantially from his health. At least young hearts heal swiftly. Let us hope Jonathan's wound of honor does as well.*

"Young hearts heal swiftly," Jane murmured. So many claimed—mostly the old, who had forgotten much. Jane, however, could not forget that she and her dear Charles had very nearly been kept apart by misunderstanding. He had left the area, and the two of them had not laid eyes upon each other for upward of six months; not once in all that time had she ceased thinking of him as the most amiable man of her acquaintance, the very sort of man she had always hoped to marry, and perhaps the only one she would truly love. When Bingley finally returned, and shortly thereafter proposed, he confessed that it had been exactly the same for him. Nothing had healed their hearts save the reunion, and then the wedding that ought to have been their destiny from the start.

Elizabeth had ever been so clever, so forthright, but that did not mean her judgment was infallible. For Jane's part, she always tried to look for the kindest possible resolution to any problem—but that did not mean her resolution was not correct.

Of course Jane had promised her nephew discretion, but what she had meant was that she would support him. Yet her support might need to take a different form than Jonathan had requested. In this matter, Jane determined to trust her own opinion.

Dearest Lizzy, she wrote. *Forgive my not having written to you sooner, but you will understand all when I tell you of the horrid event that has taken place here at Netherfield. I do not wish to frighten you—Jonathan continues to be well and happy, and dear Bingley and I are also in health. But the same cannot be said for my late brother-in-law, Mr. Hurst, who departed for our Savior's glory under circumstances most regrettable and shocking.*

From this Jane went on to describe Mr. Hurst's death, the likelihood of poison, and Jonathan's determination to see to the case. Next she would come to Miss Tilney, and for once in her life, Jane Bingley did not intend to mince her words.

Juliet did not rejoin the household until shortly before dinner, at which time she discovered that Mr. Darcy had returned to Longbourn for the evening. Having sought so vehemently to push him away, she was remarkably unhappy with the fruits of her endeavor. Torment though it had been to hear him speak of the impossible, Juliet had also treasured the evidence that his heart remained hers.

Without him to speak to, she feared a night of isolation, or more likely, of being accompanied by Mrs. Bingley while all others ignored them. The first part of the evening did indeed pass dully, with much conversation about persons she did not know, and teasing Mr. Bingley, who once again was finishing up a bit of correspondence, about his wretched handwriting. "Truly, Charles," Mrs. Hurst said, "you are even worse than Rachel, and her letters can scarce be read."

"I do not make so many blots as my brother!" Mrs. Lofton exclaimed.

"That would be nigh impossible, my dear," said Mr. Lofton. "Your brother is indeed worse, but that is the only defense for your writing that can be made."

Such topics amused those present, but could be of little interest to Juliet, who had never read so much as one note written by anyone present. Was she to endure hours more of this?

However, shortly after the Brookses arrived, Mrs. Lofton proposed a musical evening. "If you do not think it too soon, Louisa. We could play only sacred music, if you consider it more appropriate?"

Mrs. Hurst, who like all of Mr. Bingley's sisters was extraordinarily musically accomplished, had no objections whatsoever to any chance of display. "Mr. Hurst enjoyed music, and I believe he would not wish to deprive us of any chance to hear it."

At this, Mrs. Bingley looked over at Juliet, clearly about to ask her if she was musical—but she must have sensed that Juliet did not feel equal to performance, for instead she let her young guest take a place in the corner.

I shall observe, Juliet told herself. *That is investigation, too, of a sort.*

And what was it she saw?

—Mrs. Hurst playing a song she proclaimed one of her late husband's favorites with great skill and almost undue good cheer—

—Mrs. Lofton following her sister with even greater ability, the first of three times she would perform that night—

—Mrs. Brooks muddling her way through a tune like an almost untutored girl, though she joshed herself about it, how easy it was for married women to neglect their practice—

—Mr. Lofton pointing out that Mrs. Lofton spent a great deal of time at her piano, though the comparison was made in apparent good humor, and Mrs. Brooks evidently took it as such—

—Mrs. Bingley performing a simple Italian love song that nearly brought tears to Juliet's eyes, and was to her mind lovelier than any of Mrs. Hurst's or Mrs. Lofton's showy display—

—and Mr. Brooks, who seemed to watch Mrs. Hurst throughout.

The thought came to Juliet as a shock; and at first she believed, but no, she must be mistaken, it could not be so—! Were not Mr. Brooks and Mrs. Hurst long past the period of life for such passions? Was Mr. Brooks even capable of passion?

And yet . . . Mrs. Hurst slipped out often, secretively. What if she was doing so to either meet with Mr. Brooks, or to send him messages and receive his in return? They had been noted as talking privately, conversations no one else had overheard. Mr. Lofton had even made a comment about how most wives in Mrs. Brooks's situation would have suspected their husbands, a comment that seemed more pointed the more Juliet thought of it.

I must tell Mr. Darcy, she thought, before flushing. It would not be easy to face him again, after what had passed between them. And yet, her desire to tell him of this far outweighed any other consideration, for above all else, Mr. Hurst's murder must be solved.

Very shortly before luncheon the following day, guests began to arrive at Netherfield.

First came a more local visitor, Mr. Isaac Lucas. He had come on an unusual but most friendly errand, namely bringing

Mr. Bingley the newest copy of the *St. James Chronicle*; unsurprisingly, this earned him an invitation to join the household at lunch. "Though," Bingley said, "we will be many, and it will be quite the clamor! One more cannot add to it, however, and we are always happy to have you."

"I am happy to accept," Mr. Lucas said, a certain gleam in his eyes that Mr. Bingley was too busy to properly note.

Jonathan Darcy came shortly after. He saw at once that Miss Tilney had something she wished to discuss with him, and guessed immediately that it pertained to the case, but they were not to have time to step apart. For just then, the sound of hooves on earth and stone, the clatter of a carriage, and the jingling of harnesses alerted all to the arrival of the rest of their party: the Allerdyces.

Mrs. Caroline Allerdyce was, of course, another of Bingley's sisters, and the brightest and most vivacious of the lot. However, she had not always put her wit to the best use, and her pride, once wounded, was very slow to heal. The greatest injury to that pride had been done to her more than twenty-five years prior, when her efforts at ensnaring one Fitzwilliam Darcy into matrimony had not only failed but had also been bested by the wiles of a country girl with suntanned skin and muddy petticoats. All Caroline's good fortune since had not been sufficient to erase that sting, nor diminish her desire to be made whole for it.

The best of the fortune she had known took the form of her husband. Selected by Caroline purely for his wealth and estate, he had proved to be a reasonable, affectionate, and amiable man, one who urged her to become better informed and to widen her sphere of company. This she had done, and they had in fact been very happy together for many years—until she began plotting the marital fortunes of her younger daughter, Priscilla.

No such machinations had Caroline concerned herself

with regarding her elder daughter. Frederica Allerdyce had inherited her father's height, poise, and intelligence; and most parents would have been overjoyed to see their own little girl become such a fine young woman. Caroline knew only that Frederica—despite being twenty-two years of age!—had earlier that year turned down a proposal from a baronet, refusing to wed a slave owner when she might as easily have married him and ensured that he divested himself of such holdings after matrimony. Relations between mother and daughter remained frosty.

However, Caroline's fondest hopes had always rested upon her younger daughter, Priscilla. Frederica had been born not even a full year after Jonathan Darcy; as husbands were normally at least a few years older than their wives, that put paid to Caroline's firstborn as potential mistress of Pemberley. But Priscilla! She was the perfect age, and lovely in the fair, rosy way that was called "classic English beauty." By the time she had turned ten, her mother's ambitions were firm. Priscilla would do what Caroline had not: become the wife of the heir to Pemberley. If the heir to Pemberley did not see the necessity of this yet, Caroline intended that he would soon.

Caroline had in her youth and early adulthood been rather close to her sister, Mrs. Hurst, and had spent a great deal of time with the late Mr. Hurst, including in earlier years, when his penchant for wine had not yet been so pronounced, and his company therefore more pleasant. So her dismay upon hearing of his death was unfeigned. Yet whatever sorrow she might have felt for her brother-in-law was quickly replaced by shock at the news that his death was in fact deliberate murder, and then by anger at realizing that the Tilney girl—despite all Caroline's best efforts, which had been very effective indeed— was again close at hand, again playing investigator while trying to catch the younger Darcy for herself.

"I am so glad we are come here at this difficult time," Caroline said, embracing her sisters and Jane in turn. "How good it is that we should be here, to help and to support you all in this time of travail! Rest assured, no evil influences will be allowed to do harm to this family." Her gaze traveled from her family to the distant corner of the room, where Miss Tilney stood quietly. "No, that shall not be borne."

For her part, Juliet Tilney's feelings upon being described as an "evil influence" can well be imagined. So, too, can the displeasure Jonathan Darcy experienced upon hearing the same. Such emotions are understandable, and so it is hoped that the reader will forgive most of those present for temporarily forgetting the fate of Mr. Hurst—or the fact that the person responsible for that fate most likely stood in their company at that very moment.

They would not have the luxury of such forgetfulness for much longer.

Chapter Nine

Priscilla Allerdyce, though not fundamentally wicked by nature, had been fashioned by her mother as a weapon in the combat of courtship as surely as any naval architect had drafted plans for a man-o'-war. She had been informed that Jonathan Darcy would be visiting Netherfield at the same time as she; no further instructions had been required. Priscilla understood what her mother wished her to do and felt confident of making progress. If she could not yet bring Mr. Darcy to the point of proposing, she could at least set the stage for an appropriate avowal of love in the relatively near future.

Given this, Priscilla's sentiments upon seeing Miss Juliet Tilney were not so unpleasant as might be imagined. For one, though she understood her duty to catch Mr. Darcy and make him her husband, her heart was not touched by him in the slightest. This sort of sentiment, she had been given to understand, most often awakened after matrimony, so its absence at this stage did not concern her. Therefore, although Miss Tilney might represent a tactical menace, Priscilla could look upon this coolly, absent sorrow or despair.

Second, and more significantly, Priscilla was cognizant of the attendant risks following the murder of Mr. Hurst. In London, the deaths within the Rushworth family had not unduly unnerved her—grisly to think about, to be sure, but one expected evildoing in the city. Nor had she any but the most glancing acquaintance with those who had died. How different it was to encounter a murder among one's own family! (Her uncle Hurst had never been a favorite, given his pre-dilection for drink, but he was nonetheless kin.) And how shocking to have such a thing take place at Netherfield, a house Priscilla had always thought of as particularly peace-able. Worst of all, this threatened to bring disgrace upon her uncle and aunt, and such disgrace might in time even touch *her*. If Miss Tilney could assist in the resolution of this mur-der, by all means, she should be allowed to do so. Once that purpose had been fulfilled, then it would be time for Priscilla to push the competition aside and fix her attention on her future.

Her elder sister, Frederica, unencumbered by any need for strategical thinking in this matter, had gone to Miss Tilney almost immediately, greeting her with warmth and without the slightest allusion to February's scandal.

So Priscilla followed her sister, wearing a similar smile. "Miss Tilney. I trust your journey here was not unpleasant?"

"The worst of the summer heat has passed, thank good-ness," Miss Tilney replied. "Yet traveling great distances by carriage is always somewhat wearying. You must be much in need of rest."

"True, but for us, why, Netherfield might almost as well be home. It is not so tiring coming to a familiar place as it is to go to an unfamiliar one, because in a new place, one can never entirely be at ease, can one?" This was civil, and generally truthful, and yet would remind Juliet that she was an outsider here at Netherfield—that she would ever be so—while Pris-cilla herself belonged here, amid her family, her social class, and her future husband.

To judge by the way Miss Tilney's gaze drifted downward toward the floor, the message had been received. Pleased with herself, Priscilla went on to greet her aunt Jane—who, silly and sentimental though she might be, could not but be a favorite of anyone who had in childhood known her comforting ways.

Priscilla remained just young enough to hope that Aunt Jane, in defiance of the seasons, would have asked her cook to make a bit of the wonderful Netherfield gingerbread.

Juliet had in fact been trying to think of a suitable rejoinder to Priscilla Allerdyce, but as is so often the case, the perfect bon mot would not arrive until hours later, when she was trying to fall asleep. Her frustration was diverted when Jonathan Darcy came swiftly to her side.

"You choose your time wisely, Mr. Darcy." Juliet nodded toward Priscilla, deep in conversation with Mrs. Bingley. Inwardly she was proud of herself; she had remained poised, had even been witty, as the slight smile on his face demonstrated.

Mr. Darcy said, "I wish to apologize for my departure yesterday. It seemed important to—"

"Forgive my interrupting you, Mr. Darcy, but I made some observations last night that I feel I must share, and this may be our best opportunity for some time."

He heard her out, with interest but also with disbelief. "That is not a pair I should ever have thought likely—in any context, truly, but least of all in the one you suggest."

"Yet they meet privately. Yet Mrs. Hurst slips out early in the morning. And she travels into Meryton at that same hour, presumably to meet with someone." Juliet raised an eyebrow. "Who else might it be?"

"At this point I will concede only that we must investigate the point further," Mr. Darcy said. "For if that connection is true—"

"Then we know of two people who would have reason to wish Mr. Hurst out of the way," Juliet concluded, glancing around. Luckily their position in the corner and the general hubbub in the room concealed the content of their conversation, any element of which alone would have silenced all present with shock.

Except, perhaps, Mr. Brooks and Mrs. Hurst.

The person nearest Mr. Darcy and Miss Tilney was Frederica Allerdyce, who overheard nothing, largely due to distraction. She had originally intended to keep an eye on her younger sister. As Frederica was the superior in age, temperament, and sense, she often found herself obliged to soften the edges of some of Priscilla's sharper remarks. Given her mother's plans for Priscilla and Mr. Darcy, Miss Tilney would inevitably be a target.

However, Frederica had many others to greet upon her arrival at Netherfield, including one gentleman she had not expected to see so soon. "Mr. Lucas!" she said brightly. "How good of my uncle and aunt to invite you to this very first luncheon. It is always such a delight to see old friends."

"I agree entirely," said Isaac Lucas, for indeed he and Frederica had known each other almost since their infancy. The various connections between their families meant that they had been brought together once or twice a year; and one of Frederica's first memories was of toddling through the lavender that grew on one of Netherfield's low hills, young Isaac at her side, the two of them pointing out butterflies darting amid the fragrant plants. He had matured into one of the finest young men of her acquaintance, one she privately considered as the ideal of amiability.

"How very civil you are, too." Frederica gestured vaguely at Mr. Lucas's dark clothing. "You need not have donned mourning for the sake of our uncle, but let me express for all my family how much your gesture is appreciated."

"I deserve no such appreciation, for I have been wearing mourning these past nine months. You would not have heard, then, that my father passed away."

Frederica gasped at her ignorance, and her own inadvertent unkindness. "Indeed I had not! How very sorry I am to hear it. Mr. Lucas, please accept my deepest sympathies."

"Thank you, Miss Allerdyce. He was the kindest of fathers and the best of men."

Other childhood memories had filled her mind. "Do you recall when he made us the kite? The scarlet one with the long tail?"

Mr. Lucas's fond smile said more of his filial love than words could ever have done. "I think we ran up and down the length of the garden a hundred times that day. It was not windy enough for a kite after the first hour or so, but we wished it to fly, and he did not wish to disappoint us."

"A very kind father, indeed." Frederica glanced fondly at her own papa, who was deep in conversation with her dear uncle Bingley. Yet the greater implications of what Mr. Lucas had told her had begun to clarify within her mind. "So you have become head of your family and inherited your house?"

"Yes, Miss Allerdyce. I have. It is a great responsibility, and one I had thought would not fall to me for many more years to come. Yet with that responsibility come certain advantages."

Mr. Lucas's eyes met hers, and Frederica felt a flutter deep within, as tiny and bright as those long-ago butterflies in the lavender. She said only, "I am sure you fulfill your new role admirably, Mr. Lucas."

He inclined his head by way of reply, and they set to speaking with others who had to be greeted, but neither Mr. Lucas nor Frederica thought of much else for the better part of an hour.

Always, she had liked him—enjoyed his company, admired his person, recalled with pleasure the few occasions upon which they had danced together. Mr. Lucas had ever seemed to be as taken with her companionship as she was with his. Once or twice, Frederica would admit, their conversation had taken a turn toward the flirtatious.

Yet she had not allowed herself to dream of more. It had always been made tacitly clear to Frederica that Mr. Isaac Lucas was not a viable prospect for matrimony. He was only one year her elder, which in and of itself—while unusual in a milieu where husbands were generally five or more years older than their wives—did not disqualify the match. The impediment arose due to his father's relative youth and the limitations of the Lucas family fortune. To be sure, Isaac Lucas's inheritance would be a respectable one, and although Lucas Lodge was not one of the great estates of the realm, it was nonetheless a stately and elegant home. However, the financial situation of the Lucas family would not permit a son to live very high, not even the eldest. Ergo, Isaac Lucas had not been expected to be in a position to support a wife in any degree of comfort until he was well into his thirties or forties—assuming his father lived a normal lifespan.

But this, his father had not done. Isaac Lucas had already come into his inheritance, which meant certain possibilities Frederica had long considered no more than useless fantasy suddenly appeared very real indeed.

As it happened, the information regarding the death of the elder Mr. Lucas had been deliberately kept from Frederica by her mother. Caroline Allerdyce had never bothered to check the friendship between the Lucas boy and her elder daughter, certain that both families, and even the children's own good sense, would lay to rest any notions of matrimony between them. So ineligible a match did Caroline think it that she considered the death of the elder Mr. Lucas an irrelevancy—yet she had not felt entirely certain that Frederica would agree. After all, her daughter had turned down the proposal of a *baronet* only a few months prior, which signified that the girl's judgment in such matters remained impractical.

So Caroline kept one eye upon the conversation between her daughter and Mr. Lucas, but without any real sense of alarm. Even if Isaac Lucas were impudent enough to strive to marry so far above his level, and even if Frederica were foolhardy enough to wish to wed so far below her own, Mr. Allerdyce would certainly forbid it.

Cheered by this expectation, Caroline devoted herself to speaking with her sisters, who had in childhood and early adulthood been her closest friends and companions. Once, she had enjoyed no pastime more than chatting and laughing with Louisa and Rachel.

Yet not all the frolics of youth remain equally enjoyable throughout life.

"It is disgraceful," Mrs. Lofton whispered, "absolutely *disgraceful* that Louisa still has not put on mourning. Anyone would think her unmoved by the death of her husband. Not that it is any great wonder she would not miss him, given that he rarely moved from that divan, and more rarely still could be found sober any later in the day than luncheon. But the appearance of it! Shocking, very shocking indeed, particularly given the circumstances of Mr. Hurst's death. Of course I think no ill of Louisa—*that,* to be sure, is beyond question— but the *appearance* of it! Furthermore, she is constantly speaking with Mr. Brooks in places where others cannot hear—and be sure I have tried! There can be nothing in it, of course, but appearances. Appearances! Husbands and wives must think of such things."

Caroline agreed with all without considering a single word, for it was necessary to ensure that Mrs. Lofton's voice did not rise above a whisper and stir discontent, if not actual scandal. As swiftly as the flow of conversation allowed, she steered herself toward Mrs. Hurst, closest to her in age and for many years, her best friend. A good explanation for the lack of mourning was sure to follow.

Instead, she found herself listening to Mrs. Hurst's own whispers: "Rachel thinks she is being very subtle, but indeed she is not. One does not wish to make assumptions about the state of a marriage, but with such behavior as hers—! Well, let the Loftons look to each other as best they can. I have written to our solicitors to learn what is to be done; his cousin inherits, of course, but I understand that I am to have a life estate upon nearly all the family holdings, and an ample jointure of my own. So I need not fear any deprivation, which is a great comfort."

Many widows would have considered the deprivation of their husbands' companionship to be a loss beyond almost any comfort, a fact that did not fail to strike Caroline Allerdyce.

"The Brookses, as you see, are much with us," Mrs. Hurst said, pointing toward the corner where both Mr. and Mrs. Brooks were speaking with Mr. Lofton. "Did you ever imagine we should be so long haunted by the sisters Bennet?"

Caroline could but nod. The lack of grief evidenced by Mrs. Hurst was indeed shocking, but so, too, was the lack of compassion shown by Mrs. Lofton.

In some ways, most astonishing of all was the realization that, when she had been younger and more callow, not yet wed to Mr. Allerdyce, Caroline might have responded in exactly the same manner. She did not often think of herself as changed by matrimony, but she had been.

Once, after a long dinner at the Allerdyce residence in London, during which Mrs. Hurst and Mrs. Lofton judged the character of half of their society and found it wanting, Caroline had turned from her farewells at the end of the night to see her husband attempting—and failing—not to laugh.

"Caroline, my dearest, they are your sisters, and I know that you love them," Mr. Allerdyce had said, "but are you altogether certain that you *like* them?"

She had reprimanded him then—but, perhaps, she had been too quick to do so.

As she could not be avoided forever, Jonathan elected to greet Priscilla Allerdyce on his own terms. "Miss Priscilla. I trust your journey went well?"

Priscilla, who had been laughing at one of Mrs. Lofton's observations, was pleasantly surprised by this. "Indeed, Mr. Darcy, though I must say the best part has been our arrival, especially finding you here. You will be staying throughout our visit?"

"Actually, I have moved to stay with my grandparents at Longbourn," Jonathan said. "I wished to give my room to Miss Tilney." Had he not been so overwhelmed by the crush of persons, he might have taken amusement in Priscilla's poor attempt to disguise her chagrin at this news.

Mrs. Lofton had apparently overheard. "It is only right and proper that you should spend time with your mother's family as well, Mr. Darcy. Why, the Brookses should come to dinner with you there some night soon. A true reunion for you all!"

Jonathan could not see the point of a "reunion" when all persons besides himself lived within two miles of the same village, but as was often the case when Mrs. Lofton spoke, it did not appear that any reply was necessary.

Luncheon, large and noisy as it was, grated against Jonathan's every nerve. To his profound relief, once the meal had ended, all the Allerdyces went to refresh themselves after their journey, and the others went to rest. This left him alone with Miss Tilney, more or less, and gave them some time to work.

"I was thinking that we should speak with more members of the staff," he suggested to her. "Now that Netherfield hosts even more guests, they will all be even busier than before, and for some days if not weeks to come. This may be our last opportunity to have the cooks' and maids' undivided attention, if indeed that opportunity is not already lost. We did not ask about Mr. Brooks and Mrs. Hurst before, and it is possible there is much there to be learned."

"The opportunity is indeed lost," Juliet said, "for I noticed this morning that preparations are being made to finish the monthly laundering, which means the dyeing is soon to begin."

Every death within a household called for many garments to be dyed black. If a family had been visited with tragedy repeatedly, the wardrobe might already hold mourning attire enough—but this was not the case at Netherfield, and Jonathan could well imagine the enormity of the task ahead. Even servants normally unassociated with laundry and related tasks would be pulled into the effort.

"If we cannot immediately make progress in the investigation, then let us give you some time away from Netherfield," Jonathan said. "Just an evening, so that you may face the morning fresh and better able to bring your powers of concentration to bear upon our investigation."

"I would not mind that," Miss Tilney said, "but how? Do you mean for— Would Mr. Lucas—"

"Not at all. I will send a note to my grandparents. Longbourn is but three miles hence, and if I ask, I am sure they will invite you to dinner. We may allow Mr. Bingley some time with his sisters, may we not?" Perhaps Mrs. Lofton had had a point. "I shall see if they can ask the Brookses as well. That will at least give us a chance to observe them out of the company of all the others."

"An excellent point." She brightened. "If—if you truly think it would be all right—then, yes, Mr. Darcy. I should welcome the change."

So encouraged was Jonathan by this opportunity to introduce Miss Tilney to more members of his family that he had written the note and sent it to Longbourn before he fully considered how the meal was likely to go. His grandmother's contempt for him and his grandfather's lack of understanding were difficult to bear at the best of times; how much worse would it be if they were to display such in front of Miss Tilney!

Yet his grandparents always behaved better in company than they did among the family alone. With this, Jonathan consoled himself.

Even when we are most in need of comfort and special care, we tend not to wish to think of ourselves as being "coddled"— no matter how much coddling might be secretly desired! So Juliet Tilney could not wholly reconcile herself to abandoning Netherfield for Longbourn until she recollected that not all the most important elements of investigation confined themselves to the scene of the murder.

The observations of those beyond Netherfield may prove as insightful as the observations of those within it, Juliet mused as Becky quietly buttoned the back of her dinner dress. *I may learn much, if Mr. Darcy's grandparents can be persuaded to speak freely.* (From this, it can be discerned how very little Juliet yet knew of the Bennets.)

At least she looked well, for her mother had purchased

nice dresses for her in London earlier that year, which—given Juliet's near exile from polite society—had been worn but once or twice, if at all. This particular gown was made of the same white satin that might have been seen in ballrooms twenty years prior, yet its ornamentation was lushly up-to-date, with ruffles and bows, without erring toward the gaudiness displayed by Mrs. Lofton or Mrs. Hurst. As she gazed at herself in the mirror, Becky said, "You look very pretty indeed, miss. Prettier than either of those Allerdyce girls could ever be."

"Oh, you must not say such things." Juliet felt herself blushing. "Besides, beauty is as beauty does."

"Well, Miss Allerdyce might be as pretty, then, but Miss Priscilla hasn't a chance."

Juliet laughed despite herself. "Be careful, Becky. Ladies' maids must be discreet."

This gentle, commonplace advice seemed to strike Becky as far more noteworthy than Juliet would have thought. "Indeed, miss. One has to know when to keep one's mouth shut, and when to open it again. A time for all things, as the Bible says. Heard that from Mr. Brooks himself."

"When?"

Becky cocked her head. "From the pulpit, miss."

"Oh. Of course." Juliet felt foolish, but remembered another question that Becky might be able to answer more forthrightly. "Do you know of anyone connected to the Bingley family who has the Christian name of Nancy?"

"Let me think. Mrs. Mount in town, who has the fabric shop—I believe her name's Nancy, and of course Mrs. Bingley does a great deal of shopping there. And Stewart's got a new granddaughter named Nancy, a wee dear thing. The Bingleys gave her parents a whole pound as a christening present."

"Most generous," said Juliet honestly enough, as few masters would even know if their servants had grandchildren, much less pay such a sum upon their births.

"There was a horse called Nancy," Becky went on, "but I do not suppose you are much interested in the stables."

"Human Nancys are of much greater importance, I believe." Juliet's thoughts had turned to Mrs. Mount. Could she be the "Nancy" of which Mrs. Lofton had overheard?

She might have asked Becky more about Nancy Mount had Juliet not then heard the carriage being brought round, and when she went to the window, she saw Mr. Darcy already at the front step, waiting for her. How could her heart not be touched by such a gesture?

But she could not forget their history, any more than she could forget the writing desk that sat nearby, nor the chamber within that held the letter from Mr. Follett.

Longbourn proved to be a smaller but handsome house. From past insinuations of Lady Catherine de Bourgh, Juliet had been led to think that Mrs. Darcy's origins must be humble indeed, but this was unquestionably the residence of a gentleman.

The Bennets themselves were an elderly couple, not robust but apparently in reasonable health, aside from the fact that Mr. Bennet walked with a stick. Their furnishings and attire appeared somewhat out of date, yet this was hardly unusual among persons their age, and nothing in their style of living suggested any lack of comfort.

In attendance also were the Brookses. Their simple attire showed to better effect here than it did amid the elegance of Netherfield. Mr. Brooks's cool demeanor did not seem much changed, but Mrs. Brooks seemed pale and inattentive.

Would not you be distracted, Juliet thought, *if you suspected your husband of indiscretion?* Though possibly Mrs. Brooks thought no such thing.

"You have laid a very nice table for us, Mother Bennet," said Mr. Brooks, as they sat to table. "Entirely charming."

"Of course it is all as nothing compared to Netherfield," said Mrs. Bennet. "You must have seen, but Miss Tilney will not yet know, they have three full services of silver! And did you know, four settings of china? Each one enough to entertain the entire town at one of their balls. Though they have not held a proper dance since Sarah married, but mark my words, as soon as little Martha Elizabeth has her coming out, Netherfield will again be the center of all that is elegant and refined."

"I would say it is that center even now," said Mrs. Brooks. She seemed to wish herself there.

Mr. Bennet smiled slightly. "This is ambition indeed for a grand coming out, given that Martha has always been fonder of climbing trees than practicing at the pianoforte, and I am given to understand her petticoats are perpetually in a state of ruin."

"Oh! Mr. Bennet! You will not speak of petticoats at dinner!" Mrs. Bennet's voice could be sharp when she chose—or cloying, as it became when she returned to one of her more favored subjects. "Our good Jane has proved herself more than equal to being a fine lady. I always knew it would be so."

"In point of fact," Mr. Bennet said between his sips of wine, "she despaired of any of our daughters marrying at all, at least twice a week and often twice a day, until after the first one wed—and that, by far, the worst match of the lot."

Mrs. Bennet made a face. "You are always so unkind regarding poor Mr. Wickham, even now that he is in his grave with our dear Lydia and Susannah."

Memory flashed within Juliet's mind—Donwell Abbey late at night, lightning illuminating the long gallery, and Wickham lying dead upon the floor—but she closed her eyes for a moment, then set it aside.

Yet her reaction had been perceived by Mr. Darcy. "You forget, Grandmama, that it was Miss Tilney who found Mr. Wickham after his death. It cannot be a pleasant recollection for her."

"But you have seen no end of murder since, have you not?" Mrs. Bennet said, undaunted. "Bodies strewn hither and yon. I cannot think how anyone should contrive to be near so many murders."

"The obvious solution, of course," said Mr. Bennet, who seemed only to speak when he had a witticism to make, "would be to murder 'em yourself, but we do not go so far as to accuse you, Miss Tilney."

Juliet could not help but smile. Finally she had been absolved of one crime!

Mrs. Brooks had apparently been considering another of her mother's remarks for some time. "At least Jane is a fine lady," she repeated. "Elizabeth, too, of course."

"And *Mary*!" Mrs. Bennet exclaimed. "She, become the wife of a dean! Who would ever have thought it?" Her exclusion of her only other living daughter was painfully clear to all at the table except Mrs. Bennet herself. Mrs. Brooks lowered her face and attended only to her food.

Many husbands or fathers would have come to Kitty Brooks's defense at that moment, but Mr. Bennet wished to tell humorous tales of his daughter Mary's bluestocking ways as a girl, and Mr. Brooks simply helped himself to more potatoes. Mr. Darcy, who seemed to be struggling with his grandmother's loudness, was endeavoring to keep his own peace. No help was to be had for Mrs. Brooks.

She is angry, Juliet thought as she watched Mrs. Brooks sullenly dine. *Angrier than I believe anyone else suspects. At least some of the reasons why are obvious—but we may need to learn the others.*

Chapter Ten

Louisa Hurst had never troubled herself overmuch regarding housekeeping. When Mr. Hurst had inherited his estate, more than two decades into their marriage, she had simply accepted the existing housekeeper, a Mrs. Russ. In the general way of things, this action would have been both practical and considerate; however, as Mrs. Russ had been hoping for a small bequest in the late owner's will, and was reaching an advanced age, the choice was a careless one. Having had time enough to assess her new mistress, Russ had promptly begun skimming small amounts from the household funds to create her own nest egg, generally by hiring new servants at even lower wages than the disgraceful ones the Hursts believed they paid. This meant that all in their home was done poorly, which irritated Mrs. Hurst, which meant she spent even less time thinking about the house and arranged for more months away visiting family—almost always Charles and Jane Bingley. The state of affairs worked well for no one save Mrs. Russ, for whom it functioned so smoothly that she planned to retire within a year's time.

So it was no very great wonder that, when Mrs. Hurst awoke the next morning, she did not at first recognize the acrid scent drifting through her open window. A momentary fear of fire roused her thoroughly, when she saw (to her mingled relief and dismay) that the servants were, at long last, preparing the vats of black dye that awaited nearly all her clothes for transformation later that day.

Mourning must be worn, of course. This was society's rule, and Mrs. Hurst was not one who questioned such rules. Yet she could hardly stifle a cry of dismay at the thought of her pretty dresses being made funereal. It was not as though wearing black would ease her mourning; if anything, she thought, the inconvenience and ugliness of it all would make her sadder rather than happier. So what could be the point of that?

(Remembrance, it will be seen, was not one of Mrs. Hurst's virtues.)

Already she had given the maids instructions for the proper handling of her clothes, but Mrs. Hurst felt the need to ensure nothing had been forgotten. She rang the bell and commanded her maid to dress her in the brightest day dress she owned—an apple-green one trimmed with dark gold embroidery—in order to spare that, at least. Emerging from her room, she almost immediately came upon her favorite sister in the hallway.

"Well, Caroline, the stench will have told you that my mourning is to begin tomorrow," Mrs. Hurst cried. "Like as not, the servants will ruin every garment they touch. If I did not know better, I would think Jane meant to shame me for not having had the foresight to pack all my black things in case Mr. Hurst were to die."

Mrs. Allerdyce frowned. "That is not very like Jane." Yet that could be only morning disagreeableness, for she swiftly took on a more becoming smile. "Within the family circle, I think it rather mean to pay undue attention to such strictures. Of course you would never be seen beyond this estate without donning mourning, and what can your clothing signify while you are in the company of those who know your sorrow!"

Mrs. Hurst *had* ventured past Netherfield a few mornings prior—but that had been nothing with which to trouble her sister. More pertinent news had already presented itself. "I believe the eager suitor is already on his way, Caroline. And breakfast hardly even set out!"

Yet the sight of Jonathan Darcy riding toward Netherfield did not brighten Mrs. Allerdyce's spirits as might have been expected. Surely she did not think the disgraced Tilney girl to be an obstacle in Priscilla's path—but as Mrs. Hurst looked further, she understood. Not a quarter of a mile behind Mr. Darcy rode Mr. Isaac Lucas.

Laughing gaily, Mrs. Hurst said, "Do not fret about *him*, Caroline! To imagine, that either of your girls would ever be tempted to become mistress of *Lucas Lodge*!"

At that Caroline's smile became real, and they went down to breakfast arm in arm as they had in days gone by. There was no need to think further upon black garb until tomorrow, and no need ever again to consider the errand that had taken Mrs. Hurst into Meryton, none at all.

Through the lace curtain at her window, Juliet watched the arrival of Mr. Darcy and Mr. Lucas. She intended to come down to breakfast as late as possible, so that she might have more time to finish a letter.

Dinner with the Bennets had given her many thoughts regarding the investigation, but one lesson shone brightest among them all: To marry without love was not only a mistake, one destined to cast shadows over one's whole life (poor Kitty Brooks!), but in truth, a sin. Thus she had resolved to act immediately.

Returning to her desk, Juliet prepared to conclude the letter to her grandfather she had begun shortly after daybreak. Within it she had already written the usual conversational niceties and an extremely vague summation of their investigative efforts thus far, in which she knew he would have no interest. The conclusion was all that remained, and it was this that frightened her.

> *When I received the Bingleys' invitation to Netherfield,*
> *Grandfather, you suggested that this visit might spark*
> *the renewal of any addresses Mr. Jonathan Darcy*
> *might have been inclined to pay me. Though I have*
> *been here but a few days, I am already very certain*
> *that Mr. Darcy's family will never consent to our*
> *engagement. My hopes were long dead; I must now put*
> *an end to yours. It is quite impossible, even if—*

Juliet paused, quill in hand, remembering the tone of Mr. Darcy's voice when he had spoken to her of hope. Then she shook her head.

> *even if one person within that family were to agree to*
> *the match, total acceptance will not be forthcoming.*
> *Mr. Darcy is a loving and devoted son, and he*
> *would never countenance an engagement under such*
> *circumstances.*
>
> *Despite this, I must also decline the proposal of*
> *Mr. Follett. Ours would be a match without either*
> *love or fortune to recommend it; it could only begin*
> *in folly and end in misery. Nor do I believe that the*
> *marriage would achieve even its most modest aims, as*
> *the scandal attached to us both through his cruel trick*
> *with the portrait would be aired anew at our marriage.*
> *Nowhere we went, at no point in our lives, would we*
> *be introduced to new acquaintances without the tale*
> *being told to them almost immediately after. Thus*
> *the disgrace of the entire affair would be renewed in*
> *perpetuity.*

I write this fully understanding that Mr. Follett's may be the only proposal I shall ever receive. My material well-being will surely be damaged by it, as for a woman there is no surer preserver from want than marriage. Yet I do not hold with the raillery that decries old maids as meaningless persons, the fit subjects of ridicule. If I end my days as aunt and caretaker to the children Theodosia will someday have—or living in one of the favor cottages near Northanger upon the charity of either my brother or a future cousin—then I am satisfied that I shall nonetheless lead a respectable life, one of service to the family I cherish so dearly.

Would this be sufficient to end her grandfather's demands? Juliet knew him too well to believe that he would receive her missive with anything but the bitterest anger—yet he was not an unintelligent man. He had served in the wars; surely a soldier should understand when a battle had been lost.

Jonathan had resolved to keep drinking coffee, extending his time at breakfast, until Miss Tilney arrived. By the time she descended, he felt as though he might leap out of his own skin; indeed, he startled at the sight of her.

"Mr. Darcy?" she said. "Are you quite well?"

"Entirely, Miss Tilney." If the words came out too quickly, he trusted no one else would take note. "We have much to discuss. There has been a great deal of change and tumult these past few days—I felt we should review all from the very beginning, and this is as good a time as any to speak with the magistrate of our efforts so far."

This same magistrate, Mr. Isaac Lucas, happened to be at breakfast, but his attention was much for Miss Allerdyce at present. However, he recollected his duty once Miss Allerdyce had gone, and joined them on their side of the table, sitting on the other side of Miss Tilney. "Is this a good time for us to review what you have already learned?"

Miss Tilney nodded. "Indeed, sir, we are even now preparing to do so."

Thus Jonathan felt encouraged to bring out the piece of paper and sketching pencil he had tucked into one pocket. As the others had finished eating and were exiting, he, Mr. Lucas, and Miss Tilney could now be quite alone (save for Becky, obediently standing in the corner), and so he could share the notes he had already taken.

Those suspected in the death of Mr. Hurst

Mrs. Hurst
Mr. Lofton
Mrs. Lofton
Mr. Brooks
Mrs. Brooks
Mr. Bingley

"I note you have not included your aunt Jane," Miss Tilney said, but before Jonathan could protest, she smiled. "Although I believe we should be prepared to defend our reasoning, I must admit that I, too, have come to believe it impossible that Mrs. Bingley could be guilty of murder."

"Good—we need waste no more time there." Jonathan took up the pencil. "Now, let us consider these in turn. Mrs. Hurst is, I think you would agree, the person whose potential motive could most easily be guessed."

"An unhappy marriage has driven many to terrible acts," Mr. Lucas agreed.

Miss Tilney interjected, "Yet Mrs. Hurst's behavior—so

thoughtless, even callous regarding the loss of her husband—must be said to be a point against her being the guilty person."

Jonathan frowned. "You think she did not kill him *because* she does not mourn him?"

"Consider, gentlemen. Had Mrs. Hurst done it, would she not be at pains to demonstrate her innocence? What better demonstration of this could there be besides her grief? Would she not be the first to weep, the loudest to wail? Instead, she behaves in a way that draws attention, and to me it seems that no person guilty of murder would wish *more* attention paid them, rather than less."

"Your point is well-made," Jonathan conceded. "Yet other explanations are possible."

She raised one eyebrow, a familiar and tantalizing challenge. "What would one of these explanations be?"

How could this be tactfully put? "Mrs. Hurst has never struck me as a particularly insightful person, either regarding herself or others," Jonathan replied. "She lacks curiosity about those around her, and insofar as she thinks of them, in my experience, she tends to regard them as universally lesser than herself—both in class and in understanding."

Miss Tilney took a sip of coffee as she weighed his words. "You mean, she may not be considering the opinions of others because they do not matter to her, and she does not consider them intelligent enough to deduce much from her actions."

"Precisely."

"Very well. And there is the possibility of the . . . connection we had discussed."

"What connection is this?" Mr. Lucas asked. Jonathan whispered the words, to his listener's evident surprise. "You cannot mean it? Truly?"

"I remain dubious in that regard," said Jonathan, "as it would seem to suggest a depth of feeling neither has much evidenced."

"Yet they have had occasion to speak in confidence, a confidence they apparently wish to maintain even amid the mystery regarding Mr. Hurst's death," Miss Tilney said. "It may or may not be illicit, but we cannot know that until we discover what it is."

This seemed both reasonable and intriguing to Jonathan. "Then there we will press."

Miss Tilney tapped at his uncle's name upon the list. "No motive suggests itself for Mr. Bingley, save that Mr. Hurst did not appear to be an especially attentive husband, which could, I suppose, lead a brother to feel protective of his sister. Yet we have heard nothing of Mr. Hurst that would suggest he was cruel, nor that Mrs. Hurst felt oppressed by him in any respect. I should not think Mr. Bingley a man to interfere in such a situation unless his sister's situation was terrible indeed."

"Agreed," Jonathan said. "Yet he *is* keeping some manner of secret from my aunt. I overheard him giving instructions to his steward regarding the sending of a check, I know not to whom, but he stressed that Aunt Jane must not know."

"The mysterious 'Nancy'?" Miss Tilney murmured. She appeared nearly as dismayed by the idea as Jonathan felt. "Mr. Lucas, do you know of a 'Nancy' particularly attached to this house?"

"It is a common name," Lucas replied, "and there are many so called in Meryton, but I cannot name one I know to have connections to this house or family."

Miss Tilney shook her head. "This is not one of our main points of curiosity, for we have nothing to link this secret to Mr. Hurst's death. Nor can I think of any reason that, in such a case, Mr. Bingley should speak freely of the matter to his steward."

This was well reasoned, Jonathan felt. "As to the Loftons—Mrs. Lofton overhears much, which has been of a benefit to us. Yet could this not, in its own way, be a kind of concealment?" He was particularly proud of this last insight.

"Perhaps? Though it seems more artful than I would think her capable of being. Yet I fear we must learn from her example." When Miss Tilney became amused, she wrinkled her nose slightly, which Jonathan found charming. "Mr. Darcy, I fear we shall have to become quite *nosy*."

Jonathan smiled back at her. He disliked looking into the eyes of others for more than an instant, but with Miss Tilney, this lifelong aversion often melted away. "We so often do."

Then she seemed to catch herself, or to remember Mr. Lucas, sitting up straighter and attending to the list once more. She turned her attention to the servant girl Becky, who still stood near the sideboard. "I fear we are keeping you rather late. Breakfast hours must be over."

"The job's to stay as long as anyone wants to eat, miss." Becky did not seem dismayed. If anything, Jonathan thought, the girl seemed happy. "A servant does as she's bid."

"Nonetheless," Miss Tilney said as she rose, "we can move our conversation elsewhere."

Becky's wide smile remained bright. "As you like, miss."

Jonathan hastily gathered list and pencil to follow Miss Tilney from the breakfast room. Mr. Lucas, having attended to his duty, now felt free to find Miss Allerdyce elsewhere in the house. After excusing him, Jonathan told Miss Tilney, "I suppose our discussion was very nearly at an end regardless, for that is everyone we need to consider."

Miss Tilney stopped in the hallway to face him. "Not at all, for we have not spoken of Mrs. Brooks."

"Aunt Kitty?"

His consternation must have been clear, because Miss Tilney became firm. "I know you are fond of all your family, but—"

"That is not the source of my objection," Jonathan insisted. "In truth, I do not know my aunt Kitty very well at all. Yet she is not a guest in this house, there is no reason to believe she entered it on the morning of the murder, and most importantly, she lacks any possible motive for Mr. Hurst's death."

"Your first two points I concede," she replied, "and I am not even certain of the third. All I am certain of is that Mrs. Brooks is very, very angry. So much so that she bites back almost every word she wishes to say. Knowing, as we do, that her husband may be tied to this matter in ways that are not yet revealed, we cannot discount that the wife could be as well."

Jonathan could scarcely credit this. "I trust your impressions," he said carefully, "as you often possess an insight I lack into certain subtleties. Yet what do you believe to be the source of my aunt's anger?"

"Envy," Miss Tilney said. "She envies your aunt Jane so much she can hardly bear to look at her. Truly, have you not seen it?"

He had not. "Do you mean that she envies the wealth the Bingleys possess? A clergyman with a small parish necessarily lives a more modest existence than that of an independent gentleman, but the Brookses are hardly impoverished."

"Wealth may be a part of it, but not the most important part. I cannot be sure—but I feel so strongly—Mr. Darcy, it is not Mrs. Bingley's fortune that Mrs. Brooks envies. It is her *happiness.*" Miss Tilney spoke more softly with every word, conscious that they stood in a broad Netherfield hallway, their voices capable of carrying almost anywhere, though in truth Jonathan suspected the regular thunk and tick of the nearby longcase clock erased their words for any but a near and avid eavesdropper. "Mrs. Bingley married well in every sense. Yes, Mr. Bingley is a gentleman of property, but he is also warm, generous, affectionate. These are all qualities Mr. Brooks appears to lack."

"Not every person's behavior is the same in company as it

is at home," Jonathan pointed out. "Though of course, many behave better when observed, not worse."

"For a woman, the question of who to marry is perhaps the most vital of her life. We are given fewer choices. So much of our fate must lie in the hands of our future husband, and to have one's hopes thwarted—to live, always, with the knowledge of what might have been—"

She caught herself again, and the silence between them seemed to yawn wide, as if to swallow them both. Jonathan did not know whether this was danger or opportunity, but he would not let any chance go. Stepping closer to her, his voice low, he said, "My dearest hope is that you will never face such a difficulty, Miss Tilney."

"You have not heard me at all, Mr. Darcy." With that, she turned to leave.

If only it were seemly to run! Juliet stalked away across the back garden. She wanted to run with all her strength and might to the edge of the grounds, into the fields, to find some patch of shrubbery or trees that would allow her to hide from every person in the world. But to be seen running as a grown woman was—

Then again, she was already shamed beyond redemption, was she not? Who cared if she ran? Indeed, Juliet would have broken into a sprint the very next instant had Mr. Darcy not come running out of the house after her. "Miss Tilney! Please, we must speak."

Juliet might have braved herself to run despite disapproval, but her nerves were not up to creating such a spectacle as being chased. Instead she diverted her steps toward the Grecian folly, where they would at least have some small measure of privacy.

She ascended its steps, then rested her hands against two of the pillars, refusing to look back at Mr. Darcy. "You insist upon tormenting me."

"It is you who insists upon torment, both for yourself and for me," he replied with uncommon spirit. "How long do you intend to let a mere painting dictate our fortunes? How much more time will you spend on this pretense that either of us cares what the rest of the world has to say, so long as we are together?"

"I—" Juliet knew not what to say. "You know there is no hope."

"I agree," Mr. Darcy said. "I agree that there is no hope, for 'hope' suggests uncertainty, and I possess none. I have known—I believe, truly, that *we* have known for years that between us lies an . . . an uncommon affinity. We possess such candor, such understanding, and such harmony in each other's company that it is unthinkable to me that we should ever part."

How this wrenched Juliet's heart! "You have come very close to saying what you must not."

"Enough of 'scandal,' of shame, of ruination! I put no stock in them and would not give sixpence for the good opinion of anyone so small-minded as to think otherwise. Tell me truly, Miss Tilney: Do you feel that Follett's wrongdoing should reflect upon you?"

"No. No, I do not." How bracing it was, to look upon the question so simply. Could it be so easy? This seemed impossible to Juliet—but why? Had the pettiness of society infected her more deeply than she had ever realized?

Mr. Darcy became quieter then. "If your doubts are rooted instead in the duel—and in the weakness in my judgment exposed therein—"

"Do not blame yourself!"

"Is that to be your privilege alone?"

Juliet had rarely felt so fluttery, so unsure of where to look and what to say, and yet so certain as to what to do. "Let me say only what I have said before: Your parents do not approve the match. You are a loving son, and would never be guilty of disobedience."

"I would."

She gasped. "Mr. Darcy! You cannot mean what you say."

"I do, for I have considered the question time and again since we first discussed it. Thus I am wholly certain: If we must defy our families, if I am disowned of Pemberley and all else I would otherwise someday possess, then—yes, Miss Tilney. Still I would disobey my parents to marry you. Would you disobey yours to marry me?"

Juliet gripped one of the stone columns, for its strength alone kept her steady. "I—I do not think they would disapprove of the match merely because your parents do not approve. But they would ask—oh, how would we live?"

"That I know not," Mr. Darcy said, "but I have some small savings, should it come to that. And perhaps it would not. I do not suggest an elopement, Miss Tilney. Merely an engagement. My parents would be angered that I had proposed without permission, but that anger would subside in time. It is unfair, I know, to ask you to take on such uncertainty—but is not this our truest path? The one likeliest to lead us to each other? Can we not wait together?"

"My parents did," Juliet whispered. "They waited for each other, for my paternal grandfather's consent. It was years in coming."

"Yet it came." Mr. Darcy smiled once more, and this time, Juliet found herself smiling back.

"Can this be happening?" She scarcely knew she spoke aloud. For his part, Mr. Darcy seemed to have lost his earlier forcefulness, but in its place was a sentiment more gentle, and even sweeter to behold. It could only be called wonder.

Then he seemed to startle. "Oh. I—I seem to have neglected to actually propose. Even though we must wait, my dear Miss Tilney, will you do me the honor of consenting to be my wife?"

She knew every possible objection, and knew that each came from a place very distant from them both, one that could claim no position here. "With all my heart."

Mr. Darcy brightened with joy. Even as he smiled, he continued to correct himself: "I think I did not ask correctly. I ought first to have expressed the appropriate sentiments—assured you of my expectations—"

Juliet laughed, giddy with astonishment and delight. "You were accepted, sir, so you must have asked well enough."

"I was accepted." He took her hand, and she gladly surrendered it. Juliet had run out of doors without gloves, which meant the thrilling warmth of his skin pressed directly against hers. "We are to be married."

The reader will forgive Miss Tilney and Mr. Darcy for being quite overcome at this juncture and for many hours afterward. While they remained alone together, they promised to very shortly inform their families (yet at such a time and place as to invite as little immediate opposition as possible), to attend to the investigation at hand to the fullness of their abilities, and other such worthy sentiments—though none will be astonished to learn that all these words flowed past swiftly, adrift within the spell that joy and expectation had woven between them. Once they returned to the house, they attended as best they could, fitting into the activities of those around them and making such observations as they were then capable of. Few would blame them for being overcome; and even the most zealous advocate for justice would accord the young couple these hours of happy inattention, for the investigation would surely be waiting next morning for them to resume.

How long Juliet lay awake that night, embracing her pillow, laughing to herself from joy, even once or twice coming to happy tears. Mr. Darcy was willing to defy his parents for her! She knew the anger they would feel at the disobedience shown by such an engagement—but did not time heal all? If scandal was forever to be attached to them, if their union reminded society in perpetuity about the portrait and the duel and all the other ugliness of London, why, then . . . then she and Mr. Darcy would close themselves up inside Pemberley, read Walter Scott side by side, have half a dozen children, and be happy forever. What need had she of society?

Not all of Juliet's imaginings were so giddy. She knew her parents would have grave misgivings, for their own lengthy engagement had been difficult in many respects, and in truth her grandfather General Tilney still resented her father's willfulness and her mother's willingness to accept him on such terms. (Her grandfather, at least, normally so fearsome, would be gleeful at the news that she was to wed a Darcy, so much so that it almost pained Juliet to please him so well.)

As for the Darcys, their response would be graver still. Yet she felt that where Jonathan loved, his mother would inevitably follow. Would his proud father do the same? Juliet was willing to be the most obedient daughter-in-law, the most grateful, if only Mr. Darcy would consent in the end!

Yet her happiness overcame all, and she had fallen asleep with thoughts of the wildflowers that grew near her family's parsonage, and which ones she might pluck for a wedding bouquet.

Then, but a few hours later, came the screams.

Chapter Eleven

Jolted from slumber, Juliet sat upright in her bed, at first believing her pleasant dreams had inexplicably turned to nightmares, but then a second shriek convinced her that a very real person cried out in terror, or horror, not far away.

She leaped from bed, clutched her dressing gown, and hurriedly donned it as she dashed from her bedroom to the stairs. Within the other bedrooms, she could hear faint sounds of confusion and dismay—Mrs. Hurst saying, "Who can it be?," Mrs. Lofton moaning in dread, the Allerdyce girls crying out in fear. Juliet's bare feet thumped upon the stairs as she hurried down. By this time the cries from the ground floor had turned to those of sorrow, and she recognized the voice as that of Jane Bingley.

Although it seemed years to Juliet, she reached Jane within seconds and found her on her knees by the door that led to the servants' stairs. There, crumpled on the floor, half in and half out of the doorway, lay Becky, quite dead.

"Oh, she has fallen and broken her head," Jane said through tears. She held the dead girl's hand tenderly. "How terrible, how very terrible! I do not believe she was yet eighteen years of age. How shall I tell her poor mother?"

Juliet crouched low, the better to both comfort Jane and look more closely at Becky. It did appear that she had tumbled down the stairs, for her neck and head lay at an unnatural angle, and the dishevelment of her dress also suggested a fall. Yet Juliet noted that Becky had been wearing her nightdress with only a shawl over it. Why would a servant descend the stairs without first donning her uniform?

It was then that Mr. Bingley appeared, responding to his wife's cries. He looked nearly as stricken as she. "Becky! Good heavens. Is she—?" Jane nodded as she continued to sob.

Uneasy, Juliet rose to her feet, murmuring, "Please do not disturb her person just yet." The Bingleys must have been too overcome to question her reason, but they obeyed, which allowed Juliet to step over Becky's body and enter the servants' stairs. This was a narrower passageway than the one afforded to the masters of the house and their guests, and even allowing for the weakness of the dawn light, the single small window half a landing above could not ever have provided much illumination. So where was Becky's candle?

The Bingleys pay generous wages and are very kindhearted, so probably they do not scrimp on candles even for their maids, Juliet mused. *If so, might Becky have had one with her?*

Perhaps, but perhaps not. Juliet imagined most servants, accustomed to making their way down dark stairs, were capable of ascending or descending by touch alone. So Becky might not have bothered to bring one.

Unless . . .

Juliet took the first few steps, looking for signs of spattered wax or tallow, but what she found instead turned her suspicion into wretched certainty. There, tied at ankle height across the stairs, she saw a sort of ribbon or sash, artfully knotted in place. The sash was a dark green, very like the color of paint on the stairs themselves. This item could only have been placed there to trip someone—and it had, fatally so.

"Mr. Bingley," Juliet said, "you must send word both to Mr. Darcy at Longbourn and to Mr. Lucas, for I fear Becky has been the second victim of murder at Netherfield."

For his part, Jonathan had scarcely slept at all, so elated had he been by the success of his suit. He remained aware that great difficulty lay ahead of them, and yet that awareness had been for the time being exiled to the very furthest reaches of his mind, like a distant range of mountains that is both a formidable boundary and yet no more than a shadow upon the horizon.

When the horse came galloping up the Longbourn path, Jonathan sat upright to see; upon recognizing the servant atop it as one of the Netherfield staff, he smiled. His first thought—happy lover he!—was that Miss Tilney had concocted some excuse for conversation, probably relating to their investigation, that he might return to her all the earlier. Thus all the greater was his guilt upon receiving word of what had happened.

"You see, Mr. Bennet?" Grandmama cried, in her wrapper, the hastily donned mobcap crooked upon her head. "I told you we should all come to ill ends with a madman on the loose, and Jonathan the only one looking for him!"

Grandpapa, in his nightcap, simply shook his head. "My dear, you dwell too much upon the incapability of our grandson. The Tilney girl has failed grievously, too, a subject I am certain you would not wish to neglect."

A disinclination to hear any more of this, though indeed a strong sentiment, was not Jonathan's primary reason for hurrying from the house. He was much struck with remorse. *Could I have but waited another day to ask Miss Tilney*, he thought as he rode toward Netherfield Park, *would we have detected any signs of danger?*

Yet even that sharp regret was not so strong in his heart as fear—for whatever killer lurked within Netherfield had now proved a willingness to take life again. Were his uncle and aunt safe? Was Miss Tilney?

Jonathan had imagined it would be difficult, the next time

he met with Miss Tilney, to conceal their joy from any others present. Instead, he was reunited with her as she stood next to the fallen body of a servant girl.

"Becky was only seventeen," Miss Tilney murmured, gazing down at the terrible scene. "She worked as a parlormaid, but had ambitions of becoming a lady's maid—Mrs. Bingley let her dress me, that she might have practice. That future and every other is stolen from her."

"Did she not stand upon service at breakfast yesterday?"

"Yes. The Bingleys, it seems, allow their servants far more liberty than most. Sometimes this means that they trade duties with one another, should one wish for a different period of rest or any other reason. So long as no formal affair is at hand, one might find a valet polishing woodwork, a stableboy fetching coals, or even a parlormaid in the breakfast room."

Jonathan remembered this from the past. "That was but an occasional practice, if I recollect rightly. We should find out if Becky was expected to serve in the breakfast room yesterday, regularly, or whether she asked to do so."

Miss Tilney gathered his meaning almost immediately. "Of course. Did she change her day's plan on either occasion? If so, did her action lead to this end, or was that no more than circumstance?"

It was then that Isaac Lucas arrived, clearly much astonished. "Another murder?" said he, as he came walking toward the servants' stairs. "Are you quite certain?"

"Indeed, for a strip of cloth was affixed between the railings, so that someone would trip over it." Miss Tilney pointed the way for Mr. Lucas to see the unlikely weapon for himself. Though he paled as he edged around the dead girl, he resolutely went to see. Young and new though he was, he seemed to have more interest in the proper role of a magistrate than most others Jonathan had met.

"Whoever planned this crime would likely have been

familiar with the servants' stairs," Jonathan pointed out. Did that eliminate the Brookses?

"They further would have had to know that Becky would be coming down in the middle of the night, rather than any other servant," Miss Tilney said. "Probably the killer is the person who suggested that she do so. But what could have persuaded her?"

The local constables, seldom called upon to do any duty, arrived rather awestruck to remove the poor girl's body. As they rolled her over, Miss Tilney leaned down, then pointed at the floor. "Her candle—there." It lay in a little sooty spatter of melted wax.

"What of it?" Perhaps Miss Tilney thought it odd that a servant would have wax instead of tallow. "My aunt and uncle give the servants any candles that have burned unevenly, and they are rather generous when determining what is to be considered uneven."

"I mean, Mr. Darcy, that a servant probably learns the way up and down her stairway in the darkness." Miss Tilney looked grim. "If she brought a candle, it may well signify that she intended to meet with someone—and, unfortunately, it seems that, in a sense, she did."

Juliet took upon herself the sad task of examining Becky one last time, to ensure that no other signs of violence were upon her person. Indeed there were not, and for this small mercy Juliet tried to be grateful; like as not Becky had known no more that a moment's confusion, and none but the briefest pain.

Once Becky had been taken away, Juliet returned to Jonathan. She did not dare think of what had passed between them the day before; neither the great felicity of a new engagement nor the delicate work of solving a murder allowed for many thoughts on other topics, and the investigation must take all priority.

Mrs. Bingley aided them in their first determinations by identifying the sash used to trip Becky upon the stairs as her own. "I set it out as one of the garments to be dyed black for mourning," she said. "As such it would have been among the heaps of clothing set out yesterday for the laundry maids." Juliet nodded, noting that those same maids would need to be spoken to, in order to see if they had observed anyone unusual poking around.

"I take it almost as a given," Mr. Darcy said, "that you, too, feel certain that the murderer of Mr. Hurst is the guilty party in Becky's death as well."

With a nod, Juliet said, "It would be remarkable for two killers to be afoot within Netherfield at the same time. So we may eliminate the Allerdyces." She was glad not to have to question Mrs. Allerdyce, as this would have required Juliet to spend more time in her company. "Therefore we must speak with all our previous suspects."

They first conversed with Mr. Lucas, who was much shocked and dismayed. "I left Netherfield last night around ten, and arrived home before ten thirty," he said. "My mother and the servants will all attest to my presence at Lucas Lodge between that hour and the messenger's arrival this morning, and the groom can further swear that no horse nor carriage was taken from our stables."

Mr. Darcy hastily said, "It is not that we suspect you, Mr. Lucas. Yet given that another murder has occurred, we cannot know whether you would wish us to continue the investigations or take over yourself."

"Please do continue," said Mr. Lucas, "for I should have little idea where to begin, and neither of you can be faulted for failing to predict that the killer had not finished this blood-thirsty work."

Next they spoke to Mr. and Mrs. Bingley together. Here, Juliet had little thought of guilt for the husband, and absolutely none for the wife, who wept more for her parlormaid than Mrs. Hurst had for her husband. Yet, as master and mistress of the house, they would know more of what comings and goings, which sounds and sights, would be commonplace at Netherfield and which would merit further attention.

"Becky so hoped to improve her station in life," Mrs. Bingley said as she dabbed her eyes with a lace-trimmed hand-kerchief. "I do not mean that she believed herself *above* her station—she was not at all an impudent girl, you must not think so—but she was eager to learn more, to do more, to move up within the household. I think it admirable when a young person shows such endeavor."

"Indeed," said Mr. Bingley. "I daresay she would have become a lady's maid in time, and perhaps later in her life, she might even have become housekeeper at an estate."

Juliet asked, "It would not have been unusual for her to have a wax candle?" This already seemed likely, but she wanted to be as certain as possible that the killer had not been the one who gave Becky the candle.

Mrs. Bingley shook her head. "The tallow ones smell so strong, and you know, the servants' quarters are not very large. Only think what the odor of tallow must be in such confines!"

Few enough mistresses ever thought of this consideration; Juliet guiltily realized she never had herself. Her parents were kind to their servants, but she doubted any of their number had even once been given a candle of beeswax.

Mr. Darcy said, "You set the sash out to be dyed yesterday?"

"I set it out the night prior, for yesterday's dyeing," Mrs.

Bingley said, unexpectedly precise. "But as you see, it was never dyed."

Although Juliet still doubted the killer would be a servant, the death of a servant meant the situation downstairs had to be considered anew. "There were, so far as you know, no hard feelings between Becky and any of the other staff?"

"No, not to my knowledge, and I would wager not at all," Mr. Bingley said. "She was always quick to help others, the better to learn more tasks. Again, as I say, Becky always thought of the future. Poor girl!"

"What about a former servant?" Mr. Darcy said. This was apparently a new notion, but not a bad one, in Juliet's opinion; a person recently departed from the household would have all necessary knowledge of the premises and its workings, and perhaps certain grudges as well. "Did you recently let anyone go? Or did anyone give notice?"

The Bingleys looked at each other in apparent befuddlement. "We have not had occasion to dismiss anyone since—oh, four or five years ago, was it not?" Mr. Bingley asked.

"Five years at least," Mrs. Bingley said.

Juliet said, "No one recently left their position?"

"Neither recently nor otherwise," Mr. Bingley said. "Do you know, I do not think we have ever had a servant leave, either here or at our house in Staffordshire?"

"No, I do not believe we have," Mrs. Bingley added, and Juliet could not wonder at it.

The Loftons came next, together as a pair. Though Juliet thought it better, as a rule, to speak to all suspects separately, she believed it might be interesting to see how the two of them acted with each other.

Furthermore, Mrs. Lofton seemed almost incapable of even remaining upright on her own, much less facing questioning. She fanned herself, and sweat dampened her brow. Mr. Lofton kept one arm around her shoulders, either through affection or the sense that propriety would be strained if his wife collapsed upon the floor.

"Had you interacted much at all with Becky?" Juliet asked.

"Why should I know anything of a parlormaid?" Mrs. Lofton asked in genuine bewilderment.

"You recall, dear, she served at breakfast yesterday," Mr. Lofton said. "Always seemed ready to lend a hand. Even brought me my hat before I rode to Meryton."

"Charles and his wife are so eccentric." Mrs. Lofton waved her fan even harder. "I do remember a girl there, for strange it was to see, but until this moment, I did not even know it was she who had died."

"And you, Mr. Lofton?" Mr. Darcy said.

Mr. Lofton shook his head vehemently. "I know there are some gentlemen, or so society calls them, for truly they are rascals and worse, who pester the maids in their own household or wherever they happen to be staying, but I assure you both, never have I so importuned a young woman." The force of his assertion suggested to Juliet that he was honest—though she noted he could not imagine speaking to a young woman not of his class in any other circumstance. Yet there was nothing very strange in that manner of thinking.

Juliet said, "Did either of you rise during the night and leave your bedroom? Did you hear anyone else doing so?"

The Loftons looked at each other. It was Mr. Lofton who said, "I think I did hear something in the the hall at one point, but I cannot even say what, much less when. Only that my slumber was slightly disturbed. It might not have had to do with the girl's death at all. And you, my dear, you were fast asleep throughout, were you not?"

Mrs. Lofton nodded. "I sleep very deeply. Never before

have I been sorry of it—but I can tell you nothing more. Which I suppose is nothing at all."

After the Loftons left, Jonathan said, "We shall need to talk to every servant who helped with the dyeing, to see if they saw who took Aunt Jane's sash. Furthermore, ought we not speak to the Brookses later? Though I can hardly imagine them making their way to Netherfield in the dead of night."

"It is almost impossible to imagine any of the possible suspects committing this crime," Miss Tilney replied, "yet one of them must have done so. Poor Becky! I keep thinking of her at breakfast yesterday. She was so cheerful, so very bright."

Jonathan had indeed been struck by Becky's smile the day before, but now even more so, as suspicions began to form in his mind. "She said it was a maid's job, to do what was asked. Did she not?"

Miss Tilney frowned. "Yes, she did. But what of it?"

"Becky spoke with enthusiasm, even pleasure, of a maid's obligations. She had ambitions to improve her station." Jonathan wondered if he was being fantastical, but surely there was something to it. "Miss Tilney, do not you think that Becky spoke like someone who did not expect to be a maid very much longer?"

Miss Tilney's confusion remained a few moments longer, long enough for him to doubt this insight, but then she put her hand to her mouth. "I do not know if we can assume that much . . . but she had some expectation, something that elated her and she thought would change her situation. You suggest that her killer had made some kind of promise to her?"

"Such a promise—whether of money or of some other advancement—could have lured her downstairs in the night, do not you think?"

"And I can think of only one inducement she could have offered to not only draw out the killer, but also persuade that individual to kill again," Miss Tilney said. "I believe Becky knew who the murderer was. She elected not to tell us. Instead she played a very dangerous game . . . and lost her life."

Jonathan knew it had been Becky's choice not to speak, but had they been truly ready to listen? "I feel so wicked. Had we not been so—though we could hardly have been otherwise— yesterday, might we not—?"

"Shhh." Miss Tilney lay her hand atop his, an intimacy too thrilling to be entirely lost even amid this extremity. "That was not until later."

Their eyes met, and once again he felt almost overcome by her mere presence. They could not linger in the same romantic daydreams as yesterday, but their union remained constant. Today, they would attend fully to the investigation.

They did not attend to the far end of the hall, where Priscilla Allerdyce saw the two of them standing close, nor watch her eyes narrow as she realized they held each other's hands.

Chapter Twelve

There can be no perfect day for a funeral. When the sun shines, the contrast between outer brightness and inner gloom renders that gloom yet more unbearable. When rain falls, the grief-stricken imagine that the very heavens cry with them, and so cry all the harder. When snow falls and ice rims every window and river, the frozen ground resists the gravedigger. The consequences of summer heat do not bear thinking about.

Yet it must be said that some days are more appropriate for a funeral than others. For instance, Mrs. Hurst—whose late husband's residency in various icehouses had endured near two weeks, and for whom one day more or less would have made little difference—might have chosen a date that did not conflict with the burial of the unfortunate Becky.

"You would attend the funeral of a *servant*?" The incredulous Mrs. Hurst stared at her brother. "You compare that to the need to lay *my husband* to rest? He who was your brother for so very long?"

"Of course there is no question that we shall attend Mr. Hurst's service," Charles hastened to say. "Yet given Becky's youth—the terrible nature of her death—"

"The very same nature of Mr. Hurst's death," retorted Mrs. Hurst, who was now fully sheathed in mourning black and a hat veiled with crepe, and in all the worse temper for it. "Unless you have forgot already?"

"No, dear Louisa, I shall never forget these wretched days

so long as I live. Yet, were Mr. Hurst's service to be but one day the later, what could be the harm?"

"You would slight him for the sake of a girl in service!" Mrs. Hurst took out her handkerchief, which she considered as good as weeping. "How cruel, how very cruel!"

All ended as she willed it, with simultaneous funerals, one to be presided over by Mr. Brooks and attended by Mr. Bingley, the other to be foisted upon a hapless curate.

Most funerals were held at night, a custom more rigidly adhered to in some parts of the nation than in others, but nearly invariably so in the environs of Meryton. Thus both Becky and Mr. Hurst were laid to rest in the dark: Mr. Hurst ensconced in a place of honor within Mr. Brooks's church, his stone laid very near the front, to be engraved with his name, his family, and HASTEN, OH BLESSED HOUR OF REUNION; Becky in a humble graveyard overlooking the meadow, not far from a dogwood tree that flowered in the spring. The reader may judge whose was the finer monument.

Mrs. Hurst seemed to take comfort in the custom in which only men attended the funeral itself. "Women's feelings are so very delicate," she said, dry-eyed, to the ladies who sat around her in the drawing room, silent amid candlelight, while the men were gone. "We cannot endure the agony of it. Men's constitutions are stronger, and they must bear the burden."

Priscilla and Frederica Allerdyce exchanged a glance, which spoke much of their mutual doubt that their aunt was enduring any agony whatsoever. Their mother observed this but could not, under the circumstances, bring herself to chastise them either in the moment or later.

Juliet Tilney whispered to Mrs. Lofton, "I have been to a funeral, and there other women were present."

"It is not the done thing in the city any longer," said Mrs. Lofton, whose relative good humor had understandably faded much since the second murder at Netherfield. "One would never hear of such."

"I had thought that was to protect ladies from the villainy of thieves." Juliet had read the newspaper tales of women who had worn their finest jewelry to honor the dead, only to be brutally robbed as soon as clods of earth began to fall upon the coffin.

"I suppose *you* would not know much of feminine delicacy," Mrs. Allerdyce said, and Juliet was obliged to stare at her hands and think of her father's kindest words for the dead, lest unkind words issue from her mouth.

The next morning, other than for the black garb worn by all, might have been any other breakfast at Netherfield. Charles and Jane Bingley were much downcast, and Juliet's careful eye observed the dispiritedness of the servants, but it appeared that Becky was the more greatly mourned of the two recently deceased.

Visitors came soon to call. Mr. Isaac Lucas arrived first, eager as ever. Having been informed by Mr. Darcy of Mr. Lucas's intentions toward Miss Allerdyce, Juliet wondered that she had not seen it for herself before. On this occasion, Mr. Lucas attended more to Mr. Allerdyce—but was that not the wisdom of a suitor?—and Juliet noted how, from time to time, his gaze would drift toward Miss Allerdyce, who always saw it, and smiled.

Swiftly following Mr. Lucas came the Brookses. Mr. Brooks showed no sign of weariness, despite having performed the service for Mr. Hurst the night before. Juliet watched Mrs. Hurst carefully, and indeed, she did become restless after the Brookses arrived. She made a show of noticing her niece. "Why, Priscilla, what a lovely cross you wear. Are they amethysts?" Although Priscilla had scant interest in her aunt, she cared very much about her personal ornamentation, and so began speaking of her little cross with much animation. Mrs. Hurst nodded and smiled, but her efforts to avoid so much as glimpsing Mr. Brooks were all too apparent.

Does Mrs. Brooks see nothing? Juliet wondered. It appeared she did not, for she sat in a group with Mr. Lofton and Miss Allerdyce, chatting easily about the weather. Juliet noted that Mrs. Brooks was wearing a new pair of gloves: butter yellow, trimmed with fine cord. They would have been notably handsome regardless of the wearer; as much of Mrs. Brooks's attire was modest and plain, the gloves stood out all the more. Could the gloves have been a gift from Mr. Brooks—an unusual show of affection—meant to allay any suspicions his wife might harbor within her breast?

How Juliet longed to discuss all this with Mr. Darcy!—and of course, as all young lovers, she could not be entirely at rest until she could look upon his face once more. Yet, by midmorning, still he had not appeared. Where could he be?

As it happened, breakfast at Longbourn had been delayed that morning at Mr. Bennet's request.

"At my time of life, I have laid to rest too many friends to be glad of the opportunity of burying a man I hardly knew," he said, hobbling toward the breakfast table. Jonathan steeled himself and offered his grandfather his arm; the effort of attending the funeral had cost the old man and made his infirmity more apparent than was customary. "This Mr. Hurst slights my daughters in their youth, drinks all the wine one of 'em can offer him for years thereafter, then gets himself poisoned, and so I am obliged to be out in the night and the damp."

Mrs. Bennet was displeased, for she considered complaints about the night and the damp to be solely her province. "You knew that you must go. It would not be proper, would not be civil, for you to have remained home. I will not have those dreadful sisters of Mr. Bingley's saying we have no manners."

"Then you have enforced your edict poorly, my dear, for they have been saying as much these twenty-five years." Mr. Bennet settled into his chair and smiled up at Jonathan; he could be kind to his grandson when not jesting about his particularities of temperament. "Come, come, my lad. Let us eat, and then you can return to your investigations."

When at last Jonathan was freed, he rode toward Netherfield. October had come, and a slight morning chill still lingered over the fields. How bracing it felt! With health and liberty restored to him, and all the triumph of the successful lover in his heart, little wonder that Jonathan should be of good cheer even on his way to find a murderer.

His horse came up the path just as Aunt Jane was preparing to go in the carriage to Longbourn. She waited for him and greeted him warmly.

"Do you return already?" Jonathan said.

"Mamma sent a note this morning, telling me how difficult the funeral was for Papa, so I am bringing wine and cake, and will read him the newspaper." The recent issue of the *Chronicle* was tucked within her basket. "I would have gone even earlier, yet I wished to wait for you."

"For me, Aunt Jane? Why?" He stepped closer and lowered his voice. "Have you thought of another observation regarding the death of Mr. Hurst? Or of Becky?"

"Would that I had." Aunt Jane smiled gently and said, "I have at last written your parents. Please forgive me, Jonathan, for ultimately I knew that I must speak of Miss Tilney's presence here. The letter was posted two days ago."

Deeply as Jonathan had trusted his aunt Jane to keep the

secret, he found he could not consider himself betrayed. His parents' learning of this was inevitable, and now that he and Miss Tilney had become engaged, he no longer feared his parents' power to separate them. "I understand, Aunt Jane. You did as you thought right."

"I told your mother that if she does not allow a match between you and Miss Tilney, she is a fool."

Jonathan required some moments to be certain of what he had heard. He felt some chagrin that his aunt had been so very aware of his sentiments, though of course she would have received letters discussing Miss Tilney in the past. Yet chief among his astonishment was the idea that his aunt Jane might, in any way whatsoever, be critical of his mother. "You told her this?"

Aunt Jane nodded. "Do not mistake me—I love my sister greatly, as I always have and always shall. Nor do I doubt that she has been acting out of the tenderest love for you. Her judgment is often superior to mine; her cleverness and wit have revealed much to me that I would otherwise never have comprehended. But even dear Elizabeth may make a mistake, and she has fortitude enough to endure being told so. She is wise enough to prefer honesty, so this I have given her."

"You have realized the depth of my feelings for Miss Tilney," Jonathan said. "And you agree that the matter of the portrait should in no way influence our future?"

"Indeed not. Who could put any stock in wicked rumor?"

"My mother and father, it seems," Jonathan said. "Not that they believe the calumnies against Miss Tilney, but they are convinced others shall always do so and that I am better off forgetting Miss Tilney. I cannot make them comprehend that she is the one person I could never forget."

Aunt Jane put one hand over her heart. "You must understand, Elizabeth was never greatly crossed in love. The path to matrimony she and your father tread was not smooth, but for your mother, at least, her true feelings went unrecognized almost until the moment they became engaged. She was tender toward me in my own travail, but the painful sentiments involved . . . these she has never known for herself."

This suggested that Aunt Jane had suffered some manner of romantic disappointment in her youth, a fact of which Jonathan had previously been unaware. However, his curiosity on this point was understandably subsumed by more immediate concerns. "Their complaisance about public opinion—their willingness to bend to that which they know to be unjust—it is this I find most difficult to accept."

"Your father is among the best of men," said Aunt Jane, "but he is very conscious of his family pride, possesses a very great delicacy of feeling in that regard. Why, he has never even allowed the beautiful portrait of your mother to be publicly displayed. There, I think, may lie the source of his refusal. As for Elizabeth . . . like so many of us, she can forget the sorrows of the unhappy when she herself is happy. And your mother has been so very happy all her married life. Forgive them and trust that in time they will see true."

Jonathan sensed much truth in his aunt Jane's words and resolved to remember them well, for within them might lie the key to his parents' ultimate persuasion. Pushing past his reluctance to touch most persons, he leaned forward to kiss his aunt's cheek. "I shall never forget your kindness, Aunt Jane."

"I will demand to be repaid, mind you," she said with an impish smile. "You must save me a piece of the cake."

Juliet's joy upon Mr. Darcy's arrival she concealed as best she could, though to any who were attending—in particular, Priscilla Allerdyce—she seemed very nearly aglow. More notice might have been taken of the pair had they not swiftly turned their attention to the important task at hand, the next stage of the investigation: learning all they could about the theft of Aunt Jane's sash, for this delicate length of green satin had been fashioned into a weapon of murder.

Mrs. Mulgrew led them into the laundry, a sort of room Juliet had never entered even as a child; to judge by Mr. Darcy's avid curiosity, he had not done so either. On this day, the large metal tubs were still being scrubbed by the scullery maids after the work of dyeing so many garments black. The smells of soap and dye mingled in the air. Metal and wooden washboards hung on the walls, and lengths of clothesline were coiled around hooks.

"All the clothes set out for dyeing would have been brought here directly from each person's room," said Mrs. Mulgrew. "Here, they would have been separated by fabric, for some materials must soak longer than others for the color to take."

"Did all the dyeing take place in this room, Mrs. Mulgrew?" Mr. Darcy asked.

The housekeeper laughed. "Goodness, no. We should all be overcome by the fumes until we were in a faint!" Given the memory of the acrid scent on the breeze that day, Juliet could well believe it. "No, the dyes would all be mixed in the tubs in the side yard, beyond the stables, where all should be out of sight. Then each batch of clothing would be taken there and dyed in its turn."

"How many batches were there?" Juliet asked. "Were they all dyed at once, or in shifts?"

"We had four tubs of black dye and at least ten or eleven batches of clothing," said Mrs. Mulgrew. "Eleven, I believe. So we were at it all the day. After each batch had been turned black, every garment was hung out to dry, and thank goodness we had a fine sunny day—but I understand *that* is not of particular interest to you."

"That is correct, Mrs. Mulgrew, for the sash was stolen before it was dyed." Juliet went toward the door that led from the laundry to the yard and opened it; the path uphill toward the dyeing and drying area was soft brown soil worn through the grass, evidence of the feet of many servants over many years. "Am I correct in believing that the clothing would have remained entirely unattended from the time it left this room to the time it entered the dyeing tubs?"

Mrs. Mulgrew then seemed somewhat uncomfortable. "Well, we've no laundress here at Netherfield—the task is one undertaken by many, and their other tasks ever remain to be done. So it is possible that one of the girls might have taken one batch or another out to the field early—before another batch had finished its time in the tub—and left it there to see to something else. Mind you, the clothes are fully scrubbed during and after their dyeing. So there's no question of them being made dirty."

"We would not for the world criticize your methods, ma'am," Mr. Darcy hastened to tell Mrs. Mulgrew. Juliet's heart, in a state to seize upon every merit of his being, swelled at this simple courtesy. "Thus we must turn to the question of whether anyone from upstairs was seen to be in or near the basement earlier that day."

"Mrs. Hurst came down twice to tell us to take care of particular items," Mrs. Mulgrew said. "I of course told her we take care of every piece entrusted to us, but that would not suffice for her. Yet Mrs. Hurst took nothing away with her at that time."

Juliet asked, "Would it have been possible for Mrs. Hurst to come down here at a moment when you were not supervising and none of the maids were present?"

After a moment's consideration, Mrs. Mulgrew nodded. "Yes, this could have happened, but if so, I saw no sign of it."

Next Juliet turned her attention to the maids, who had

continued their scrubbing while ill-disguising their avid interest in the scandalous subject at hand. "Did any of you see Mrs. Hurst here, or anyone else? Or anyone near the actual dyeing and drying who would not normally have been there?" The girls exchanged glances, and Juliet hastened to add, "We will not share with anyone beyond this room how we have learned of it." She wondered whether any of her reassurances could bear much weight, given that they were investigating the murder of one of their fellow servants.

However, one finally said, "Mrs. Brooks was out on the lawns once, looking at all the black clothes on the line. Staring like she'd never seen black before, ma'am—I mean, miss. Stayed a good long time, too, and neither saw the moment of her coming nor her going."

Another maid chimed in, this one very young. "I saw Mr. Lofton walking near the stable, too—that's close to the yard! And Mr. Bingley went not long after."

Mrs. Mulgrew scoffed. "Did you ever think the gentlemen might have been going to the stable, child?"

Mr. Darcy said, "Every piece of information is potentially useful to us, Mrs. Mulgrew, so we are grateful to the girls for telling us this."

Had either of the gentlemen gone out riding that day? Juliet could not immediately recall. Oh, if only the necessities of etiquette and propriety did not so slow their investigations! Still, this could be found out. "Yes, indeed. Thank you all very much."

Upstairs that afternoon, Caroline Allerdyce sat in the parlor, pretending to embroider, while across the room, her daughter Frederica was once again deep in conversation with Mr. Lucas. Jane Bingley sat in the room as well, returned from visiting Longbourn and happily engrossed in a book, but Caroline took no particular notice of her sister-in-law, as was her custom. Nor could Jane have engaged in any activity that would have distracted a mother from such matrimonial danger.

He would not have the effrontery, Caroline told herself. *Surely not. It pleases his vanity to gain the attentions of a girl so far beyond his expectations, but he is not insensible.* As yet Caroline had formed no new plans for her elder daughter, still stung as she was by the loss of the baronet, but assuredly she could turn up a potential suitor more deserving than this.

While Caroline tallied up the various sons of her acquaintance—and had not Mr. Biggs-Dawson been widowered in early summer? He should be again eligible come springtime—Priscilla came to sit by her mother. Caroline said to her, "Are you wishing to go into the town, dear?" Mr. Allerdyce had given both the girls five pounds, so that on this trip they might buy themselves as many niceties as they wished—a rare but not unheard-of fatherly indulgence. "Your money would be better spent in a larger place than Meryton, which has little to choose from."

"I am not thinking of going there," Priscilla murmured. "Do you not wonder, Mamma, that Mr. Darcy and Miss Tilney should be allowed so much time together all but unattended?"

She replied in the same low voice her younger daughter had used. "Such, I am given to understand, is the nature of their investigatory endeavors. You should not worry, Priscilla. Whatever danger *she* may have represented, that is no more. The match is not only impossible; it is unthinkable."

"To you, and to me," said Priscilla. "But certainly not to Miss Tilney, and perhaps not to Mr. Darcy."

Caroline set down her embroidery. "Whatever do you mean?"

Now speaking in almost a whisper, Priscilla said, "I have glimpsed small touches and attentions between them that make me wonder— Mamma, you have said often enough that preying girls will stoop to any level, any at all."

Was it possible that the Tilney girl would stoop to entrapping Jonathan Darcy? That she would offer certain liberties that would then require him, in honor, to propose to her despite her enduring disgrace?

As Caroline considered this with mounting alarm, the sound of an approaching carriage was heard. Jane lifted her face from the book of poetry she had been reading with a frown. "Whoever can that be? We expect no one."

Both women rose and went to the window, and thus shared in the astonishment of realizing that the carriage coming toward them was manned by servants wearing the distinctive livery of Pemberley.

Chapter Thirteen

The Bingleys scarcely had time to hurry out of their home before the coach had come to a halt and one of the liveried footmen had opened its door to reveal Mr. Fitzwilliam Darcy.

"Mr. Darcy!" exclaimed Mr. Bingley, holding out his hands to his old friend. "How excellent to see you!—but why did you not tell us you were coming?"

"I believe he wished to surprise us," said Mrs. Bingley, who instantly sensed that her letter had done the work of summoning Mr. Darcy hence.

Despite the inevitable dust and weariness of travel, Mr. Darcy maintained his usual correctness. "When we learned of the shocking deaths here, Mrs. Darcy and I felt one of us should be near to support Jonathan in his endeavors. She has remained with Georgiana. Given the grave circumstances, I trust you will forgive me this impetuosity."

"You need never ask forgiveness for visiting us," Mr. Bingley said, "though I must prove a poor host on this occasion, for every bedroom at Netherfield is currently occupied. I fear you shall be obliged to stay at Longbourn."

Only someone who knew Mr. Darcy very intimately would have recognized how he absorbed this blow. "Ah. Then I shall send notice to the Bennets immediately. They will then have at least one afternoon's notice, which is more than I offered to you."

"Come in, come in," urged Mrs. Bingley. "You will wish to refresh yourself."

As she had feared he would, Mr. Darcy replied, "First of all, I must speak with my son."

One moment, Jonathan had been as happily engaged as it was possible to be, both in the sense of being secretly affianced and in expending all his mental energies in the worthy service of investigating a murder. In the next, he had been snatched from these endeavors and delivered to the study to face his newly arrived, and very much aggrieved, father.

"Jonathan, we must talk," said Mr. Darcy, though he then hesitated. "You are feeling—you are well? Your wound does not—?"

"I am fully recovered, as I have been for some time, Father," Jonathan replied. He knew what was coming, knew the justice of his own position, and yet the suddenness of it all, and its extremity, threatened to overwhelm him. Already his heart beat faster, stray noises seemed louder, and his eyes would not fix upon his parent.

Reassured of his son's fitness to be castigated, Mr. Darcy began. "Given the circumstances, I do not intend to chastise you for not informing us of the murders here at Netherfield. Although I would have been well able to hear it, your mother's fear for your well-being—heightened as it has been these many months—would have been unendurable. You no doubt wished to protect her."

"Of course," Jonathan said, though the words were but a way to fill the brief pause. He could not collect himself. For Miss Tilney's sake, he must, but everything was happening so very quickly!

Mr. Darcy clasped his hands behind his back, a sign that a lengthy lecture was forthcoming. "What troubles me far more is that your silence has also been the concealment of Miss Tilney's presence. Knowing our objections, knowing the impossibility of any further connection between you, you have nonetheless brought the girl back into a situation that can only add to her infamy."

Though Jonathan remained much overwhelmed, he found his tongue. "You know that we conduct these investigations together. Her thoughts, her observations, add greatly to the understanding of such mysteries as we attempt to unravel. Furthermore, many questions must be asked of ladies that I could never presume to speak aloud. Without Miss Tilney's assistance in these matters, I do not know whether the truth should ever be known. Would you deny my uncle and aunt the best help they could be given?"

Mr. Darcy tilted his head, acknowledging the point without softening his stance. "Miss Tilney's ability in such matters has never been in question. The salient point is that the connection, though an assistance to the Bingleys, is not beneficial to the young lady's reputation, which has been damaged enough already. Nor can it be conducive to your own peace of mind."

How Jonathan wished he could loosen his cravat. "If I wish to risk my peace of mind, and Miss Tilney does not consider this a blemish upon her honor—which I would not think likely for any person of worth—then that is the end of the matter, is it not?"

"No, for gravest of all is the fact that you have been dishonest," said Mr. Darcy. "You have kept a secret from me and your mother, knowing that we would wish to have this information, solely because you did not want to hear what we would then have to say. This secrecy is beneath you, Jonathan. To lie by omission, to be so dishonest with your parents, is a sin against your filial duty."

All of this was true, and its truth silenced all else that Jonathan wished to say, even that which was most important—for he knew he now kept another secret, one far greater, and thus the even more serious sin. Before he could collect himself, his father simply inclined his head and left the study, so that Jonathan stood alone.

For her part, Juliet felt all aflutter—worried for Jonathan, worried that the investigation should be interrupted, worried even that Mr. Darcy would upbraid her for her impudence. Given the secret engagement between herself and Mr. Jonathan Darcy, his father's opinion meant a great deal to her, and she feared this sudden appearance meant that his disapproval was more severe than she had feared—and she had feared much.

However, when Mr. Darcy emerged from the study, he came immediately to greet her. "Miss Tilney. I trust you are well?"

"Yes, Mr. Darcy." She was proud that her voice did not tremble. "Thank you. I trust you and Mrs. Darcy keep well also?"

"Indeed. Thank you for your assistance to the Bingleys in this matter. I am certain it is much appreciated." With that, Mr. Darcy walked away, the conversation ended. He had been entirely civil—no less, but also no more. Juliet resolved to be content with this for the time being.

When Jonathan Darcy came forth, however, he looked so pale, so overcome, that she was reminded of his pallor after the shooting. As he came toward her, she said, "And now, Mr. Darcy?"

"And now—" He swallowed hard, then collected himself. "Now let us return to our investigations." All else, she realized, must wait. This alone would clarify their thoughts, steady their purpose, and ease some small measure of the suspense occasioned by his father's arrival.

Given their mutual state of mind, Juliet thought it wisest that they should begin by questioning the two persons who had been seen near the stable on the day of the dyeing, for they seemed likeliest to have good reason to have been there.

"Yes, Miss Tilney, I did travel into Meryton that day, as I have on some other occasions since we arrived at Netherfield," said Mr. Lofton. Juliet and Jonathan had reclaimed the study as their own, though the open door felt more intrusive than it had before. "Mrs. Lofton wished for a few trifles, so I visited the shop of Mrs. Mount. My wife would have happily gone herself, but like as not would have purchased half its contents. Furthermore, I wished to ride. One should relish the fine days of autumn." He smiled as though remembering the scent of fresh air. "All these particulars can be confirmed by Mrs. Lofton, Mrs. Mount, and the stableboy, if need be."

This forthrightness was, rather unexpectedly, not echoed by Mr. Bingley, who submitted to their questions afterward. "Ah. Yes. Well. I needed to speak with the head groom, and with Mr. Burton. On matters of estate business, you know."

Jonathan Darcy asked, "Would you not normally meet with them in your study?"

"Of course, but on that day, well. Given everything going on." Mr. Bingley appeared positively sheepish.

Juliet had never thought of her host as a likely suspect in either of the murders, but his failure to be forthcoming she found both displeasing and ominous. "Will you not tell us what you met with them about?"

"A new horse, of course." Mr. Bingley then leaned forward and whispered, "You must both understand that there are certain secrets a gentleman must keep from his wife. Let us not discuss that further. But of course none of this had aught to do with the fate of poor Becky."

After Mr. Bingley had gone, Juliet said, "I must confess I am . . . disappointed in Mr. Bingley."

"I cannot believe he conceals anything so wicked," said Mr. Darcy, "though I admit there is no reason he could not discuss the acquisition of a horse in front of my aunt."

"Still," she said, "that, too, can be confirmed with the groom or the steward."

Juliet further considered that even with such errands as these two gentlemen had described, it would have been but the work of an instant to step toward the dyeing area and steal the sash. But seeing Jonathan so forlorn—still so very uncertain after the terrible interaction with his father—she felt the point could be raised later. For now, she simply laid her hand on his arm for a moment, so that they might find some brief measure of peace together.

Never let it be said that the appearance of Fitzwilliam Darcy failed to delight Caroline Allerdyce. Though her aspirations now rested upon her younger daughter rather than herself, her zeal remained unabated; and where this was the case, she tended to fall back into unfortunate conversational habits.

"Mr. Darcy! How fortunate for us all that you have joined our party!" Caroline gestured toward the chair near her and her husband. "We have become a very sad lot, and the honor of your company is just the thing to cheer us."

"I should imagine cheer to be very far from possible for the bereaved at present," Mr. Darcy replied. "Good afternoon, Mr. Allerdyce."

"Good afternoon, Mr. Darcy," said Allerdyce. "No, indeed, we are not to be cheerful, but we can be companionable, and I am sure the Bingleys are glad of your support."

"As must your son be," Caroline said. She lowered her

voice. "One must be ever cautious regarding certain . . . *preying* individuals. Jonathan is so noble-minded that he does not consider all he should take into account."

"Those who are predatory in certain matters are indeed to be avoided," said Mr. Darcy. "If you judge my son's mind more noble than my own, I shall not argue the point."

Caroline found this answer dissatisfactory, as she did the peculiar look Mr. Allerdyce then gave her. She glanced about the room, looking for Priscilla, that she might call her over and give Mr. Darcy a chance to be charmed by her—but Priscilla was not near, and in that short instant, Mr. Darcy had made good his escape.

For the time being.

By the time Jonathan Darcy judged himself ready to question Mrs. Brooks, both wife and husband had already returned to the vicarage for the evening. Juliet could hardly bear the chagrin. "So distracted have we been by your father's arrival, we did not even let your aunt Brooks know we wished to speak with her."

"It is of no great moment," he said wearily. "We can speak with her on the morrow."

Juliet knew this to be true, but it did not soothe her. She found that, were his father to bear witness, she wished to be quicker, brighter, more intelligent, more of every good thing it was possible for a young woman to be—so that he might better forget the scandal occasioned by Mr. Follett. Still, the error was made and could not be remedied yet, so she would not compound it by failing to use the last hour of the afternoon to speak once more with Mrs. Hurst.

"How many such interviews of this sort must there be?" Mrs. Hurst demanded as she took her place. "I declare, I have scarcely spoken as much to my sisters as I have to the two of you."

How fortunate for them, Juliet thought. "As we learn more, more questions arise, Mrs. Hurst."

Mr. Darcy interjected: "For instance, we have learned that you went repeatedly into the laundry downstairs on the day the household clothing was being dyed for mourning."

"Do you think I would let my best things be ruined?" Mrs. Hurst protested. "Of course most will never be fit for anything but mourning ever again, but the pelisses and spencers, those at least could be salvaged for regular wear. One of the pelisses is true China silk!"

It appeared that Mrs. Hurst believed her argument unassailable on this point. Juliet would allow her this. "Did you always speak with one of the laundry maids when downstairs, or with Mrs. Mulgrew? Or did you ever go down and find yourself alone?"

Mrs. Hurst shook her head. "No, I did not, though I might as well have done for all that they heeded me. One of my lace caps is entirely spoiled."

"Did you ever bring anything up from the laundry room, madam?" Mr. Darcy asked.

"Why should I do that?" Mrs. Hurst asked, in evident puzzlement. "Why should I begin fetching laundry like a servant girl?"

Juliet realized he had asked that particular question not for the sake of the answer they would receive, but to observe Mrs. Hurst's response. In this, Juliet could detect no hint of guilt or evasion. Though, as she had reason to know, murderers were often also excellent liars.

"If you ask me, which you have not, the first suspects in the death of a servant should be other servants," Mrs. Hurst continued. "I wonder that you have not spoken to more of them."

Mr. Darcy replied, "I wonder that you have not considered

that Becky's murderer and that of Mr. Hurst are almost surely one and the same."

How wary Mrs. Hurst looked then! *If she did not do it*, Juliet thought (though far from convinced on that point), *who* does *she think guilty?*

Once Mrs. Hurst had gone, Juliet raised this point. "We have not always asked those around us whom they believe to be responsible."

"Do you feel that we need them to guide us?" Mr. Darcy asked. His spirits were indeed poor.

"Not in the slightest." Juliet could not imagine where Mrs. Hurst could possibly guide her that would be worth the going. "But if we wish to understand their actions, it may benefit us to understand their suspicions—for these may be more influential than we have yet realized."

Mr. Darcy rallied then. "Of course you are correct. However, I believe we have more pressing priorities—first, speaking with Mrs. Brooks."

"Naturally. Then, though I hate to admit it . . . Mrs. Hurst has given me a good idea. Accidentally, I am certain. But we need to know more of who was speaking with Becky outside of the normal range of her duties. Anyone might have reason to speak to a servant for a moment, but we may learn much from finding out who did."

"Agreed," said Mr. Darcy. "How I wish we could begin immediately!"

"But you must return to Longbourn," Juliet said, her heart sinking as she added, "with your father."

"Wish me strength, dear Miss Tilney." He took her hand as he said it, a touch so thrilling that she found herself emboldened to ask a question that had been much on her mind since the night of their engagement.

"Mr. Darcy—though it is very forward, it is not so unusual as once it was to—" Juliet summoned her courage. "Mr. Darcy, do not you think we might, when in privacy, call each other by our Christian names?"

How the idea delighted him! "We shall have to be careful of being overheard, but I confess, it would be my greatest pleasure. My dear—my dear Juliet."

Thrilling as this was to hear, it would be yet more thrilling to speak. "My dear Jonathan," Juliet replied, and how glad she was, on this trying day, to have given her beloved a reason to smile.

Juliet, Jonathan thought, over and over again that evening. *Juliet, my Juliet.*

He would likely have been as enamored of this new intimacy under any possible circumstances, but it was also a great comfort to him over dinner at Longbourn.

Fitzwilliam Darcy had not been an overnight guest at Longbourn above three times in his life, this by the mutual consent of the man himself, his wife, and his mother-in-law. Mrs. Bennet had never developed any great liking for Mr. Darcy, though his long-ago slights toward her daughter had been compensated for by his subsequently having married her. His fortune and his hauteur equally intimidated Mrs. Bennet, and so in his presence she vacillated between long periods of goggle-eyed silence and bursts of her usual chatter. As this chatter was sometimes nigh unendurable, even for persons far more tolerant of noise and nonsense than Mr. Darcy, it was to the mutual satisfaction of all that he had either stayed at Netherfield or simply hosted them at Pemberley, which had more than enough room to give all necessary space to breathe.

Longbourn offered no such spaciousness, as Jonathan was keenly aware that night while they all sat to table.

"Had you given us more notice, Mr. Darcy, we could have had partridges for you," said Mrs. Bennet. "Pine is terribly good with partridges. Or a turkey! There are often turkeys to be had in town, you know. Not so fine as those you have at Pemberley, and to be sure, I imagine you dine on turkey nearly every night!"

"This roast pork is more than satisfactory, Mrs. Bennet," said Mr. Darcy. "Please give my compliments to Mrs. Pine."

As this constituted a successful conversation between the two of them, Mrs. Bennet fell silent for a while in sheer relief, though this emotion might have been felt in even greater measure by the others at table.

Mr. Bennet, never unwilling to make a bit of mischief, said, "We had the pleasure of Miss Tilney's company a few nights ago."

"Did you?" Mr. Darcy said, but his even tone did not deceive Jonathan. His father was but further angered that Juliet had been introduced to Jonathan's grandparents—under most circumstances, a pronounced show of family favor. That was not entirely the case here, but Jonathan knew better than to argue it. "I trust the evening was an enjoyable one."

"Indeed, for she is a bright young woman, with some wit about her. Little enough has there been in this house since you took our Elizabeth from it." Mr. Bennet winked. "A shame, the things people will write in newspapers without any cause whatsoever."

Mr. Darcy said, "All aspects of the incident in London last February are deeply regrettable."

Mrs. Bennet dearly wished to hear more of the scandalous events, but feared to ask Mr. Darcy of them. No doubt he would be more communicative than her peculiar nephew or obstinate daughter, but the cast of his face and the tone of his voice suggested more conversation on this topic was unwelcome. From this rare insight, she gleaned only that she must say something else, about nearly anything else, right away. "We would have a better pudding to offer you at the end of the meal, sir, had we known you would be joining us, but we do have a sponge cake. One made with orange water—do not you remember how that was Susannah's favorite? And Lydia's before her. Ah, my poor lost girls."

"Yes, I remember," Mr. Darcy said softly, thinking of the child who had been so very like a daughter to him. For Jonathan's part, he was silenced by the reminder that he kept more than one secret from his father.

Chapter Fourteen

Jonathan Darcy elected to breakfast at Netherfield. This was not only to be with Miss Tilney—*Juliet*—but also, given the choice between dining in a place which had recently been host to a poisoning and spending more time seated by his silently glowering father, he felt that inspecting coffee cups was not so great a burden.

However, his father chose to ride with him; and as Jonathan could not concoct any plausible reason to gallop at top speed, instead of escape, he was obliged instead to be glowered at on horseback.

Yet after only minutes, his father said, "You are riding exceptionally well, Jonathan."

"It is scarcely a difficult path."

"I meant to refer to your health. Your stamina, your bearing. After you were wounded, your mother and I feared your recovery might never be complete—as indeed it is not for many persons."

Gunshot wounds were indeed perilous long after the fateful pull of the trigger. Wounds that neither destroyed organs nor caused fatal bloodshed could fester into gangrene or lesser infections that nonetheless forever caused pain, limping, or loss of strength. Even now, years after the end of the Napoleonic Wars, men who had been wounded in that conflict could still be seen hobbling, walking bent, wearing eye patches and the like. Jonathan's frustration with being coddled had obscured to him the breadth of the risks he had taken, the severity of the fear he had occasioned within his parents. "I was fortunate, Father," he said. "I have given thanks to the Lord many times for my deliverance."

"As have I." Mr. Darcy's smile encouraged Jonathan somewhat, until he added, "A father cannot protect his son against every danger, but he cannot be prevented from trying."

As Jonathan interpreted this to be an allusion to Juliet as the "danger" afoot, he did not respond to this, but looked toward the horizon, where Netherfield could just be seen upon the low hill.

Jonathan and Juliet had sent a note the night before, requesting Mrs. Brooks's return on the morrow, and he had scarcely entered Netherfield before the Brookses' carriage arrived. From the window he marked the small size of the carriage; well-kept as it was, any observer would see that it was of an older style. His aunt had driven herself, which was not particularly noteworthy when covering such short distances in the countryside, but Jonathan knew none of Mr. Bingley's sisters, nor even his aunt Jane, would ever have done so. The Brookses could not have had servants enough to employ a coachman—no doubt other men working for them performed this task when possible, but when one could not be spared, Aunt Kitty must be obliged to convey herself.

"She wears her lovely new gloves," said Juliet, who had come to his side at the window without his even realizing it.

"So she does," he replied. "Good morning, Miss Tilney."

"Good morning, Mr. Darcy." She smiled slightly, and some measure of his inner disquiet was soothed. He could neither fear nor resent any difficulty necessary to have her forever beside him.

Aunt Kitty came to the study and greeted them with civility, but no warmth. Her reserve chilled when she heard their question. "You want to know why I should happen to see my sister's laundry?"

"It was hung largely out of sight of the house, Mrs. Brooks,"

Juliet pointed out. "You would have had to go to some trouble to see it."

"Unless," Jonathan proffered, "you had some other reason to be in the vicinity of the stables?"

To his surprise, Aunt Kitty seemed to soften. She appeared younger to him in that instant, her face more like the one he remembered from the earliest days of childhood. "No. You are correct. I went to look at Jane's things, and those of Mrs. Lofton. And Mrs. Hurst. They have clothing of the latest fashions, especially Mr. Bingley's sisters. Their garments are of finer materials than anything that could be obtained from Mrs. Mount's shop. A woman wishes to know these things, even when she cannot aspire to have the same."

Juliet said, "It is indeed difficult, ma'am, to have desires above one's income."

Aunt Kitty laughed. "Yet it is not above our income! That is the rub."

"I would not have thought this a prosperous parish," said Jonathan. Did the Meryton church have a generous patron he somehow knew nothing of? Or perhaps Mr. Brooks was eventually to inherit more than Jonathan had previously suspected.

"It is not a prosperous parish," Aunt Kitty replied. "We would be obliged to live on little in any case, and yet, Mr. Brooks will not allot our household but a half of that. He squirrels it all away, for what purpose I know not. He does not care how shabby—my feelings—he does not care."

Jonathan, who had never had any particular reason to practice economy, could not guess at Mr. Brooks's motivations, and it appeared that Juliet was even more struck. "Only a half! This goes beyond thrift."

"It is miserliness," said Aunt Kitty. "My misery is only made greater by beholding what my sister may have that I may not. Yet still, sometimes . . . I must look."

After she left the study, Juliet said, "This would explain why the Brookses come here so often."

"So that Mrs. Brooks should have more occasion for envy?"

"If she is obliged to run her household on half of what a country parson receives, that house cannot be a very comfortable one," she answered. "Mr. Brooks's demeanor is cold, unwelcoming. Perhaps any amount of envy is easier to endure."

Jonathan could well imagine that this was so, but nonetheless he added, "Yet still, she has her new gloves."

During this time, Mr. Darcy had little to occupy him save to talk to the other visitors in the household; and, as this would expose him to Mrs. Allerdyce, it seemed an entertainment not worth the risk. Ultimately, in defiance of the hour, he asked Mr. Bingley for a game of billiards.

The billiards room at Netherfield was not a large one, and it was farther from the study than Mr. Darcy would have preferred. Though he had no intention of eavesdropping, he somehow felt as though his proximity would help his son remember what was owed to his family. Yet he could imagine how Elizabeth would have laughed at his foolishness—such sense of humor as Mr. Darcy had about himself came always in her voice—and therefore the game was to be played.

Mr. Bingley, through their long friendship, could privately ask Mr. Darcy much that would never be spoken in wider company, as he did when he said, "I take it Georgiana still needs Elizabeth near?"

"The companionship of another woman is very welcome to my sister. Rarely have I been as thankful that Elizabeth has become a sister to her in every sense but blood."

Bingley, so unassuming in most respects, became ruthless

with a cue in his hand. He sank a difficult shot easily while saying, "Jane little anticipated such a response to her letter."

Mr. Darcy would not have admitted as much to nearly any other person, but to Bingley he said, "Elizabeth was not so alarmed by its contents as I. She even attempted to dissuade me from coming, but it is better that I am here."

"Has not Jonathan previously investigated murders without your being present?"

"Yes, of course. That is not the source of the difficulty." Mr. Darcy tapped lightly, nudged a red ball into the pocket. "I fear Jonathan's lack of prudence regarding Miss Tilney may lead him to make a grievous error."

Mr. Bingley looked up from the green felt of the table. "You mean, you are afraid that he will not ask Miss Tilney to marry him?"

It took a moment for Mr. Darcy to be certain of what he had heard. "I am afraid that he *will* ask her. Bingley, you know of the scandal—the duel—"

"Yes, yes, all of that." Bingley banked a shot off the side of the table before it spun into the hole. "Unfortunate and distressing, I know. However, we have come to know the girl a bit during her time here, and it requires very little acquaintance to realize that any rumors against her in such regard are without merit. Jane likes her very much, and I confess, I do as well."

"It is not a matter of liking her," Darcy said. "She has ever been a regrettable influence upon Jonathan." He had not forgotten how, when they had all first become acquainted, Miss Tilney had persuaded Jonathan to slip away and sneak around their host's study like thieves—a breach of etiquette so shocking it could have ruined her reputation then and there.

Mr. Bingley tutted the shot Darcy then missed. "To us, Jonathan seems much improved these past few years. Of course we have always loved him, and his character and heart have ever been excellent. Yet he is more confident now. Better able to navigate changes and troubles. Easier in his conversation with people he does not know very well. Some of this may only be greater maturity, but do you not feel Miss Tilney's influence in these changes?"

"*That*, I put down to his success in the investigations."

"Is she not his partner in those?" Mr. Bingley struck one ball into another, sending them both straight into their targets. "In the greatest confidence, Darcy, I will tell you—Miss Tilney has received an offer of marriage, one she has been urged to accept. She confessed as much to Jane. The same painter who so insulted her honor believes he can best repair it by wedding her."

The relief Mr. Darcy felt at that moment! "Then she is not ruined forever. She will be respectably wed elsewhere. That is the best, most rational end to the entire business."

Mr. Bingley put down his cue. "Darcy, are you quite mad? The best end to this is a girl forced to marry a man she cares nothing for, only for the sake of gossip?"

When put that way, Mr. Darcy could not answer. He had not changed his mind—but he saw, for the first time, how very much his reason had diverged from his decency.

Those gentlemen and ladies who keep only to the genteel areas of their house—who never enter the servants' domain—know less than half of what truly happens beneath their own roofs. Much of what occurs in the scullery or the attics is best left unrealized. Yet this can also lead to a level of ignorance about one's own abode, as Jonathan had realized when asking the Bingleys how long it would take to move from the laundry to a bedchamber.

"Let me consider," Aunt Jane had said. "Of course it would

depend upon which bedchamber. The Loftons and the Hursts stay at the far end of the hall, so they would require another minute or so compared to, say, Miss Tilney, who is so very near the stairs."

"That is not so great a difference in time as to concern us," Jonathan replied.

Yet Aunt Jane had few other insights; as kind a mistress as she was, she spent little time belowstairs. Jonathan had made the trip with Juliet by his side, but not while attempting either haste or discretion. Therefore they spent a portion of the afternoon hurrying from various bedrooms down into the laundry, or from the house to the place where clothes were dyed. Dark clouds hung low overhead, presaging the autumn rains that were soon to begin. So odd was it to see a gentleman and lady repeatedly dashing up and down stairs, or along such a length, that a handful of the servants found a moment to stop and watch them, even out of doors despite the encroaching damp.

"I think the murderer must have been obliged to steal the sash from the laundry, rather than the dye tubs," Juliet finally said. They stood upon the back lawn, breathing hard; Jonathan liked the rosiness of her cheeks. "It is not that the trip could not be swiftly made, but surely the person would have been seen."

"The stables were far closer," Jonathan pointed out, "though both Mr. Bingley and Mr. Lofton were able to give accounts of their reasons for being there, and were witnessed doing precisely what they had reported."

"A momentary step away might have been possible, nevertheless." Juliet peered upward. "I believe the first raindrops have begun to fall."

Once inside, the inevitable obligations of being a guest in a country house superseded the investigation for a time. Stewart the butler handed Juliet a letter, one she did not take up immediately, but instead asked to have brought to her room. When Jonathan looked at her curiously, she said, "It is from my grandfather, which means it will be unpleasant. I am in no haste to hear what he will have to say."

"Is he always unpleasant?" Jonathan asked. He knew he would have to gain General Tilney's approval one day.

Juliet considered this. "Nearly always, yes. In this case, I am certain he is replying to my letter, informing him that I"— she glanced about, but though Priscilla Allerdyce watched them closely, the others in the drawing room were paying them little heed—"that I declined a certain invitation I recently received."

Jonathan understood and felt no further concern. Whatever displeasure the general might express regarding Juliet's refusal would dissipate as soon as he learned of her engagement to a far more eligible suitor—which Jonathan, in all modesty, knew himself to be. The heir to Pemberley would be a match for any young lady, potentially even among the nobility.

But if I do not convince my father, Jonathan thought, *if he becomes too angry that I dared enter into an engagement without his approval, I may be the heir to Pemberley no longer.*

Another game of cards was to begin, and as the tables were made up, Jonathan first thought to give his usual excuses. He then realized that Mr. Brooks's table still lacked a player. How better to assess the character of someone so taciturn than by observing them in such a context?

As soon as Jonathan had taken his chair, Mr. Brooks said, "Mr. Darcy, I believe I recall your extraordinary talent at cards."

"The rest of us shall have our share of luck, never you fear," said Mrs. Hurst.

"Cards are not a matter of luck—or, I should say, not only of luck," Jonathan replied. "Probabilities are all that matter."

"Precisely so," said Mr. Brooks. "I find that the moment one begins to feel 'lucky'—to gain enthusiasm, to lose one's head—that is the moment to lay down one's cards."

"To quit just as one has luck?" Mrs. Hurst exclaimed. "Do not think I shall surrender my good fortune so easily!"

"I am sure you will not, Mrs. Hurst," Mr. Brooks replied civilly.

The fourth at table, Mr. Allerdyce, said, "You have a cool head, Mr. Brooks. That is a benefit in many circumstances, not only cards."

"I find it so," said Mr. Brooks.

"What are some of those circumstances?" Jonathan asked. His hand was poor, enough so that he knew to risk little. One achieved greater success by looking toward victory of an evening entire, not that of a single round. "In which you feel calm, reasoned consideration to be of the greatest benefit? I should imagine this especially important for a clergyman."

In truth he wondered whether Mr. Brooks could truly be as unimpassioned as he appeared and proclaimed. Jonathan had always assumed miserliness to rise from a place of fear that the future could not be as prosperous as the past.

Mr. Brooks drew a card. "Investments, Mr. Darcy. In investing, it is critical to keep one's head. One reads in the paper of speculators building fortunes within a week and losing them within a day. This is worse than folly." His face never shifted expression as he spoke. "One must look toward the more distant future. This Stockton and Darlington company I have bought into—they will make little profit at first, but I believe great potential lies there."

Mr. Allerdyce assented, saying, "Your policy is exactly right, sir."

Was Mr. Brooks simply saving money to invest? But why so much of it? And if he was making a great deal of money in investments, should not at least some of that fortune have gone to Aunt Kitty for the maintenance of the household? What was the point of hoarding such wealth?

"Oh, no," cried Mrs. Hurst as Mr. Brooks lay down his successful hand.

Juliet spent much of the evening pretending to read one of the fashion periodicals, though she could not avoid conversation on this point altogether.

"That magazine is half a year out of date, is it not?" Priscilla Allerdyce said.

"I suppose," Juliet replied, "but fashions do not change as quickly as all that."

Mrs. Allerdyce interjected, "To those who truly attend to matters of fashion, I assure you, a *great* deal of difference can be seen season to season. Though for those who will not be in London, I suppose it could not be of any consequence."

Juliet turned to her hostess. "You take quite a few of these publications, do you not, Mrs. Bingley?"

"My dear husband subscribes to them for me, for he knows I enjoy seeing how pretty the designs all are," said Mrs. Bingley. "But I do not need to own a great deal of finery. It is simply that I like to look at beautiful things."

The two Allerdyces nearby exchanged stares of disbelief, while Juliet desperately wished they would all leave her be. In truth, while she felt she had chosen wisely in electing to read her grandfather's letter only at the end of the evening, increasingly her curiosity and dread had begun to overcome her. Suspense was no one's friend. At the earliest possible hour, Juliet excused herself to retire.

As she left the room, she glanced back at Jonathan and saw

that he was watching her leave. Juliet could not help but smile, though this expression faded as she realized the silent, wary Mr. Darcy had witnessed this exchange and disapproved of it.

Still, such disapproval as that, she thought while ascending the stairs, *is unlikely to compare to whatever my grandfather will have to say.*

Yet all Juliet's dread had been inadequate to the truth, for she opened General Tilney's letter to find herself disowned.

Chapter Fifteen

Miss Tilney—

*You have, through your misconduct, your lack of
discretion, and above all through your obstinate
disobedience, forfeited the right to call yourself my
granddaughter—to visit Northanger Abbey or the
parish I have allowed your father to have—to be
considered as any member of the family.*

*As you are so certain of yourself in Hertfordshire,
remain there, or go elsewhere, but you shall not return
here. Nevermore shall you be admitted to our presence,
and if you or your parents attempt to defy me in this
matter, it will go all the worse for them.*

*May your regrets be as bitter as are mine for putting
trust in a faithless child.*

General Tilney

Juliet had ever known her grandfather to be an unkind,
uncharitable man. He had not been good to her mother during the courtship of Juliet's parents, and he oversaw his holdings with all the dictatorial arrogance of a lord of the realm,
though in truth many lords were far better behaved. Yet never
had she foreseen such a consequence as this.

If only she could write back to her grandfather, tell him
that she was engaged to Jonathan Darcy! Once he knew this,
she was certain all would be forgiven—for even though she

felt she had done nothing wrong to forgive, even though she knew her grandfather's reversal would arise from purely selfish motives, it was impossible to read evidence of such anger and not wish it gone. However, this she could not write, for their engagement remained secret, and to judge by Mr. Darcy's demeanor at Netherfield, the secret would have to be kept far longer.

What frightened her most was the strong hint that, if her parents attempted to support her in her refusal of Mr. Follet's offer, they, too, would be punished. Her father's parish was one over which her grandfather's influence ruled; if General Tilney wished another minister to be appointed there, then this would occur, and Henry Tilney would lose his living. This would not be a fatal blow to the family, for Catherine Tilney made more income from her books than could ever be decently acknowledged—but it would materially hurt their circumstances, as well as those of Theodosia and Albion.

Juliet did not doubt that her parents would nonetheless choose her. Yet she could not bear the thought of this sacrifice. If her mother and father could but be assured of her well-being elsewhere, they might not defy General Tilney to such an extent that they would share Juliet's fate.

But where should such a place be?

"Miss Tilney?"

She startled from her place in Mr. Bingley's study—though she had read the letter many hours before, after a long and sleepless night, its words remained before her, a shadowy screen through which the entire world had been made unclear. "Oh. Yes, Mr. Darcy?"

"Are you quite well? You have not been attending very closely this morning." Jonathan had been attempting to review and align what was known of various suspects, but she had proved unable to assist in any meaningful way. "Forgive me—you seem quite pale—"

"My grandfather's letter was difficult to read," she said, but no further would she yet speak. To pressure Jonathan into telling his father of their engagement immediately, when they could have no chance of success—it would not improve her circumstances. He would only be made as unhappy as she, a fate Juliet would have wished on no person. "I did not sleep much. What were you saying, of the staircase?"

Jonathan gazed at her, clearly unsure that he had heard the whole truth, but he did her the honor of taking her at her word. "My thought was that tripping a person upon a stair, though very dangerous and as we have seen sometimes fatal, is by no means an assured method of committing murder. It would have been equally likely—nay, more so—that Becky would have tripped and been injured, yet survived. Given this, does it not strike you as an extraordinary risk for the murderer to have taken?"

Juliet considered this carefully. "It may be," she said slowly, "that the murderer's purpose might have been fulfilled by injury equally as well as by death. If, as we speculate, Becky knew who the guilty party was, and hoped to obtain money from them—such a fall would have done more than hurt her. It would have frightened her badly and made it clear that the murderer was more than willing to kill again."

"Very possible," Jonathan agreed, "though I confess, my thought was yet more disturbing: that the killer might have gone downstairs after Becky's fall to ensure that she was dead. Had the tumble not broken her neck, he could then have dispatched her by other means."

"How terrible!" Juliet shuddered. "I am glad for her sake that, if she had to die, it was by the fall. That at least was swift."

Jonathan touched her arm briefly. "If the incident upon the staircase was as much warning as murder, then I fear we cannot be certain we shall not receive such warnings ourselves."

Meanwhile, during a stroll through the garden but a few minutes' steps away, another young woman was enjoying a far happier morning, and a far more conventional courtship.

And courtship it most definitely was, as Frederica Allerdyce was learning to her delight.

"We have always been friends to each other," said Isaac Lucas, his expression open with artless hope. "I have always admired your strength of character, your goodness, and your loveliness. We value the same principles, the same sorts of people, I believe; we wish for the same good life. So I ask you, my dear Miss Allerdyce, will you share that life with me?"

"Yes," whispered Frederica, a brilliant smile illuminating her face more brightly than the weak October sun. "Yes, Mr. Lucas, I should be so very happy to become your wife."

Mr. Lucas took Frederica's hand, a thrilling touch. "Then let me go to your father at once."

"When you do, tell him that you have my entire heart," Frederica said. "Then he will not be able to refuse you."

Very daringly, Mr. Lucas stole a kiss upon her cheek, then hurried inside the house, unwilling to wait even one moment longer than necessary before making their engagement entirely official.

Frederica spun about in place amid the goldenrod and gentian, laughing out loud for pure delight. It was then that Priscilla—who had been following her sister and spying from a distance—dared to approach.

"You are very giddy this morning," said she as she came

up to Frederica, who remained flushed with happiness. "Is Mr. Lucas paying you court?"

"He has already done so, and we are to be married. As soon as he speaks to Papa, which he has already gone to do. Oh, Priss, I have never been so happy!"

"Have you always liked him, then?"

Frederica nodded. "Though I never gave the notion serious thought, so clear did it seem that the match would be entirely impossible. Now that he has inherited his house and fortune, however, nothing should stand between us."

Priscilla was of two minds about this news. Her mother's snobbery had formed enough of her character for her to think Isaac Lucas of Meryton less than her sister deserved; also she had a better notion than did Frederica of Mrs. Allerdyce's likely reaction to this news. However, she liked her sister well enough to take some pleasure in her happiness. Furthermore, it was always said that talk of one wedding brought on another. Would the announcement of this match perhaps make Jonathan Darcy think more seriously about his own future?

Or had the Darcy heir already made a very grave mistake?

"You cannot have allowed it," said Caroline Allerdyce, whose husband had drawn her into their Netherfield bedroom to share what he had believed to be excellent news. "Tell me you sent him away. Tell me you refused him!"

"By no means did I refuse him." Mr. Allerdyce possessed as strong a will as his wife when he chose to exercise it, as he did now. "Isaac Lucas is a likable, intelligent young man with an income of almost three thousand a year and a fine estate."

"Not even three thousand a year? For a girl with a dowry

of ten thousand pounds?" Caroline paced the length of the room, which was not so long as to keep her from turning and turning and turning again. "You cannot think that a sensible match. To go from a member of the nobility to this!"

"To go from a baronet Frederica could not respect to a young man closer to her age, who cares for her as deeply as we could wish, of whom we know only good? To me, Caroline, that seems an excellent change."

She had rarely felt so at odds with her husband as she did at this moment. "If it must be, it must be," Caroline said. "To think, *my daughter* to be mistress of *Lucas Lodge*—oh, Louisa will never cease laughing at it."

"Is it Mrs. Hurst's good opinion we should be seeking above all else?" Mr. Allerdyce, though an even-tempered man by nature, had begun finally to anger. "I listen to my own reason, which tells me this match will make our daughter happy without depriving her materially. If you are sensible, you will keep your own counsel as well, instead of listening to Mrs. Hurst."

Caroline was not even truly listening to him, so outdone was she. "I suppose our greatest hopes have always been for Priscilla. When she weds Jonathan Darcy, any wagging tongues mocking us for Frederica's match will be well and truly silenced."

Mr. Allerdyce's surprise on this point was great indeed. "Whatever can you mean? The young Mr. Darcy shows no particular attachment to Priscilla that I have seen. It is the Tilney girl to whom he attends."

"The Darcys will never consent to that match. Mr. Darcy's appearance here proves that at least."

"Because of the rumors surrounding the girl," said Mr. Allerdyce. "But we know whence these rumors spring, Caroline—from an incident that you yourself brought about."

"I did not convince that painter to portray her so! Others

had begun to recognize her well before I ever saw the work for myself, you know."

"I further know that what would otherwise have been a resemblance remarked upon by only a few was made very public by your taking Miss Tilney to the gallery yourself and ensuring that a crowd could see both girl and picture at the same time. A small rumor was made a great scandal by your mischief. This you did believing that the Darcy heir would then have no other choice but to wed Priscilla, regardless of his lack of interest in her."

"She will be mistress of Pemberley!" Caroline insisted. "I will have it so!"

"Because *you* did not become its mistress," replied Mr. Allerdyce, and his anger had fled from him then. In its place was something far worse: sorrow. "From past jibes of Mrs. Hurst, I had already determined that you once aspired to wed Mr. Darcy. I could not fault you for attempting to make an eligible match, for what else do we all do during the time of life when courtship occurs? Yet I had believed these many years that it was I who had won your love, and this was what mattered most in the end. It appears that this is not what matters most to you."

With that, Mr. Allerdyce left, and Caroline was left alone with both her disappointments and her dread of what had become of her husband's love for her.

Unsurprisingly, that night at dinner, both Miss Allerdyce and Mr. Lucas practically shone with happiness, and every person present wished them joy. Mr. Bingley insisted that some of the best wine be brought up from the cellars, and he and his wife, at least, genuinely shared in the young couple's satisfaction.

Yet the spirit at table did not rise to the heights that might normally have been expected. The deaths of Mr. Hurst and Becky still cast their pall, but added to this were the glowering disapproval of Mr. Darcy; the resentment of Jonathan Darcy; the wan languor of Juliet Tilney; the petulance of Caroline Allerdyce; the depression of her husband; the dark amusement of Miss Priscilla; and the wary gazes of the Loftons, who sensed that much strife lay all about them in every direction but knew not what. Mrs. Hurst was primarily interested in the partridges, which were excellent.

Mr. Bingley truly believed he would be helping to jolly the evening along by civilly asking, "Miss Tilney, did not you receive a letter from your grandfather yesterday? Is all your family in good health?"

The question was unremarkable, for letters were often read aloud in general company, even when the letter writer was unknown to most others present. When Juliet blanched, however, it became clear that she could not give him an equally unremarkable answer. "My grandfather . . . he asked of me something I know my parents would not wish me to do. He can be severe. Forgive me, but I can share no more."

"Oh dear." Mr. Bingley could scarcely bear the thought of having hurt another through his own imprudence. "How terribly sorry we all are to hear it."

Caroline, goaded by her own misdeeds, said, "I suppose he has many concerns about your prospects at present."

This was most rude—even Mr. Darcy thought so—and only deepened the breach between Caroline Allerdyce and her husband. Yet Juliet accepted it in silence; and, angry though Jonathan was on her behalf, he knew that to make more of the comment would only worsen Juliet's shame.

So this gibe might have gone unremarked, had it not had a most unusual, even astounding effect upon another person currently seated at the table.

Somebody had finally, truly, made Jane Bingley mad.

Of course, Jane's natural sweetness meant that she did not shout, or say anything unkind. Instead she gave her decided opinion: "I think it very wrong that a young woman's reputation should be considered sullied only because a trick has been played upon her."

This astonishing forthrightness, particularly given its source, stunned most into silence. It was Mr. Darcy who said, "Nonetheless it is the way of society."

"I am not certain it should be so," replied Jane. "In fact, I am not certain it *is* so. For, you see, a trick was once played upon me. Do you not remember, Mr. Darcy? And you, Mrs. Allerdyce, Mrs. Hurst? It has always been my understanding that each of you had a part in it, though if I am incorrect, I humbly beg your pardon."

Mr. Darcy, Mrs. Hurst, and Caroline Allerdyce had all turned various shades of red. The younger persons present were in a state of consternation, and for many, also an avid curiosity. "What trick?" Priscilla asked. "What sort of trick do you mean?"

Juliet said, "You cannot mean—no painting of you—"

"Oh, goodness, indeed no!" Jane exclaimed. "I should not have had your fortitude in that case, Miss Tilney. This trick was not so elaborate. It was only that I loved Mr. Bingley, and Mr. Bingley loved me, but it did not suit his sisters or his friend that we should marry. So they gave him reasons to be in London, and when I visited London as well, I was informed that he knew of my being present in the city, yet he never came to call. Given this, I could only surmise that he no longer cared for me. How heartbroken I was! Yet it was all a trick, you see. Mrs. Hurst and Mrs. Allerdyce concealed my presence in London from Mr. Bingley, with the knowledge and support of Mr. Darcy."

"Well," said Mr. Bingley, as surprised as anyone else could be by his wife's sudden display of spirit, but not displeased. "We sorted it all out in the end."

Jane smiled at her husband. "We did indeed, for I believe that where there is true love, it can triumph over any obstacle. But I have not yet posed my question. Mr. Darcy, do you feel that my good reputation was sullied by the trick you played upon me?"

Nothing in the previous quarter century could have prepared Mr. Darcy for this from Jane. He had long since confessed his wrongdoing in the matter to Bingley, and had been heartily ashamed of his behavior. Only now did he realize he had never apologized to Jane herself, and that he should have done. "Of course not, Mrs. Bingley," he managed to say. "I am most grievously sorry."

"You are not sorry enough to give credit to another girl who has had a trick played upon her. So I cannot think the lesson has been truly learned. Forgive me, Mr. Darcy, for speaking of an event so long past, but I could no longer be silent."

With this, Jane turned her attention back to her food. No one could speak. Jonathan stared at his father in shocked disapproval, as the Allerdyce girls did their mother. Juliet's gratification in her hostess's defense was tempered by the private burdens she still bore. Mrs. Hurst, who had never been ashamed of her machinations regarding her brother's courtship, simply turned her attention back to the partridges.

The elder generation felt well and truly shamed before the younger after dinner that evening. Caroline could hardly face her daughters, and her husband did not want to face her. Juliet Tilney, though still dazed with horror and uncertainty, found she could walk past Mr. Darcy without the slightest concern for his opinion.

Yet most troubled of all was Jonathan Darcy.

Forever, he had looked up to his father as the epitome of everything that was good, right, and gentlemanly. Whenever Mr. Darcy had urged his son toward different behaviors, Jonathan had endeavored mightily to behave as his father wished—even when his particular character was profoundly distressed by doing so. All this he had done because he honored his father above all other men.

Then to learn this!

The two Darcy men rode back toward Longbourn in silence until they had very nearly reached the house, when at last Jonathan could not but ask, "Does Mother know?"

Mr. Darcy sighed. "She learned of it at the time, and gave me such an upbraiding as I shall never forget. I am deeply ashamed of my behavior toward your aunt and have been ever since that day."

"Yet you say that I am the one who has behaved dishonorably," Jonathan said, "because I sought to stand by the woman that I love when wrong was being done to her."

"The situations are not at all the same!" Mr. Darcy insisted, though inwardly he became less certain of this every day. "Whatever errors I have made in judgment, they do not justify your having kept secrets from me."

"Then I shall no longer keep them," said Jonathan. He had much to tell his father, but he knew what had to be said first, before anything else, for it was the burden he had carried longest. "Father—you must know—what happened to Susannah, the reason Mr. Wickham took her from us—it is my fault. I am the reason she is dead."

Chapter Sixteen

Fitzwilliam Darcy was one of the rare individuals in this world who had been given nearly everything he had ever wanted in life. He understood this, though in his reckoning, he did not even include so much of the good fortune he possessed: caring and attentive parents, health even through the perilous years of early youth, an estate that freed him from all financial cares. These had ever been such a part of his existence that he scarcely understood them as separate from himself.

He did, however, give thanks for those blessings he was more conscious of receiving. Young Fitzwilliam had hoped very much for a sister, and just as he had reached an age when any future siblings seemed unlikely, his mother had unexpectedly presented the family with Georgiana. Like most boys above the age of ten, he could not allow himself to be wholly preoccupied with a baby sister, but whenever he was home from school, he doted on her as much as his youthful dignity allowed.

(Never had he been as eager to have a brother, and Darcy had occasionally reflected upon why this would be. It pained him to recognize that this might have been that the need for boyish companionship had been fulfilled by the steward's son, George Wickham. His memories of Wickham had been stained by what came to pass in later years—but there had been a time when they were not so unlike brothers. How sad, that all should have ended as it did!)

Other gifts he recognized, as the years went on: the Oxford

education that had broadened both his mind and his acquaintance, his parents' survival into his early adulthood, and friendships with such men as George Knightley and Charles Bingley. Thus he had been ill-prepared for any refusal of his heart's desire when Elizabeth Bennet had rejected his first proposal—yet even this, Darcy came to see, had proved to be invaluable to his happiness. Had she not spoken her mind fully, not called his attention to the defects in his character, they could never have shared so strong a union. His love had not been denied, merely delayed.

In truth, it could be said that Fitzwilliam Darcy had only ever faced one great unfulfilled wish in his life: his longing for a daughter.

He cherished each of the three sons Elizabeth bore him, but they had both so hoped that a little girl would come to join them. Yet, as the years went on, slowly he and Elizabeth had come to realize that their family was complete. Given their boys' health and strength, this could not be mourned . . . but there remained within Darcy a need he could not have named, the need for such tenderness as the age would only allow a father to give to a daughter.

Then Susannah had come into their lives, first on its periphery, then more and more. Wickham and Lydia's lack of interest in her had allowed Darcy to bring the girl into his home, to rear her with every privilege and pleasure, and to love her almost as though she had been born to them. Given that Susannah strongly resembled the Bennet side of her family, Elizabeth could so easily have been her mother. After Lydia's death from smallpox, Susannah had come to live with them with no definite date to return to her father, and for the longest time, it had seemed that date would never arrive.

Darcy had never fully understood the circumstances that had led Wickham to change his mind—with such fatal consequences for Susannah—until this night.

"What can you mean?" he said to Jonathan. "How could you have been responsible for Susannah's death?"

His eldest son faced him; the moonlight revealed Jonathan's face to be pale and drawn. Their horses shifted restlessly between them, recognizing the unease of their riders. "I mean," Jonathan said, "that while I was visiting the family here in Hertfordshire, I had occasion to be at the Brookses' vicarage at the same time as Mr. Wickham. Aunt Kitty—she always had more time for him than the rest of the family, as you recall—"

"Do not digress." Darcy could scarcely recognize his voice as his own.

This seemed to brace Jonathan, for he continued more forthrightly. "In those days, I had not made as much of a practice of understanding how others behave. It did not occur to me that Mr. Wickham would take such great offense to hearing that Susannah had begun to call you Papa."

"So it was you who told him."

"Yes, Father."

Wickham's letter had explained why he demanded Susannah back, more or less: *You have taken from me a great deal through the years, Darcy. You stole the parish that ought to have been my living. You stole your sister's love from me and the marriage I ought to have had. You stole from me the choice to marry any other and perhaps improve my position by forcing me to wed Lydia. I will not have you steal my daughter, too. Never again will she address you as her father! Susannah will know who her true father is, and precisely how he has been wronged by you and your family.*

The majority of these accusations were both familiar and unjust. It was the final point that had been new, and had proved disastrous. For Susannah had at that time only just recovered from a putrid fever, one that had greatly weakened her. Darcy and Elizabeth had summoned physicians, had rubbed her limbs and kept her room warm and free of drafts, and prayed day and night until at last the little girl could sit up once more, could speak, could wish to hear stories. On the very day Wickham's letter had arrived, she had even begun to smile again.

Darcy had delayed Susannah's return for two weeks. His reply to Wickham had included no rebuttals to the man's petulant grievances, only the information regarding Susannah's illness and the need for her to recover more fully before traveling. This had produced only an even more furious response.

Ultimately, they had sent Susannah away warmly dressed, in their finest carriage, with a nurse to tend her and a basket of good things to eat. (The nurse had been paid to remain at the Wickham home, but returned almost immediately, informing the Darcys that Mr. Wickham had not even allowed her to enter the dwelling.) They had thought Wickham would see Susannah more burden than possession ere long, that she would be sent back very soon.

Wickham had not bothered to write and tell them of her death until Susannah was already in the cold ground.

"I should have understood," Jonathan said. "Wickham's pride—I knew enough of that to have been more cautious."

Darcy had been so open with his son, who had hidden so much from him. "Yes, you knew. You should have been. And it is Susannah who paid the price for your error. The dearest price, I should say, for your mother was very nearly killed by her grief." Of his own grief, he did not trust himself to speak.

Jonathan exhaled sharply, a sound Darcy recognized from the first days following the duel, when Jonathan's wound had still been fresh. "I have repented of it every day since."

"Repent of it you should." Darcy had nothing more to say to Jonathan. Shock, anger, and sorrow battled for dominance within his breast, and he knew only that he could not bear even to look at his son—his beloved son—one moment longer.

He rode to put up his horse. Jonathan had tact enough

to wait to do the same until Darcy had entered Longbourn, foisted off the Bennets with the bare minimum of civility, and shut himself up in his room.

The next morning dawned gray and harsh, which befit Juliet Tilney's mood. She had lain awake again, wondering what on earth she was to do once this mystery had been solved and her visit at Netherfield therefore come to an end.

If Juliet attempted to return to Gloucestershire, her grandfather would strip her father of his living and cast out the entire family from their home. Her father would eventually have an independent fortune from his mother's estate—but only after her grandfather died, and General Tilney remained in dismayingly good health. Juliet did not doubt that the kindly Mrs. Bingley would allow her to remain, perhaps in perpetuity, but to request as much was to invite a family quarrel that would no doubt cause the Bingleys much strife. Aunt Eleanor was not as beholden to General Tilney as was Juliet's father, as her husband held both estate and title, but there, too, would come a family rift likely to be of great duration.

Beyond her own family, Juliet had only one intimate friend with whom she might have been able to stay indefinitely—Marianne Brandon of Devonshire. Twice, Juliet's investigations had overlapped with the Brandon family, and both Colonel and Mrs. Brandon had proven their true friendship and proclaimed their lasting gratitude. However, Marianne's most recent letters had included hints that she was soon to be delivered of her second child. Juliet could scarcely invite herself to another woman's confinement. She fretted on this until the sun had risen far enough in the sky that she need feel no qualms about ringing for the maid to make her ready.

This, in turn, reminded her of poor Becky. As Juliet's stays were draped around her, she asked the new maid, Kate, "Are they very sad belowstairs?"

"About Becky, miss?" Kate sighed. "She was always fun to have around, ready to do anything. But there's those as say she poked her nose in where it didn't belong, and that's why she's come to a bad end."

Juliet had considered this. If Becky had truly known who killed Mr. Hurst, and had been willing to keep that secret for the sake of money, then it could not be denied that this was sinful. Yet, in her newly disowned state, Juliet could better appreciate how someone might jump at a comfortable living that would otherwise be forever denied her.

However, that had been a matter of not speaking. "Poking one's nose in" would refer to action rather than inaction, would it not? "Where did they think she was poking her nose in, exactly?" Juliet asked. "If you don't mind telling me."

Kate shrugged. "She was talking with upstairs folk too much of late. It's one thing to exchange a friendly word now and again, like you and me here, but over and over? Just asking for trouble, I say."

"Who, exactly, was Becky speaking with? Do you know?"

"Well, she was delivering messages for Mrs. Hurst. Why Mrs. Hurst had so much to say she couldn't say in the post, I could not begin to guess, but Becky carried notes for her at least three times. I know she *delivered* at least one message to Mr. Lofton."

Is this more evidence of a connection between Mrs. Hurst and Mr. Brooks? Juliet wondered. *But who should be attempting to contact Mr. Lofton in secret?*

Kate, having warmed to her subject, continued as she buttoned the back of Juliet's dress. "Seems as Mrs. Lofton must have found whatever note it was, because Stewart and I saw her giving Becky a piece of her mind once, maybe the day before Mr. Hurst died." She paused as she finished, then added, "Of course, Becky talked to Mr. Bingley for a bit the day before she died, but that's not so unusual, I would suppose."

"Thank you, Kate," Juliet said. She had been given much to think upon, and her mind, weary of its own troubles, was eager to return to the investigation at hand.

No sooner had she descended to breakfast than Jonathan Darcy arrived at Netherfield. Juliet's first response was joy at seeing her beloved—then an eagerness to talk through much of what she had just learned—but as he sat at the table near her, she saw how very much downcast he was. "Mr. Darcy?" Juliet said. "I trust you slept well?"

"I do not think I slept a single hour, Miss Tilney." This was not mere wit, she realized; something weighed heavily on his heart, even more heavily than anything of which she had already heard.

They should have to absent themselves very shortly, she realized. Her first impulse was not merely to hear Jonathan's troubles but also to share her own. Could they not console each other, find greater strength together than either could alone?

Yet Juliet feared that perhaps they could not. Jonathan could become overwhelmed so very easily, and if a surfeit of sound and movement could undo him, how much more difficult must it be for him to bear troubles that would strain any person to extremity? So she resolved to carry her own burden alone for a time longer, the better to aid he whom she loved.

Jonathan was grateful for the speed and tact with which Juliet hastened their retreat into the study, for his spirits were too low for much pretense at normality. How glad he was that he had long ago told Juliet the whole truth regarding Susannah! He did not think he could've borne recounting it all again.

"You are not to blame," Juliet insisted gently. "Your mistake was made in innocence."

"No, I did not know how angry Mr. Wickham would be, but I *ought* to have known."

"Many would have suspected he would be displeased to hear of his daughter's change of affections, all the more because he would have known that change to be justified. But I can scarcely believe that anyone would believe a father to risk his daughter's life for that alone. The extremity of Mr. Wickham's response, the unfeeling selfishness he then displayed—*that*, I do not think any person would have expected."

"My father does not see it so," Jonathan said. "He turned from me as though he never again wished to see me. Perhaps he does not. Perhaps he will always and forever think of me first as the person who caused Susannah's death."

Juliet shook her head. "You are his beloved son. He will know that again. In truth, I am sure he knows it even now. You must give him a chance to reckon with the grief he must still feel for your poor cousin."

"I hope you are right. You usually are."

She reached out her hand, giving Jonathan the choice of whether or not to take it. He found that he did wish for physical contact—that he would find such comforting, rather than distressing—but felt as though he were on the precipice of being overcome. So he moved very slowly to take her hand in his, to raise it toward his face, and then, very gradually and gently, to press it against his cheek. In that moment, for the first and last time in some while, Jonathan felt some measure of true peace.

Once he had calmed himself, Juliet told him of her conversation with the maid that morning. "The delivering and receiving of messages, we ought to have guessed at before," she said. "It would, for instance, explain why Mrs. Hurst sometimes ventured out of doors early in the mornings."

"I saw her once returning in a carriage, also early in the day," Jonathan replied. "Perhaps that, too, was a day on which she had important information to convey—most likely to Mr. Brooks—but Becky was caught up in her duties and unable to help."

"We should speak to everyone about their conversations with Becky, to learn more about what sorts of messages she carried."

Jonathan saw the sense in this immediately, but found he could not abide the thought of remaining in Netherfield throughout the day. The previous night's turmoil had rendered him both weary and restless. Worse, his father was likely to come to Netherfield no later than afternoon. They had avoided each other this morning, and Jonathan felt sure the desire to continue such avoidance was mutual.

When he explained as much to Juliet, she reflected for a few moments before saying, "You cannot forever delay meeting your father again, but perhaps it is best that you both have some time to gain calm."

"I should go into Meryton," Jonathan suggested. "We have not done so thus far, but I could confirm that those who have claimed to be at that town on certain days were in fact there." Already they had confirmed goings and comings with the groom, but it did not follow that because a person had left Netherfield, they had necessarily gone to Meryton; other destinations were possible, and could prove enlightening.

Juliet agreed immediately. "You must also find out more of this Mrs. Mount. If she is the 'Nancy' of which your uncle and aunt have both referred—"

"It could have nothing to do with the murders," Jonathan

said. The mere thought of duplicity from his uncle unnerved him.

Understanding this, Juliet replied, "Then more investigation of it is for the better, so that Mr. Bingley's innocence could be proved."

So it was that by midmorning, Jonathan had ridden into Meryton. In his boyhood, he remembered the place as bustling and lively, and his mother had often said that during the militia's stay there, Meryton had very nearly become a city. Yet it seemed quiet to him now, almost sleepy. Was this merely because he had more basis for comparison? Or were more people leaving Meryton than being born into it?

This demographical question, though mildly interesting to Jonathan, was a matter for another day. He went from inn to pub to stable yard, asking those in employ there about persons from Netherfield who had been seen about of late. Mr. Burton, the steward, had indeed come through on business for Mr. Bingley, though no one knew for what. Both Mr. Lofton and Mrs. Hurst had been seen traveling through town on the western road that led toward the church.

Next to the church was the vicarage inhabited by his aunt Kitty and Mr. Brooks.

I believe the Brookses have played a bigger role in this than Juliet and I had yet reckoned with, Jonathan thought.

Finally he resolved to stop at the shop operated by Mrs. Mount, to determine whether Mr. Lofton had in truth purchased items there on the day he claimed . . . and to see whether this "Nancy" could possibly be the one who might have come between his uncle Bingley and aunt Jane.

Chapter Seventeen

Juliet, left to her own endeavors at Netherfield, began her inquiries as soon as Jonathan had ridden away. Besides her desire to find definite answers for the sake of the Bingleys, she required no more time alone with her thoughts, which at present were not easy company.

First she spoke to Mr. Bingley, who remained as cordial as ever. "Poor Becky! Yes, I suppose I would have spoken to her at some point during those days. You must not think it a slight on Mrs. Mulgrew that I sometimes speak with the parlor-maids, the kitchen maids, and the like. She is an excellent housekeeper and well able to manage on her own. Yet when I have a minor thought or request, I find it more expedient and more natural to simply speak directly with the servant at hand."

General Tilney, Juliet felt certain, had never spoken to any but the most senior staff at Northanger Abbey even once in his life. "Of course, sir. Do you remember what you asked Becky about in particular?"

Mr. Bingley had to consider. "I believe I asked her how she liked being a lady's maid, if it was still an ambition of hers. My idea was that, if she did, I would see whether she might assist Miss Allerdyce or Miss Priscilla during their stay. The Allerdyces generally only travel with one maid for both girls, you see. Alas, it was not to be."

Can he possibly be as kindly a man as he seems to be? Juliet wondered. *Is anyone so truly and wholly good?*

Mrs. Lofton came next. She, more than most persons at

Netherfield, had become only more anxious over time rather than less. (Although all others in the house possessed some uneasiness, each day without an additional poisoning or other violence no doubt reassured them that they did not seem to be among the murderer's targets.) When asked about her confrontation with Becky, Mrs. Lofton was much offended. "How can it be any of your business how I speak to the servants in the house of my brother? When you are just a guest, and at that—but *there*, it is best to be silent."

Such a minor jab as this no longer counted for much with Juliet. "It is your brother who has charged me with discovering who murdered Becky, and all those who spoke with her in the days before her death might have valuable insights to share."

Unfortunately, Mrs. Lofton was little mollified by being thought valuable or insightful. "The girl was too familiar. She spoke to her betters as though they were her equals. In particular, I caught her speaking to my husband, and near our bedchamber! Many a servant girl has sought to entrap a wealthy man, Miss Tilney. You are no longer too innocent to learn that."

This information was not new to Juliet. Furthermore, she understood that more often it was wealthy men who "entrapped" young women who relied on them for their livelihoods. Yet Juliet sensed that this was not a problem Becky had suffered, bright and cheery as she had been; certainly she had not been oppressed during the final few days of her life. "So you were objecting to her behavior, no more?"

Mrs. Lofton scoffed. "What else could there be to say to such a creature? I saw the game she was playing and put a stop to it."

That could have been done in more than one way, Juliet realized. Had Mrs. Lofton simply chosen her words unwisely, or had that been a telling slip of the tongue?

Mr. Lofton's reaction to being asked was gentler and more rueful. "I remember speaking with the girl on two occasions in particular—anything beyond that would have been too commonplace to recall. Once, I asked her to take a note to Mrs. Brooks."

Although married men and women might, with propriety, correspond with persons of the opposite sex not their spouse, it was generally understood that such communication must be of the most respectable nature: a mother eager for news from her son's tutor, perhaps, or a man giving family news to his brother's wife, or other messages of that nature. Juliet knew no such pretext existed between Mr. Lofton and Mrs. Brooks. "Will you tell me the subject of your letter, sir?"

"It was a letter of apology," Mr. Lofton confessed. "My wife had been rather sharp with her—she is sharp with many, as you will have noted." Juliet had very recent proof that this was true. "I felt that I ought to have interceded on the night in question, curbed Mrs. Lofton's excesses, taken her up that we might retire early. Instead I did not, and I believed Mrs. Brooks to be very much wounded. I apologized for both my wife's behavior and my own negligence."

A letter of apology was perfectly respectable, though Juliet thought that might more easily have been sent through the post, or simply handed to Mrs. Brooks with discretion while all the family was together. This, however, she kept to herself. "On what other particular occasion did you speak with Becky?"

"Well." Mr. Lofton appeared even more sheepish than before. "It seems my wife saw me hand the note to Becky and drew the wrong inference. She scolded the poor girl within an inch of her life. For this, too, I felt obliged to apologize. That was the day before she died—small a thing as it was, Miss Tilney, I am glad I spoke. I should not like to have left that apology unsaid."

Last came Mrs. Hurst, whose sentiments regarding the interrogations were not improving with practice. "Why would you not ask all your questions at once, instead of bothering everyone all the time?"

"I beg your pardon, Mrs. Hurst, but we cannot ask questions about events before we have learned of them. We only very recently heard that you had been in conversation with Becky shortly before her death."

"She took down some of my things to be dyed black," said Mrs. Hurst, who evidently still very much resented the dark garb she would be obliged to wear for an entire year more. "I gave her very specific instructions, in case Mrs. Mulgrew should forget. And little good it did! Did I tell you what became of my lace cap?"

"You have indeed mentioned it, ma'am."

Jonathan returned in somewhat better spirits than when he had left, for he had learned at least one fact of value. To judge by Juliet's brighter smile, she had as well. Though, perhaps, this might be attributed primarily to the pleasure of the reunion alone.

Yet their discussion was not to be a private one, for Jonathan had no sooner dismounted than Mr. Isaac Lucas was seen to be approaching Netherfield as well. He of course greeted Miss Allerdyce with great affection, but he had not come primarily to visit her. "I am sure you understand why I have been so distracted, these past several days," he said, all smiles. "Indeed, I am very certain of it."

Has he guessed? Jonathan thought with alarm—before realizing that Mr. Lucas did not allude to the actual secret engagement to Juliet, only their evident affection for each other.

Mr. Lucas continued, "Yet my happiness cannot erase my

duty. Let us discuss the investigations, as I am sure you have made much progress."

So it was that Jonathan, Juliet, and Mr. Lucas gathered in the study. He spoke first, explaining that all errands in town seemed to hold true, including the fact that Mr. Lofton had bought a few things from Mrs. Mount. "Mrs. Nancy Mount," he said, with a significance only Juliet would understand, "is a widow almost seventy years of age, who has continued running the shop her husband founded. This she has done mostly on the strength of her renown as a mantua maker, from which flows dealing in fabric, ribbons, gloves, and the like."

Juliet sighed with evident relief, which Jonathan shared. Whatever truth lay behind his uncle's secretive behavior, they need fear no indiscretion with the elderly dressmaker.

"Yes, Mrs. Mount manages quite capably," Mr. Lucas said. "Strange though it may seem to have a woman in charge of a business, both she and the shop are so familiar in Meryton that no one thinks much of it, here."

"Many dressmakers and milliners are women who govern their own concerns," said Juliet, "but I digress. Now let me tell you of what I have learned."

Jonathan listened to Juliet's report alongside Mr. Lucas. When she had told all, he agreed. "It is strange that Mr. Lofton should send a letter to Aunt Kitty via a servant or, at least, a servant who would not generally be tasked with delivering notes and such to other houses."

"I thought of this," Juliet said, "but I also know that here at Netherfield, servants may trade certain tasks once in a while. Perhaps it was no more than that."

Mr. Lucas cleared his throat. "May I interject?"

"Of course, Mr. Lucas," Jonathan said. "As magistrate, you have granted us authority to investigate, but you have not surrendered your own."

"I should not say this, as a man so recently and happily engaged," Mr. Lucas said, "but it seems to me from my reading of the London and Manchester papers that in most cases, where violence is done to a person by someone of their acquaintance—the nearer the acquaintance, the greater the danger. In other words, no one is so likely to murder a husband than his wife. Vice versa, of course, but that is not the situation at hand."

Juliet said, "You mean that, in your opinion, our suspicion should first go to Mrs. Hurst."

Little as Jonathan liked Mrs. Hurst, and knowing as he did that it was his duty to be as open with Mr. Lucas, he nonetheless found it difficult to say the next aloud: "She seems to have some manner of connection with Mr. Brooks that cannot be spoken of openly, and about which she has gone to some efforts to be secretive."

"Presumably Mr. Brooks has been secretive as well," said Juliet, "but if so, he is much better suited to deception."

"Good heavens," said Mr. Lucas, evidently considering the possibility. Jonathan had only ever felt true attraction toward Juliet Tilney, but he understood what elements society considered to be beautiful. Mrs. Hurst possessed these in abundance despite her years. Mr. Brooks would be, he guessed, not so very much younger than she.

Juliet's thoughts must have been very like, for she said, "Mrs. Hurst always dresses very well, and her hair is immaculately styled. She cares for nothing but wine and cards—in other words, for fun, of a certain sort. I even suspect that she"—Juliet lowered her voice yet further—"dabbles in rouge."

Cosmetics! These were meant to be solely the province of actresses and prostitutes. Then Jonathan wondered why he should find that shocking while also considering Mrs. Hurst as potentially capable of murder.

"The appeal of Mr. Brooks is, I confess, less apparent to me," Juliet continued. "He is not an ill-favored gentleman, but he wears his years heavily. However, it is certain that Mrs. Hurst still wishes to be appealing."

"He also enjoys cards," Mr. Lucas pointed out. "That is not much—"

"Still, it could have been a beginning," Juliet concluded.

Jonathan considered the plight of his aunt Kitty. "The others are all very careful of Mrs. Brooks. Perhaps they suspect something—or, at least, know that she is sad."

"Sad, and also angry," Juliet said. "If this be true, who could wonder at it?"

Meanwhile, Mr. Fitzwilliam Darcy—incapable of yet facing his son, much less the entire lot currently housed at Netherfield—found himself obliged to remain at Longbourn. From this, the extremity of his need for privacy could readily be surmised.

Unsurprisingly, Mrs. Bennet did not surmise it. "We do not have much to offer you at luncheon," she said, "as we do not take much food at midday. Nothing like you must have at Pemberley. I wager you offer pheasant and goose nearly every day!"

His mother-in-law's belief in Pemberley as an equal to Xanadu, a place from which all earthly pleasures might flow had not been shaken by her many visits, during which she had been generously—yet quite normally—entertained. "Not at all, madam," Darcy said. His voice sounded flat, even to himself. "We dine lightly at midday as well."

"Well then, let us do so, too!" Mrs. Bennet said, forgetting in her zeal to please her wealthiest son-in-law that she had already explained this to be their plan. Mr. Darcy did not trouble to correct her, and Mr. Bennet was so absorbed in his newspaper that he did not even hear.

Darcy had first seen Susannah in this very house, when she was scarce a year old. Lydia, feeling herself much burdened without the luxuries of nurse or nanny, had come to stay with her parents. Mr. Bennet, by this time, had possessed grandchildren enough to be happy and yet reasonable regarding the arrival of another. Mrs. Bennet, on the other hand, could scarcely contain herself, for Lydia had always been her favorite, and she could not be made to see—or could not be made to admit to see—the many deficits in Mr. Wickham's character. A child born to them both had pleased her no end.

"Look, Mr. Darcy," she had said just after his arrival on that occasion, coming toward him with Susannah in her arms. "Is she not an angel? Have you ever seen such a darling little girl?"

"No, madam," he had said, in all truth.

Darcy's gaze traveled to the place in the room where they had been standing when Mrs. Bennet showed her off, and for one terrible moment, he thought he might lose all composure.

Then the sound of a carriage drew their attention. This proved to be the modest equipage of Kitty Brooks, who had arrived with an apple pie.

"Well, at last you have remembered us," said Mrs. Bennet. "Jane is forever bringing nice things to eat and drink, or flowers cut from the gardens, but it has been a long time since you favored us in this fashion."

"Jane has gardens," Kitty replied. "She has such a large staff that people can make more food than she and her guests could ever eat."

"Now, now, child," Mr. Bennet said. "Do not begrudge your sister her position. As the Good Book tells us, and your own husband has recited from the pulpit, 'A sound heart is the life of the flesh: but envy the rottenness of the bones.' Is not that correct, my dear?" At this, Mrs. Bennet—who possessed only commonplace piety and no learning—attempted to look as though she, too, had had the verse upon the tip of her tongue.

Though a clergyman's wife, Kitty seemed to take little solace from the Bible. She took the pie through to Pine with no further comment. As Kitty returned, Mrs. Bennet said, "Will you go to Netherfield again today, Kitty?"

"Yes, I will." With that, Kitty smiled more broadly, more happily, than Darcy was accustomed to seeing upon her face. "May I take a message from you to Jane?"

As Mrs. Bennet began reciting the many necessities her eldest daughter was to send, Darcy reflected upon what he had just witnessed. It struck him as odd that Kitty should be so openly envious of Jane—and yet so happy to go to Netherfield, the very embodiment of the wealth and luxury Jane Bingley possessed but Kitty Brooks did not.

I should speak of this to Jonathan, Darcy thought, before catching himself and remembering that he could not trust himself to speak with his eldest son today, or for some time to come.

The afternoon did indeed pass pleasantly at Netherfield. Jonathan went to the library. Juliet did not follow, both to avoid attracting comment and because she understood that Jonathan intended to soothe himself by reading some of the ancient Roman history that so intrigued him. He had explained that, when he gave his full attention to the subjects that interested him the most, it felt as though all else in the world dropped away. She could not blame him for wishing it to do so, not after the terrible conversation with his father.

Juliet had meant what she had said to her fiancé: She fully believed that Mr. Darcy would forgive his son, and sooner rather than later. The first reaction of a man who has lost a daughter in all but fact could not be expected to be rational, moderate, well judged. Nor could it be expected to endure forever.

Juliet instead took her place in the drawing room, choosing the seat nearest Miss Allerdyce. Mr. Lucas had only just departed, and Frederica's happiness nearly shone from her.

"You are very well, it seems," Juliet began.

"Never so well in all my life!" Frederica moved closer to Juliet on the divan. "However, my mother—though she has consented to the union—is not satisfied. I believe she wished me married to nobility, regardless of my own sentiments or those of whatever hapless nobleman she contemplated as my future husband. And now I know as never before how ruthless she can be in such matters. What a cruel thing they did to Aunt Jane!"

"Your father has consented to the match with Mr. Lucas, however, and so your happiness is assured." Juliet could not resist a sigh.

Frederica, in an even lower voice, said, "Where parents genuinely desire the happiness of their children, they will do right in the end. I am trying to believe that of my mother, and . . . I should not say it, but . . . I will believe it of Mr. Darcy, too."

Her kindness moved Juliet greatly. "Your sister would not wish it so."

"Priscilla's heart is untouched. Of that I am certain. She wishes only to please our mother, who is not easily pleased." Frederica's smile faltered slightly. "Yet more troubles you, does it not?"

Although Juliet trusted Frederica implicitly, she knew she could not confess having been disowned. It would be wrong to tell anyone before she told Jonathan—and yet she could not tell Jonathan until he was less distressed, lest he become overwhelmed. She said only, "My position is a difficult one for my family to understand."

"It is all just as Aunt Jane said last night," Frederica replied. "A trick was played on you. That is all."

"When others see it as you do," Juliet said, "how happy I shall be!"

The two young women speaking so earnestly upon the divan did not notice that, in the doorway at the far end of the room, Mrs. Allerdyce and Mrs. Hurst stood together, observing.

"If only we could hear them!" Mrs. Hurst whispered.

Caroline Allerdyce—who, whatever her faults, was not given to eavesdropping—frowned at her sister. "Do not be *common*, Louisa. I imagine they are discussing lace and flowers and all other accoutrements of a wedding. Frederica, for the poor marriage she has stooped to, and Miss Tilney, for the exalted marriage she aspires to still. This, although the elder Mr. Darcy clearly cannot bear the sight of her!"

Mrs. Hurst hooked her arm through Caroline's, a gesture of affection that had not been offered for a very long time. "We must stand firm, and we must stand together."

"Of course," said Caroline, pleased by this show of loyalty, though she could not understand to what Mrs. Hurst specifically referred. "Yet what can we do but wait?"

Mrs. Hurst drew Caroline away, into the hallway, whispering, "Perhaps it is time for a . . . sisterly conspiracy."

Chapter Eighteen

Caroline Allerdyce had spent more of her life in Meryton and its environs than she would have readily admitted even to herself. Within Netherfield, she could pretend the country folk and their country manners were much farther away than in fact they were. It followed that, while she attended such local functions as passed for "society," she made few friends and called on nearly no one. Caroline had even prided herself upon this, as it had never occurred to her that the people of Meryton might have as little use for her company as she had for theirs.

So it felt strange, very strange indeed, to summon her family's coach and horses from the stables in order to go into Meryton—but so her sister had asked.

"The engagement between Frederica and Mr. Lucas is indeed unfortunate," Mrs. Hurst had said, patting Caroline's arm as they walked through one of the long hallways at Netherfield. "Mr. Allerdyce does not comprehend it, I know. Men are not always so mindful of such things, are they? Let me do what I can to improve the situation for your family. Let them see what others see."

From this, Caroline understood that Mrs. Hurst would speak to Mr. Allerdyce about the evils of the match between Frederica and Mr. Lucas. Instead of an argument between husband and wife, this could perhaps be a rational conversation about the expectations of society. If Frederica could be persuaded to call off the engagement herself, or

Mr. Allerdyce to do so for her—before they had written any of their other family or friends, so soon that no one would suspect impropriety—then all could yet be made right. Caroline hoped for this, but even more did she hope that, when Mr. Allerdyce heard Mrs. Hurst, he would realize that these concerns had merit.

Then, perhaps, he would think better of her again.

As the carriage made its way into Meryton, Caroline observed the autumnal gold settling over the countryside. Leaves had not yet begun to fall, but they trembled and rustled upon their branches. Yet the autumn flowers still bloomed—gentian peeking pink from the greenery, violet-blue harebells drooping low, and bright yellow hawkbits studding the ground with sunbursts. She remembered noticing them the very first time she had come to Netherfield in the very same season . . .

It struck her that, at that time, she had been more interested in the reactions of the people they drove past, how awed and envious they must feel to see so fine a carriage, such elegant people! Caroline did not feel that way any longer, but she had not reflected upon why this might be.

She reached her destination, Meryton vicarage, in the middle of visiting hours—yet when Caroline was received by Mrs. Brooks, she found the lady much surprised to have a caller. "Is it so very strange that I should come, Mrs. Brooks?" Caroline asked. "I had not thought I would startle you so."

"I am not startled," Mrs. Brooks insisted. "It is only that the day is so gray, I should hardly have thought anyone would venture out of doors."

The sky, though cloudy, was not so gray as that. Caroline was so accustomed to the inanities of customary visiting discourse that her mind remained at liberty enough to notice other potential reasons for Mrs. Brooks's isolation. Meryton vicarage, though not deficient in its size and in repair, nonetheless remained plain and cheerless within. All furnishings had clearly arrived in the house decades before the Brookses would have resided there. Though old-fashioned, the furniture might easily have been freshened with new upholstery, but every seat and arm showed signs of wear. This could not be the fault of Mrs. Brooks's housekeeping, for the residence was immaculate; Caroline thus attributed it to a lack of taste, and was not surprised.

Mrs. Brooks mentioned that her husband was visiting a sick member of the parish, in what Caroline took to be a rare display of attention to his larger clerical duties. This was a great relief to her, as otherwise she would have been obliged not only to say hello to him but to attempt to speak with him alone. As it was, however, Caroline had only to wait until Mrs. Brooks had to briefly excuse herself to speak to one of her few servants. This gave Caroline time to slip down the hallway, find the room that could only be Mr. Brooks's study, and place Mrs. Hurst's note upon his desk.

How strange, that they should communicate via letter! Caroline had told herself before, and now again, that this must in some way relate to the death of Mr. Hurst. Perhaps her sister was disguising the grief she actually felt but wished to speak of only to a man of the cloth. Knowing her sister as she did, Caroline could scarcely believe it—but even less could she believe any alternatives.

By the time Mrs. Brooks returned to the morning room, Caroline sat once again in her chair, smiling brightly. The qualms she felt about what she had just done were assuaged by the thought that, even at this moment, Mrs. Hurst would be fulfilling her part of their arrangement; she might come home to find all set right with Mr. Allerdyce, and her family happy once again.

As it happened, Mrs. Hurst was indeed doing her duty to her sister. However, Mrs. Hurst's idea of that duty was not at all what Caroline had conjectured.

Juliet Tilney sat in the drawing room at the little writing desk, finishing the task that had led to her disownment. So adamant had she been about refusing Mr. Follett that she had never got around to actually sending the refusal. This she was resolved to do without further delay.

> *I thank you for your kind offer, and am conscious of the honor you have bestowed upon me. However, I cannot accept. The connection between us could not support a marriage, as I believe you fully understand. Your painting career has suffered due to your own actions; I am not obliged to repair it; if that is an end to your career as a portraitist, then perhaps that is for the best, lest you be tempted to treat another subject as you did me.*
>
> *Your apology is accepted, however, and I do believe you when you say that you did not intend such harm as resulted. With this we must both be content.*

Was this too frank? Young ladies were not supposed to be so firm or forthright in their communications. But as this was in support of a delicacy that society had already decreed Juliet no longer to possess, why should she not speak her mind?

"Why, whom should you be writing to, my dear?" Mrs. Hurst had not spoken until she stood almost at Juliet's elbow, startling her greatly. "Your parents, I am sure. How much you must have to tell them!"

Juliet made sure to angle the paper away from Mrs. Hurst's view. "I am certain they will scarcely believe all that has transpired," she replied, which was certainly true.

Mrs. Hurst tilted her head, as though in thought, then

whispered, "Miss Tilney, I feel I must in decency tell you something I have heard."

"About the murders?" This was a surprising source of investigatory information—or, Juliet wondered, might this be an attempt at deceit by the guilty party herself?

It was neither, as Mrs. Hurst's next words made clear. "No, nothing of the sort. Yet I overheard Charles speaking with Jane last night. It seems he and Mr. Darcy corresponded yesterday."

This will have been about Jonathan, about the death of his little cousin, Juliet thought.

Mrs. Hurst continued, "Mr. Darcy intends to leave for Pemberley very soon, and if his son does not come with him—I fear there will be a great breach between them. Charles was not certain, but he suspected Darcy might even decide to settle his estate on his second son instead."

This was grave indeed. Mr. Darcy seemed to blame Jonathan greatly for the death of Susannah Wickham, far more than was rational. Still, to him the girl had been all but a daughter; such grief could render anyone irrational for a time. What concerned Juliet was how much that blame would hurt Jonathan. "That is very shocking, madam, very unfortunate."

"Too true," said Mrs. Hurst. "You know Mr. Jonathan Darcy well, through your shared endeavors, do you not, Miss Tilney? You should tell him to leave with his father; he is a peculiar sort, but he appears to listen to you. If this is done, the breach might yet be healed."

Juliet found this confusing. Why should shared travel make a difference to the Darcys' grief? She said only, "The investigation must be completed first, ma'am."

"Then tell him to leave as soon as this occurs. Perhaps that will not be too late."

This conversation deepened Juliet's concern for Jonathan but had no other effect. Mrs. Hurst would have been surprised indeed to know this, as she believed she had just scared the girl away from Jonathan Darcy. Why should Miss Tilney continue to scheme for the hand of a peculiar young man who would have no money, no house, nothing to recommend him? Knowing nothing of Susannah or the revelation of Jonathan's unwitting role in her death, Mrs. Hurst had thought it obvious for the Tilney girl to assume his father's anger was entirely her own fault.

How pleased Caroline would be! Though, thinking upon the favor Caroline was performing for her at this instant, Mrs. Hurst knew she had got the better part of the deal.

Of course Fitzwilliam Darcy had made no such proclamations. At that time he remained at Longbourn, unaware of the scheming around him and still greatly preoccupied with his memories of Susannah.

He had spent the morning on horseback, riding for hours with no particular destination in mind, crisscrossing the countryside. Though the day was gray and cool, Darcy found his vigor refreshed by the exercise and his mind calmed by both the bucolic surroundings and the absence of Mrs. Bennet. This, perhaps, was the time to consider Jonathan.

How could you have made such a mistake? Darcy could picture the scene at Meryton vicarage: Wickham lounging about as though he were the master of the house; Kitty scurrying around to please him for Lydia's sake; and Jonathan, guileless, blurting out all that he knew. So clear was it within Darcy's mind that it seemed to him that he could step back through time, into that moment, and stop Jonathan. One step, one careful word, and Susannah's life might have been saved.

It had been so little a thing. That made matters so much the worse, to know the girl had lost her life to so little a thing.

At noontime, Darcy took his horse back to the Long-bourn barn and entered to find Mrs. Bennet upstairs for the day. "For, as she says, her nerves do plague her," explained Mr. Bennet, "though what she has to be nervous of at our time of life, I cannot imagine. The natural assumption would be that no great risk remains to befall us, other than our natural surcease, and for all Mrs. Bennet's aches and complaints, I do not think she has any intention of dying for many years to come."

"Would that intention alone were enough," said Darcy.

"Were that the case, sir, I believe we should still be much plagued with Buonaparte." Mr. Bennet folded his paper. "I must say, Jonathan seems much improved of late. He is less particular, less fastidious, less overbearing regarding his own personal concerns."

"I should not say Jonathan's character has ever been over-bearing. He is particular, yes, but this is a matter over which he has very little control. Accepted as he is, he is a most obliging, dutiful son."

A wag of Mr. Bennet's eyebrows revealed that he still did not believe Jonathan's peculiarities of temperament to be anything but the willfulness of a wealthy young man. Darcy knew Elizabeth had attempted to convince her parents otherwise on many occasions; where she had failed, he would not be successful, and so he remained silent.

Mr. Bennet said only, "You are an affectionate and patient father. Yet I cannot but notice that you seem to have spent the last two days avoiding your son, quite as successfully as he has avoided you. Has there been some manner of disagreement between you? You see that I claim the privilege of the elderly grandfather to pry into matters that are no business of mine."

There could be no question of speaking of Susannah's death with Mr. Bennet; Darcy knew he would be overcome.

He said only, "I would not term it a disagreement. Jonathan and I will speak again when we can be rational again."

"Hm! Well, let me say only this, Mr. Darcy. If this muddle between you and Jonathan pertains to the girl, I must speak as I find and tell you that I like Miss Tilney. She has sense, character, and an elegance of person I find very pleasing. What I like best in her, however, is the same quality I first liked in you."

"I hesitate to ask."

"It was that you valued my Elizabeth for herself," said Mr. Bennet. "As I believe Miss Tilney values Jonathan. This deeper affinity is a far better basis for matrimony than the weighing of various estates and dowries, and certainly superior to mere attraction."

Mrs. Bennet's bell again rang upstairs. As Pine scurried past to see to her mistress, Mr. Bennet sighed and returned to his newspaper, leaving Darcy alone with complicated thoughts.

Jonathan, meanwhile, continued to spend as much time as possible at Netherfield. He was able to meet with Juliet near the end of visiting hours, and accepted from her—with pleasure—the letter to Mr. Follett carrying her refusal. "I cannot be seen to leave it to be posted, of course," she said, "but I would have it sent as soon as possible."

"I shall ride into Meryton to the postmaster's this afternoon," Jonathan promised. The weight of his conversation with his father still lay heavy upon him, she could see, but how bravely he still wished to do his duty! "Have you made any headway this morning? I confess I have not one theory the more to offer."

"Mrs. Hurst and I had a most curious conversation this

morning," Juliet said. She then recounted all that Mrs. Hurst had said.

Jonathan received this news with both shock and dismay. "I knew him to be angry," he said, "but I should never have dreamed my father would go so far as this."

"There is every chance that Mrs. Hurst misunderstood what she heard." Juliet leaned closer to him. "Or there is another possibility we must consider: that the entire tale is nothing but Mrs. Hurst's invention."

"Why should she lie in this matter?"

"To distress you, and therefore to distract you. If Mrs. Hurst is the murderer we seek—or even if she only wishes to conceal the nature of her connection to Mr. Brooks—she has every reason to invent such a story."

Despite his agitation, Jonathan saw the sense of this. Determinedly he thought through exactly what Juliet had told him, then weighed it with what he knew of his father's character. At last he said, "You are correct to doubt Mrs. Hurst, though I could not say whether that is because she imagines too much or invents too much. My father is displeased with me at present, and I could conjecture circumstances in which he would consider such steps—but he would never do such a thing without speaking to me seriously, urging me to correct my conduct. Only after such an effort failed would he consider so drastic a step as this. I am sure of it."

"What circumstances do you conjecture?" Juliet asked. From the tone of her voice alone, Jonathan knew that she felt a secret engagement might constitute reason enough for the breach. Unfortunately—particularly given the distress his father felt regarding Susannah's death and the reasons for it— he tended to agree.

They were speaking together at the far end of the drawing room, while the Allerdyce girls and Mrs. Hurst all chattered away near the door. Aunt Jane sat in the middle, serenely embroidering a handkerchief. All these activities were interrupted by the appearance in the doorway of his uncle, who announced to everyone, "I have been keeping a secret."

Aunt Jane looked up from her needle and thread. "What do you mean, Mr. Bingley?"

Mr. Bingley smiled wide. "You shall have to come and see."

At this Aunt Jane rose, and Mrs. Hurst, Frederica, and Priscilla declared they should have some share in this revelation as well. Jonathan and Juliet shared a look—whatever secret he had been hiding clearly had not been as nefarious as they had feared!

They reached the entry hall just as Mrs. Brooks and Mrs. Allerdyce were announced—Mrs. Allerdyce apparently having brought Mrs. Brooks back to Netherfield with her in the carriage. "Whatever is astir?" Mrs. Allerdyce exclaimed. "Where can you all be going?"

"Did not you notice when you arrived?" Mr. Bingley led them all outside, to see the Allerdyce carriage being taken away . . . and both Burton the steward and the stable master standing on either side of a small gray mare. Aunt Jane gasped, and Mr. Bingley clasped her hand. "Yes, she is for you."

"Oh! How lovely she is!" Aunt Jane hurried forward, though she slowed her steps so as not to startle her new horse. "And I have needed more exercise since poor Nancy died. How lovely indeed!"

"The perfect size for a female rider, would not you say?" Mr. Bingley did not attempt to conceal his delight in having surprised his wife and made her happy.

Jonathan managed to say, "Nancy was the name of her horse?"

If the phrasing of this question struck Mr. Bingley as odd, he did not consider it worth commenting upon. "Jane rode a few days a week when she had Nancy. Your aunt is not a bold rider; she is only truly comfortable upon a smaller horse, and then Burton told me a fellow in Watford might have one that would suit perfectly." He sighed in satisfaction. "How she has missed riding!"

Aunt Jane, still petting her new acquisition, said, "I think a more botanical name would suit her. What do you think of Bellflower?"

"Bellflower she shall be," said Mr. Bingley.

Jonathan and Juliet exchanged a glance that spoke volumes—of his relief, and her wonder, that his uncle had proved to be wholly trustworthy, a man with no secrets more nefarious than a gift for his beloved wife. Juliet murmured, "Becky did mention the horse."

"A lesson for us to discount nothing, and to inquire into everything," Jonathan replied.

Aunt Kitty suddenly turned and stalked into the house, as though she were intent upon something. Her haste, and her unmistakable air of dissatisfaction, drew some manner of attention from all. Jonathan made to follow, but Juliet stayed him, whispering, "Her words, I think, will come more readily to a female hearer."

Kitty Brooks could not think where to go, or what to do, only that she must be alone, away from the scene upon the drive. The drawing room would soon be filled again by the others— the servants had begun readying the dining room for the evening meal—and so she made her way into Mr. Bingley's study, a room she had never entered save to answer questions from her nephew and the Tilney girl. Even as she sank down upon the bench, Kitty realized that Miss Tilney had followed her. "Leave me in peace. I have no time for your questions now!"

Yet Miss Tilney instead sat next to her. "I have no questions now, Mrs. Brooks. Yet I am willing to hear you, if you wish. I think you have needed a listener for a very long while."

To Kitty's horror, tears welled in her eyes. "Mr. Bingley is forever searching for little gifts to make Jane happy. Sometimes I wish my husband would bring me a gift, but then I remember how little it is the thing itself that matters. It is the sentiment behind the gift that I so long for."

Miss Tilney's evident sympathy was a balm, one Kitty needed badly and might have availed herself of at great length, had Jane not then appeared in the doorway.

"Kitty, dearest," Jane said, "whatever is the matter?"

When bitterness is dammed for too long a time, once loosed it will flow beyond any containment. "For you, Jane, nothing is the matter. You have everything, and I have nothing."

"But your children," Jane said. "You have them, and surely they are dearer to you than all else."

"They are in school and gone above half the year. The house is now so quiet." Kitty stared at her eldest sister, who still—still!—held much of her beauty, the silver strands in her hair mixing gently with the gold. "Lydia and I always had to make our own fun, you know. You and Elizabeth cared little enough for us, and Mary cared only for her books."

Jane looked wounded, and Kitty's heart was hard enough to relish it. "Kitty, forgive me if I slighted you. It is only natural that sisters nearer in age should be closer friends to each other. It never occurred to me that you felt neglected by us."

Truly, Kitty had not felt that way often, beyond the ordinary envy of young girls when their elder sisters are first able to put their hair up. Yet in the aftermath of Lydia's elopement, Kitty had come to understand how much their friendship had cost her intimacy with the rest of her sisters, for afterward she often felt much alone.

She did not admit this, saying instead, "I always knew you

would marry well, beautiful as you are. And I always knew Elizabeth was too clever not to catch herself someone eligible. Yet you both married even above my wildest fancies." Kitty wiped her face with her handkerchief. "But then Mary? *Mary?* That she should marry into fortune and position? How could that be so?"

This was not what truly rankled Kitty, not the source of the resentment that had corrupted her sisterly feeling so. It was that even Mary—plain, bookish, staid Mary—had been able to wed for love.

Miss Tilney, perhaps finally recognizing how inappropriate it was to witness such an intimate conversation, rose from the bench. "Forgive me. I did not mean to intrude."

"You did intrude, as did Jane." Kitty got to her feet. Having humiliated herself, she could only think of quitting Netherfield even more swiftly than she had arrived. "I will walk back to the vicarage. The air will clear my head."

Mercifully, Jane did not try to stop her as she left. Kitty was all too aware of the chatter in the drawing room from all others present, as well as the excruciating lowering of that chatter as her footsteps echoed past them. Her cheeks flamed.

Yet as she walked out into the dull October afternoon, unheeding of the wildflowers around her or the gentle breeze, Kitty told herself that even if everyone at Netherfield now knew of her envy and resentment, she had a secret they did not know and never would, no matter how many questions her nephew and Miss Tilney tried to ask.

Chapter Nineteen

The difficulties of the evening began just as the soup course was being served.

Charles Bingley would have been horrified by the thought that he might distress his guests in any way, especially given how disturbing the past weeks at Netherfield had been. If anything, he meant to help. As soon as the tureen of mulligatawny had been put in front of him, he said to his nephew—not speaking too loudly, even in this way attempting to be polite!—"I say, we have neither seen nor heard from your father for days, not since the last night we all dined together. He is neglecting us most shamefully, and I intend to have a word with him."

By this, he meant that he had sensed the tension between the Darcys, recognized that the matter must be of some seriousness, and intended to speak with Darcy as a friend. (Mr. Bingley recognized that Jane's story that night had weighed heavily upon the considerable pride of Fitzwilliam Darcy, but he also knew the man well enough to be certain Jane would not be resented for having told the simple truth.)

However, the comment had quite a different effect on Jonathan than Bingley had intended. "You mean, you have not spoken to my father at all since that night? You have not even corresponded?"

"No, we have had not a word from him," Bingley said.

Miss Tilney had taken a great interest in this as well. "That is very strange, sir," she said, "for just this morning, Mrs. Hurst told me she had overheard you talking about correspondence you had with Mr. Darcy—one that apparently never occurred."

Bingley's first thought was that his eldest sister had misheard him, though he could not imagine what she had actually heard instead. However, Mrs. Hurst's face had taken on an expression he recognized all too well, even from the days when she had been guilty of no worse than stealing biscuits from his plate. She huffed, "It is very rude of you, miss, to bring up a private conversation at dinner."

To Bingley's surprise, Miss Tilney showed no sign of chastisement. "If I have erred against etiquette, no less so have you for telling me of this supposed conversation between the Bingleys. I would also point out that you had erred more gravely by eavesdropping, had the conversation ever taken place, which I now doubt."

The Allerdyce girls and their father were openly staring in amazement; Mr. Lofton seemed amused; Mrs. Lofton alone seemed to take little interest. As for Mrs. Allerdyce, she swiftly interjected, "Regardless, the dinner table cannot be the appropriate place for such remarks as these. Please, Miss Tilney, reserve your questions for my brother's study."

Jonathan said, "You will not silence me, however, for it is my father who was spoken of falsely." He spoke so seriously that all at table were taken aback, and Bingley remembered with unease that Jonathan had recently felt the need to duel for someone's honor. God forbid such would happen again!

Mrs. Hurst blurted out, "Caroline told me to."

"I did no such thing!" Mrs. Allerdyce exclaimed.

"Yes, you did," Mrs. Hurst insisted. "We agreed that—well, that Miss Tilney must go, and soon. That she and her wiles must be kept far away from Mr. Jonathan Darcy. So I told her that he was to be disinherited, knowing that when there was no more chance of a fortune, there would be no more efforts at entrapment."

"Mother!" Frederica exclaimed. "How unkind!"

Mrs. Allerdyce had gone white. "That is not at all what we agreed to, Louisa. You were to speak to my husband about the unfortunate match between Frederica and Mr. Lucas. To make him see sense."

"That is no better!" Frederica looked as though she might weep, and her father reached over to hold her hand.

Mrs. Hurst simply shrugged. "Then we did not understand each other. I apologize to those concerned. I believed I was doing my sister a service, one she was very much set upon."

"It was Mrs. Hurst who suggested she speak to my husband," Mrs. Allerdyce protested. "And she asked for a favor in return—that I might deliver secret correspondence to Mr. Brooks."

"It seems," said Miss Tilney, "that Mrs. Hurst is fond of secret correspondence."

After what seemed to Bingley an interminable pause, Mrs. Hurst rose from her chair and left the table. Jonathan said, "Aunt Jane, please do excuse Miss Tilney and me. It is imperative we speak to Mrs. Hurst immediately."

"By all means," said Jane.

By this time Frederica was weeping openly and left the room as well. Mr. Allerdyce said, florid with anger, "Mrs. Allerdyce, will you join me for a moment?" She did not seem delighted by this suggestion, but she moved to obey it.

"I cannot," Mrs. Lofton said faintly. "It is too much. It is too much."

Mr. Lofton took her arm and helped her up. "My wife is overexcited. Forgive us, please."

With that, Bingley was left alone with his wife and only one guest, his niece Priscilla. After a long and uneasy silence, Priscilla ventured to say, "The soup is delicious."

Let us first follow the Allerdyces to their bedchamber, the only room Mr. Allerdyce trusted for their privacy. As soon as he had shut the door behind them, Caroline began, "I meant only for her to have a conversation with you. No more than that."

"That alone is more than you should have done," he replied. "To deliver secret correspondence? You have to have known that this was wrong, that there could be no moral justification for this sort of message between your sister and Mr. Brooks. Yet you were willing to do so, all because you hoped she might interfere in a match that has already been made for our eldest daughter, a perfectly respectable match that has rendered her very happy. Does your pride truly extend so far? Or does it stretch back even farther, so that you still feel yourself deprived of the title of mistress of Pemberley?"

"It is not that," Caroline said, hoping it was true. "Yet Frederica can do better. You know that is so."

"Here we differ, my dear." The tone of Mr. Allerdyce's voice made the last word less affectionate than Caroline had imagined it could be spoken. "I believe that a match that satisfies both prudence and passion to be the best possible. For so many years, I had believed we made such a match. I do not know whether I can believe this any longer."

Caroline felt as though the floor kept dropping beneath her, settling lower and lower, an unending sense of sinking. "What do you mean?"

Suddenly, Mr. Allerdyce seemed very weary. "I mean, Caroline, that after Frederica has been wed to Mr. Lucas, I intend to travel for a time. Perhaps I shall bring Priscilla along, to broaden her mind and her interests past the trivialities to which you have limited her. I know only that you will not be joining us."

"For how long will you be gone?"

"Months," he said. "At least."

Then he departed to go to Frederica, and Caroline was left alone, her only companion the bitterest of remorse.

Meanwhile, Jonathan and Juliet had followed Mrs. Hurst to her room, where she had barricaded herself nearly as well as the besieged city of Orléans. It took some minutes of persuasion to convince her that her dignity would be more greatly assaulted by questions shouted through a door than by another conference in Mr. Bingley's study.

"I do not wish to speak of it," Mrs. Hurst began, rather unnecessarily in Jonathan's opinion, given how reluctant she had been to quit her bedchamber. "The correspondence between Mr. Brooks and myself is of a private nature."

Jonathan replied, "We have had to ask many questions regarding private matters in this investigation, ma'am, which I will remind you concerns the death of your late husband. Had you told us the truth from the beginning, we might know his killer by now. Or is that precisely what frightens you?"

Mrs. Hurst drew herself upright, despite everything still capable of righteous indignation. "I will not sit here to be accused!"

"Then help us, Mrs. Hurst." Juliet spoke more gently than the events warranted. Why should she suddenly behave so sweetly toward one who had behaved so poorly toward her? "We only want to understand. If you will but give us the truth, then we need trouble you no longer."

This achieved the amazing effect of calming Mrs. Hurst, if not entirely, at least to the point of rationality. "If you must know," she said stiffly, "Mr. Brooks and I have had occasion to correspond because he has won more money at cards than I have had in my possession."

"May I ask how much?" Juliet said.

"Most recently, I lost eight hundred pounds to him."

Jonathan was very much startled. Such a sum was more than he had ever considered risking at a table; he had once won one hundred pounds at Oxford, in a game where the others had urged heavy betting, and his reward had been not only the money but also the severance of the few strands of friendship he had formed there. Yet his surprise was not so great that he failed to notice how Mrs. Hurst had qualified her statement. "'Most recently,' you said. Will you tell us how much you owe Mr. Brooks, in total?"

Mrs. Hurst winced. "Twelve thousand pounds."

That was more than Jonathan's father had as income for a year! Juliet's gasp revealed she was equally surprised as he. "How?" she asked. "How is such a thing possible?"

"It began with a few hundred here or there," Mrs. Hurst said, careless that this alone was a sum greater than most people saw in a year's time. "Mr. Brooks is very good at cards, you know, a cold and disagreeable man but very good indeed. Yet I am good, too! In London, at my friends' tables, I am rarely the poorer. And I know that someday, I shall surely beat Brooks, too. He gives me a tick for my whole debt and lets me bet that as well. More than once, I have cleared my debt to him so— once when it had got as high as fifteen hundred pounds! That was a fine evening."

"Why did you not stop then, madam?" Jonathan said.

The expression upon Mrs. Hurst's countenance made it clear she had never considered such a thing. "It is not enough to be out of debt. I wish to win. Someday I shall win, and get back every penny I have lost to the man and as much again in profit. Until then—why, I must try."

She is a gamester, Jonathan realized, *one of those who cannot ever put down their cards.* This had led to the disgrace of many persons of a higher class than she, and to the ruination of fortunes larger than the one she possessed. Yet reason would do no good here; rational prudence had no part in Mrs. Hurst's decisions. She would always and ever determine it best to play, and no amount of losses would stop her—unless and until she became a bankrupt.

One thing still puzzled him, however. "My uncle does not allow large bets to be placed in his house. He is firmly against gambling such sums."

"Ah, Charles," she scoffed. "He is not nearly so much fun as once he was, I must say. Let me add only that Charles cannot sit at every table set up for cards, nor hear everything said at other tables. Mr. Brooks and I have quite a code together by this point, you see, so even if Charles is with us, sometimes we are able to play for real stakes."

Juliet said, "Did Mr. Hurst know of your debts?"

It took Mrs. Hurst some time to answer. "To some extent. Enough to be displeased. He would be sharp with Mr. Brooks after he won, though Mr. Brooks never took any account of it. Mr. Hurst would sometimes scold those who had lost to me, even were it but a few pounds, because he wished for me to pay Mr. Brooks back very soon. Some night, though, I shall clear the debt in one stroke. How I wish Mr. Hurst could have lived to see it!"

This last bit of sentiment rang false to Jonathan, but he would not challenge it at this time. "Madam, we know that you have sent secret messages from this house before, even that you have traveled into Meryton early in the morning without informing anyone of your plans. Were these all messages to Mr. Brooks, or is there other correspondence of which you wish to inform us?"

"If there is more," Juliet added, still gentle, "tell us now, so that all the unpleasantness can end."

Mrs. Hurst nodded. "He says he will charge me interest. I argue that is not fair. We go back and forth on this matter—on times and methods of payment—I tell you now, that man never tires of speaking of money! Though it is so horribly vulgar."

She was then released to return to her room, there to retrieve her offended dignity. Jonathan and Juliet were left alone. He said, "I feel certain she is telling the truth about the debts. Do you think she is also being honest about the correspondence, that it was solely between them and on that topic?"

"I agree with both your certainty and your doubt," said Juliet. "We have learned at least one more thing of value— Mrs. Hurst and Mr. Brooks were not so intimately connected as we had feared."

For Aunt Kitty's sake, Jonathan was glad of this. "How I wish we were not so lost in this . . . maze of suspicion. Guilt and secrets touch everyone, but surely only one is a murderer. Still we know not what to think."

Juliet considered this for a moment before saying, "Then let us learn what others think."

"What do you mean?"

"Tomorrow morning, let us question everyone again—but this time, we will ask them only one question: Whom do they believe to be guilty?"

At first, to Jonathan, this seemed a terrible dereliction of duty. Why should they ask others to solve a mystery they themselves had not? Yet only a moment's consideration persuaded him of the idea's merit. The guilty person would be among those questioned; the reaction might tell them much.

Juliet suggested that they begin with the two people she and Jonathan both considered to be innocent: the Bingleys.

They went to Mrs. Bingley first, speaking with her in the small room upstairs that she used to speak with her housekeeper and sometimes write letters. "Oh, I could not say," she replied, "for I am sure I do not know."

"You must have wondered, Mrs. Bingley," Juliet said. "It would be impossible not to."

"Of course I have asked myself this, but—Mrs. Hurst has been an intimate of this house for so many years, and though she and I think differently about so many things, surely she would not stoop so low as murder. Mr. Lofton has always been very congenial, very charming, to my family as well as to others in town, and I cannot think how he would benefit from harm befalling Mr. Hurst or poor Becky. And Mrs. Lofton frightens so easily! I should think she would be terrified by the very prospect of something so horrid. As for the Brookses, why, I do not think they could ever slip into Netherfield without being announced." Mrs. Bingley paused, no doubt thinking of Mrs. Brooks's great resentment, but she shook her head. "There is no one, no one at all, that I can bring myself to believe capable of such wickedness."

Jonathan said, "You must realize that at least one person here was capable of it, and remains so."

"I do," said Aunt Jane, "but still, I cannot *believe* it."

Mr. Bingley, though generally as good-natured as his wife, proved to have thought more seriously upon the matter than she. "It pains me to say this," he said in his study, which he had for a few moments reclaimed, "but my thoughts return to Mr. Brooks."

"Truly?" Jonathan said. "Why so?"

"Of course it would be dreadfully difficult for him to enter the house at odd hours—but if he and Becky had been speaking in some way, to this purpose, she could well have let him in," Mr. Bingley pointed out. "But Mr. Hurst had been very difficult with him about some gambling debts involving Mrs. Hurst, very difficult indeed."

Juliet could tell from his tone of voice that Mr. Bingley had no idea of the scale of the debt involved; he considered Mr. Hurst to have been overreacting. Instead, the strife had been occasioned by a sum far greater than others had been willing to kill for. "Do you mean that Mr. Brooks might have been frightened of Mr. Hurst?"

Nodding, Mr. Bingley replied, "Quite possibly. I hate to say it, for Brooks has been Mrs. Bingley's brother-in-law these many years, but he is a cold sort of fellow. Practical to a fault. I do not wish to think him capable of murdering a man to protect himself . . . but I can think of no one else at Netherfield with even so much motive as that."

To Juliet's surprise, Mrs. Hurst appeared more congenially inclined toward the two investigators this morning, talking with them easily over breakfast while no one else happened to be present. Either she felt safe now, because her only secret had been exposed, or she had more reason to want their good opinion. "To my mind, it could only be Mrs. Brooks."

"Why do you think so, ma'am?" Jonathan asked.

"Well, she used poison, didn't she? All know that poison is a woman's weapon. And that servant girl—Betsey or Becky or whatever it was—was she not murdered with a sash? Would a man be likely to choose a satin sash to commit a murder?"

Juliet had to admit this was somewhat persuasive. "Why would you think Mrs. Brooks wanted your husband dead?"

Mrs. Hurst shrugged, nonchalant even in the matter of Mr. Hurst's murder. "Perhaps only to bring scandal to her sister. To somehow shame this house, for she is quite bitter enough for that, let me assure you."

Mr. Lofton they spoke with again in Mr. Bingley's study. "You must look carefully at Mr. Brooks, I think."

This was the first time someone had been named twice, but Juliet was determined not to let this sway her. "Why so?"

"He and Mr. Hurst had some manner of strife between them—I thought it a small thing at the time, but I could well have been wrong. As you know, Mr. Hurst drank to excess, often to a stupor. When not stuporous, however, he could become very angry, very belligerent, make entirely irrational decisions." Mr. Lofton sighed. "Rarely was Hurst in such a state, but when he was, his behavior could become very unnerving indeed. If he threatened Mr. Brooks in that way, Brooks may have believed he must protect himself—at all costs."

Mrs. Lofton proved the most elusive of those they sought to question. Despite the autumnal chill and gusty winds, she had chosen to take a turn along the pathways that lined Netherfield Park. Juliet and Jonathan set out to meet her on the path, Juliet holding on to her bonnet as the wind whipped the edges of her pelisse. Mrs. Lofton must have seen their approach from quite a distance, and yet she made no move to acknowledge them or hurry their meeting. When they reached her side, Mrs. Lofton simply inclined her head. Her gaze remained fixed on the tree limbs lashing the sky overhead and did not lower until Jonathan asked her the fateful question.

"You believe that I know who did this?" Mrs. Lofton said.

"If you knew beyond all certainty, of course you would tell us," Juliet said, omitting the possibility that Mrs. Lofton could be very certain if she had done it herself. "We only want to know what you think."

"I find that an outrageous question. It is you two who have undertaken to determine this, not I, and if you have failed at it, you should admit as much." Mrs. Lofton clutched the side of her bonnet, perhaps to keep her ribbons from lashing her with the wind, perhaps only to keep Juliet and Jonathan from seeing her face. "I will not be baited into accusation. You will excuse me." With that, she walked away.

Once Mrs. Lofton was out of earshot, Jonathan said, "Do you think it means much that she has been the only one to refuse to answer?"

"We will not know," Juliet said, "until we have an answer of our own."

Chapter Twenty

Poison is a woman's weapon.
A cold sort of fellow.
His behavior could become very unnerving indeed.

The many theories Juliet had heard with Jonathan the night before preoccupied her greatly during luncheon. Eager was she to go into Meryton afterward, to visit the Brookses and hear their theories. She found it particularly intriguing that the couple had been named by several persons—this, despite the fact that they would have had to slip into Netherfield.

With Becky's help, that would not have been so difficult, Juliet thought. She had even contemplated the idea that it might have been Becky herself who placed the poison in the coffee cup on the morning of Mr. Hurst's death; the money the killer might have offered her might not have been only to keep silent but also to complete the deed. Becky had seemed so amiable and cheerful that Juliet did not like this thought—but she had met amiable murderers before.

Just as the meal ended, one of the Netherfield servants returned with the post, which included a letter for Juliet. She recognized upon its address her mother's hand, as familiar to Juliet as her own.

"Mr. Darcy," she said to Jonathan, "if you will forgive me, I must read this before we are away to Meryton."

Jonathan seemed puzzled, as well he might be, but he excused her warmly. Juliet hurried up to her bedchamber, cracking the wax seal even as she went through the door.

Dearest Juliet—

We returned home from our travels with Theodosia and Albion to discover first that you had gone to Hertfordshire, then to our great distress the cruel edict laid down upon you by General Tilney. Your father has of course rebelled against this, but your grandfather has thus far held firm, and it is my belief that he will continue to do so.

First I must reassure you that we do not and will not consent to your disownment. We would never do such a thing, ever, under any circumstances; you are our daughter, our firstborn, and more precious to us than we can express. That General Tilney should have been a father himself and yet failed to understand this! His decision says nothing of your character and everything of his.

Do not think that your father and I are so without resource that we must comply with your grandfather's wishes. The copyrights of my last and next books will keep us from poverty; your father's future expectations from his mother's estate may allow us some measure of credit; beyond that, there are other parishes in the nation of England, and not all of them are equally susceptible to the influence of wealth. Your father has already written to the bishop about the possibility of another living, and if worse comes to worst, there is of course the one at Foxley.

Foxley, Juliet knew, was the parish connected to the estate that belonged to her uncle, the viscount Lord Astwick. Sir David and her aunt Eleanor were happily wed; and if her aunt wished for Juliet's family to have that living, it would be so. Yet Juliet also knew that Foxley was a very scanty living indeed. Aunt Eleanor had sighed over the smallness of its vicarage and the difficulty of keeping a parson for very long, for the income produced by the parish was generally not enough to support a family. If Juliet's mother already thought of their moving to Foxley as a possibility, matters were grave. In this way, Catherine Tilney's efforts to comfort and console her daughter worked entirely the opposite effect of what was intended.

Juliet folded the letter and put it in her writing desk, but though she did not carry the paper with her, its burden still lay upon her. She descended the stairs into Netherfield's great hall, where Jonathan waited for her, wearing her best attempt at a smile. Yet within an instant, Jonathan's answering expression had become a frown of confusion. "Are you unwell in some way? Did your letter contain bad news?"

She found she could not lie to him. "Please, Mr. Darcy. We have an important task before us—let us first attend to that, before we discuss any other matters."

"The task is most important," said Jonathan, "and that is all the more reason that we must approach it with clear minds."

Juliet hesitated, but this could not be kept back any longer. "Let us talk in the carriage."

The rain that had begun to patter the countryside this afternoon was their friend, for normally so short a journey would have called only for an open carriage. Instead, the coach had been made ready, and within but a few steps they were both ensconced inside, safe from both weather and prying ears.

As soon as the coach door closed, Jonathan turned to Juliet in concern. "Please, will you not tell me the difficulty?"

"My mother wrote to tell me that neither she nor my father will comply with my grandfather's wishes regarding me. You see, in the last letter my grandfather wrote— Jonathan, I am disowned by him, for rejecting the proposal of Mr. Follett."

His astonishment was great. "Utterly and completely? Merely because you would not marry a man you do not love?"

"Also because I refused to entrap you into marriage." Juliet struggled against tears. "If he but knew! Still, it is done, and I know my grandfather well enough to know that he will hold fast, both against me and anyone in the family who dares to support me. He threatens to take away my father's parish, and if he does so, we shall be nearly penniless. I have proved the ruin of us all."

Jonathan took her hand. "Do not say so. It will not come to this. As you yourself said—if your grandfather knew of our engagement, he would forgive all, would he not?"

She considered this carefully. "Forgive, no, for he is a hard man. Yet his vanity would eclipse his ire in this matter. He would find it very pleasing to be so connected to the Darcys of Derbyshire."

"Then this is but a brief tempest," Jonathan said. "We will reveal the truth soon."

"The break between you and your father—it will not long endure, surely, but—"

"But after you leave Netherfield, you will have no place to go." Jonathan's spirits had sunk as well. "I shall have to inform him earlier than I would have otherwise, to be sure. But perhaps that is for the best. Even in anger, my father would not see you so hard done by. We will find a way, this I promise. I will not see you so hard done by—it is not to be borne, and it shall not be."

Juliet nodded, hoping it to be true. For a moment she simply held Jonathan's hand and watched the raindrops speckling the coach windows. The countryside all around had become blurred, silver, like a transparency that had been too long exposed to the sun.

Then Jonathan said, "Did not your grandfather's last letter arrive some days ago?"

"Yes, but I did not wish to burden you. I know that at times you become overwhelmed, and given the difficulty with your father, I feared it would be too much."

To her surprise, Jonathan said, "You must not ever do this again. You must not hide your fears and travails, only for my sake." He lifted her hand and kissed it; even through her glove, Juliet felt the warmth of his mouth. "Throughout my life, I have had to struggle to be as others would wish me to be. In these past few years, primarily due to our connection, I no longer feel such a great need to do so. Yet I am capable of endeavor, capable through long experience, and there is no purpose more worthy of that endeavor than of supporting and caring for you."

Again Juliet fought back tears, for different and far better reasons. "My dear Jonathan. You are so good."

"Do you promise?" Jonathan said. "You will trust me to be as strong as you may need me to be?"

"I do promise. I do trust you. I trust you more than I have ever trusted any other person, with my very life."

These words touched Jonathan deeply. To be cared for was one thing, to be trusted another—and only in this moment did he realize how little he had been trusted. Almost no one had ever doubted his character, but almost everyone had doubted his capacity. Juliet alone saw him true.

She smiled at him, their hands still joined, and a warm tide of feeling made Jonathan acutely conscious how little he minded being touched by her. How much he actually wished to touch her. This desire had never moved him before knowing Juliet Tilney, and he had but little explored it. Now it struck him afresh that marriage would mean an end to all restraint in such matters. That he had never felt the pain of such restraint so sharply as he did at this moment.

Yet an engagement, even a secret one, allowed for considerably less restraint than before.

Jonathan leaned nearer to Juliet, caressing the hand he held while using his other to trace a fingertip along the line of her jaw. She gasped, in surprise but perhaps for other reasons as well. Certainly she did not pull away.

"I hardly know what to do," he whispered.

His finger found the corner of her small answering smile. "Nor I, sir. Yet I would gladly learn."

He brought his face closer to Juliet's, felt her breath against his lips, and finally dared to kiss her.

At first the touch was strange to Jonathan—thrilling, but strange—and he was not at all sure he was doing things correctly. The delight of it, however, prompted him to try once more, then again. Juliet's mouth seemed to soften against his, her lips parting slightly. Jonathan parted his own, kissed her more slowly, and began to think this might be more the proper way of going about it . . .

And then, as their kiss deepened, Jonathan forgot about such concerns altogether, which was the proof that he had got it right after all.

After a few such moments, they broke apart. Jonathan's breath came quickly, and Juliet's cheeks were flushed. He said the only words his mind could fix upon: "We must marry soon. Very soon."

Juliet laughed, ducking her head as she whispered, "I should like that very much."

The Meryton vicarage remained as cheerless as Jonathan recalled it, and Aunt Kitty admitted them warily. He wondered whether she saw him more as nephew or as investigator. Furthermore, he suspected Aunt Kitty might see Juliet as a young woman angling for the kind of marriage that she herself had failed to make.

His first question seemed to be answered when Aunt Kitty said, "If you come with a message from Jane, tell her none is necessary. She could not scold me any worse than I have scolded myself."

Jonathan could only remember Aunt Jane scolding one person, her youngest daughter, Martha Elizabeth, who had climbed a tall tree and could well have hurt herself. Even that had ended with a tender embrace. "I do not think she would be harsh with you. Regardless, we come on our own business."

When Juliet put the question to her, Aunt Kitty's initial reaction surprised him: She looked almost pleased. Had she been waiting to be asked her opinion about this? Perhaps she had been waiting, in vain, for anyone to ask her opinion about anything.

"I have thought about this a great deal," she said, "as one can scarcely hope to do otherwise, in the circumstances. Of course I do not know, and I would not wish anyone else to take my thoughts for mere gossip."

Jonathan assured her, "We will ask everyone, and their answers will never be heard by any ears but our own."

Aunt Kitty folded her hands in her lap slowly, as though with care. "My suspicion is all for Mrs. Lofton."

"Mrs. Lofton?" Juliet said, a note of surprise in her voice. "Why should you think so?"

"I could not say what did or did not pass between herself and Mr. Hurst, but I know that ever since the murder of Becky, Mrs. Lofton has been behaving very strangely. Perhaps even since Mr. Hurst's death, but we were all in such a shock then that I would say we were none of us entirely ourselves. She has been highly inquisitive about the behavior of all involved, yet very secretive regarding her own."

Jonathan had not forgotten that Mrs. Lofton had been the only one to refuse to answer their question, and upon consideration, he realized that his aunt was correct about the lady's behavior having changed following Becky's death. He ought to have noted for himself that Mrs. Lofton had become quieter and more nervous. Yet was that not a natural consequence, not only of guilt but also of sharing a house with a murderer? "This is the sole basis for your suspicions?"

"It is suspicious enough," Aunt Kitty said, "but I have noticed that Mr. Lofton seems eager to . . . observe her movements, to question her whereabouts. I believe he suspects her, too."

In fact, Mr. Lofton had claimed he suspected Mr. Brooks. Could this have been a falsehood? Merely a way to divert their attention from his wife?

Jonathan had expected more resistance when they went to the church office to speak to Mr. Brooks, but he alone seemed to have been expecting such a question. "It is a great puzzle. I can well imagine that you have not yet worked it out. You have a fine mathematical mind, Mr. Darcy; the equations will be solvable in time."

Juliet said, "Yet we wish to know what you think."

Mr. Brooks steepled his hands before him upon his desk. "I think that Mr. Lofton is the cleverest among them. I think Mrs. Lofton the most excitable, the most unsteady. I think Mrs. Hurst had the most to conceal."

"She conceals one truth no longer," Jonathan replied. "She has admitted the extremity of the debt she owes you."

"Extraordinary, is it not? Yet she is the one who always asks to play again, to bet again, to risk once more." Ever mild, Mr. Brooks shrugged. "If she insists upon losing money, why should I not be the one to win it?"

"Forgive the indelicacy," Juliet replied, "yet we have noticed, and Mrs. Brooks has confirmed, that you live on very little money, only half of what you are paid. You have also spoken of investments, and now we have learned of your considerable winnings at cards. How are we to reconcile this discrepancy?"

Mr. Brooks remained unbothered. "There is no discrepancy. Between my savings, my investments, and money I have won from Mrs. Hurst and a handful of Mr. Bingley's other acquaintances from afar, I have amassed a fortune of almost twenty-five thousand pounds."

This was a staggering amount. Jonathan found himself unwillingly impressed. Juliet did not seem to be. "Does Mrs. Brooks know of this?" she asked.

"It is I who oversee the household accounts, so she does not know the precise details, but she understands the principle, the general result, of my efforts. When we were first married, she would so often importune me, asking for frippery such as dresses and hats or luxuries like extra servants, that I found I could have no peace until I explained the importance of my investments."

"Investments do not preclude leading an ordinary life, one in which your wife might live in comfort," Juliet replied. "Why do you begrudge her nearly every pleasantry of living?"

At once Mr. Brooks became cold. "My house is my own, as is my money and my family, and I will thank you not to comment upon matters that are none of your concern. Or do you believe that my *housekeeping* could have anything to do with these deaths?"

In the coach, on the way back, Juliet said, "He is miserly, capable of taking joy only in the hoarding of money, none in the many small comforts and satisfactions that can be purchased with it. No wonder Mrs. Brooks has so many resentments! She might not begrudge her sister a good fortune that seemed entirely beyond reach—but to have a fortune at hand that one is forbidden to use? That must be vexing indeed."

"It must be very hard on Aunt Kitty," Jonathan agreed.

His hand entangled again with Juliet's, and they caressed fingers and palms. She murmured, "We must remain cautious."

"Of course." He understood her reluctance to kiss again, as much as they had both enjoyed it, for now he realized how very difficult it could be to stop.

The various upsets of the previous day had led to another withdrawal of companionship, similar to that which had immediately followed the death of Mr. Hurst. Once again, dinners were mostly to be sent up on trays, and the only person lingering in the drawing room was Mr. Allerdyce—and this, Juliet suspected, mostly to avoid being in the same room as his wife. She wished Frederica Allerdyce at least were here to speak with, once Jonathan had returned to Longbourn, but both sisters were attending a dinner at Lucas Lodge, where Frederica was becoming more acquainted with those who would become her new family. Juliet wondered how long it would be before Frederica would be obliged to host Charlotte Collins, and her husband Mr. Collins, whom they had come to know in Kent—and, when the time came, how much Frederica would be able to endure hearing the many virtues of Lady Catherine de Bourgh.

The quiet evening allowed Juliet to retire early. Alone in her bed, her thoughts returned again and again to the kisses she and Jonathan had shared. Her skin seemed to tingle at the memory, and she twisted and turned restlessly, longing for she knew not what.

Well. She knew a little of what it was she longed for. Like any other child of the countryside, she had watched the horses; like any other person who had ever seen a satirical cartoon posted in the city or published in the newspaper, she understood some of the common postures. When younger, she had always thought it all very strange. Upon reaching adolescence, she had begun to understand some of the appeal, though the practice still seemed quite rude.

From the instant of their first kiss, however, Juliet felt transformed. She could not dismiss such images and thoughts from her mind, nor did she wish to. So this was what it meant, the longing to become a bride! When at last Juliet drifted into slumber, she did so hoping against hope that Mrs. Darcy might convince Mr. Darcy to approve the match soon.

Having fallen asleep so late, Juliet slept late as well. Only when a shaft of warm sunlight warmed her face did she begin to stir. A glance at the clock revealed she had nearly entirely missed her opportunity for breakfast, but she would simply ring the bell and have a few pastries sent up along with some tea. Tea was translucent. One could see poison in tea. (Juliet did not specifically fear for her life, but caution seemed called for.)

She rose from her bed, put on her wrapper—then heard a low moan from one of the other bedrooms nearby. This was followed by the words, "Oh, no—oh no, no, no, it cannot be—"

The voice was Mrs. Bingley's. Juliet dashed into the hallway and down the hall, knocking against one of the little decorative tables and tipping over the peacock ornament with a *thunk*. The very next door belonged, she knew, to the Loftons, and Mrs. Bingley stood in the doorway, one hand pressed to her mouth.

To Juliet's horror, she could make out the shape of Mrs. Lofton, hanging from a noose, quite dead.

Chapter Twenty-One

Jonathan had taken even longer to fall asleep the night after his first kiss. He, who had not seen the value of physical contact for so long, now felt afire with the need to kiss Juliet again. More could not come until they were wed.

In the brief moments that passion left him, anger took its place, equally as disquieting and far more difficult to endure. The injustice against Juliet had outraged Jonathan since the moment he had comprehended Follett's foul trick, but to think that it had come to disownment! This he could not endure. The need to put this right—to undo that which should not be—tormented him, and he knew it would continue to do so until proper redress had been made.

This meant he must broach the question of an engagement with his father. Jonathan briefly considered simply pressing for permission to ask Miss Tilney, rather than admitting to the secret engagement, but he had taken his father's words about deception greatly to heart. Even as terrible as the truth was regarding his late cousin Susannah, Jonathan felt better for knowing it had been revealed at last. Honesty must be his course.

He descended for breakfast early but took his time instead of rushing off. Mr. Bennet noted this with interest. "You are not so hasty to go to Netherfield today, I see. Have you caught the fiend you sought? Are you now at liberty?"

"Not yet, Grandpapa."

"I do wish you would not dawdle so," said Mrs. Bennet as she buttered her bread. "Some madman loose, running about with slaughter on his mind, and yet you do not conclude the business."

"It is not a thing that can be rushed, Grandmama," Jonathan replied, with but slight hope of her understanding. "The truth will out. Besides, it may not be a madman on the loose, but a madwoman."

Mrs. Bennet thought little of this. "Ha! It is men that go about killing people. No wonder you have taken so long at the task, if you do not even know *that*!"

Jonathan would have gone on to tell his grandmother about the female murderers he and Miss Tilney had uncovered in the past had he not then heard his father's footsteps upon the stairs.

Mr. Darcy had expected his son to avoid him at breakfast again, but he was not sorry to have his expectations defied. "Good morning to you all," he said.

"Good morning, Father." Jonathan felt the better for even this small beginning.

Mrs. Bennet—who had been all but oblivious to the divide between the Darcy men—merely gestured at the breakfast table, from which they were to take as they desired. "I beg you, sir, enjoy as much bacon as you like, for Mr. Bennet should not always have it all."

"I entirely disagree," said Mr. Bennet, "yet I shall not resent it if I do not eat the lot today."

Mr. Darcy took the chair opposite Jonathan's, and after a pause said, "You have rested well?"

"Yes, Father. And you?"

"Quite well, thank you."

These small courtesies meant a great deal, as Jonathan well knew. His father had not gone cold; he did not reject his eldest son outright; this could only mean that forgiveness, if not already upon them, would soon follow.

The rest of breakfast was filled with idle chitchat, especially idle in the case of Mrs. Bennet. After Pine had cleared away the breakfast things, Jonathan's grandmother took herself off to call on her sister Mrs. Philips. His grandfather said, "I have a mind to visit the circulating library today. My subscription has not been put to much use of late. May as well get my money's worth, eh?"

"You will not be made uncomfortable?" Jonathan said. "You have often said that it is difficult to get about Meryton with your stick."

Mr. Bennet smiled and shook his head. "Never fear, Jonathan. I have already instructed Peck to return in the landau after depositing Mrs. Bennet at her destination, and he will convey me and my cane into town well enough." Only then did it occur to Jonathan that his grandfather meant to give the Darcys a chance to speak alone.

Indeed, no sooner had Mr. Bennet departed than Mr. Darcy came to Jonathan. "I wish to apologize," he said. "You can only have taken my silence these last days to mean that I blamed you for your cousin's death. Please know that I did not, and do not. You made a mistake, but you committed no wrong. That was Mr. Wickham's alone."

Jonathan breathed out heavily. "I do blame myself. Never shall I regret any action more, but I had no ill intent. Mr. Wickham's reaction might be predicted—his *action*, less so."

Mr. Darcy put one hand on his son's shoulder, a gesture of warmth Jonathan could not but be encouraged by. "You have always been a loving and obedient son, Jonathan. You have been honest in all your dealings, and of the most forthright character. There are those who judge you harshly for particularities of temperament; they also judge wrongly, placing their attention on that of little consequence instead of that which is most important. Please know how very proud I am of you, and ever shall be."

How much pleasure Jonathan wished to take in these words!—but his father's pride was in Jonathan's obedience.

In his forthrightness. In his honesty. Now another lie had to be revealed, another omission, and one of the greatest acts of disobedience of which any son could ever be capable. Surely his father would have pity for Miss Tilney's plight and would wish to save her from her cruel situation as much as Jonathan did, or very near. Yet if it had taken days for him to see past the matter with Susannah, how long would the next forgiveness be in coming?

Before he could even begin to untangle this Gordian knot, they heard the sounds of a horse galloping toward Longbourn. Jonathan and his father looked at each other, then stepped outside just as the rider and his mount came to a halt. "Mr. Darcy, sir!" the servant called, before realizing. "Mr. Jonathan Darcy! There has been another death at Netherfield!"

Juliet had witnessed the aftermath of murder more than once, but never the aftermath of self-murder. The latter, she felt sure, was more horrible by far.

"We must take her down," Jane had said, sobbing, overwhelmed by the pitiful state of the dead woman, who hung from the chandelier. A sort of rope had been fashioned from petticoats, ripped apart and knotted together; Mrs. Lofton would have known she did not require their service again. How horrid her face appeared!—Jonathan had warned Juliet once that she was better off not having seen a past victim who had been strangled, and now she knew why. The protuberance of tongue and eyes was grotesque. Little wonder Mrs. Bingley could hardly bear to look upon the scene.

Yet Juliet said, "Please wait, Mrs. Bingley. It is better that we do so only after Mr. Lucas and Mr. Jonathan Darcy have arrived."

"But why? Why?"

This, Juliet could not articulate. It was not common police practice, and yet she knew from past experience that much could be discerned from the immediate aftermath of any violent incident. Better, surely, to see as much as they could—in a case of suicide as much as any other.

Cries and shouts of alarm and grief came from below as Mr. Bingley informed all the others in turn, including those closest to Mrs. Lofton: her sisters and of course her husband. Juliet could only imagine how Mr. Bingley himself suffered from the death of his youngest sister. He showed great courage in thinking of others even in such an extremity.

"Please, Mrs. Bingley," Juliet said, "go downstairs and be with your husband. He needs you now, I think. Will you send Mr. Lucas and Mr. Darcy up when they arrive?" Jane, having been urged to care for another, would never fail to do so, and she hurried away at once.

This left Juliet alone in the room to behold the wretched scene. Gruesome though it was, she determined to learn what she could. Mrs. Lofton had not rung for her maid that morning, it seemed, as she still wore her nightdress of cotton lawn and her feet remained bare. Once Juliet had been able to look away from the dangling corpse, her attention was drawn to the small desk in the corner, upon which sat inkwell, pen, and paper. A note had been written before the fatal act, ink dry upon both page and the rim of the uncorked bottle. It took Juliet a moment to make out the words written there, for Mrs. Lofton's handwriting was as blotted and illegible as her sisters had proclaimed: *May God and the dead forgive me my evil deeds.*

Juliet put one hand to her lips. Was this begging for salvation after the commission of self-murder? Or . . . was this a confession?

Footsteps in the hall made her turn to see Mr. Isaac Lucas appearing in the doorway. How terrible was his shock and disgust! "May our Savior have mercy," he whispered.

"Look, Mr. Lucas." Juliet gestured to the note. "Can this mean what it seems to suggest?"

Mr. Lucas came to the desk and squinted. After a moment, "You believe her to have been the murderer? That she took her own life out of remorse?"

"That seems the obvious inference to draw." Yet Juliet had learned to be wary of such inferences.

Jonathan arrived shortly thereafter and came immediately to her side, taking her hand. Juliet could not but be glad of it, given how terrible the sight before them. If Mr. Lucas thought aught of it, or of Juliet's dishabille, he said nothing. "You must read the note, Mr. Darcy," Juliet said.

He promptly did so. "She seems to suggest guilt for the murders. Are we to believe that guilt drove her to self-murder?"

Something about the way Jonathan phrased this—*Are we to believe*—encouraged Juliet to question further. "If so, why did she not say this precisely?" When both Jonathan and Mr. Lucas turned to her, Juliet elaborated: "If she intended to claim responsibility, she might have done so explicitly. She might have explained what drove her to the act, for I still know not why she would have wished to harm Mr. Hurst. If Mrs. Lofton felt guilty enough to take her own life, why did she not bother to explain?"

"Despair, perhaps," said Mr. Lucas.

Yet Jonathan, more attuned to Juliet's thinking in this matter, said, "It is a good point. Not dispositive, but we must consider it."

Mr. Lucas grimaced. "May we first have her body taken down?"

An unlucky two of the servants had the task of doing this. It appeared that Mrs. Lofton had stood atop the high bed to tie the makeshift rope around the chandelier, then put her head through the noose and stepped away from it. Yet as the servants worked, Jonathan murmured, "Does not that seem high to you? Difficult for Mrs. Lofton to reach?"

"Difficult, yes," Juliet said. "Not impossible." Yet this detail bothered her also.

Conversations they had had with a certain Dr. Hitchcock on a prior case had taught Juliet enough to know that the phenomenon of rigor mortis began an hour or two after demise, not fully taking hold until nearly half a day. Mrs. Lofton showed no sign of it. So this had in fact happened very shortly before Mrs. Bingley had discovered the aftermath. (It had occurred to Juliet that, if Mrs. Lofton's body had been stiff, Mr. Lofton must have been suspected, for he alone would have been with her through the night.)

"I do not like this," Jonathan murmured. "I cannot say why. Not—of course I do not like seeing any such thing as this—but it seems an odd end to the matter."

The servants had begun wrapping Mrs. Lofton in a sheet, the makeshift noose still around her neck. Juliet put out her hand. "Wait. First, before you take her away, you should remove the noose."

This was done, and Juliet determinedly knelt down beside the body to look closer. Immediately she spotted the lie. "Mr. Darcy, do you see?"

"Finger marks," Jonathan said, gesturing for Mr. Lucas's sake at the unmistakable imprints of fingers on Mrs. Lofton's neck. "Thus she was strangled and killed before she was hanged from the chandelier!"

"My word," Mr. Lucas breathed. "But—the note?"

Jonathan remembered the raillery of Mrs. Hurst and Mrs. Allerdyce as well as Juliet did, for he replied, "Mrs. Lofton's handwriting was full of blots, difficult to read, as was well-known. This could be imitated more believably, perhaps, than more regular script."

Juliet realized the rest. "This may be why the note is so short. A longer missive might have betrayed the difference in handwriting, regardless of blots. A shorter one would be more likely to pass muster."

Mr. Lucas appeared grim, as well he might. "I must report this third murder to those downstairs."

"Wait," Juliet said. The thoughts formed in her mind almost as she spoke. "Do not tell them. Let them believe that this was an act of self-murder for a while longer."

"But—" Mr. Lucas's consternation was considerable. "There is still a killer among you!"

Jonathan, however, understood her immediately. "Yes, Mr. Lucas. If that murderer believes we have accepted the lie, this may lead to more carelessness about the truth. Much may be revealed."

That day was perhaps the saddest of all those Netherfield had recently known. Mr. Hurst's death had resulted in shockingly little grief, and Becky, mostly unknown to those upstairs, had been regretted more in the abstract.

Mrs. Lofton, however, had been sister to Mrs. Hurst, Mrs. Allerdyce, and Mr. Bingley. Mrs. Allerdyce was quite overcome, and her husband laid aside his recent grievances to be at her side; her daughters, though only somewhat mournful for an aunt who had never made much time for them, were not so upset with their mother as to fail to condole with her in her time of need. Mr. Bingley wept openly for his youngest sibling, whom he remembered as an infant he had held in his arms. He did so in the arms of his wife, who grieved for Mrs. Lofton more sincerely than the relationship had truly deserved, and then in conversation with Mr. Darcy, who came immediately to support his friend.

Mrs. Hurst and Mr. Lofton also appeared grief-stricken, but kept to themselves more, not even coming down to greet the Brookses when Mr. Brooks came to minister to them in the time of travail.

Juliet, who sat with Jonathan alone in the drawing room—with the door still open for propriety's sake, though no one could possibly take any notice of them at the moment—murmured, "It cannot be either of the Brookses, then."

He nodded. "No. The other murders were set into motion in the dead of night, when either of the Brookses could conceivably have entered Netherfield with the aid of an accomplice. This took place in the morning, after Mr. Lofton arose. Mr. and Mrs. Brooks could not possibly have avoided being seen at that hour."

"I have been thinking," said Juliet, "about Mrs. Bingley's cry of distress this morning, and about the little peacock ornament on the table in the hall. It fell over amid the fuss, just as it had the morning of Mr. Hurst's death."

Jonathan said, "I have been thinking about Aunt Kitty's new gloves."

She knew then that they had reached the same conclusion. The murderer remained a mystery no longer.

"Yet we have no proof." Jonathan grimaced. "We can demonstrate that Mrs. Lofton was a case of murder, not self-murder. But we cannot demonstrate who did it, not to the satisfaction of a court of law."

Juliet thought hard, until an idea came to her. This plan seemed to her to involve much risk, but it seemed their only path to justice. "If we have no proof, then we shall have to force the murderer to create it."

She went to the nearby writing desk, took up pen and ink and a piece of the fine stationery the Bingleys shared with all. Jonathan came to her side as she wrote:

I know what you have done. I would tell Mr. Lucas all, and your life would then be forfeit. However, I believe

that we can benefit each other. If you will meet me at
ten o'clock this evening at the Grecian folly, we shall
come to terms.—Juliet Tilney

"You have signed it?" Jonathan said.

"My position is known to be compromised," Juliet replied. "I am understood to be desperate. That is why the note will be believed." How great was her satisfaction in the moment when she realized her disgrace could also prove to be a weapon for truth.

The night proved to be the coldest since early March. Juliet put on the warmest pelisse she had brought and wound a scarf around her throat—though the memory of the fabric around Mrs. Lofton's neck gave her momentary pause regarding the scarf. From the drawing room, she could hear the continuing murmur of conversation: The Brookses had come to condole with all those at Netherfield just after the evening meal, and it seemed unlikely that anyone would depart the house until well into the night. Juliet considered this for the best, as it comforted her to know how many others were close at hand.

She took up a small lamp and went outside to the folly half an hour early, lest she be unpleasantly accosted on her way. Before ten minutes had passed, Juliet had begun to shiver, but this was from dread as much as the chill in the air.

Pacing back and forth kept her warmer, and helped to pass the seemingly interminable time, until the moment she heard one of the back doors creaking. Juliet shifted so that she faced the sound, and so that her back was to one of the thicker columns of the folly. Footsteps came closer and closer, until the figure came into her lamp's sphere of light.

She said, "Good evening, Mr. Lofton."

His congeniality had vanished. He said only, "What do you want?"

"I want one hundred pounds," Juliet said, choosing the amount at random. "Give me this, in notes, and I shall leave this part of the country together, to begin again someplace new. What I know will depart with me."

"You will have to allow me to visit my bank," said Mr. Lofton. "If there is one word from you in that amount of time, it will go the worse for you."

The tone of his voice frightened Juliet, for she knew what he meant by this: If three persons could fall prey to him, so could a fourth. However, she kept her head enough to recognize that as yet Mr. Lofton had admitted nothing. He might claim that he paid her only to keep her from spreading scurrilous rumors, or even out of pity for her plight, rather than to prevent the revelation of the truth.

He turned as though to go. Quickly Juliet said, "Do not you wish to know how I found you out?"

This was sufficient to stop Mr. Lofton, though still he said nothing—only glared.

"First," Juliet said, "there was the matter of the peacock."

"The peacock?"

"The little ornament on the table in the hall upstairs. Mrs. Bingley had noticed that it had been knocked over on the morning of Mr. Hurst's death. I knocked it over myself this morning when I ran to the bedroom you had shared with your wife. It is heavier than it appears, however. Only my collision with the table disturbed it, and it made a thud when it did so."

"What has that to do with anything?" Mr. Lofton demanded.

"The table sits between the doors of your room and the Hursts' room. Your dressing gown—which I saw the morning Becky's body was discovered—has long, heavy tassels. Had you been running from the breakfast room after placing the arsenic in the coffee cup, you could have collided with the table yourself, or one of the tassels of your dressing gown could have knocked the peacock over." Juliet gripped the lamp more tightly, afraid it might show her to be trembling. "Nobody else would have passed that way. I even believe the thud might have been what awoke Mr. Hurst so unusually early that morning. Had he not been disturbed, the first coffee drinker to come down for breakfast would almost certainly have been your wife."

"Unless it was she who placed the poison and knocked over this trinket," Mr. Lofton retorted. He had begun to look as though he would like to keep his one hundred pounds. "Did she not admit to it, even if not in so many words?"

Juliet shook her head. "If Mrs. Lofton had placed the poison, she would have had no idea who else would drink the fatal dose. Nor did she have any reason to wish disgrace upon the house for its own sake."

Mr. Lofton scowled at her, but he said nothing. Once again, she thought he might depart without incriminating himself.

In desperation, she said, "And, of course, there is the matter of the finger marks on the neck of your wife. Mr. Lucas, the magistrate—he lacks familiarity with strangulation, he does not know—but I know. The bruises on your late wife's neck will prove it."

A long moment of silence followed, and Mr. Lofton said, "Would you like to know how I strangled my wife? Exactly how? Then I shall show you!"

He came at her, hands raised, and Juliet cried out. Yet even as she did so, Mr. Lucas and the constables emerged from behind the folly, where they had secreted themselves, Jonathan only one step after. As Juliet went to Jonathan's side, Mr. Lucas proclaimed, "We have all heard you confess to one murder, Mr. Lofton, but I dare say you shall swing for all three."

Chapter Twenty-Two

As the constables of Meryton only assisted the populace when required, and were very seldom required, no person at Netherfield that night had any previous experience of transporting a murderer to gaol. If they had, a sturdy coach would have been made ready for the purpose. As it happened, however, both Mr. Lucas and the constables had ridden their horses to Netherfield. Their stealthier approach had its merits, but once Mr. Lofton had been apprehended and restrained, there then was some consternation about how best to remove him from the estate. Mr. Lucas was obliged to go to the stables to ask for a carriage to be prepared, certain that the Bingleys would not find this officious after all had been revealed.

The revelation came when the constables brought Mr. Lofton inside to be contained while waiting, and Jonathan and Juliet were obliged to explain to the assembled household. What little calm had settled over Netherfield was shattered in an instant, descending into an uproar. Only many minutes later could any of the countless questions be answered.

"How could you know this?" Aunt Jane said as the clamor began to subside. All were gathered in the drawing room— the Allerdyces stricken, Mrs. Hurst almost hysterical, Mrs. Brooks sobbing, the Bingleys pale, Mr. Brooks coolly disapproving, and Mr. Darcy in awe. Mr. Lofton sat sullen in one corner, his wrists in irons. "How could you be sure?"

"We are sure because Mr. Lofton has admitted to the death of his wife at least, in the presence of witnesses," Juliet replied, seizing this opportunity to shape the chaos into rational conversation. "There were signs upon her body that she had been strangled, rather than hanged, and we realized quickly that only Mr. Lofton would have been in a position to do this."

Jonathan added, "However, we also realized that evidence from the first two deaths also related to Mr. Lofton, and to the reason for his actions."

There was a moment's general consternation when Mrs. Allerdyce swooned and had to helped to a chair; but in only moments, Mr. Bingley said, "But why? Why should Mr. Lofton wish to harm Rachel or Mr. Hurst or Becky?"

Juliet said, "It is our belief that Mr. Lofton's original intent was only to murder Mrs. Lofton. He was seen downstairs that morning in his dressing gown, obtaining some toast or biscuit for his wife to have before coming down to breakfast. This was not an uncommon errand, it seems, and Mr. Lofton must have realized that one morning, it would provide him with the opportunity he sought, and so he kept the arsenic on hand. On that fateful day, he saw his chance. He poisoned the foremost coffee cup—the one he knew his wife always took in the morning."

"Yet in his haste," Jonathan added, "he knocked over the small peacock ornament on the hall table, the very one you noticed, Aunt Jane. Only the Loftons' room was farther down the hall than that table, so only one of the Loftons could have disturbed the peacock. The great irony is that the sound of the ornament falling is likely what awoke Mr. Hurst earlier than usual that morning, which is why he drank the poison instead of Mrs. Lofton."

"It was an *accident*?" Mrs. Hurst, previously so unmoved by her husband's death, had now gone scarlet with anger. "You did not even mean to do it? To kill with malice is very wicked, but to kill through mere carelessness? For shame, Mr. Lofton, for shame!"

Mr. Bingley, wan and confused, asked, "You are certain it

was not Rachel—indeed, it could not be so—but how did you determine it?"

"Becky's murder was the first to suggest Mr. Lofton more strongly than Mrs. Lofton," Juliet explained. "Mr. Lofton went to the stables on the day household garments were to be dyed black—and the stables are but a step from the area where the dyeing, and drying, were to take place. It would have been but the work of a moment for him to steal a simple sash; and even if he had been found with it before the act, he would have had a ready excuse to hand—claiming it as his wife's placed there by mistake, perhaps. Such an excuse would not have come as readily had he attempted to take some of the household rope."

"In addition," Jonathan said, "the knot on the stair was a complicated one, the sort of knot generally tied by only workmen or sailors. Mr. Lofton spoke very proudly of his father's naval past and the many lessons he learned about the sea. He himself informed us that knot tying was among those lessons."

Juliet recalled Becky's smile, her hopefulness, her dreams for the future, and the terrible end these dreams had led to. "Becky must have seen Mr. Lofton in the breakfast room that morning and realized his guilt. Days later, when she was helping me in my room, the Loftons walked by as I was questioning her, and the phrasing Becky used to reply—she said that if someone had seen something that morning, that person would have something worthwhile to tell me. Only much later did I realize that those words were spoken for Mr. Lofton's benefit. He must have promised her money for her silence, persuaded her to come down in the night to receive her payment. Had she been badly injured, she would have been sufficiently warned to remain silent; instead, she died and was silenced forever."

"But why?" Mrs. Allerdyce said, through the kerchief she held before her face to catch her tears. "Why should Mr. Lofton wish to kill our sister?"

To Juliet's surprise, the elder Mr. Darcy answered her. "Evidently he had tired of his marriage. Divorces are difficult to obtain even when there are legal grounds, and Mrs. Lofton had given Mr. Lofton no such. Yet why he should be so wicked as to prefer murder to the more commonplace remedy of living separately, I could not say."

As Mr. Darcy spoke, Mr. Lofton shifted his weight in his seat and, though still silent, glanced up from the floor for the first time. He had given up all else upon his capture, Juliet realized, but this—this, he still cared about and wished secret. However, the time for secrets had passed.

Jonathan was the properest person to speak of this, as it concerned his family. He began, "I realized the truth when I thought about Aunt Kitty's new gloves."

Every person's attention went then to Mrs. Brooks, who sobbed all the harder. She would not look up.

"Mr. Brooks does not allow Aunt Kitty even enough money to properly run their house," Jonathan continued very gently, "much less pin money that would allow her to purchase some things for herself. This, despite his having earned a fortune through both gambling and investments."

Juliet felt greatly for Mrs. Brooks despite everything, and so she spoke with tenderness in her voice. "To be so cast down, to feel so needlessly deprived of all the small pleasures of life, to have no measure of affection from her husband—how hard a fate this is for a woman! It must make her susceptible to flattery, to gifts. To any show of admiration or affection, let alone protestations of love."

Mr. Lofton burst out, "You will leave her be! Kitty knew nothing of this!"

Never had Juliet recognized the piercing stare of disapproval so sharply as she did when it was aimed at Mrs. Brooks by all present. Perhaps one had to experience it before appreciating how devastating it truly could be.

"I did not know," Mrs. Brooks managed, though her words came unevenly between sobs. "This I swear. Nor had we—had I—there has been no crime, no sin, save that of the heart."

"We noticed that Mr. Lofton always had kind words to say regarding Aunt Kitty," Jonathan said. "He had admitted communicating with her privately once, though he claimed to have sent only a proper letter of apology. This we now doubt. We learned also that he had purchased some items at Mrs. Mount's shop in Meryton. He claimed these were for his wife. But then Aunt Kitty began to wear new gloves, which she could never had bought for herself."

Juliet added, "You will recall, Mrs. Bingley, that one of your magazines of women's fashion was once left out, opened to a page about gloves. At first I had thought Becky might have looked through it covetously, but a servant would have remembered to put the magazine back in its place. Instead, I believe that Mr. Lofton perused its pages, seeking the correct gift for Mrs. Brooks."

Mr. Brooks looked upon his wife with something like disgust before turning toward Mr. Lofton. "Mrs. Lofton was not the only obstacle to your ambition, sir. What had you planned for me?"

How terrible it was to see Mr. Lofton's crooked smile. "I learned from Mr. Hurst's death. The second poisoning—no one would have guessed a thing."

At this Mrs. Brooks fainted. Amid the flutterings this caused, with her sister Jane taking Mrs. Brooks into her embrace and care, Juliet wondered whether this claimed ignorance was true or false. Mr. Lofton had defended Mrs. Brooks, whose horror and astonishment seemed quite genuine—but Juliet had not forgotten who had been the only person to suggest that Mrs. Lofton might have been the murderer.

Though that may not have been knowledge, merely desire, Juliet realized. If Mrs. Brooks wished Mr. Lofton free, how easily she could have convinced herself that her rival was a villain!

Finally the carriage sounded upon the drive, and Mr. Lucas called, "Bring the rascal out. Never more shall he set foot in this house, nor any other decent place save a court of law." He appeared in the doorway as he added, "Your fate lies in goal, and then upon the gallows."

Mr. Lofton gave Juliet, then Jonathan, a look of such hatred she would not soon forget. Yet the man could but rise, hold his shackled hands before him, and submit to his removal from Netherfield, a house which finally was once again safe.

Afterward, the group broke apart, that nearer relations might comfort one another. Mr. Bingley's grief, already great, was worsened by the knowledge that his sister had in fact been killed, and by the man who had sworn to love her forevermore. As Mrs. Bingley felt the need to remain with her sister and send Mr. Brooks home, her husband was instead consoled by his good friend Darcy. Mrs. Hurst took herself off alone, afire with indignation. If anyone were to have had the effrontery to murder Mr. Hurst, they ought to have done it on purpose. Otherwise it made him seem so very unimportant. Mrs. Hurst did not grieve her husband, exactly—a wealthy widowhood suited her as well, if not better, than matrimony— but she did not like him being thought unimportant.

The Allerdyces claimed the morning room, otherwise empty at this hour. Caroline's daughters held each of her hands as Mr. Allerdyce fetched a glass of wine. "To think of my poor sister brought to such an end," Caroline said while wiping her face. "We were not great friends to each other, but I should never have wished ill upon her in any way, much less this wretched fate."

"It is very terrible, Mamma," said Frederica, patting her mother's hand. "She is with our Savior now, and in this we must take comfort."

Mr. Allerdyce handed the wine to Priscilla, who handed it to her mother. Caroline drank far more deeply than was her wont, breathed deeply, then looked at Frederica. "My dear, never before have I truly understood how important it is to marry only where there is trust, character, and decency. Please forgive my past resistance to your engagement to Mr. Lucas. He has shown himself to be a fine young man, and he offers you a life of purpose and affection. With all my heart, I wish you both joy."

Frederica smiled through her tears. "Oh, Mamma, thank you." They embraced as Priscilla, sitting aside, began the long work of rethinking such lessons on matrimony as she had previously been taught.

When Caroline had collected herself, the family went upstairs, first ushering the girls into their room. Only once they were alone in their own bedchamber did Mr. Allerdyce say to his wife, "I am very proud of you, Caroline."

"You should not be, that it took such a terrible lesson for me to learn. To learn again, I say, for it was long ago that I discovered the value of a marriage with honor and trust." Her eyes met his, uncertain but hopeful. "I merely forgot for a time. Please say that you will not go away without me."

"I will not go away without you." Mr. Allerdyce crossed his arms before his chest—but he had begun to smile. "You forgot, eh? You were merely blinded by the grandeur of Pemberley?"

Caroline smiled back through her tears. "My dearest, most beloved husband. I would not trade you for a hundred Pemberleys."

With that he took her into his arms, and Caroline felt the last of her old self slip away, like a robe falling from her shoulders, never to be picked up again.

Once again, Jonathan and Juliet were left all but alone, propriety having temporarily removed elsewhere with Mr. Lofton. Jonathan fetched some wine for her and for himself, briefly encountering Mr. Allerdyce along the way. Afterward, they spoke in the manner of those who have recently experienced some shocking incident, telling each other everything they already knew, as if only by doing so they could make themselves believe.

"I was not so very frightened at the folly," Juliet said, "for I knew you were close with the constables and Mr. Lucas. Yet the look in Mr. Lofton's eyes was so terrible! This must have been the last thing Mrs. Lofton saw, which makes me pity her all the more."

"Despite your bravery, and the efficacy of the trap, I did not care for it." Jonathan wondered whether he dared touch her hand, but remained cautious for the moment. Movements about Netherfield would be unpredictable tonight. "To stand by while you took all the risk? I know well the reasons for it, but the fear for your safety was almost unbearable."

"I am very safe, sir," Juliet said in a tone of voice that made Jonathan wish to kiss her again.

In the very next instant, to Jonathan's chagrin, his father came into the room. "I congratulate you on another successful endeavor, Miss Tilney," said Mr. Darcy.

This was promising, was it not? Juliet may have thought so, too, to judge by her answering smile. "Thank you, sir."

"You will excuse my son?" Mr. Darcy said. "We need to have a word."

"Of course, sir." Juliet inclined her head, freeing Jonathan to walk from the room into the hallway, where his father waited for him.

Mr. Darcy kept his voice low as he said, "I have spoken with both your aunts, and we are all in agreement that Mrs. Brooks should not return to the vicarage tonight, if ever. It is thought best that she should stay at Longbourn for the time being."

"Of course, Father," Jonathan said. "We shall escort her there shortly?"

"Indeed. Tomorrow certain arrangements will have to be made, both regarding the removal of her things from the vicarage and regarding the case against Mr. Lofton. I intend to assist in both these endeavors. Then, the following morning, we shall return to Derbyshire."

Jonathan had not reckoned on this. "I do not wish to go to Derbyshire."

"You wish to remain near Miss Tilney." Mr. Darcy sighed. "We will speak again on the matter, but not at this time. She needs to return to her home, as you should return to yours."

Juliet could not return home. Yet could Jonathan tell Mr. Darcy this? Would not hearing of her disownment discredit her anew? Jonathan thought not, but was not sure; further, Juliet had not given him permission to tell any other soul. Such a profound wrong should not remain secret—how else might it be undone?—but he wished greatly to speak of it later, or at least on the morrow, when all had been able to rest and recover from the night's revelations. He ventured, "There can be no reason for haste, Father. If we were to return but a few days later, what harm could be done?"

Forgive Mr. Darcy this, for it had been a long and difficult night. "Jonathan, have we not learned this night the value of proper conduct, proper behavior, and obedience? As your father, this is my decision to make, and mine alone. There are to be no more false pretenses between us." He sighed. "As I said, we will speak again on the matter."

Forgive Jonathan this, for although he had greatly improved his understanding of the unspoken nuances of human behavior, his comprehension was not perfect. Furthermore,

Mr. Darcy could be a subtle man. Perhaps only Jonathan's mother could have heard, in Darcy's final sentence, the sense of coming change, of hopes but briefly deferred. All Jonathan heard was flat denial, an excuse, the sense that all conversation and bravery had proved unable to effect a change. He knew only that the great injustice done to Juliet seemed to be without remedy, which maddened him past reason. He drew himself upright and said only, "Of course, Father. I trust you will allow me to bid Miss Tilney good evening."

Darcy might have questioned this complaisance had he not had so many other claims on his attention. "Certainly. I must go upstairs to fetch Mrs. Brooks."

Jonathan returned to the morning room, where Juliet sat with the last of her wine. He could not have guessed what expression his face wore, but she put down her glass. "Whatever is the matter?"

"I fear my father remains resolute that I should return to Derbyshire, and that we should meet no more." He sat next to her and boldly clasped her hand. "Be assured I will not abandon you, now or ever."

"Jonathan, what are we to do?"

That which was wrong had to be put right. Jonathan, who could at times be distracted to the point of distress by a misalignment of plates or books, felt such distress tenfold at this misalignment of the moral universe. It had to be fixed; he could fix it; therefore he must and would do so. Even six hours before, Jonathan would never have seriously entertained such a notion, however briefly. After hearing his father, and understanding what he had understood about his family's resistance to Miss Tilney, a new course of action had become not only thinkable but imperative.

"My dear Juliet," he said, "we must elope."

Chapter Twenty-Three

When the word "elope" is spoken, the natural associations are disapproval, scandal, and disgrace. Juliet could not but be shocked by it, even when spoken by so proper and beloved a man as Jonathan Darcy was to her. "We cannot," she said. "The breach between you and your family will be fixed from that time on. We will never be forgiven!"

"If my parents do not forgive you, only for having had a trick played upon you, then their forgiveness can matter but little to me." Jonathan spoke haltingly at first, yet his words became surer as he continued. "As for your family—your grandfather has already disowned you, and in this way, your parents would not be forced to give up their home and living for your sake."

Juliet did not think peace within the Tilneys would be so easily achieved, but would not her parents indeed be preserved from want in this way? "Yet the two of us have no money. The pittance my grandfather gave me for this journey is almost exhausted; I can pay for the post coach home, perhaps a meal at an inn, no more."

Still Jonathan would not be discouraged. "I have some money set aside. My parents gave me a very liberal allowance at school and at Oxford, I believe so that I might be free to dine and drink merrily and have various adventures with friends. As I dined at a minimum, drank even less often, and made not one solitary friend, I always had a great deal left over in the bank, and over the years, it has compounded. To be sure, it is not a fortune. This sum will sustain us for a year, maybe two, if we live very modestly in an inn or boarding-house. Surely it cannot compare to the estate I will be sur-rendering. Yet we will be together, and this is more important than anything else."

The thoughts that rushed in dizzied Juliet, whirling her about to see possibilities she had never glimpsed before. "But the scandal of it. We are already scandalous!"

"If scandal is already so attached to our names, then let it remain so." Jonathan paused. "I should mention that I do not suggest any impropriety. We shall board separately and respectably until such time as we can be married."

"Of course, sir." Juliet had not even got so far as that. "Yet what will become of us after that year has passed? When we have money no longer?"

Jonathan did not feel so confident on this point, she could tell, but he said, "I am not without education or resource. I suppose I shall . . . work. Probably I could read law."

The law was a profession acceptable among gentlemen, though often as but a stepping stone into politics. Juliet had never even attempted to imagine Jonathan—or any other gentleman she knew—in any place so peculiar as an *office*. Could this be done? "Will not our scandal hold you back in that way?"

"Probably so," Jonathan admitted, "but it is my belief that while ninety-nine men of a hundred would object, there would also be one sympathetic to a young couple who wed for love despite disapproval. We need but one to give me that opportunity."

Was this perhaps correct? She put one hand to her forehead. "I must think—I must think."

Her disownment ought to have simplified her delibera-tions. Were Juliet to go home to Gloucestershire, the consequences for her parents would be grave. They would be cast from their home, her father from his work, made to live on such scraps as her aunt Eleanor could offer. Only by not returning could she spare them this fate.

Yet she could not ask Jonathan Darcy to surrender his legacy, to commit to a life of greater hardship, solely to protect her parents. Even so sacred a duty as Juliet owed to them could not justify a hasty or ill-thought marriage.

This is not hasty, Juliet thought. *We have known we wished to marry for years. Our affinity and understanding is far beyond that achieved by many husbands and wives well into the married state.* Or, to judge by the Brookses, ever.

She believed that the love they shared was equal to the sacrifice. If the future that lay ahead of Juliet would be more difficult than that she had always imagined, it would also be far more interesting.

Tremulous, joyful, Juliet said, "When shall we go?"

Jonathan kissed her hand. "My father wishes to take me back to Derbyshire the day after tomorrow. So—tomorrow night, we fly."

The following morning at Netherfield was much subdued. Though the inhabitants were, in fact, finally safe from the murderer who had been in their midst, all were sobered by the terrible truths they had learned. Mr. Lucas called early to be with Frederica and her family, which gave Mrs. Allerdyce her first opportunity to fully welcome the young man who would shortly become her son-in-law. It was decided among them that the banns should be read beginning the very next Sunday; Caroline even went so far as to say that, as they were all to be in mourning for some months yet, they need purchase only Frederica's wedding dress at present—the rest of her trousseau could be ordered months from now, on a future visit, when all colors would again be hers to claim. As for the more prosaic details, Mr. Allerdyce suggested he would take on the duty of suggesting to Mr. Brooks that a curate be brought in from a nearby village to perform the ceremony itself, as reminders of the fatal unpleasantness at Netherfield could only mar the happy day to come.

When Mrs. Hurst heard that the wedding should be held in Meryton, rather than some grander locale, she thought it very shabby indeed. However, she was not displeased at the thought of remaining longer at Netherfield, for she still aspired to win her money back from Mr. Brooks. (It had not yet occurred to her that Mr. Brooks would by necessity no longer be calling regularly.) Nor did she wish to display herself in her widow's black before her society friends very soon, for she looked so dreadful in it. Instead she began cheerfully to write those friends she had corresponded with regarding Mr. Hurst's death, so that they would know not to expect her at their card tables for at least some months to come, if not a year. By then, perhaps, she would have won the entirety of Mr. Brooks's fortune!

As for the master and mistress of the house, the Bingleys chose to ride out together in the morning. Jane spoke softly to Bellflower as they took one of their first rides together, while Mr. Bingley took comfort in the familiarity of his usual mount, Merlin.

Together husband and wife reached the edge of their property to gaze across the rolling meadows below. In the past few weeks, this vista had begun to dull, presaging the winter to come.

"I do not ever think I shall be free of the horror that befell Rachel," Charles said. "Never in all my days."

He expected Jane to comfort him, and she did—but not in

the manner he was anticipating. "Netherfield will never be the same to us again, I believe. Why do we not return to Staffordshire, to Whitebeam Dower? Our society is more congenial there, and the house holds only happy memories for us both."

Charles had not realized how dearly he missed Whitebeam Dower until this moment. "My sisters are less likely to visit us in Derbyshire."

Jane said nothing, which allowed the Bingleys to acknowledge silently that this consideration was but a further inducement.

Still he hesitated. "Your parents—will they not need you?"

"Kitty will be living with them for a long while, and perhaps forevermore," Jane said. She did not mention the fact that Kitty had shirked her duty toward the Bennets even after her children had gone away to school, for Jane could not see it so harshly. To her, this was surely an opportunity for Kitty to finally earn the appreciation owed to her by her parents, who would no doubt be kinder toward her once they no longer felt the need to make so many invidious comparisons. Jane's faith in her family, however unrealistic, never flagged. "Mamma and Papa will be very well looked after. When we return to this part of the country, we shall simply visit Longbourn before going to stay with Sarah or Abigail."

The smile that Jane then wore made Charles cock his head. "What is it you have not told me?"

"It is not certain yet," Jane said, "and perhaps not for another few weeks, but—very, very soon—oh, my darling, our Abigail anticipates the quickening of her first child."

Charles Bingley would have sworn, but moments before, that a very long time would pass before he felt joy again, and how wonderful it was to be proved wrong. "Then we are to be grandparents."

Jane held out her hand to him; their horses stood just close enough for him to clasp it. "When Abigail brings our grandchild to visit us, I know where I hope to welcome them."

"I agree entirely." Therefore was it agreed that Netherfield was to be let once again.

That day proved to be a very busy one for Jonathan.

He had preparations to make, and very little time to make them. He put several items in a trunk that he hoped could be retrieved even at night, but in case it could not, the clothing he liked best was packed in two valises he could carry. Yet other items had to be brought as well. Grateful was he that he had traveled with his bank book and other papers. Regardless of anything else, he and Juliet would have to first go to London for him to withdraw the rest of his savings. The weight of them would be rather heavy—and he would have to transport them in safety to a new bank, in whatever town or city they would next be.

What of hats? Jonathan wondered. *What of shoes?* He would have to pack the trunk even fuller, though this would make its removal from the house more difficult and thus more likely to be noticed.

So many risks and complications he had not previously considered! So many ways in which all could go wrong! He who so liked order and routine was putting an end to all such in his life, at least for many weeks and quite possibly much longer. The unknown was no friend to him, and yet it yawed before him. Yet Jonathan did not falter. The wrong that had been done to Juliet could not stand. That would be even more unendurable to him than all the uncertainties of the world combined. Believing what he believed, he could make no other choice.

By midday he was obliged to accompany his father to

Meryton vicarage, where Mr. Brooks waited in no good humor. The clergyman had bid the house's few servants to have all Aunt Kitty's things packed and waiting; Jonathan was appalled to see that her entire possessions came to scarcely more than he had brought on this journey alone.

Mr. Brooks said, "Am I to understand that your family intends to shelter and defend this adulteress?"

"There has been no adultery, sir," said Mr. Darcy with more surety than he could possibly possess; Jonathan admired this. "Yet your marriage has suffered a breach from which there may be no repair."

"I do not wish for *repair*," Mr. Brooks said. "I wish her gone."

"To your house she will not return," Mr. Darcy replied. "In the matter of the children—she will desire to see them, and there will be less trouble, less gossip, if you allow her to do so."

Mr. Brooks merely sniffed. "They are old enough, now, that her moral taint need not stain them." Jonathan suspected he simply did not wish to be bothered with his sons, any more than he had been with his wife, or even with the tasks involved in maintaining a pleasant home. Mr. Brooks remained alone with his one true love—money—and a pulpit he could not deserve.

As Jonathan supervised the loading of the trunks into the carriage they had hired, he said to his father, "Why did such a man ever marry? He can have no feeling for Aunt Kitty, nor for anyone, I believe."

"For the sake of respectability, I imagine," Darcy replied. "Though of the shabbiest sort. I do not condone your aunt's actions, and yet I cannot say that I do not understand her plight. At least the doings in Meryton are not of interest to the papers. Your mother will be happier knowing that Mrs. Brooks is with her parents, and that her stay is to be of some duration."

Forever, Jonathan thought. The divide, however welcome

to both parties, could not but sadden him. Aunt Kitty had not asked for much, had been given even less, and then had been made to feel the crush of poverty although her husband's circumstances did not demand it. Then she had been manipulated by a wicked man, and it had brought her to this pass. He hoped against hope that her future would be less burdensome than her past.

They arrived back in Longbourn to find Aunt Kitty sitting by the fire with her parents, eyes red. Mrs. Bennet, rather than being outraged with her daughter beyond reason, had decided instead to defend her beyond reason. "It is wicked that a man should keep such a fortune away from his wife entirely. It ought not to be the law!"

"On that point we happen to agree, my dear," said Mr. Bennet. "How seldom this occurs! Let that be taken as evidence that the opinion is truth."

Mrs. Bennet continued patting her daughter's hair, as though Kitty were a little girl again. "There, there, my dear. You are safe at Longbourn once more, and never more shall that wretched man trouble you. Why, everyone is safe from harm now, as Jonathan has finally caught that fiend. Did not I tell you, it would be a man who had done it all?"

"You were correct, madam." Jonathan could not help but smile, for his grandmother had finally paid him a compliment. Yet he could not bask in satisfaction for long, because he took the coins out to the driver—and then quietly, out of earshot of his father, hired the coach for another journey, far longer, and late at night.

Mr. Darcy, greatly wearied by the events of the past few days, briefly contemplated staying longer in Hertfordshire. To travel back to Pemberley so soon after this much upset would be uncomfortable to be sure—but he wanted very badly to see his wife again, to discuss with her all that had been learned. By this time she would again be at home, and he yearned for nothing so much as to be with her.

As fate would have it, a letter from Elizabeth arrived that very afternoon, just before Darcy and Jonathan were to return to Netherfield to dine and bid adieu to all those present. Glad of the missive as he was, Darcy determined to read it upon returning to Longbourn, when he would have more time to relish her insight and wit.

The evening at Netherfield was more pleasant than might have been anticipated. This was partly due to the evident joy of Miss Allerdyce and Mr. Lucas, the latter of whom was now being openly welcomed by his future mother-in-law. Bingley and Jane were in better spirits as well as they announced their intention to quit Netherfield within a month's time—a fact which was greatly satisfying to Darcy, for his good friend would now be only a very easy day's journey away. And how happy Elizabeth would be made by Jane's return!

Mrs. Hurst, however, did not seem so well pleased. "I do not like to visit Whitebeam Dower," she said. "It is so very much farther for me to travel, of no interest whatsoever. And if you are not here, how shall I ever return to this part of the country?"

Jonathan, apparently in all seriousness, said, "Were you to call upon my grandparents at Longbourn, they might be inclined to invite you in future." Mrs. Hurst received this in silence.

This was one of the few occasions upon which Jonathan spoke during the evening, beyond the exchange of pleasantries. Darcy noted that his son and Miss Tilney, though evidently still taken with each other, did not openly seek out each other's company; no doubt Jonathan wished to be an obedient son once more.

Darcy did not expect that obedience to require Miss Tilney's absence for much longer. Already he had decided that, after conferring with Elizabeth, he would be willing to bless the union. He wished to talk with his wife purely because it was a matter too great not to consult her; Darcy understood that she would almost certainly agree. No doubt they would only be back at Pemberley for a few days before Jonathan would take himself away again, to Miss Tilney's home, where the proposal would occur.

Still, Darcy had reservations about the way rumors would hang about his son and Miss Tilney for years to come. About the propriety of these investigations, particularly for a young lady. About the recklessness Jonathan had displayed on Miss Tilney's behalf. Beyond all this, however, he had become convinced that the affection between them was deep and true. A happily married man could not but recognize this as the proper foundation for the life he wished his son to have.

That evening, after returning to Longbourn, Darcy sat up to have a small dram of whisky with Mr. Bennet before retiring to his room, late enough that he imagined Jonathan already asleep. Only then was he able to read his wife's letter.

Dearest—

Before all else, I must tell you, for you will be happy to know that harmony once again reigns at Maidencourt. For now, at least, the troubles are past, and we may breathe more easily on that score.

Now I shall turn to the letter you sent me, informing me of all that is occurring in Hertfordshire, which arrived only shortly after Jane's own missive with this same news. It is very shocking indeed that this should be happening, and at such a peaceful place as Netherfield

*has always been! As soon as I finish this letter to you, I
shall reply to comfort my poor sister, for Jane must be
greatly distressed.*

How relieved Elizabeth would be to receive word that
Mr. Lofton had been arrested for his crimes, and how overjoyed to know her sister would soon be almost a neighbor once
more. Darcy smiled at the thought of her reaction, resolving
to tell her in person rather than writing to her, particularly as
a letter would arrive only a day or two at most before he and
Jonathan would.

> *As for the matter of Jonathan and Miss Tilney, I
> must confess that I do not share your alarm. I should
> have thought rather less of him if he had behaved any
> other way. He did his duty to his aunt and uncle, and
> he defended Miss Tilney against calumny she did not
> deserve. For our part in turning her away—oh, how I
> have regretted it! Upon learning of the duel, I became
> so afraid and angry as to lose all reason. Only days
> later, however, I had realized how unfair my decision
> had been. I did not speak, both because I sensed your
> resistance and also because I thought it remained to be
> seen whether our son's affection for Miss Tilney held
> true.*
>
> *So it has. And there, I think, is our answer.*
>
> *Were this not reason enough, I have been urged
> toward this acceptance—chastised, I should say—by
> none other than Jane. Her letter was all kindness
> and clarity, and from anyone else would have been
> unremarkable, but rarely has my sister spoken her
> mind as forcefully as she has done in defense of a match
> between Jonathan and Miss Tilney. You know, my
> love, how very rare it is for my elder sister to put herself*

forward in such a manner. Thus I feel inclined to agree with her opinion, doubly so as it is an opinion I have come to share.

Do not blame Jonathan further for his deception. Honor instead the depth of the love that persuaded him to it, for no less than that would ever make him defy you in any matter. Besides, if Miss Tilney is to be our daughter-in-law, you should make a friend of her. I think we shall all be glad of it.

No longer did Darcy need to confer with his wife, for she had sent him all he needed to know. He felt a moment's impulse to go to Jonathan's room, to wake him and tell him that consent was given.

But the boy was sleeping. Besides, impetuous young lover that he was, what was to keep Jonathan from returning to Netherfield in the dead of night to propose? Amused by the thought, Mr. Darcy resolved to go to bed. Tomorrow, after breakfast, he would delay their return to Derbyshire, take Jonathan aside, and let him know that permission was given. By the next night, they would be toasting two affianced young couples, rather than only one.

For the moment, though, Jonathan was best left undisturbed.

From such slender threads are our fates woven!

The clock chimed midnight, and Juliet opened her bedroom door to slip downstairs.

It had been a small matter to have her things packed and her trunks brought down, as both the Bingleys and the staff expected her to depart soon anyway. Mrs. Bingley had kindly asked her to stay another week or two, an invitation that, in other circumstances, Juliet would have gladly accepted.

Yet she had instead accepted a proposal, and this acceptance required her to be ready to depart both Netherfield and all the life she had ever known by five minutes after midnight.

Juliet had written a note to her hostess, apologizing for her departure and trusting her reasons would be understood; this note further requested that the Bingleys post the letter Juliet had left for her parents. In this she had explained her decision, telling them that they no longer needed to oppose General Tilney, but assuring them that she did not wed for their safety alone. *I have accepted Mr. Darcy with the greatest affection and love. Though our lives may prove more difficult than otherwise they would have been, we will face these troubles together.*

How bravely Juliet had written this, and how it contrasted with her trembling upon the stairs! Yet she had faced greater fears than these without quailing, and would not falter now.

Carrying only a candle, Juliet went to the back side door, slowly opened it, then showed the light. A small light flickered back at her: That would be the carriage, waiting at the far end of the drive, so as not to awaken the others. Heart racing, Juliet blew out her candle and set it down.

Within a few minutes, Jonathan had come, along with the coachmen who—having been warned regarding silence— wordlessly took her trunks to be loaded.

"You are certain?" Jonathan whispered to Juliet, taking her hands.

"I am."

"You are ready?"

Juliet laughed softly. "That, I do not know! But this is the hour, and—"

A third voice said, "I thought so."

Jonathan and Juliet turned in unison to see Priscilla Allerdyce emerge from the butler's pantry in nightdress, wrapper and curling-papers, a lamp in one hand.

"Miss Priscilla," Jonathan said, "I beg of you, please do not alert the others."

Priscilla raised an eyebrow in consternation, then turned to Juliet. "Here. It is all that I have." With that, she handed Juliet five pound notes. When Juliet gasped, Priscilla said, "You are eloping, are you not? You will need the money."

Both of the young lovers were stunned into silence for a moment. It was Jonathan who finally said, "I had believed you intended to marry me."

"I did, when my mother wished it," Priscilla said. "She now has very different ideas about matrimony and desires that I should have thoughts of my own regarding the matter. I find that I have no interest in wedding any man who is not equally interested in wedding me."

"How did you know we planned to elope?" Juliet asked.

"It was not so very hard to guess, for anyone who was truly watching you. I think I am the only person who did." Priscilla smiled at them both. "In honesty, I find your adventure rather thrilling."

Juliet could only say, "Thank you." Priscilla shook her hand, then Jonathan's, an unlikely sort of friendship finally struck up among them.

Priscilla glanced toward the stairs not so very far away. "Make haste, for there are too many people in this house to be certain of not being overheard. Good fortune to you both!"

With this, Jonathan and Juliet took hands and dashed along the long drive that led from Netherfield to the main road, where the carriage awaited them. Jonathan helped Juliet inside, joined her, shut the door, and thumped it softly. At this signal, the driver began leading them away.

In that moment—when the act had been committed, when

the unthinkable had become the irrevocable—Juliet whispered. "I am so frightened."

"So am I," Jonathan said. "But you do not wish to turn back?"

Juliet took his hands. "No. We shall not turn back."

Acknowledgments

Nobody writes and publishes a book alone. Absolutely no one. The only difference is how well the authors involved know that—and how well the people around those authors provide support. I am tremendously fortunate to both have wonderful people around me and to be completely aware of the value of that gift.

My first thanks go to my immediate team: Laura Rennert, my wonderful agent; and Sarah Simpson Weiss, my miracle-working assistant. They've constantly made themselves available for help, advice, or near-therapeutic levels of psychological support, regardless of how busy they are. Never, ever do I take that for granted.

Then there's my fabulous editor for this series, Anna Kaufman, whose wisdom, humor, and insight has made every single book better—possibly every single page. It's the editing experience every author dreams of, and not one every author receives; I'm still in awe of her skill, her tact, and her kindness.

Thanks also go to the rest of the team at Vintage: Tina Nouri-Mahdavi, who sits at Anna's right hand; Melissa Yoon, the production editor; copyeditor Martha Schwartz; proofreaders Nancy Inglis and Louise Collazo; Kelsey Curtis, our publicist; Julianne Clancy in marketing; interior designer Nicholas Alguire; and, of course, the cover designer, Perry De La Vega, who is endlessly patient with notes like "Could they be more kissing while still not kissing?" or "Maybe green?"—and surfaces from this tsunami of suggestions with beautiful, inspiring work every single time.

I'd also like to thank Kimberly VanderHorst of Salt & Sage Books, whose authenticity reads have guided this series since its inception, and whose insights have greatly enriched the characterization of Jonathan Darcy. Any inaccuracies remaining are mine alone.

And thank you to the many fans who have spoken about this series on social media or directly to their friends, and to the booksellers who have championed the Mr. Darcy & Miss Tilney mysteries! Seeing how many people have become invested in these characters and their journey is always a thrill.

Finally, I am endlessly grateful to my family, my friends, and, above all, my husband, Paul, who supports me at every stage of this process. Writing can be a solitary profession, but thanks to him, and to all the others listed above, I never feel alone.

At the conclusion of the two dances, Ada found herself, she knew not how, seated very near the Osborne set. She was immediately struck with the fine countenance and animated gestures of the little boy, as he was standing before his mother, wondering when they should begin.

"You will not be surprised at Nicholas's impatience," said Mrs. Blake, a lively, pleasant-looking little woman of five or six and thirty, to a lady who was standing near her, "when you know what a partner he is to have. Miss Osborne has been so very kind as to promise to dance the two first dances with him."

"Oh, yes! We have been engaged this week," cried the boy, "and we are to dance down every couple."

On the other side of Ada, Miss Osborne, Miss Carr, and a party of young men were standing engaged in very lively consultation. Soon afterwards Ada saw the smartest officer of the set walking off to the orchestra to order the dance, while Miss Osborne, passing before her to her little, expecting partner, hastily said, "Nicholas, I beg your pardon for not keeping my engagement, but I am going to dance these two dances with Colonel Beresford. I know you will excuse me, and I will certainly dance with you after tea." Without staying for an answer, she turned again to Miss Carr and in another minute was led by Colonel Beresford to begin the set.

If the poor little boy's face had in its happiness been interesting to Ada, it was infinitely more so under this sudden reverse. He stood the picture of disappointment, with crimsoned cheeks, quivering lips, and eyes bent on the floor. His mother, stifling her own mortification, tried to soothe his with the prospect of Miss Osborne's second promise, but though he contrived to utter, with an effort of boyish bravery, "Oh, I do not mind it!" it was very evident by the unceasing agitation of his features that he minded it as much as ever.

Ada did not think or reflect; she felt and acted. "I shall be very happy to dance with you, sir, if you like it," said she, holding out her hand with the most unaffected good humor. The boy, in one moment restored to all his first delight, looked joyfully at his mother, and stepping forward with an honest and simple "Thank you, ma'am," was instantly ready to attend his new acquaintance. The thankfulness of Mrs. Blake was more diffuse; with a look most expressive of unexpected pleasure and lively gratitude, she turned to her neighbor with repeated and fervent acknowledgments of so great and condescending a kindness to her boy. Ada, with perfect truth, could assure her that she could not be giving greater pleasure than she felt herself, and Nicholas being provided with his gloves and charged to keep them on, they joined the set which was now rapidly forming with nearly equal complacency. It was a partnership which could not be noticed without surprise. It gained her a broad stare from Miss Osborne and Miss Carr as they passed her in the dance. "Upon my word, Nicholas, you are in luck," said the former, as she turned him, "you have got a better partner than me," to which the happy Nicholas answered, "Yes."

Tim Munro, who was dancing with Miss Carr, gave her many inquisitive glances. After a time Lord Osborne himself came near, and under pretense of talking to Nicholas during slower moments of the dance, stood to look at his partner. Though rather distressed by such observation, Ada could not repent what she had done, so happy had it made both the boy and his mother. Her little partner, she found, though bent chiefly on dancing, was not unwilling to speak when her questions or remarks gave him anything to say, and she learnt, by a sort of inevitable inquiry, that he had two brothers and a sister, that they and their mama all lived with his uncle at Wickstead, that his uncle taught him Latin, that he was very fond of riding and had a pony of his own given him by Lord Osborne.

At the end of these dances, Ada found they were to drink tea. Rose gave her a caution to be at hand, in a manner which convinced her of Mrs. Edwards's holding it very important to have them both close to her when she moved into the tea room, and Ada was accordingly on the alert to gain her proper station. It was always the pleasure of the company to have a little bustle and crowd when they adjourned for refreshment. The tea room was a small room beyond the cardroom, and in passing through the latter, where the passage was straitened by tables, Mrs. Edwards and her party were for a few moments hemmed in. It happened close by Lady Osborne's cassino table; Mr. Howard, who belonged to it, spoke to his nephew; and Ada, on perceiving herself the object of attention both to Lady Osborne and him, had just turned away her eyes in time to avoid seeming to hear her young companion delightedly whisper aloud, "Oh, uncle! Do look at my partner; she is so pretty!" As they were immediately in motion again, however, Nicholas was hurried off without being able to receive his uncle's suffrage.

On entering the tea room, in which two long tables were prepared, Lord Osborne was to be seen quite alone at the end of one, as if retreating as far as he could from the ball, to enjoy his own thoughts and gape without restraint. Nicholas instantly pointed him out to Ada. "There's Lord Osborne; let you and I go and sit by him."

"No, no," said Ada, laughing. "You must sit with my friends."

Nicholas was now free enough to hazard a few questions in his turn. "What o'clock is it?"

"Eleven."

"Eleven! and I am not at all sleepy. Mama said I should be asleep before ten. Do you think Miss Osborne will keep her word with me, when tea is over?"

"Oh, yes! I suppose so," Ada replied, though she felt that she had no better reason to give than that Miss Osborne had not kept it before.

"When shall you come to Osborne Castle?"

"Never, probably. I am not acquainted with the family."

"But you may come to Wickstead and see Mama, and she can take you to the castle. There is a monstrous curious stuffed fox at the castle, and the biggest badger that was ever caught; anybody would think they were alive. It is a pity you should not see them."

On rising from tea, there was again a scramble for the pleasure of being first out of the room, which happened to be increased by one or two of the card parties having just broken up, and the players being disposed to move exactly the different way. Among these was Mr. Howard, his sister leaning on his arm. No sooner were they within reach of Ada, than Mrs. Blake, calling her notice by a friendly touch, said, "Your goodness to Nicholas, my dear Miss Watson, brings all his family upon you. Give me leave to introduce my brother Mr. Howard."

Ada curtsied; the gentleman bowed and smiled. "Your kindness does you credit, Miss Watson. Though I fear I cannot match my nephew's excellence in dancing, I am eager to make the attempt. May I have the honor of your hand in the next two dances?" To this a hasty affirmative was given, but they were immediately impelled in opposite directions.

Ada was very well pleased with the circumstance; there was a quietly cheerful, gentlemanlike air in Mr. Howard which suited her. In a few minutes afterward the value of her engagement increased, when, as she was sitting in the card-room, somewhat screened by a door, she heard Lord Osborne, who was lounging on a vacant table near her, call Tim Munro toward him and say, "Why do not you dance with that beautiful Ada Watson? I want you to dance with her, and I will come and stand by you."

"I was determining on it this very moment, my lord," replied Tim. "I'll be introduced and dance with her directly."

"Aye, do, and if you find she does not want much talking to, you may introduce me by and by."